DAMNING
TRIFLES

DAMNING TRIFLES

by

MAURICE C. JOHNSON

RAMBLE HOUSE

ISBN 13: 978-1-60543-751-4

Preparation: Fender Tucker

Cover Art © 2014 by Gavin L. O'Keefe

I

AT SIX O'CLOCK on Saturday afternoon, November 18, 192—, the reporters' room in the Chicago *Leader* Building was almost deserted. Only two of the staff had remained after the last edition of the paper had gone to press.

"I can't see it your way at all, Rollins," remarked Griffith Dawson, shaking his head. "Nobody can convince me that a man has a better chance to get away with a killing if he does it on the impulse of the moment. That statement doesn't make sense nor sound reasonable to me. Why, if—"

"Hold on a minute, Griff!" interrupted Rollins. "I know just what you're going to say. You believe that a really clever chap should be able to plan a murder and foresee every possible contingency. You think he could take such exhaustive precautions that not even the most trifling item which might furnish a clue would be overlooked. That's what you are thinking, isn't it?"

"That," replied Dawson "is precisely what I mean. I'm not forgetting for a minute that you pulled off two big murder beats for the *Leader* a year ago. I don't claim to be any good as a sleuth, either. But it stands to reason that the more brains a man puts into any crime, the less apt he is to be caught. According to your say-so, that isn't true at all. You think that a man who commits deliberate murder has no chance on earth to avoid conviction. Well, maybe you are right, Bob, but I don't believe it. Anyhow, I wish you'd explain."

"All right, Griff, I will. You and I have been good friends for 3 years. Let's suppose we go out walking together in the country through some woods. Suppose then you thoughtlessly make an insulting statement about a girl whom I am crazy about. Of course I get sore and come back at you good and strong. Let's say I call you one of those names that you *must* smile when you say. Then you become angry too and lambaste me with further insults about the girl and myself. We both get fighting mad in a minute and curse each other to a fare-you-well. Then I pick up a club or a piece of wood or a rock and bang you over the head with it, kill you, leave you there, and come straight back home without speaking a word to anybody.

"The whole incident was unpremeditated. It was a crime of passion pure and simple, and unless some witness saw us together or my conscience forces me to betray myself, there isn't one chance in a thousand of my being caught. The reason is that no living man but myself knows of a motive for the killing. There's the distinction, Griff. A planned murder always presupposes a motive, and when the true motive is known, it's always possible to find the man who committed the crime,"—and Rollins paused for Dawson's comments.

"I understand all that, Bob," retorted the latter. "But suppose I had a secret motive for bumping you off and that nobody on earth knew I had such a motive except myself. Suppose I inveigled you out into the woods and then cracked you over the bean just as you said. If I did that, I surely would have cooked up some sort of alibi beforehand, and that is something I would *not* have done if I had killed you in the heat of anger. How do you dope it out that the killing could be traced to me more easily because I had planned the whole thing beforehand? Tell me that, will you?"

"There are several reasons, Griff. The first is that a real motive *did* exist before we took our walk together. Any pre-existing fact *can* be found if the fellow who is looking for it searches long enough and hard enough. Here, too, is a second *reason.* You would surely have planned in advance *all* the details of the murder. You would have made sure, before we started out, that a club, slung shot, or rock would be waiting handy for your use. You would have taken excessive care not to be seen with me before the crime. Your prepared alibi—no matter how carefully arranged—would be a false one and could therefore be proved fictitious on thorough inquiry. Probably, too, you would wear gloves or erase your fingerprints from whatever weapon you used and would have *overdone* your precautions in other respects. It is this *excessive* care which would be likely to betray you.

"Now let's look at a third reason. It is almost certain that some unexpected happening which you could not possibly have foreseen would occur. It might be only the veriest trifle, but it would upset your plans to some extent, if you observed it, and you would be forced to find some quick way to make it jibe with your program or wipe out its evidence. You couldn't wait and study over it. You'd have to do it instantly. Let's suppose that little trifle passed without your notice. Then it would probably indicate to the searchers for evidence that the killing resulted from a *motive*—and it might eventually point to you as the slayer. No, sir! Successfully premeditated murder is *impossible* if the investigators of the crime have good brains and use those brains correctly."

"I hear what you say, Bob, but that doesn't mean that I'm convinced," remarked Dawson. "Anyhow, there's no use arguing about it. What have you got on for tonight? It's only six thirty now. I say let's eat and take in a show after dinner. Are you game, old sox?"

"Can't do it tonight, Griff. I've got a date with my best girl for a party and I'll have to clean up and dress before I go. By the way, look at this note from old Bostock. Wonder what he wants to see me about on Monday. I fluked pretty badly twice this week. Maybe I'm getting canned."

"Don't worry, Bob! Bostock's bark is a darn sight worse than his bite. You'll smooth his fur down all right. Well, here goes nothing! See you on Monday, Bob. Good luck and so long!"

"Good-bye, Griff! I'm going to take the L for the North Side. Take care of yourself and don't murder anybody until I see you again."

Less than two hours after Robert Rollins and his friend had parted company at the *Leader* office, a well-dressed gentleman, whose rugged features and iron-gray hair denoted middle age, came slowly round the corner of Clark and Adams streets and strode westward. The electric clock in the lobby

of the Meyers Building—a somewhat superannuated structure, located on Adams Street a short distance west of La
Salle—pointed to eight thirty as the man entered.

As the chill autumn air breezed through the open doorway,
John Harvey, the trusted and trustworthy night watchman,
looked up and smilingly greeted his incoming visitor.

"Wull! Wull! Is it ye comin' back agin, Maister Stevens?
Are ye wurrkin' late the nicht? Shall I take ye up to yer shop
or wull ye set here awhile?"

"Take me up, please, Harvey. I shan't stay in the laboratory more than a couple of hours, but I've got some reactions
to watch that can't wait over till Monday,"—and presently
the pair were transported by a waiting elevator to the topmost floor.

As Harvey descended in the car, his visitor walked
thoughtfully down the dimly lighted hallway toward the rear
of the building. No office showed any sign of occupancy;
only the ribbed glass transom of the lavatory showed light.
The incomer stood before a door which bore above it the
number 713 and upon its massive oaken panel a heavy brass
plate, engraved on which were the words:

ALEXANDER F. STEVENS
CHEMIST

Taking then from his trousers pocket a leather key-
container, Stevens selected a long, thin, finely corrugated
key, applied it to the lock, shot back the bolt, and entered the
room. A moment later a light gleamed through the transom
above, the door was closed and locked—and Stevens was
alone.

Inasmuch as the laboratory office of Alexander Stevens is
the stage upon which many of the strange events of our
drama will be enacted, it may be well to describe it fully.

Had some stranger accompanied the chemist in room 713
on that fateful evening, he would have observed that a photographic dark-room, about six feet square, occupied the left-
hand corner, just behind the entrance door.

On the right and toward the front of the laboratory four long shelves upheld many neatly labeled glass-stoppered bottles, flasks, and containers, each with some powder, crystal, or liquid within. Upon the shelves were also retorts, test-tubes, siphons, mortars, scales, vacuum tubes, and other chemical or electrical apparatus. Beneath the shelving reposed a good-sized dynamo and electric motor. Adjoining the shelving and near the door stood a porcelain sink, with gleaming metal faucets. A table stood beside the sink, and another beneath the rows of shelving—all this along the eastern wall.

At the far end of the room, facing a wide alley, were two windows, glazed with frosted glass. Outside these windows, imbedded in the stone sills of the building, were ten thick steel bars, five to each window, spaced about six inches apart. In fact, the room was a veritable fortress, well calculated to defy entrance to any invader not equipped with sledges and dynamite, for the door and transom were of three-inch oak and the lock was of massive type, such as is rarely seen outside of a stronghold containing treasure.

Between the windows stood a large oaken flat-topped desk, upon which reposed a telephone, desk fountain-pen, calendar, and blotter.

Above the desk—projecting outward about twenty inches from the wall between the windows—was a T-shaped brass arm containing electric wires. To each of the outer ends of the T was attached a green-shaded bulb for lighting.

It would be clear to the most casual observer that photography had lately been the principal occupation of the tenant of room 713. Scattered about the laboratory in somewhat disorderly fashion were two tripod cameras, several portable electric reflectors, some background screens, boxes of plates and films, a safe, a table, and four chairs. Here could be found every needful appliance for the photographic art, and these utensils had served their master well.

Such was the condition of room 713 in the Meyers Building at nine fifteen o'clock on the night of November 18,

192—, as its tenant sat before his desk in his oak swivel-chair, thinking and waiting.

At that same instant John Harvey, in the lobby six floors below, reached for his pipe and tobacco-pouch, only to find the latter empty. With Clark Street and cigar-stores only a block and a half away, it would require but a few moments to obtain a fresh supply, and that might be his last opportunity for the night. To a smoker Harvey's decision would be obvious. He went.

Scarcely had the form of the outgoing watchman reached the corner of La Salle Street when a muffled, overcoated figure, wearing a short brown Vandyke beard, stealthily crossed Adams Street, peered cautiously through the glass windows into the Meyers Building lobby, swung open the heavy door, and commenced to ascend the dim stairway. Unseen by any mortal, he reached the topmost floor, crept on tiptoe down the deserted hall, entered the lavatory, and two minutes later knocked on the door of room 713.

Although the pockets of the intruding visitor contained such unusual items as a burglar's short jemmy, a pair of chamois gloves, and a tiny paper packet wherein were certain deadly crystals, it would seem that there was no need for their use, for the tenant of the laboratory answered his knock at once, gave him hearty welcome, and ushered him into the well-lighted room.

At precisely ten thirty o'clock that same evening the corpse of Alexander Stevens sprawled in grotesque fashion, with the upper part of its torso upon the desk, and the laboratory lights extinguished.

Three minutes later John Harvey was informing a stranger who—apparently—had just entered the lobby that Dr. Wilson, a tenant of a second-floor office, could only be found at his home at that late hour. With profuse thanks the visitor then departed and Harvey resumed the half-doze from which he had been awakened.

To Robert Rollins, returning a little before midnight from the dance which he had attended with his fiancée, Eleanor Stevens, and her friend Alice Lane, the world was a delightful place to inhabit. As he parted from Nora at the door of Alexander Stevens' unpretentious home on the North Side near Lake Michigan, his final words were: "Make it soon, dearest! Please do! I'll be out to see you tomorrow evening and talk with your father. Maybe you will tell me then. How about it, Nora?"

"Honestly, I can't decide yet, Bob. You know why. You can talk it over with Dad tomorrow if you want to, but I can't promise unless he changes his mind. Good night, dear. Come around early!" and the door closed against Bob's further pleadings.

Next morning, as the gentle-faced gray-haired maid who had faithfully worked for the Stevens family for ten years was giving Nora and Alice their Sunday morning breakfast, Nora said: "Sarah, what do you suppose Dad meant by calling up last night and leaving word that he had to go out of town? I just can't imagine. It seems so queer. He never does things like that. I'm worried. Really I am."

"I don't know, Miss Nora. I couldn't hear him very well. His voice sounded sort of strange like. He just said: 'Listen, Sarah! Tell Nora I have to run up to Milwaukee on business, but I'll be home Tuesday night or Wednesday morning sure.' That's all he said, and then he rung off. I wouldn't worry about it. I'm sure everything's all right."

"What time did he call, Sarah? Did you notice?" asked Nora.

"It was exactly quarter after ten. I looked at the hall clock," replied Sarah. "I had got back from the movies at nine and worked an hour on my aprons."

"Well," commented Nora, doubtingly, "it's mighty funny. What do you suppose could make Dad want to meet somebody in Milwaukee on a Sunday, Alice?"

"Goodness! How do I know? It is kind of odd, but cheer up! I don't see anything to get anxious about. He'll surely telephone or write tomorrow. Now take your mind off of Dad Stevens and tell me about Bob. What are you going to do with that poor boy—take pity on him and name the fatal day, or keep him teetering on the anxious seat?"

Nora Stevens sat for a moment in silence. The look of worry on her face visibly deepened. Finally, in thoughtful tones, she said: "Honest, Alice, I don't know what to answer. I've known Bob and loved him since I was fifteen. I'd do almost anything for him, he's such a dear. Just about the finest boy in the world!"

"What's the idea of waiting, then?" inquired Alice. "If he's such a wonder, why hesitate? Not money enough? Is that it?"

Nora bridled up. "That's not what's worrying me at all. You know it. I'd marry Bob tomorrow, but I can't bear to leave Dad, and Dad swears he won't live with us if we get married. Says no home is big enough for a father- (or mother-) in-law. If we could all live together, it would be heavenly, but Dad says no! That means I should have to leave him if I married Bob, and I can't do that, Alice. I simply can't," and Nora paused, almost on the verge of tears.

"Doesn't your father like Bob?" asked Alice.

"Oh yes! Dad thinks he's splendid; says Bob is just as clever as he can be. That old mind of mine! Wish I could make it up!"

"Nora Stevens, you ought to be spanked. You don't know your own luck. If you don't want Bob Rollins, give him to me. *I'll* take him in a minute and go downtown this afternoon and get a license," retorted Alice, with emphasis.

"No indeed!" said Nora; "I'm not passing him along to anybody just yet. Besides that, you're a lot too anxious, young woman! You just stop bothering me about Bob. He and I will scrap it out together, somehow!"

At seven o'clock that same evening there was a threesome—Nora, Alice, and Robert Rollins—in the Stevenses' living-room.

"Now quit worrying, Nora!" said Bob. "Milwaukee is only a few steps away. Let's telephone your dad at his hotel tonight."

"But I don't know what hotel he stops at. He never went off before without telling me why he had to go. Besides, I know there has been something troubling him lately. Maybe it's that new color-process of his, but I don't think so."

"What do you mean by 'color-process,' Nora? You never spoke of it before. Is it something secret? Do you mind telling me about it?"

"Surely not, Bob, dear! I didn't speak of it before because Father asked me not to mention it to anyone until he had it perfected. Wait a minute! I'll show you a print he made day before yesterday. Here! Look at it!"

"Gee whiz, Nora! Do you mean to say those colors are printed on that paper by exposure to light? I'd swear they are painted on—and mighty darn good painting, too! Those ferns and that orchid are as natural as life. Why, if an artist could paint a picture as well as that, he could make a fortune."

"Let me see it, Nora," exclaimed Alice excitedly. "Why! It's simply wonderful. It must take a lot of time and a good many operations to do it, eh?"

"No, it's not painted, Bob," Nora assured him. "And it's not done by the sun, and it only needs one operation, Alice. Father coats the film and the printing paper with some new kind of emulsion he has invented. He exposes the film with a four-color rotating screen passing over the lens during the exposure. Each color screens the lens for a tiny fraction of a second. After that he develops the negative with a special developer. When the negative is dry, he prints directly from the film on to a special paper, but uses four intensities of light at the same time. I don't understand it at all, but this is how it comes out. Dad just got it perfect ten days ago. Oh, Bob! I'm so worried about Father! Couldn't I reach him somehow in Milwaukee tonight? There must be some way to find him. Can't you think of one?"

Rollins pondered the matter for several minutes, during which Sarah served sandwiches and coffee to the trio.

"Yes, Nora, I believe there is," he said. "Your father is the sort of man who would never stop at a second-class hotel, and there aren't so very many first-class hotels in Milwaukee. I've got a good friend there, Harry Stoddard, and he's certain to be home on a Sunday evening. I'll call him up right now and get him to telephone to all the good hotels in Milwaukee and get in touch with your father, and then Mr.

Stevens can telephone to us right here. I'll bet anything you'll be talking to your father in less than two hours, Nora, so don't worry."

Eleanor Stevens brightened up at this suggestion. "That's splendid, Bob!" she said. "I'll go out and let Sarah off from putting away the dishes, while you telephone. She's been in the house all day, poor woman, and she wants to go down and take in the movies tonight. You can go now, Sarah; I'll finish the rest."

"Thank you so much, Miss Nora!" cried Sarah delightedly from the pantry. "After Mr. Rollins gets through, I'll telephone that I'm coming. You're the dearest soul in the world."

Rollins at once put in a person-to-person call for his Milwaukee friend; Sarah quickly finished her brief phone talk in the interval, and five minutes later Harry Stoddard and Robert Rollins were on the wire together.

"I'll find Mr. Stevens, sure," he said. "Just hang on and wait for me to phone you back. Mr. Stevens may be out somewhere, but I'll get him if he is and have him call you up when he gets home. Hold your horses, Bob, and don't fret! You'll get a call from him or me before midnight, sure."

After this matter had been disposed of, the minds of all three were again at ease, and their conversation regarding the color-photograph was resumed.

"Listen, Nora! I've seen a few miracles; the radio is one; but this picture here is another. It's the most marvelous thing I ever saw. Has your father applied for a patent?"

"No, Bob, he says he isn't going to! He's going to use it himself for a year or so until we have enough to keep us in comfort, and then he is going to publish the formula in the scientific magazines. He'll detail the whole process so that everyone may use it. Dad never did care much for money, and he says the world needs all the beauty it can get."

"Nora Stevens!" declared Alice; "your father is the biggest fool on earth, but I'll say he is one of the biggest men on earth to do a thing like that. When did he first start working on this?"

"About six years ago, while he and Edward Folsom were partners. They worked together on it, but made no headway at all. After Mr. Folsom's health broke down and he had to dissolve the firm and go to California, Father kept right on. He told me often that it was pretty discouraging, but he wouldn't quit. It is only in the last two months that Dad has had real success with it."

"Nora, dear!" interposed Rollins; "you know I'm on the *Leader,* and you must realize what it would mean to me if your father would let me write up this discovery. It would be one of the biggest beats in years. Would he let me print it, do you think?"

"No, Bob, old dear! He wouldn't let you, I know. Father intends to keep it an absolute secret until he has put it on a commercial basis. He has told me so, and we must none of us breathe a word about it until he lets us. Promise me! Both of you. Will you?" The pledge of silence was readily given, but Rollins resumed his inquiry. "Let me look at that picture again. Nora, that photo is almost incredible. If your father should keep his process as a monopoly, the Stevens family would be multimillionaires in a few years. Really, it's so wonderful that it's dangerous. If some unscrupulous person should learn of it, he might stop at nothing to steal the invention. What's your opinion about it, Alice?"

"I think Bob is right, Nora. Everyone knows that there are men in this world who are like that. If it wasn't a dead secret, I'd be really frightened about it. Does anyone except us three know of this invention? Who is there besides your father who knows where he keeps the records of how he does it— or does he just remember it and keep it all in his head?" inquired Alice earnestly.

"Don't worry, Alice! Dad told me yesterday that every single item of the formulae comprising his process was down in black and white and was safely put away in his office safe. No one but a chemist would understand it anyhow, he said. Let's talk about something else for a change. This is too exciting. How's the newspaper business, Bob, old dear?"

"Well," replied Rollins, "the business is all right, so far as I know, but there's something wrong with me, that's sure. Twice last week I threw old man Bostock down, and the other papers beat us. Both times I was so concentrated on one assignment that I didn't even see a bigger story, and let it get past me. Right now I've got a note in my pocket from the old boy telling me he wants to see me the first thing in the morning. I'll sure be one lucky kid if I'm on the *Leader* this time next week. I've got no kick coming, Nora; it's all my own fault."

"Oh Bob, honey, I'm so sorry. I do hope it isn't as bad as you think. Let me know tomorrow, surely, won't you?" Nora pleaded.

Alice broke in: "Bob Rollins, I don't believe it. Have they forgotten what you did last year in that Howerton murder case? And that Garwood robbery, too! Both times you found out who it was that did it, and the *Leader* said so when they were convicted and afterwards. Don't you ever believe they are going to fire you. No, sir! They'd be crazy to do that, and if that's the kind they are, you're crazy to keep working for them. Don't you worry! They're not going to do anything of that kind, and I know it."

"I certainly hope you are right, Alice, but I wouldn't bet on it. In the newspaper game it's what you do that counts, not what you did a year ago. Anyhow, I'm not shooting any alibis. If I stay, I've learned a good lesson, and if I'm fired, I've learned two lessons. Well, here's hoping for luck when they bring the case of Robert Rollins before the court. But let's forget my little troubles for a while. Tell me something, Nora! Why does your dad keep those important records in that old ramshackle laboratory of his?"

"I don't see why he shouldn't keep them in his office, Bob. It's awfully strong, really. I never saw a stronger place except a jail."

"What do you mean by that? How could an old shack like the Meyers Building be strong? It was built before the World's Fair, if I'm not mistaken."

"Why, I guess I didn't tell you, Bob! Dad spent three hundred and fifty dollars on his office about six months ago, fixing it up. He felt pretty certain he would make a success of his process and he wanted to feel absolutely sure that no one could steal it. He had heavy steel bars put close together in each window-opening and they're cemented deep into the stone. There's a heavy oak door and transom in the entrance, and the hinges and lock are the best that money could buy. The lock came from England. Banister's superintendent got it for him and they had a special key made for it so that there can't be a duplicate. Dad told me he would have to get the Fire Department to get into his office if he ever lost that key. He even used to put his key-case under his pillow at night to make sure it was safe. There is no building within twenty feet of his office windows, and if anyone tried to get in, he'd have to use an acetylene torch to burn off those bars. His safe is a first-class one and supposed to be burglar-proof. I don't see what more Dad could do, do you, Bob?"

"No! That certainly looks as if he had used every precaution he could. I'm certainly glad, Nora. Your dad is too fine a man to lose out right after he has hit the bull's-eye. It's better to be safe than sorry; that's why I asked."

For the next three hours the conversation ebbed and flowed. Eleven o'clock struck. Then half after eleven; and still the telephone was silent. Sarah had returned from the movies. Alice was fidgeting in her chair and vainly trying to form sentences; all were without meaning. Nora had sunk into brooding silence.

Finally at a quarter to twelve the bell of the telephone rang and Rollins sprang to answer. Harry Stoddard was on the wire.

"What's that, Harry? Every one? How many? Are you sure? Positive you didn't miss one? How about the cheap ones? . . . No, of course not. Which hotels did you go to personally? Did you look at today's registers as well as yesterday's? . . . Yes, I'm awfully sorry. Can't understand it at all! . . . No, I don't see what more we can do except make another try tomorrow. Thank you, Harry! Good-bye!"

Rollins turned to the two girls, whose anxious ears had only too clearly absorbed the meaning of his talk with Stoddard.

"Harry can't find him, Nora. He's looked all over, so it's likely your father is in Chicago yet. I'm going down to Police Headquarters now and learn if Mr. Stevens has met with an accident and been taken to a hospital. I'll telephone you as soon as I find out what's happened. Don't worry, girls, I'm sure it's nothing serious. Good-bye!"

Less than five minutes later the Stevens door-bell gave forth a hesitant tinkle. Nora had already gone upstairs. Sarah, the housekeeper, had retired for the night; hence Alice was compelled to answer the feeble summons. Bob Rollins was standing on the threshold as the door was opened.

"Listen, Alice!" he whispered hoarsely. "I've got two flat tires, with only one spare, and that spare needs pumping. Looks as though I must have picked up some tacks or nails somewhere today. Anyhow, I can't drive home tonight, so I'm going to put the car behind the house, right next to Nora's garage. I'll take the L downtown, to the Sanford, and send someone to fix up the car tomorrow. Will that be all right, Alice?"

"Bob," said Alice, "I'm glad you came back. The minute you left, Nora started sobbing and moaning, and now she's almost crazy. I can't do a thing with her. She's upstairs crying this minute. I'm going to give her a sleeping-powder if I can find one—which I doubt. Anyhow, I want you to call me up early tomorrow morning and see how she is. She insists there's something desperately wrong about her father's absence, and I'm beginning to believe it myself. Will you do it, Bob?"

"I surely will, just as soon as I can, and you be waiting for it. Good night, Alice!"

For fifty yards Rollins trudged thoughtfully through the moonless somber darkness toward the Bryn Mawr station of the L and—*"Stick 'em up! Quick!"* came a hoarse voice beside him, and a hard unyielding object was pressed against his ribs.

Rollins involuntarily obeyed the command.

His eyes, not yet accustomed to the dense gloom, could only detect vaguely the form of the thug, nor had he yet fully awakened to his danger.

A strong hand grasped his left shoulder. *"Right-about face! Walk toward that tree!"* The hand pulled him partly round, and for one brief instant that deadly sharp pressure on his ribs was gone.

Quick as a flash Rollins bent forward until the tips of his right fingers touched the ground. At that same instant he shot his left foot backward and diagonally upward with all his might.

Certain bygone lessons from an old French comrade in the deadly Gallic art of *savate*—foot-fighting—were now to serve him well. As Rollins bent double, while delivering this tremendous backward kick, which apparently landed solidly on human flesh, he received a smashing blow on the upper muscles of his back. Had he been standing upright, as before, his skull would surely have been shattered.

Before another second had elapsed, his assailant had secured a football tackle around Rollins' knees, and both men were rolling on the gravel beside the walk, locked in desperate embrace.

II

THE LEFT ARM of his unknown assailant had entwined itself completely around Rollins' head, with fingers wildly clawing for his eye, but this movement somewhat relaxed the pressure of the grappler's other arm around Bob's ribs.

"Foul fighting!" thought Rollins. "Here's something that'll take care of your damn gouging stuff,"—and he jerked his right knee vigorously upward into his opponent's groin. A smothered grunt was the only answer, but the attempt at gouging abruptly ceased. The hand which had vainly sought Bob's eye now dropped downward and clutched his throat.

"If I can only get my left forearm under his jaw," thought Rollins; and, with one tremendous rolling lunge, the thing was done. The head of the bandit went back; Rollins' right arm was released; and *smash* went a hard right fist into the unseen chin. It was a beautiful punch, but too far from the "button" to finish the job. At that instant footsteps sounded on the walk.

Because of being on top for the moment and thus confident of winning—combined, perhaps, with belief that whoever approached must needs side with him—Rollins' attention was distracted for a fraction of a second. That was enough! The earth seemed to upheave beneath him. His head struck the curb. A million stars rushed toward his misting eyes— and all was dark.

"Gesh ya better have a drink of this, ol' top! That's the real goods, partner. Never go round without your medicine! 'At's the way, ev'ry day, keepsh the doctor far away." And Bob's throat was flooded with some concoction which might well have dissolved the flask that held it.

Satisfied that his work of rescue had been thorough, the good Samaritan pursued his kindly though wavering way, while Rollins weakly trod the long blocks leading toward the Elevated.

Before the hands of the clock at the Sanford Hotel pointed to one, he sank, almost incapable of thought, into the embraces of the most delightful mattress in the world.

"Did I leave a five-thirty call?" he muttered. "Oh yes, I remember. Gee, this bed is fi-i-ne!"

Promptly at five thirty on Monday morning came the ringing of the telephone in Bob's room, and, despite last night's battle, he answered it almost before the sound had ceased. Youth is a marvelous physician.

As he rose, Rollins glanced at his money on the dresser. "Nine dollars and thirty-five cents. That hold-up bird last night was sure one poor picker!"

At six o'clock he was on his way to breakfast, and at a quarter to seven he telephoned directly to the Stevens home. Good old Sarah Vasch answered the call, and in three minutes he was talking with Alice Lane herself.

"Hello, Alice! How is Nora? What kind of a night did she have? How does she feel now?"

"Bob," said Alice, "I never in my life put in such a night! Nora didn't sleep an hour, and neither did I. She sat up in my room all night, rocking, and wringing her hands. She wasn't hysterical and she didn't say much except 'I know something's happened. I just know it!' This morning she's pretty much the same. Have you heard anything more, Bob?"

"Not a thing, Alice! How could I? I'll get on the job this morning, though. Tell Nora not to worry a bit. I'll have her talking to her father before today is over, sure. Tell her so, Alice, and make it strong! And Alice! Don't either of you stir out of the house today. I may want to call you any minute, and be sure you always answer the phone. Is that a promise?"

"All right, Bob! I'll tell Nora—and that's a promise. Good-bye!" And Alice hung up.

At seven fifteen Bob was talking to Desk-Sergeant Ryan, at Police Headquarters. They were old acquaintances and

Bob had no fear that any reasonable request he might make would be refused.

"Listen, Sergeant! Here's my story. I've got a good friend, Alexander Stevens. Known the family ten years. He's fifty-two years old, smooth-faced, gray-haired, with dark-blue eyes, five feet ten, strongly built, and weighs about a hundred and seventy-five pounds. He lives on the North Side, on Myrtle Avenue. He's a chemist and an expert photographer. He has an office in the Meyers Building, on Adams Street. He's a widower, but a home-loving man, and doesn't go out of town on the average more than once or twice a year. Last Saturday night, at about ten fifteen, he telephoned (supposedly from his office) that he had to go to Milwaukee on business that night and wouldn't come back until late tonight or tomorrow forenoon.

"His daughter was so worried last night that I got a friend of mine in Milwaukee to canvass all the reputable hotels there. We can't find hide or hair of him. Stevens is one of the finest men I know. Absolutely clean-living and moral and wouldn't lie if he could make a million. He said on the phone that he was going to Milwaukee, and he's not the sort of man who would go to any hotel but the best, so I'm certain he didn't go to Milwaukee as he intended.

"Another thing! He idolizes his daughter. If he didn't go out of town, he's somewhere in Chicago right now. If that's so, providing he was well enough to do it, he would surely have telephoned his daughter and told her where he was and why he couldn't get home. Don't make any mistake, Sergeant. I *know* he'd have done just that."

"Well, Rollins," said Sergeant Ryan, "whaddya want me to do about it?"

"Just this, Sergeant!" said Bob. "I'll appreciate it tremendously if you'll do two things. Here's the first. Send somebody over to the downtown telephone exchange that connects with the Meyers Building and see if they have a record there of a call from Stevens' office phone to his home on Saturday evening, November 18. Find out the exact time if there was such a call. Second, give me one of your men to go with me over to Stevens' office and see if we can find out anything there. Let me have the man right now if you can. Will you do it, Sergeant?"

"Sure I will! Glad to oblige you, Rollins," said Ryan. "I'll look into the telephone matter right off, but you'll have to wait until later for the other thing. I can't do that until the day shift is ready to go out. Tell you what I'll do. I'll have Detective O'Connor meet you in the lobby of the Meyers Building at quarter to nine. You know him, and he knows you. How's that, Rollins?"

"Fine!" said Bob. "Sergeant, you're a prince! Here, smoke this! I'll guarantee you never slipped a better one into your face! So long!"

"Well," said Bob to himself, as he strode in the direction of the *Evening Leader* offices, "so far, so good! And now for the battle with General Bostock. Gosh! I sure hope the old man won't fire me. Maybe I deserve it, but, as the fellow says, 'I didn't go to do it'—and I have pulled off some good stunts for the *Leader*, if I do say it myself."

Promptly at eight o'clock Robert Rollins stood at attention in the office of Editor Ralph Bostock, as that redoubtable personage looked up from scanning a dummy of Sunday's news for Monday's paper.

"Sit down, Rollins," he said. "I'm sorry, but we can't use your services after this week. You've done fine work—in fact, excellent work at times, and I've appreciated it. You are one of the keenest men I know, when you want to be, but when you've got your nose buried in one job, you're blind and deaf to anything else that happens. If some kid should explode a giant fire-cracker behind your back while you were doping out one of your day-dreams, you'd never hear or smell it. You know we got scooped twice last week by every evening sheet in Chicago, just because you were sleeping at the switch, and the thing just can't go on. You can do police and court news this week, but we'll have to part company on Saturday. Nothing personal, you know, Rollins! You're a nice boy and I like you, but we've got to have *news*—hot news—and not alibis. Come in and shake hands Saturday, before you go. That's all."

"Whew!" thought Bob as he reached the street. "So that's that! Fired! Canned! Dismissed! Discharged! Booted out! And all without even one chicken-hearted peep from yours truly. I s'pose if I'd recited a few paragraphs from the *Leader's* columns of a year ago telling what a sleuth-hound I was, and what 'marvelous insight' I displayed in that 'crime unsolvable,' as he called it, he might have weakened. But I couldn't do it. No, sir, I just couldn't.

"Well, anyhow, I've got almost eight hundred dollars in the bank, and this week's salary coming, and—let's see— nine dollars and a few dimes in my pocket; so it might be worse. 'Police news,' he said. That's right in my mitt. Maybe this will be a 'Missing Man Mystery,' though I sure hope not. Well, I'll be just in time to meet O'Connor if I start over there now, so here goes."

Detective Sergeant James O'Connor and Robert Rollins shook hands in the lobby of the Meyers Building at a quarter to nine o'clock, and the "Glad to see you, old scout!" which came from both pairs of lips in unison was like a well-rehearsed duet.

"I suppose Sergeant Ryan told you all that I told him, didn't he, Jim?" said Bob.

"Sure! I've got the whole works to date. But what's the big idea of comin' here? You don't expect to find old Stevens waitin' for you an' apologizin' for wastin' your valuable time, do ya?"

"No," said Bob, "of course not! But here's the last place that we're sure he was at, and seems to me here's the only logical place to start hunting for him."

"Guess you're right, Bob," said the Sergeant. "Where's his office? No use going there, though. He wouldn't be in before nine o'clock if he's in town, as you think, would he?"

"Of course we're going there, Jim. It isn't likely he's there, but he might be. First, though, I'm going to telephone to his office before we go up. If he's there, he'll answer—and then we can make some excuse so he won't think it's strange we're looking for him. Wait a minute, Jim; I'll call him."

Three minutes later Bob was back, shaking his head. "No use, Jim! No answer. Let's go up."

Their trip to the top floor and repeated knocking on the door of room 713 brought no result, and both returned to the lobby. "We're not getting anywhere by this," said the Sergeant.

"No," said Bob. "Come on! Let's see the superintendent of the building. There he is. I know him. Good morning, Mr. Donovan! How are you? This is my friend Jim O'Connor. Can we see you for a couple of minutes?"

"Of course you can, Mr. Rollins, and I know Mr. O'Connor already, by sight. Glad to meet you, Sergeant. What can I do for you?"

Rapidly Bob explained matters as he had done before to Sergeant Ryan, and Superintendent Donovan was much interested. "Mr. Stevens has been our tenant for over five years," he said. "I never met a finer man, and I'll do anything I can to help. What do you suggest, Mr. Rollins?"

"I'd like to ask your boys here when any one of them last saw Mr. Stevens," said Bob. "I suppose most of them know him?"

"Surely! All of 'em do," said Donovan.

A few moments of inquiry developed that one of the elevator men had seen Mr. Stevens leave the building about six o'clock on the Saturday evening before.

"Did he come back that night?" said Bob.

"I dunno," said the lad. "If he did, John Harvey mighta seen him. He's our watchman. Goes on at seven every night. He's here now. Just come back from the bank a minute ago. Had to draw out some money. He'll be goin' home in a minute. Wanta see him?"

"Sure!" said Bob. "Get him, will you, please?—and here's a cigar to help the game along."

John Harvey was a big, good-natured Scotchman of about sixty years. To the inquiries of Bob and Detective O'Connor, he told all he knew.

According to his version, Mr. Stevens had come into the Meyers Building at about half past eight Saturday evening, taken the elevator, and gone up to his laboratory. He frequently worked there until late at night, Harvey said, and, in the watchman's opinion, "The Lord ne'er gie the wurrld a mair bonny mon."

"Did you know when he left here that night?" asked Bob. "And was anyone with him when he came or when he went?"

"Weel, noo, yon's a verra queer thing. I didna see Maister Stevens leave at all—though he might well hae left aroond nine thirty or sae when I was oot for a bit o' tabaccy."

"How long were you gone for the tobacco, Mr. Harvey?" asked Bob. "As I understand it, you were the only one here, and I don't believe Mr. Stevens would walk down six flights of stairs when he only had to ring and you'd go up with the elevator and get him. Did the elevator annunciator over there in the corner show any calls from the seventh floor, or any other floor, while you were gone?"

"I was awa' aboot twelve minutes or sae, but it's sair brainless I must be gettin'. Ye're raight, Maister Rrollins! There wasna ony seegnal on that annoonciator at all. Yon Stevens mon wad nae ha' walked doon the stairs. Not him! Naiver in a thousand years! Laird save us! There's summat wrong here! Save for the wee bit I was oot for the 'baccy, I war here all the nicht throo, an' he did na gae out."

"Listen, Mr. Donovan," said Bob; "I agree with Mr. Harvey here that there's something wrong. We've just got to have a look into Mr. Stevens' room—and do it now. I want you to get a step-ladder and an ax, so that we can smash that *transom* and take a look-see into room 713. Please don't argue! I'll pay all damages. Get your ladder and ax and we'll do this job right now. From what Stevens' daughter says, the door can't be forced. It's too strong. Let's get busy! Game on!"

Before the clock in the near-by Stock Exchange that morning marked the hour of ten, three persons—Building Superintendent Donovan, Detective Sergeant James O'Gannor,

and Robert Rollins—had demolished the glass in the transom
of room 713, viewed the gruesome spectacle within, secured
a short ladder, thrust it inside by way of the transom,
squeezed painfully through its narrow opening, and descended the ladder, and stood beside the body of the missing
Alexander Stevens, sprawled half-recumbent on his desk—
silent, unseeing, lifeless.

For a moment not a word was uttered. Then O'Connor
spoke. "Well! Here's the answer, fellers! It's too damn bad. I
guess this is the end of our job. Looks like a clear case of
suicide to me. See! Here's a note on the desk right under his
hand. Pen right alongside of it! Look at that whisky-glass
there! It's got some frosted crystals at the bottom of it yet,
and I'll bet a million it's some kind of poison. Not a thing in
the room disturbed as far as I can see! Safe looks all O.K.!
See those bars on the windows! Are them windows both
locked? Yeah! Let's take a look at the door! Gee! No spring
lock on that. She won't budge. Reckon we'll have to climb
out the way we got in and then get the Fire Department to
smash that door so we can take out the body!

"Listen, you fellers!" O'Connor continued. "Don't you
touch one damn thing in this shop! Don't put a finger on
anything! I'll climb out through the transom after I've telephoned headquarters, and get a locksmith. Mebbe there's
some way of openin' that door. *Hey! Look here!* See this key
right in the middle of the desk. Mebbe it's the key to that
door. Looks as if it might be! Lemme try it an' see. Wait till
I get a handkerchief to handle it with."

O'Connor held the key down upon the small desk-blotter
and carefully traced around it with a sharp pencil. Then,
picking it up with cloth-covered fingers, he tried it in the
massive lock of room 713. The bolt shot back. The door
opened.

"That settles it!" he asserted. "Of course I can't say offi-
cially until we have made an autopsy, analyzed the crystals
in that glass, and finger-printed this whole joint, but it sure
looks like suicide. When a man dies of poison—if it is poison—in a regular prison like this, and the key to his own pri-

vate jail lying within a foot of his nose, if that ain't suicide, I'm crazy. Come on, Donovan! You stay here, Bob, till we come back, but *don't you touch a thing, not a thing*—and don't let a soul in until I come back with the other lads!"

"Wait a minute, Donovan! When was this room last cleaned?" said Rollins.

"Friday afternoon," said Donovan. "Stevens wouldn't let us in on Saturday."

O'Connor and Donovan left. Bob sat on the edge of a chair, alone with his thoughts. The scene through which he and his companions had just passed had shocked him deeply. It seemed incredible that Alexander Stevens, immediately after having perfected an invention on which he had expended years of labor, should destroy himself.

Stranger still was it that he should have betrayed to the daughter whom he idolized not even the slightest advance warning that such was his state of mind. Bob recalled his conversation with Nora on the previous evening. She had mentioned that her father had been somewhat worried lately, but the whole tenor of her remarks indicated that Stevens was tremendously enthusiastic over his successful results in color-photography. Why should he now take his own life?

Then, too, there was that bogus Milwaukee trip! What earthly reason could there be for a deliberate falsehood such as that? Possibly Stevens had meant to go to Milwaukee on Saturday night and some vitally serious happening had caused him to relinquish that plan and remain in Chicago— and then commit suicide. Yes, such a theory was within the bounds of possibility; but Bob found himself unable to believe it.

He remembered the scores of pleasant social meetings between Stevens and himself, usually in Nora's presence, but sometimes alone. The poise, clear-headedness, optimism, and likability of the man whose inert body now rested motionless only ten feet away!

No, the thing was incredible! The personality of Stevens refuted even the supposition—and yet, there was his corpse.

Bob thought again of Nora. How could he tell her? Yet he must. But not now! Better wait until the official inquiry had been completed. That would be soon enough.

Unable to remain quiet longer, Bob rose and paced the room, with hands in pockets, still thinking.

Strange how neat and orderly the laboratory was now! Ten months before, when he had visited Stevens in this same room, while following up a news item, the floor had been well littered with paper, rubbish, pieces of string, and the like. Now it was as clean as the deck of a yacht, and even the waste-basket beside the desk was empty.

He noted, too, the desk-top, shining as if new! Why should it seem less clean close to the body? The janitor service in the Meyers Building must have improved lately. Yet those little glasses on the shelf were thick with dust—except one. Why should that one be so shiny?

Bob wondered what was written on that little piece of paper lying beneath the desk fountain-pen on the blotter. Though O'Connor had read it, Bob had not, but now he could do so, for it lay face-upward.

Yes, that was Stevens' handwriting beyond a doubt! Just a small slip of blue writing-paper, evidently cut from Stevens' letter-head. It was only three inches long, and upon it were the words:

I BID THE WORLD GOOD-BYE.
Alexander F. Stevens

What a strange message! Not a syllable to Nora! Not a phrase or line telling her or anyone else why he had gone unbidden into the unknown! Yet the writing and signature were indisputably those of the man whose name appeared on the bottom of that small piece of paper. Bob had seen Stevens' writing dozens of times. He knew.

But why had it been *cut* off? There were no shears in sight. Where was the rest of the sheet? He looked, but could not find it.

Still nervously pacing the floor, Bob started to open his cigarette-case, but refrained. It would be like desecration to smoke in that room. Bob recalled how Stevens had often remarked that he had never smoked in his life; he did not object to the practice in others, but disliked it himself.

What beautiful hair Stevens had! Thick and heavy, with a slight natural wave. Its iron-gray mass rested like a mop on his left arm and contrasted with the mixed blue and black color of his attire. Times without number Bob had seen Nora thrust her fingers through that silvery hair and laugh tantalizingly at her father's protest. Never would she do it again!

How immaculately well garbed was that recumbent form! Bob remembered a piece of advice once given him by Stevens: "Good tailoring is the best possible economy. An ill-fitting collar and baggy trousers have exploded many a business deal." No artist could have done a better job upon Stevens' suit—yet for order and cleanliness of surroundings Stevens, like many geniuses, had cared little.

But what was *that?* There under his eyes! Not much larger than an ant! He must be mistaken. Absurd! Impossible! It simply could not be what it seemed.

Touch it? No! "Don't lay a finger on anything in the room," O'Connor had said, and Bob would obey—but his eyes were his own to use. He came still nearer. Yes! There it was! Not a shadow of doubt about it! And what did it mean? *What could it mean?*

III

BOB TOTTERED BACK to the chair just vacated, fairly weak from his imaginings. His head was reeling. A thousand thoughts swept lightning-like through his brain. O'Connor and his associates were due to return within an hour. Should he tell them what he had noted and what inferences had crowded into his mind? Jim O'Connor was a fine upstanding officer, but Bob knew well his mental proclivities. Unless a glaring fact stood boldly forth, discovered by himself, O'Connor was likely to belittle it, seek an illogical explanation, or refrain from following it through to the uttermost end.

Perhaps some explanatory fact might develop during the coming police inquiry which would throw a somewhat different light on this incredible thing. If Rollins mentioned what he had noted, and if his statement should leak into print—as well it might—through O'Connor's somewhat unguarded tongue and liking for publicity, all chance of pursuing an investigation concerning it would be irretrievably lost. Perhaps by a confidential talk he could influence the coroner to adjourn the inquest? No! If that were done, it would be equivalent to a trumpet signal that the police had a "mystery" at hand. The press then would play it up to the limit.

Possibly the department investigators might also observe what he had seen! Rollins sincerely hoped that they would, for that would release him from his quandary. The decision would then be out of his hands.

How about the coroner's inquest later? Should he be asked whether or not he had learned any fact not previously brought out in his testimony, he would, of course, tell the truth. But if such a question were not asked! Being then in the position of withholding an inference—but not evidence—

his would be the responsibility for persistent personal inquiry until justice was done.

Meanwhile, since this astounding thing had crashed the portals of his mind without voluntary effort, might there not be still more to learn if he were earnestly to seek?

With this intent Rollins now applied intensive scrutiny to every surface and object in the room. Concerning each he made definite mental queries and comparisons with things of similar sort, there or elsewhere. Particularly were all bottles, flasks, and containers studied, though none were touched. Objects on or around the desk, safe, and walls were viewed from every possible angle, and a brief synopsis of his mental queries was scribbled in his note-book.

The summary was amazing—incredible, even to himself.

How long this quest of facts continued Rollins could not have told, for suddenly his ponderings were broken by the opening of the door and the entrance of four police officials. All were in plain clothes, and all were known to Bob through his past reportorial experiences.

One of the men was the head of the finger-print bureau, George Downing. The second was the department medical examiner, Dr. Frank Alston, a man who also had frequently qualified as an expert in anatomy and toxicology in numerous criminal-court sessions. Detective Inspector Gregory Devine was the third to enter, and William Hackett, department photographic expert and analytical chemist, brought up the rear. Hackett and Rollins had been friends for many years.

Each one of these four men ranked high in his respective department of crime investigation. Inspector Devine had now, apparently, taken charge of the affair, for his first words to Bob were a brusque "O'Connor had to go to court. Witness in an auto smash-up. I'm handling this case. Sure you haven't touched anything here, Rollins?"

Bob repressed a slight irritation at the Inspector's lack of suavity in voice and manner and assured Devine that he had touched nothing in the room save the chair he sat in.

"All right!" said the Inspector. "O'Connor gave me a full report of all you and he had done. Thinks it's a simple case of suicide! Maybe he's right. We'll see! I understand you knew Alexander Stevens, Rollins. Do you identify this body as his? Will you swear he's the man who owns this shop? Sure about that, eh, Rollins?"

"Absolutely sure, Inspector. I can only see a part of his face now, but that's enough. I know it's Alexander Stevens all right!" said Bob.

"Any of you others know this man?" snapped Devine to his companions.

"I do," said Hackett. "Met him half a dozen times and liked him fine. He was a peach of a chemist and a wizard at photography. It's Stevens—no doubt about it, Inspector."

"All right, then," said Devine; "we'll consider the identity established. Now, Doctor, you make sure that he's dead— and try to guess how long since he died, if you can. Don't touch him, except with your stethoscope, if you can help it."

In a moment Dr. Alston had verified the fact of death. "I can't say precisely how long he's been dead until we make an autopsy; but I should say off-hand it is at least thirty-six hours," he said. "Perhaps longer!"

"Very well, Doctor," said Devine. "Now let me look around for a minute. All of you stay right where you are, while I get familiar with this room."

For the next few minutes the Inspector, with hands in pockets, explored every nook and cranny of the laboratory. It would seem that nothing could have escaped that keen-eyed scrutiny.

"Well, that's that!" he said. "Come here, Hackett! I want four pictures of this shop. One from the doorway, looking toward the front; and three photographs of the desk, chairs, and body. Take one from each of the three sides of the desk. Be sure you get sharp details on the last three. You can use several of these reflectors here for extra light and give your plate a fairly long exposure. That'll save the smoke and smell of a flash."

It was clear that Hackett knew his business. The four pictures were taken almost before Bob realized it. Hackett handled his big camera like a master, and two exposures were made in each position.

"Now, then!" said the Inspector. "Let's see what was in that glass"—and he bent over to smell it. "Huh! Smells like whisky! Here, Downing, go over the glass for finger-prints first, will you?" Carefully Downing picked up the glass with a pair of large tweezers, dusted it with his camel's-hair brush and gray powder, blew away the residue, and remarked: "There you are, Inspector! As fine a set of prints as I ever saw."

"All right, Downing! While you're at it, you'd better fingerprint the desk and everything on it! Start with the loose things here and then we can go over the desk when the other stuff is off."

In ten minutes Downing's job was over, and every article on the desk—telephone, note-paper, desk-pen, onyx holder, door-key, blotter, the face of Alexander Stevens' last message, and finally the entire desk-surface had been dusted with lamp-black or gray powder, and any existing finger-prints made visible.

"Huh," said Devine, "looks like the same prints all over! See, here they are! Same on the pen, on the writing-paper, on the note, and on the desk-front as on the glass. No prints on the phone or the other side of the desk. Better take pictures of each one of these prints, Hackett. Then we'll be done with them.

"Now, then, Downing, get me a good set of prints from Stevens' fingers. Better take two from each hand to make sure. After that, Hackett can photo them, too. Be sure you do a good job, both of you!"

Although not impressed favorably by Inspector Devine's personality or his dictatorial tones, Bob was forced to admire his systematic methods. Here was a man who knew his business, handled the details of his job in proper sequence, and did his work with thoroughness.

A half-hour later Hackett had finished his task, winding up with a photo of the safe-front and dial, although the latter gave no evidence that any hand had ever touched it.

"Now for the stuff that was in that glass!" said the Inspector. "Seems to me, Hackett, you might make a rough analysis of it here! Looks like Stevens had half the chemicals in the world on those shelves. Doctor, what would you say caused Stevens' death, from the looks of him?"

"Well," said Dr. Alston, "that's a tough question! It might be any of several things; but, from his color, lips, facial strain, and position, I'd make a guess at potassium cyanide—though I may be wrong and probably am."

"Very well, Doctor. We'll try it, anyhow," said Devine. "Hackett, you take that glass, use distilled water, dissolve that scum around the bottom and sides, put your solution in a sterilized bottle, and test a little of it for cyanide of potassium. We'll save the rest of the solution for a complete laboratory test later. Go ahead! Let's see what you find."

Another twenty minutes had gone before Hackett looked up from his labors. "You're right, Doc, it's potassium cyanide, and if I'm not mistaken, it was taken in whisky, though I can't be sure about that until I get to the laboratory. Anyhow, it's cyanide that did the job. There's enough left in this bottle to kill a man right now."

"Good for you, Hackett!" said the Inspector. "Doctor, I congratulate you. You're a mighty good guesser. Hackett, you may as well develop your plates right here, and then if anything's wrong, we can have a retake before things are disturbed. There's a dark-room there in the corner and you can do the whole job in an hour or so, I guess. Meanwhile we'll hold a gab-fest and talk things over while you're working. How about it, Hackett?"

"Right you are, Inspector! I'll take the stuff in and get busy," said Hackett, and he retired to the small dark-room with his paraphernalia.

"Now, then, gentlemen," said Inspector Devine, "sit down. Let's see what we've got. Let's take the whole proposition first and the details later. Here's this man Stevens dead in a chair in his own office. In front of him is a glass containing some cyanide of potassium—probably dissolved in whisky. His appearance indicates that cyanide caused his death. In front of him is a note saying he is bidding the world good-bye. By the way, can anybody here identify the handwriting on that note?"

"I can," said Bob. "I'd swear that is Mr. Stevens' writing and signature. I've seen his writing fifty times at least."

"All right, Rollins. Well, let's get on! The glass that held the doped whisky shows Stevens' finger-prints and only his. The pen shows the same. So does the note he wrote before he died. So does the desk in front of him. Plenty of his finger-prints and not one of anybody else.

"Now, then! Stevens pulls off this stunt all alone. The proof of this is that he's locked himself up in an office that's pretty much like a jail. It's got steel bars on its two windows that would hardly leave room for a cat. Both windows are locked tight. The dust on the window-locks show no finger-prints. He's got a lock on the door that's mortised into three-inch oak. It's a special lock without a spring. You've got to turn that key every time you lock or unlock that door, whether from inside or outside. The key is lying there on the desk in front of Stevens when we find him, just where it is now. *Nobody* could have put it there but Stevens, for both windows are absolutely tight, the door and transom fit as close as wax, and the walls are solid brick, without a panel or any possible opening. You can't dematerialize keys and ma-terialize them again, so it's clear that Stevens closed and locked that door himself, from the inside, before he wrote that note and before he died.

"There seems to be no evidence of robbery, although we haven't gone through Stevens' pockets yet, for the safe is locked and there's no indication that it has been tampered with. If the autopsy discloses—as I'm sure it will—that Ste-vens died of cyanide poisoning, I'm asking you, gentlemen, can you suggest any other solution to this case, except sui-cide?

"As far as I'm concerned, that note and this key settle it, but we'll all have to testify at the coroner's inquest tomorrow morning, and we may as well consolidate our facts and opinions before then. We'll inventory Stevens' pockets now, and then I'll ask you for your opinion—subject, of course, to the findings of the autopsy."

The inventory of articles found on Stevens' person consumed but little time. Inspector Devine grasped the collar and one shoulder of the dead man and raised the body to an upright position in its chair. As he did this, Rollins cried: "Wait!" but Devine ignored his exclamation. George Downing then searched all of Stevens' pockets, removed from them the dead man's belongings, using gloves while handling them, and placed them on the desk.

The first item of importance was a Hamilton open-faced watch with its crystal broken. This had reposed in the upper left-hand vest pocket of the dead man, together with a fountain-pen and pencil. It seemed evident that when the body had fallen face-down upon the desk, the pressure of pen or pencil had broken the crystal. The hands of the watch pointed to nine twenty-eight. The broken crystal fragments or their pressure, or both, had evidently stopped the watch; hence it seemed probable that 9.28 A.M. or P.M. had been the exact moment of death. On removing the broken glass, twelve full turns of the watch stem were required to rewind the watch, which at once started running.

The Inspector then remarked: "Most men wind their watches at night before they go to bed. This watch had pretty nearly run down. It was due to be rewound in four or five hours at least. We know from the condition of the body, according to Dr. Alston, that Stevens died somewhere around thirty-six hours ago. I'd say, then, that he must have committed suicide at nine twenty-eight Saturday night. That is, on the assumption that he wound his watch at night. Does that seem logical to you?"

Before Devine's question had fully left his lips, Rollins was on his feet, trembling with emotion.

"Stop a minute, please, Inspector! What you say about that watch is perfectly logical and I don't doubt that it registers the hour of Stevens' death—if it was keeping accurate time when he died. Of course we aren't sure of that. However, Stevens' housekeeper, Sarah Vasch, told me that she received a telephone message from Stevens at exactly ten fifteen last Saturday night, about a trip to Milwaukee, which Stevens didn't make. She will swear to the time, for she noticed it on Stevens' hall clock. How could Stevens telephone to his home three quarters of an hour after he was dead? Can anyone here tell me that?"

Looks of incredulity and amazement appeared on every face except one.

"That's excellent information, Rollins, and I'm grateful for it," said the Inspector; "but it seems to me you've answered your own question. How does anyone know that Stevens' watch and his clock at home were *both* keeping the same accurate time last Saturday? How can we be sure that they synchronized? Another thing! How do we know that Stevens' watch didn't stop of its own accord at nine twenty-eight Saturday morning, and that the watch wasn't running when the crystal broke that night? I congratulate you on your shrewd inference, Rollins, but you can readily see it's impossible to prove its accuracy. Now, then, I ask you all again: does my reasoning seem logical?"

There was no dissent to this conclusion, and Devine continued: "Doctor, you make a list of all these things and then we'll know precisely what Stevens had on him when he died. We can turn the stuff over to the family after the inquest."

Dr. Alston's list comprised the following items: watch, vest-chain, small locket, fountain-pen, pencil, bill-fold (containing fifty-two dollars in bills and some business cards), a dollar and eighty cents in loose change, pocket-knife, handkerchief, key-container, with five keys in clips, three old letters, a small memorandum book, two unpaid current bills, several receipts for office supplies, and a longhand draft of some uncompleted rhymed verses, in Stevens' handwriting.

Inspector Devine and his three associates glanced at the bills and letters. "Nothing here to help us, apparently," he said. "If you don't object, we'll finger-print this memo book first. Then I'll put all this stuff in an envelope and we'll hold it for the inquest, subject to the coroner's orders. We'll leave the watch out, for we know that will be needed to establish the probable hour of death. Here, Rollins, get me one of those heavy Manila envelopes on the safe."

Bob did so, and the Inspector placed within the envelope all articles listed on the inventory. After Downing had dusted the memo book without result, Devine sealed the package, wrote his name across its flap, and pocketed it, together with the watch.

"Well, gentlemen, I guess we've finished. Now let's have your conclusions. What do you think, Dr. Alston?"

"Suicide, without a doubt, provided the autopsy confirms my diagnosis of cyanide poisoning," said the doctor.

"What about you, Downing?"

"Same conclusion," said the finger-print expert.

"And you, Rollins?"

Bob sat silent for a moment, started to speak, then stopped. The silence became intense; Dr. Alston and George Downing fidgeted in their chairs; one could almost have heard the proverbial drop of a pin. The face of Inspector Devine grew rigid, and color mounted to his cheeks.

"Well, we're waiting for you, Mr. Rollins!" he said.

"I won't believe it!" Bob almost shouted. "Alexander Stevens never killed himself. He wasn't that sort of man. I could give a dozen reasons why I can't believe he did it. I realize what the evidence seems to prove as well as you do, and I'm not blaming any one of you for your opinion, but I knew Stevens well; I know his family; I know how much he loved his daughter, and no man on earth can make me believe he'd have committed suicide without some written or spoken word to her.

"Stevens had a heart as big as himself," continued Rollins. "His thought was always of others. He was planning to do something for the world that meant a sacrifice of millions to himself. He had practically accomplished what he was after. I can't disprove one atom of this evidence here, and I'll say again that you are fully justified in thinking as you do—but I *know* it isn't as it looks. What's more, I'm going to do my damnedest to *prove* that Alexander Stevens did *not* take his own life. *This is a murder.* That's my judgment and I mean it. I'm sorry, gentlemen, that I've had to be so emphatic about this, but that's how I feel, and you'll have to take it or leave it."

Bob stopped speaking, and after a few seconds of silence the Inspector quietly observed:

"Can you produce any evidence now, Rollins, to warrant your present opinion? We shall certainly welcome it if you can, and I'm not blaming you for your feelings."

"No, I can't," said Bob. "But, believe me, I'll get some!"

"Very well," said Devine. "I most sincerely hope you are successful. It's a terrible thing for a man to leave the stigma of suicide as a heritage to his child, but, so far as I can see, your friend Stevens has done it."

Then turning toward the dark-room, in which Hackett had been busy during all this period, he inquired: "How are the negatives coming along, Hackett?"

"Just finished 'em, Inspector. Ready to go now any time as soon as they're dry."

"All right, gentlemen," said Devine. "Dr. Alston, will you please phone for the ambulance and have the body taken to the mortuary at once? Downing, I want you to notify the watchman, Harvey, the elevator boys, Donovan, and any others who may have been in this room to be present at headquarters promptly at nine tomorrow morning. We'll hold the inquest there. Of course all of us will be on hand. Dr. Alston, I assume you can complete the autopsy this afternoon and be able to report in the morning. Hackett, you bundle up all the other pieces of evidence and bring 'em along after they've taken Stevens' body away. Lock up when you leave, but stay right here until then and let nobody in. You may as well make two prints from each of your negatives before you go, so that we'll have everything needful at the inquest. Come along, gentlemen. You too, Rollins."

"If you don't mind, Inspector, I'll stay here until they take the body away. You see, I feel pretty bad about this thing—and, besides, I've got to tell Mr. Stevens' daughter about it. She doesn't know a thing yet."

Inspector Devine hesitated a moment. "Very well," he said. "It will be necessary that Miss Stevens be present at the inquest tomorrow. You probably can help her between now and then to arrange for her father's funeral. Good afternoon"—and Dr. Alston, Inspector Devine, and George Downing went out. Robert Rollins and William Hackett were left alone.

Hardly had the Inspector and his associates vacated the scene when Bob, his mind alert for action, said to his companion: "See here, Hackett! I'm supposed to be a reporter and I haven't sent in a stick of copy today. I'm going to phone the *Leader* now and give 'em what we've got so far. Meanwhile be a good sport and help me make a rep for myself. Let me have an extra print from one of those three negatives showing the position of the body. That one taken from the rear, facing the desk-front will do. I won't publish it until you say so. Word of honor, I won't."

"All right, Rollins. I'll make an extra print for you on that distinct understanding, but if you throw me down on this, it'll surely mean losing my job. You promise to hold the print until I give you permission to publish. Maybe old Bostock can fix it with the department to let loose of it right away, but don't say I gave it to you."

For the next ten minutes Bob was busy on the phone, giving to his paper a rapid but conservative account of the finding of Alexander Stevens' body. The possibility of suicide was not even hinted at in his write-up. Accidental poisoning might be inferred by the reader as the probable cause of Stevens' death. His news was barely in time for the *Leader's* last edition, but its readers were promised full details on the morrow.

This duty performed, Bob called up the Stevens home, and

was promptly answered by Alice Lane. Almost before a word of greeting could be uttered, Bob said: "I'm coming out right away, Alice. I'll be there in two hours. Don't say a word to Nora except that her father has met with a very serious accident. Remember, not another word. I'll tell her all about it when I get there. Be sure, now! Good-bye!"

Next Bob telephoned to the undertaker who had buried Mrs. Stevens eight years before, telling him briefly of Alexander Stevens' death and of the inquest on Tuesday morning, and asking him to stand ready to assist on the morrow, if needed.

By this time Hackett had completed the extra print, which he handed to Bob with the comment: "I hope it helps you, Bob, but remember your promise."

"I surely will," said Bob.

While Hackett was assembling his photographic paraphernalia and the articles designated by Inspector Devine, the ambulance arrived, and soon room 713 in the Meyers Building contained only living occupants.

Bill Hackett locked the door of room 713 and silently accompanied Bob to the elevator. As the car descended, the Negro elevator boy remarked:

"Ain't it terrible about Mr. Stevens? Somebody killed him, huh?"

"Of course not," said Hackett. "What makes you ask that?"

"Why," said the boy, "I know Devine's a peach of a detective and I wouldn't think he'd tackle anything less'n a murder or somep'n. Gee! I wish't I was a detective like him; every time I see him I envy him, honest!"

"You're away off, kid!" said Hackett. "Don't peddle around any of that murder dope. Mr. Stevens probably took some poison by accident, that's all!"

Then, as the car reached the ground floor: "Good-bye, Rollins, old man! I sure don't envy you your job of breaking the news to Miss Stevens. See you in the mornin'," and Hackett was gone.

Not a morsel of food or drink had passed Rollins' lips since breakfast. Suddenly feeling weak and a trifle giddy, he stopped in a lunch-room, consumed a sandwich, with two cups of coffee to wash it down, and hurried to the L. At half past six he was ringing the bell of Alexander Stevens' desolated home.

When the door opened, Alice met him and, with finger on her lips, commanding silence, led him at once to the kitchen.

"Listen, Bob," said Alice. "You don't need to tell Nora or me what has happened. Mr. Stevens is dead. I know it, for Nora has insisted on it ever since morning, and I just had to believe her. She made me. Is it true, Bob?"

Bob nodded his head. He was speechless.

Alice went on: "Don't worry about Nora, now, Bob. She's wonderful! I wouldn't believe it if I hadn't seen it myself. She hasn't cried once all day. Right after breakfast she calmed down and said: 'Alice, *I know* Father's gone. Nothing we can do will bring him back. Crying and worrying isn't going to help. Just leave me alone, Alice, until I get used to it. When Bob comes tonight, he'll tell us'—and that's how she's been all day. Shall we go in and see her, Bob?"

"Yes," said he; and they entered the living-room together. Nora was sitting in a deep overstuffed chair, but rose instantly as they came in. Lifting her head, she looked straight into Rollins' eyes with a wan half-smile and quivering lips. Placing both her hands on Bob's shoulders, Nora stood for a long, long minute, looking—looking—looking. At last she broke the silence.

"Bob! Bob, dear! I know you'll tell me the truth. You'd never lie to your Nora, would you, darling? It's so, isn't it? Daddy's gone. Don't be afraid to say it, for I know it now. It's so. Poor, poor Daddy! He'll never come back. It's true, isn't it, sweetheart? Please tell me if it's true!"

Rollins tenderly took the pleading form of his beloved in his arms, drew her head upon his shoulder, and stroked her forehead.

"Yes, Nora, darling, it's true," he said.

Nora, sobbing, nestled her cheek and brow closely in the angle of her lover's neck and shoulder.

"I knew it, dearest. Daddy's hopes and troubles are over now. They're all done with and I'm alone with you. You are all I have, sweetheart. Nobody else in the world to live for! Don't worry, dear! I won't break down again. Alice will tell you that I can be brave if I have to. Only don't leave me any more, Bob, dear! Please, please, don't leave me, ever!"

"I'll never leave you, Nora, so help me God!" was Rollins' solemn response. Their lips met. To the youth, whose arms enclosed the most precious burden in all the world, it seemed that yielding kiss should last forever.

The aspect of living changed for him from that instant. Since his adolescence Nora Stevens had been the one girl whom he had adored. More than two years had passed since he had first asked her to marry him. Nora had frankly told him that she loved him very dearly and had assured him that there would never be another in her affections. Could she have been united to Rollins and still continued to live with her father, she would have assented joyfully, but Alexander Stevens was insistent that this should not be. Too many marriages had been wrecked by that arrangement, was his emphatic comment, and the adoration of his daughter had thus far dominated her love for Bob.

But now, in one short day, all this was altered. The father whom Nora had almost reverenced was gone. All the ardors of her being—love, affection, passion—*all* had merged into one great overwhelming wave, which swept upon its crest the hearts of both.

The fact that Alice, open-eyed and wondering, stood beside and viewed this tremendous unloosening of emotions, and that Sarah, also, was in the room adjoining, seemed of less moment to those two than the ticking of a clock.

They were alone. To them life was an oasis in a desert, and theirs the only feet which trod therein.

An hour later, after dinner had become a memory, all three—Nora, Bob, and Alice—sat together in the cozy den which had once been sacred to Nora's father. Alice and Bob reclined in deep leather chairs; Nora chose a footstool. It was easier there to hold a loved one's hand.

"Nora," said Alice, "I never believed that sorrow and happiness could exist in one mind together, but they can. The greatest sorrow of your life is here, but real whole-hearted love has come with it. You know it's so, Nora dear, and you ought to thank God that you have found it."

"I do," said Nora. "If it weren't for Bob here, I shouldn't want to stay. Life wouldn't be worth the living with Daddy gone forever. But now I've got two things to live for. I must make Bob happy and he and I must prove to the world that Father was no quitter. He went away only because he must. Bob, you've told us most of it, but not all. Now tell us the rest."

"Nora, dear," said Bob, "there's just one thing I can't tell you yet—but only one. The proof of that one thing was wiped out today, and nobody on earth can bring back that evidence. Every other detail seems to show that your father destroyed himself. The strongest evidence of all is that key to room 713, which we found lying on your father's desk within a foot of his hand. *How did it get there?* The windows, door, and transom are each as tight as a drum. The desk is twenty feet from the door. The transom is screwed tight from the inside with eight long screws. There isn't enough space for a good-sized ant to crawl in anywhere, and you yourself tell me that your father had only one key to that room and kept it constantly with him.

"Nevertheless, I know that some other person besides your father was in room 713 last Saturday night. My job—our job—is to *prove* it, and prove who that person is. We're going to do that job, Nora—you and I. I haven't got a fingerprint or a shred of evidence yet to work from. Not a shred! We're not going to find out who murdered your father by running round aimlessly. We've got to do this thing by study, analysis, and logic, and that's how we're going to do it. We've got to get *all* our facts, not part of them. Do you feel able to answer some questions, Nora dear—or would you rather wait a few days?"

"Now, darling!" said Nora. "I'll answer any question I can. Don't be afraid! Ask me anything! Let's talk now!"

IV

"NORA, DEAR," SAID ROLLINS, "I want you and Alice to know that I'm not doing this questioning because I want to. I feel precisely like a surgeon who is operating on his own daughter to save her life. Your father was murdered two days ago, Nora! We don't know the motive, or the name of the man who did it, although we can guess at his reason. Two days have been lost already, and each added day we delay will make our job harder. I propose to learn all I can from you, from Alice, and from Sarah about your father's life, his habits, his associates, his friends, and his methods of work. With these facts we'll have a base on which to build.

"Oh, Sarah! Come in here! That's right! We want you to help us on this job. I know you thought the world and all of Mr. Stevens, and you may possibly have heard him say something or seen him do something which none of us know. Now, then, my shorthand is none too good, but I'm going to write out my questions and your answers just as if you were witnesses in court, and then I can study the facts later without depending on memory. Alice, will you get me some paper? All right! Thank you! Now, Nora, here's where we start. This is the first question:

"Up to last night, when you told Alice and me about your father's new process, who else in the world do you think could possibly have known he had nearly succeeded in perfecting it?"

Nora: "No one but myself and Sarah, except possibly in the last ten days, when he had got the process perfect. His old partner, Edward Folsom, knew he was working on it, but Father hadn't anywhere near succeeded then."

Bob: "Do you know Folsom's last address, or where he's likely to be now?"

Nora: "Mr. Folsom was living in Los Angeles a year ago, and it seems to me Father spoke of getting a letter from him lately, saying he was coming east. I'll hunt for that letter tonight."

Bob: "Please do! Find every letter from Folsom that you can. It's mighty important. What kind of a man was Folsom, Nora?"

Nora: "Very quiet and reserved. Rather cold and unsympathetic. 'Frozen-face' is what I used to call him when talking to Father. But I think that was because he suffered so sometimes from arthritis. He was awfully anxious to make money. When the firm of Stevens and Folsom dissolved, he screwed Father down to the last cent. He didn't seem to trust anyone. He had a very keen mind, and Father thought him one of the brainiest men he'd ever met, but I didn't like him a bit, and I'm sure Father didn't care for him personally."

Bob: "Did your father carry any insurance, Nora?"

Nora: "Oh, yes, Daddy had ten thousand dollars that he took out fifteen years ago, and another twenty-five thousand he bought almost two years ago—two years next January. The last he took was in the Marathon Life—the same company that Mr. Folsom was insured in. Mr. Folsom liked his policy so well that Father took one just like it."

Bob: "What kind of a policy did your father take, dearest?"

Nora: "A twenty-payment life policy, Bob. It's in his safe downtown. You get through paying premiums in twenty years, and if you get killed by accident, the company pays double."

Bob: "Have you ever seen or read his last policy, Nora?"

Nora: "Oh yes! It's very nice. I read it over twice when it came."

Bob: "Did you notice anything in it about suicide, dear?"

Nora: "Yes, Bob! It said the company would pay back only the premiums if the insured died by suicide within the first two years."

Bob: "Listen, Nora darling! Don't you see what a difference this makes? If your father was poisoned by someone else, as I'm certain he was, that last policy is worth fifty thousand dollars. If we can't prove that he did *not* commit suicide, the policy is of *no* value—except the two years' premiums paid—for he hasn't been insured two full years under that policy. That's another reason, sweetheart, why we just must prove your father was killed by somebody and didn't do it himself."

Nora: "Bob, dear, I don't care if I never get a cent so long as we find out who poisoned Daddy."

Bob: "We'll do it, honey! Now, Nora, tell me, do you think Edward Folsom is still keeping up his insurance in the Marathon Life?"

Nora: "Yes, I feel sure he is. He thought a lot of that insurance, for he's got one sister in California and two nephews—I don't know where they are. Besides that, he couldn't get any other insurance if he dropped the Marathon policy. He has arthritis, you know, and no company would take him."

Bob: "You said, Nora, that your father's policies were in the safe in his office. Do you know the combination of that safe?"

Nora: "Oh, yes! Father had a terribly poor memory for figures. He couldn't remember telephone numbers, or even street addresses. He always had to put down the figures somewhere so he wouldn't forget. The safe-combination used to bother him a lot, and he always had to look at his little memo book every time he opened the safe."

Bob: "Was that the little black memorandum book he used to carry in his inside vest pocket, Nora?"

Nora: "Yes, Bob. The combination is in there. It's 42-86-9-23. You turn the wheel four full turns to the right till you get to 42; then you turn it three full turns to the left and stop at 86; then twice to the right and stop at 9; then once to the left and stop at 23. The safe will then open. If you can't open it, Bob dear, I can. I've done it twice when Father was ill and wanted some papers from the office. Besides that, there's a lot of addresses and telephone numbers in the book, too."

Bob: "That's splendid, dearest. Do you know where your father kept the formula for his process?"

Nora: "Oh, yes! That's in the safe too—in a brown enve-lope, on six little cards. Five of the cards are about chemicals and things, and the last one tells how to use the lights. All about the rotating color-screen, the voltage, oscillations, wave-lengths, and all that. It's funny! Father could remember every one of all those chemicals, but half the time he'd forget our own telephone number. And he never could remember anyone else's."

Bob: "Would you mind if I opened the safe and used your father's office sometimes, Nora?"

Nora: "Of course not, Bob! Do anything you think best, dear. I'm trusting myself to you, and surely I can trust every other thing I've got."

Bob: "God bless you, dearest! You'll never need to worry about me. Now tell me, Nora, did your father ever make an enemy? Is anyone ill-disposed toward him that you know of?"

Nora: "Not a soul, Bob! I'm sure of it. He would do almost anything to keep from hurting the feelings of anybody."

Bob: "Well, then, here's another thing. They found some rhymes—some poetry—in his pocket, written in pencil in his own handwriting. Do you think he wrote them, or did he copy them from somewhere?"

Nora: "Oh, they're his all right, Bob! Father loved to write verses for folks. I've got lots of his poetry. At Christmas and every time one of his close friends had a birthday, he'd write a little poem, made up just for them. He'd keep a typewritten copy of the verses in his scrap-book, but he'd always write the poem in longhand, because that was more personal, he said. It showed that his own hands as well as brain had willingly helped to bring somebody happiness. Some of his poems are lovely, Bob! Should you like to see the book?"

Alice: "They certainly are beautiful, Bob! Nora isn't exaggerating a bit. Shall I get the scrap-book, Nora? I know where it is."

Nora: "Please do, Alice dear! Bob can take it with him when he goes and read the verses when he has time. I know you'll enjoy them, Bob."

Alice: "I'll go and get it now and come right back," and she left the room.

Bob: "I'll surely read the verses, sweetheart, and don't forget to hunt up all of Folsom's letters. Now there's just one thing more I want you to do. We'll both have to be at the inquest tomorrow morning at nine o'clock, but I want you and Alice to come separately, and you two girls sit together. Don't pay any special attention to me or talk to me except to say good morning. We may as well make up our minds, dear, that the coroner's jury will render a verdict of suicide. We mustn't blame them, for every atom of evidence points that way.

"Now, here's what I am asking," Rollins continued. "Just as soon as the verdict is given, you go to the coroner and ask him to give you every one of your father's effects that the police took away. Most of them are in a brown envelope which Inspector Devine took with him. The memorandum book is there, with his key-case and with other papers. So is his last good-bye note. Besides that, the police have his watch and chain and the key to his office. Get them all, Nora dear. Insist on it! Demand it! The police have no right to them after a verdict has been reached. As soon as you get outside, hand me all the things quietly, so no one sees us.

"Ah, thank you, Alice!" he went on, as Alice returned with the scrap-book. "I'll read this just as soon as I can. Now, Alice, can you tell us anything that would help? I know you've only been visiting Nora for a week, but you might have heard Mr. Stevens make some remark about somebody that would give us a lead."

Alice: "I've been trying to think, Bob. Last Friday Mr. Stevens and I were talking about being rich or poor and things like that, and he said, as near as I can remember: 'Alice, I just can't understand this craze some people have for money. Happiness doesn't come from having a lot of money, yet most people seem to think it does. Why, right now there's a chap doing his best to make life miserable for me, just on account of some money that he hasn't the slightest right or title to. He even became so threatening that I'm having a friend of mine intervene and try to make him quit.' That's the only thing I can think of that might help, Bob."

Bob: "Alice, that may help a good deal! Now, Sarah, what can you tell us? Are you absolutely positive that it was a quarter after ten o'clock last Saturday night when Mr. Stevens telephoned that he was going to Milwaukee?"

Sarah: "Absolutely, Mr. Rollins! I could swear to it."

Bob: "Are you sure the hall clock was correct, Sarah?"

Sarah: "Mr. Rollins, that clock is always right. It don't vary ten minutes in a year. It's never stopped once in the whole ten years I've been here. If you'll look at your watch, you'll see it is correct now."

Bob: "Thank you, Sarah. Now, of course you have often heard Mr. Stevens talking to Nora about his color-photographs, and you heard me say, a little while ago, that I believed Mr. Stevens had been murdered. I think the man who killed him was trying to learn the secret of Mr. Stevens' invention. Did you mention to anyone, outside this house, Sarah, that Mr. Stevens had at last succeeded in making really excellent color-photographs? Think, Sarah, please!"

Sarah Vasch was visibly distressed, but it was evident she was doing her loyal best to speak the truth. Finally she answered:

"Mr. Bob, my tongue rattles on so that I don't really know what I say. I'm a regular old-maid gossip, that's what I am. I'm pretty sure I spoke of that last beautiful photo-picture to several of my friends, but I can't remember just now what I said or who I spoke to."

"Do try to remember, Sarah!" urged Rollins, "and tell me the names of *all* whom you told, as soon as you can. Don't you see that nobody could have had a motive for killing Mr. Stevens unless he knew that the invention was successful? There can't be many who know about that, so it's tremendously important that we learn the names of *every* man or woman who has become aware of that fact. Now, Sarah, one last question, please. I am certain that Mr. Stevens was killed three quarters of an hour before you took that telephone message, which you thought came from him. You said his voice sounded strange and not as usual. Sarah, I am convinced that Mr. Stevens' *murderer* spoke to you over the telephone last Saturday night. Can you describe that voice, Sarah? Would you recognize it if you heard it again?"

While Rollins was propounding his last question, the effect of his words upon Sarah Vasch was pitiable. Her cheeks became almost ashen in color; her knees and hands trembled; she seemed on the verge of collapse.

Finally, in sobbing accents, she wailed: "Oh, Mr. Bob! It can't be that I was talking to the man who killed poor Mr. Stevens. It isn't so! It can't be! Oh, I don't know—I can't think—oh!—" and Sarah Vasch, sweet, lovable woman of sixty that she was, slid nervelessly from her chair and fainted.

Rollins and Nora carried the senseless form to her room on the floor above and with the aid of restoratives soon brought her back to consciousness, but Bob refused to question her further.

"Poor old Sarah! No wonder she couldn't stand it," he said as he and his beloved returned to the library. "The very idea that the murder of her dearest friend might possibly have been instigated through her thoughtless words, and that she had unknowingly talked with the murderer, would be enough to knock the props from under any sensitive woman. Let's leave poor Sarah alone, girls! I'll talk to her again in a few days, when she's calmed down and is used to it.

"By the way! I forgot to tell you, girls, that some nervy lad tried to hold me up last night, only half a block from here. We had quite a scrap for a minute and he didn't get away with any money, but he got away himself, worse luck! Anyhow, I wasn't hurt, but I didn't get much sleep, so I'll just take this scrap-book and these notes and run along. I'm glad the car is fixed up, so I won't have to walk away over to the L again. How did the tires come to be flat, Alice?"

"I can't say, Bob," replied Alice. "The man who fixed them said they had a dozen little holes in them, about the size of a bradawl, but he couldn't find any nails or tacks. It's mighty funny, isn't it?"

"I'll say it's funny—and so was that hold-up. Something to think about, believe me. Well, good night, Alice! Do you mind going out into the kitchen and rattling the dishes a minute while I tell Nora something that's been on my mind for two hours? . . . God bless you, Nora darling! I love you with all my heart and soul and body. Good night, beloved! Remember tomorrow!"

Seven o'clock Tuesday morning found Rollins working hard at his desk in the *Leader* Office. At eight he had written nearly a column of copy on the Stevens case, concluding with a brief but kindly obituary of his dead friend. The next hour he devoted to rounding up minor police items for his day's story, and at nine o'clock he stood outside the room wherein the inquest on the body of Alexander Stevens was to be held.

Nora and Alice were just arriving as he entered the hallway, and in passing them Bob received from Nora two envelopes which she deftly slipped into his hand, after which both girls entered the room. Not a word was said by either of the three.

Bob himself was about to step inside when a harsh and most unfriendly voice accosted him. "Hey you, Rollins! Come here a minute. You're a fine hunk of cheese, you are! A hell of a friend! Oh, yes! A nice truthful, Sunday-school guy, I don't think."

It was Hackett, the P.D. photographer.

"What's the trouble, Bill?" said Bob, wonderingly.

"Don't 'Bill' me, you low-down lying tramp! You couldn't keep your damned trap closed twenty-four hours, but had to spill the beans about the extra print I gave you, and you couldn't wait even one day to do it! An' now I'm canned! D'ya get me? *Canned!* Just because I tried to do a friend a favor."

"Listen, Bill Hackett!" said Bob. "May the Lord strike me dead if I've ever told any man, woman, or child on earth about that print. I'll swear it on a stack of Bibles, Bill! For Heaven's sake, believe me! See here, Hackett! We've got to thresh this out. Both of us have got to attend this inquest now, but as soon as it's over, you meet me on the northwest corner of Madison and Clark, and I'll prove that I'm no liar. Will you do it, Bill? Be a good scout and say yes."

Hackett looked Bob in the eyes for a minute. "All right, Rollins! I'll be there. Ten minutes after this shindig adjourns. Remember, now! No crawfishing, or I'll smash your face for you, if it's the last thing I do." Hackett turned and entered the inquest chamber.

Bob followed, utterly dazed by this encounter. He had told Bill Hackett the precise truth, and at that moment the extra print reposed safely in his own inside coat pocket.

Every person who had even in the most remote degree been connected with the tragedy of room 713, Meyers Building, in the twelve hours before and after nine thirty on Saturday evening, November 18, was called to testify at the coroner's inquest. As far as Bob could judge, each one of them told the truth without reservation. Nora's testimony was brief and entirely of negative character. The coroner's questions to her were voiced with discretion and sympathy, and in ten minutes Nora's ordeal was over. The report of the four Police Department investigators was read aloud, and each man, including Hackett, orally confirmed all the facts set forth therein, amplifying some of the items.

Bob himself was astounded that so few questions were propounded for him to answer. He was asked regarding Stevens' telephone call, and the message that he was going to Milwaukee, and he stated the time it had been received, according to Sarah Vasch. He was questioned about the visit of Sergeant O'Connor and himself to room 713 on Monday, their forcible entrance through the transom, the finding of the body, and their joint request for police assistance. The coroner appeared on the point of making further queries of Bob, regarding the precise time of the telephone call and other details of the department report. After a brief period of indecision, however, he desisted, saying: "That's all, Mr. Rollins." Again Bob attempted to speak, but without avail. "That's all," the coroner repeated.

An employee of the telephone company confirmed the fact that a telephone call had been made from Stevens' office to his home on Saturday evening, but the exact time of the call was not shown on their records.

Dr. Alston's autopsy disclosed poisoning by potassium cyanide. "Stevens took enough cyanide to kill ten men," he said. In the doctor's opinion, death was almost instantaneous.

Sarah Vasch, the housekeeper at the Stevens home, had not been summoned to the inquest. Recalling her statement that on the fateful Saturday night she had talked with Alexander Stevens over the phone at ten fifteen—after Stevens was supposedly dead—Rollins could not understand it.

"A fine sample of somebody's idiocy!" he thought. "Sarah Vasch is the most important witness in this case, and yet she isn't summoned to the inquest."

Inspector Devine's testimony presented the facts brought out in the police inquiry in masterly fashion, and at half past ten the jury rendered a finding of suicide, without discussion or even leaving their seats.

A few minutes later Bob saw Nora and Alice talking to Coroner Howard. He noted with immense satisfaction that all of Stevens' belongings were handed by Howard to Nora, despite a protest from two other officials.

Bob stood waiting on the sidewalk near the door when the two girls left the building, and again Nora slipped a package to Bob in passing. Nora and Alice then proceeded to the undertaker's to arrange for Stevens' funeral.

The package was a small paper bag, which apparently Nora had secured for that purpose prior to the inquest. A swift glance into the bag told Bob that all he wanted was within; best of all, the brown envelope containing Stevens' memorandum book had not been opened.

The jury had evidently been satisfied with the police report and its accompanying photographs, without viewing the original articles, which would normally have been produced in evidence.

The first smile that had crossed Bob's face for two days broadened to a grin. He could have shouted for joy.

Stopping a moment at the *Leader* office, to turn in his inquest story (which he had scribbled in the inquiry room), Bob found Hackett waiting for him at Madison and Clark streets, as agreed.

"Bill," said Rollins, "don't let's talk here! Come on over to Stevens' office with me. I've got the key to it. We can talk there and get down to the bottom of this."

Five minutes later they had arrived at their destination, and Hackett began:

"Listen, Rollins! I don't know whether to believe you or not, about that print, but let me tell you just what happened this morning, and then I'll listen to you. I got to headquarters at ten minutes to eight. Inspector Devine was the first man that met me as I stepped in. The minute he saw me he snapped: 'Hackett, come into my office!' I could see he was mad, but he was as cold as ice. As soon as we got in, he closed the door and said: 'How many prints did you make from each one of those four negatives in that suicide case yesterday?' 'Two,' says I, which was true—almost. 'Which negative did you make an extra print of and give to Rollins?' says he. Well, sir, he had me! I didn't dare to lie, for he looked as though he knew I'd done what he said. If I lied to him and swore I *hadn't* made an extra print—and if he knew I had—why, then the stuff was all off and I'd be fired sure. If I didn't lie, but 'fessed up and tried to smooth it over, I had a bare chance to get by with a call-down. So I owned up an' told him I'd loaned you an extra print of the rear view of the body, and that you'd promised faithfully not to use it without my permission."

Hackett paused for a moment and then resumed: " 'Hackett!' says Devine, 'this is your last week on the Chicago Police Department. On Saturday you're through—and you know why. What's more, you can tell your friend Mr. Rollins that he'd better destroy that print and do it now. It is not his property. He obtained it by subterfuge. He has no right to it, and he's no better than a thief if he keeps or uses it! That's all.' Now," said Hackett, "what have you got to say, Rollins?"

"Just what I said this morning, Bill. Here's your print. It's been in this coat pocket of mine ever since you gave it to me. Only once have I taken it out. Not once have I whispered or breathed a word about it to anyone, so help me God! Devine's question to you was pure bluff, but it worked. Do you believe me, Bill? Will you shake hands on it, old scout?"

"All right, Bob! I believe you, and I'll shake, but that don't give me my job back," said Hackett.

"Bill, I'll gamble every dollar I'll ever have on earth that you'll have your job back before Christmas—if you'll stick by me and work with me—and keep your mouth shut. Will you do it, Bill? Are you game?"

"By thunder, I'm game," said Hackett. "I'll do it! My word of honor, Bob! Now shoot the works!"

"Good boy, Bill! We'll start right now. You're good at shorthand. Take this pad and put down these things I'm going to tell you as I reel 'em off to you. Ready?"

"O.K., Bob! Let her go!"

V

"BEFORE you take down these questionable items, Bill, let's talk over some of them. We'll start with this one first.

"There was no electric light in this room when O'Connor and I came in here and found Stevens' body. Stevens couldn't have turned out the light after he drank that cyanide on Saturday night. The poison worked too quickly for that. He must have had an electric light turned on when he put the whisky and cyanide in that liquor-glass or he couldn't have seen what he was doing. The first question, then, is: Why did Stevens turn out the light before he poisoned himself? What sane reason could there be that a man should desire to commit suicide by poison in the dark? Can you think of any sound, logical excuse for it, Bill?"

Hackett studied the query for a moment. "No!" he said. "The more I think of it, the more idiotic it seems. The light-switch is twenty feet away on the wall beside the door. Stevens would have to come back from it in the dark, feel his way around all these reflectors, chairs, and tables, sit down in that swivel-chair, reach for the glass with the poison in it, and then drink the dose. No, Bob! The thing isn't reasonable. That's all."

"All right, Bill! Put that down as query number one. Now let's discuss the next point. I want you to examine all the bottles on those shelves and in the dark-room. See if you can find any flask, bottle, or other receptacle which has any whisky in it now or has *ever* held whisky. Go over the whole room, Bill, and be absolutely sure you don't miss any possible container. Smell all of them and see what you find."

After twenty minutes of exhaustive search Hackett reported: "Can't find a sign or smell of whisky in the whole shop, anywhere. There never has been any. I'll swear to it."

"All right, Bill. I looked all over the place yesterday and couldn't locate anything which had ever held whisky, but I wanted to be sure. You and I also know that Stevens had no flask on his person. The question is, then, how did Stevens transport that whisky—in which the cyanide was later dissolved—from outside this building into this room? In what receptacle did he carry it? He certainly didn't carry a glass full of liquor in his hand all the way from some downtown speak-easy, through the streets, into the elevator, and up here into this laboratory; yet we know positively, from analysis, that the poison which he took was dissolved in whisky. How, then, did the whisky get here? Put that down as query number two, will you, Bill?"

"Will I? I'll say I will. Sufferin' Moses! I'd never have thought of that in a million years. Go ahead, Bob! Give us some more!"

"Sure! Here goes the next one. If you were a first-class chemist, Bill, and knew the physiological effect of a poison like cyanide of potassium—were aware that a small dose of that drug would kill a man almost before he could taste it—would you go to the trouble of dissolving that cyanide in whisky? Or would you use plain water as a solvent? What's the answer?"

"Huh! I'd use water, of course. Anybody would."

"So would I, Bill! Put that down as query number three, please. Why is it that Stevens didn't use water as a solvent for the suicide dose he is supposed to have taken?"

"She's down, Bob. I've got it and it's a pippin. What's the next one?"

"The next is about that desk. Take a good look at it. Anybody could see that it has been thoroughly cleaned off within the last day or two. See how nice and shiny it is on the entire side opposite where Stevens sat and also on each side of where his body lay. Downing couldn't find a single fingerprint anywhere on that desk except on the portion which was covered by Stevens' body, and all the prints on that portion had been made by Stevens' fingers. Not one made by anybody else. Rather extraordinary, isn't it?

"Now, Bill, I ask you if there can be any logical reason why an intelligent man should polish up four fifths of his desk and leave the other fifth greasy and grimy—if he had access to the entire surface of the desk while he was doing his polishing?"

Hackett shook his head, and Rollins resumed:

"I can only conceive of one reason for doing such a sense-less thing, and here is my inference: The person who wiped off four fifths of that desk could not possibly wipe off the other fifth because Stevens' body and left arm covered that fifth while he was wiping it. Another thing, Bill. Look at that towel there under the sink. It's filthy with dirt and grime. Worse than if somebody had cleaned off a dozen shoes with it. That towel must have been freshly laundered last Friday, for Superintendent Donovan told me that this room was last cleaned on Friday. This means that the towel acquired its grime on Saturday—the day Stevens died. From that, of course, my inference is that the towel was used to wipe off that desk and that the wiping was probably done to erase any possible finger-prints. I think you had better put down as the next query: Who polished off four fifths of Stevens' desk and left the other fifth uncleaned; and why was this done?"

Hackett was fairly trembling with excitement. "Got it all down, Bob! Shoot your next question! Come on! Make it snappy, old man!"

"All right, Bill, I will. It seems to me that practically the same query should apply to the floor and waste-basket as to the desk. Stevens used this room all day Saturday. We know that. He must have torn up and discarded some papers and created some other litter. Nevertheless you can't find even the smallest scrap in the waste-basket or on the floor. Both are as clean as a new-built house. Somebody, therefore, must have swept up the place and carried off all the waste and lit-ter which accumulated Saturday. I should say, then, that query number five ought to be: Did Stevens—or somebody else—destroy and remove *all* of Saturday's litter; and *how* did he dispose of it? Did he personally carry it out of this room before taking poison—or what?"

Only three words escaped Hackett. "Go on, Bob!" he gasped hoarsely.

"Let's tackle that good-bye note of Stevens next, Bill," said Rollins. "Here it is. Look at it! You'll notice it has not been *torn* off from a letter-head, but has been *cut* off by means of a knife or a pair of scissors. Look at the line 'I bid the world good-bye'! See how very close it is to the top margin of the paper! Nobody would normally write as close to the margin as that. Stevens had ample room on this paper slip to write four or five lines instead of only one line and his signature. Don't forget, too, that he had dozens of *whole* letter-heads in his desk to write on."

Bill nodded, and his friend continued his series of deductions. "There is absolutely no doubt that Stevens personally wrote that line and signed his name to it, but I'm certain he did *not* write it as a notification to the world that he was going to commit suicide. The whole thing is so abnormal that I think query number six should read: Why didn't Stevens use a whole letter-head, or space his message on the paper in normal fashion, and why did he write an ambiguous rhythmic message such as this?"

Rollins paused for a moment, thinking.

"Is that all, Bob?" inquired Hackett as he gazed admiringly at his partner. "Seems to me we've got more than plenty to prove you were right when you told the Inspector this was not a suicide, but a murder. What more can you dig up, I'd like to know."

"We've hardly scratched the surface yet, Bill. I'm going to read off a long list of other queries which I put down while I was here alone, after O'Connor had gone to headquarters to make his report on Monday morning. Just scribble these down, Bill, as I give them to you. I'll call them off in numerical order as I wrote them.

"Number 7. Why did Stevens remove the key to this room from the remainder of the keys attached to his key-container? His daughter tells me this particular key is the *only* one which fits the lock of this laboratory door and that her father always kept it in his key-case.

"Number 8. Why should he put that key in front of him on his desk before he died and what special reason had he for selecting that location?

"Number 9. We know that Stevens used his safe daily, and Miss Stevens tells me that his most important records were kept there. Why is that safe-dial entirely devoid of *any* finger-prints—and who polished them off—and when?

"Number 10. Since *all* prints were undoubtedly wiped off that dial, why were the prints so erased?

"Number 11. Notice those two shiny glasses on that shelf—one large glass and one liquor-glass! Why are those two so clean and shiny while all the other glasses are dusty and dim? Both of those two must have been recently polished. When—and by whom?

"Number 12. Why should Stevens select a liquor-glass to take his fatal dose from instead of a water-glass?

"Number 13. Stevens' desk and fountain-pen were polished thoroughly, except the portion of the desk we discussed. Why is that onyx penholder so dusty and unclean? Was there a reason for polishing the pen, but not the holder?

"Number 14. Why are there no finger-prints of anyone on that telephone receiver, when the evidence would appear to show that Stevens called up his home last Saturday night?

"Number 15. Since so many of the objects in this room appear to have been wiped off so recently, and probably within two or three days at most, was this wiping done before or after Stevens died?

"Number 16. There are dozens of large photographs in this room, but absolutely no small ones. This indicates that the large camera was often used and the small camera but rarely. Why, then, is the small film-camera completely free from dust, while the large plate-camera is thick with it?

"Number 17. I happen to know that Stevens never smoked in his life. Notice that someone has pinched off the fire from a lighted cigarette on the rim of that cuspidor there. Who did it—and when was it done?

"Number 18. Stevens was never a man to do manual labor such as building fires, shoveling snow, sifting ashes, washing dishes, or cleaning up of any sort. Why, then, should he go contrary to his nature and clean, sweep, and polish innumerable articles in his laboratory?

"Number 20. Stevens idolized his daughter, Eleanor. She was always first in his mind. *Could* a man who loved his child so dearly destroy himself by committing suicide without a last spoken or written word to her?

"Number 21. Why should Stevens, having no intention of going to Milwaukee, telephone a lie to his home? And how could he, when all indications seem to prove that he died forty-seven minutes before that phone call?

"Number 22. Within the last ten days Stevens had achieved his greatest ambition. Is it reasonable to believe that a man who has reached the very pinnacle of his life's aim should take his own life?

"Number 23. Stevens had a twenty-five-thousand-dollar life-insurance policy which contained a clause making the policy invalid and worthless if he committed suicide within two years from its date. The policy is now twenty-two and a half months old, and the two years will expire on January 2 next. By waiting six weeks to commit suicide he would have bequeathed to his daughter fifty thousand dollars in cash. Could any sane man, knowing that fact, kill himself and wipe out that inheritance to his beloved child?

"Number 24. Are all these seeming trifles accidents or coincidences? Or did some person who was in this room with Alexander Stevens last Saturday night *murder* him and try to cover his tracks?

"I think you had better tackle that last question first, Bill. What is your answer? Have I proved my case?"

"My God, yes! You've *more* than proved it. It's *murder!* Nothing else."

"I knew you'd see it that way, Bill. But you must remember that all of these things we've discussed are only inferences—not evidence. What I want to know is—will you stick by me and help me turn them into evidence? Will you do it—and bring some damnable hound to justice?"

"I'll stick till hell freezes over. You know it, Bob," replied Hackett.

"All right, Bill! Here's the motive of all this. Stevens was a potential millionaire. He would have assuredly been one if he had lived. He had just perfected an invention—in color-photography—that is simply marvelous. My theory is that somebody murdered Stevens to get that invention for himself and keep Stevens from using or selling it."

"How's that? Where did Stevens keep his dope?" inquired Hackett.

"I happen to know, through Stevens' daughter, that his whole discovery and the formulae for using it are written on six cards and locked up in that safe," answered Rollins. "His daughter told me the combination of the safe and also said that Stevens carried a record of that combination in his black memo book. His memory for numbers was very poor. You remember the memo book we took from the inside pocket of Stevens' vest yesterday. It's in this brown envelope here right now. Stevens had to look at it whenever he opened the safe. Memory was bad. Now, Bill, I'm going to open that safe and see if those six cards are there yet. I'm also going to see if there are any finger-prints on any of 'em except Stevens'. He surely would never have shown those cards to anyone. My idea is that the murderer wanted to copy or steal those cards, and I shouldn't be a bit surprised if they were missing." The safe soon stood open, and the envelope containing the formula cards was disclosed at once, in a small compartment.

Bob removed the envelope gingerly, handling it by its edges. "Better use our handkerchiefs in handling these cards and the envelope, Bill. We don't want to mess 'em up with any of our finger-prints. Have you got your powder and brush with you? All right! Just dust all the cards and envelope—both sides—and we'll see what shows up."

A little later Hackett remarked: "Did you see that other card, Bob? I don't find it here."

"What other card?" said Bob.

"Why, card number six—I've got five cards here, each one numbered from one to five. There isn't any number six and you said there were six altogether."

"Let's stop right here, Bill!" said Rollins. "I know there were six cards, for Nor—I mean Miss Stevens—told me the sixth card explained how to use the color-screens and lights. Isn't it here, Bill?"

"Nope! Not here! All these five cards show nothing but chemical formulae. Nothing at all about lights or anything like that."

"Isn't there a card headed 'Method'?" asked Rollins.

"Not here! Look! See! That's all there is in the envelope!"

Bob studied the envelope and cards for a few seconds. "Look here, Bill! There's no logical reason on earth why Stevens should have removed that one card and put it somewhere else. That card was vital to his color-process. The whole thing was N.G. without it. The chances are a thousand to one that Stevens put all six cards in that envelope together, and that he locked that safe before he died, knowing that all were there. He *couldn't* have taken out that one card, and since he didn't, we've got to believe that somebody else did."

"That looks like common sense to me. But what are we going to do about it?"

"The first thing," replied Bob, "is to see if there are any fingerprints on the cards or envelope besides those of Stevens. You've studied Stevens' prints so often you must know 'em at sight now. Do you find any strange prints?"

"Not a single one! Not one anywhere!" said Hackett. "Every one on these cards was made by Stevens. I'll swear to it. But I do notice something else, Bob! Look at this third formula on card number one. That chemical symbol there represents potassium ferro-cyanide. Just below it you'll notice the symbol HCl, which means hydrochloric acid. The formula indicates that twenty drops of the acid are to be added to the potassium solution. No chemist could possibly do such a thing. The fellow who would do that is bug-house. Why, he'd knock hell out of the potassium solution and have a lot of precipitation at the bottom of his test-tube the instant the acid went into the mess. This man Stevens was a bird of a chemist. He knew that would happen if he stuck to the formula as it's written here." Hackett resumed his study of the cards and then exploded further.

"Say, Bob! Here's another mess almost as bad on card two. That HNO_2 means nitrous acid, and the Lord pity the man who monkeys with nitrous compounds like that. They're all unstable and more or less explosive, and it's courting death to handle 'em, unless you know just what you're doing. Stevens knew that as well as I. Hey! Here's another one on card three. Say, Bob! This is damn-foolishness! Either Stevens was bug-house, or somebody has changed some chemicals on these cards."

"All right, Bill. I'm not surprised. Here, take this pocket microscope and see if you can find any indication of a change in symbols at those three points you just mentioned. Maybe a letter or figure has been added or scratched out."

"Nothing scratched out, Bob," said Hackett, "but some of the letters are a little different in shape. In some places, too, the ink looks fresher-like and just a little brighter in color. Wait a minute! I'll test the ink on this one! Look's to me as if there were two kinds of ink here. If that's so, I'll have the answer in a jiffy. Shut up, Bob, and let me work!"

Bill applied his testing alkalis carefully at five or six points and studied the results. Then, turning to Bob, he said slowly: "You're right! They've been changed in all these five places with a different ink, and, I believe, a different handwriting."

"Good boy, Bill!" said Rollins. "Here's conclusive proof that the murderer opened this safe and changed these formulae. Say, Bill, before we go to lunch, I want you to test the ink in that desk fountain-pen there. See if it's the same sort of ink that was used in making these alterations on the cards. Test the ink on this 'good-bye' note too. Was *that* written by this desk fountain-pen?"

"Right you are, old sox!" said Hackett ten minutes later. "Same ink on the card-alterations, but the note was *not* written with this ink. I'll bet a million that damned skunk sat right at this desk and altered those cards with Stevens' dead body square in front of him. Some nerve, I'll say! But why in hell should Stevens write that suicide note with another kind of ink? I'm frightened, Bob! That guy won't stop at nothin'. He don't care any more for a man's life than a cigarette butt. If he ever gets wise to what we're doin', we'll have to lock ourselves in a room an' cook our own meals or emigrate to China. Believe me, Bob, that's so!"

"I think we've both good reason to be careful—mighty careful! Come on, Bill, let's eat and we'll come back right after lunch. Give me that key. It's a good thing you can't forget to lock the door with this sort of lock. The key won't come out of the keyhole unless you've turned it and shot the bolt out first. It's a nuisance, but it certainly prevents a fellow from leaving the door unlocked if he's absent-minded."

After the comrades had returned, Rollins inquired: "How long can you stay here with me and help, Bill? Won't you have to get back to headquarters?"

"To hell with headquarters! I'm fired anyhow, and if they don't pay me for the rest of this week, I'll only lose four days. I'll phone 'em now and tell 'em I'm sick and likely to be laid up two or three days longer. It's true, too! I'm so damned sick about this whole rotten business that I can hardly eat—an', believe me, when I can't eat, there's somep'n wrong. Gimme that phone." Hackett delivered his message and hung up the receiver. "What's next?" said he.

Rollins sat thinking. Finally he started. "Let's reason about this a little! We know that Stevens must have used all these cards every day while he was experimenting. That includes last Saturday, when he was murdered. He'd have noticed instantly if the formulae had been altered before Saturday, so the alterations must have been made after Friday, anyhow. That fixes the approximate time." Rollins looked at Hackett, who nodded comprehension.

Bob continued: "The next thing is that the altered cards are in the safe; the safe is locked tight; the lock hasn't been injured, and, finally, Stevens was *not* the man who opened and closed the safe to put those cards back. If Stevens had put them back, the six cards would all be there, and he would surely have noticed those alterations on them. You'll agree to that, Bill, I'm sure."

"Absolutely!" was the prompt reply, and Bob resumed his analysis of facts.

"That proves that the man who made those alterations *must* have possessed the combination of that safe. Only two people knew that combination—Stevens and his daughter—and it's a cinch neither of them ever told it to anybody. There's only one other way that the skunk who opened that safe could learn the combination, and that is from Stevens' memorandum book, which we've got in this envelope here. If he got the combination from that book, he must have handled the book, and if he handled the book, there's a fair chance of our finding his finger-prints somewhere on or in the book."

"Ain't you forgetting something, Rollins? Don't you remember how we dusted that book and couldn't get a finger-print of any kind off it?"

"Yes," said Bob; "you dusted the outside, but I noticed nobody dusted the inside. In fact, as I remember it, nobody even opened the book and looked inside of it."

"By thunder, you're right! And say! Somebody must have wiped off the outside of that book before the last time it went into Stevens' pocket, or else Stevens' finger-prints would show somewhere on the covers. Let's get at that book right now, Bob! Shall we?"

"Yes, that ought to be our next move, Bill! Let's be mighty careful we don't get any of our prints on it, though. I'll open up this envelope, and you take out the book with your fingers in your handkerchief. I wish we had some silk or rubber gloves here. We sure need 'em.

"There we are, Bill!" said Rollins. "Now leaf the book real carefully by its edges. Hey! Stop! See that page where the book sort of opens itself a little—just as if it had been stretched out flat recently? Now open it at that page real slow, Bill. See that little bit of grayish powder between those two pages and near the binding? Dump that bit of dust out here on this clean sheet of writing-paper! Now! What would you say it is?"

Both men stared at the tiny grayish flakes resting so innocently on the pure blue-tinted surface of the letter-head.

"If that ain't a tiny bit of cigarette ash, I'll eat my hat!" said Hackett.

"That's just what it is, Bill! And please notice two things. The first is that those ashes were right in the crevice of two pages—and on one of those pages are the combination numbers which open that safe. See 'em! There they are, right there! The second thing is that Stevens never smoked in his life. Do you see what this means, Bill? *He* didn't spill those ashes. The last man who opened that book did so to learn the combination of Stevens' safe—but he left his calling card. Those ashes! I'm thinking possibly he might have left another card or two here besides the ashes. Just dust those two pages real carefully, Bill, and see whether there are any finger-prints on 'em besides those of Stevens."

Hackett was too excited to speak. He worked feverishly over the book for a few minutes and, without looking up, whispered hoarsely: "Don't look yet, Bob! I'm gonna dust these three or four pages which come just before an' just after these two. There might be something on them."

Five minutes later, still holding the book through his handkerchief, Hackett was prancing round the room like a howling dervish. "We've got him, Bob! We've got the . . .! Here's five dandy prints! A thumb and two fingers of his right hand and a thumb and one finger of his left. That settles his hash! Sufferin' cats! I wouldn't have missed this for a million dollars. We'll find that damn skunk now, if it takes ten years. Believe you me, I'll spend every darn cent I got, and I don't give a cuss whether I ever get another job or not. Here! You hold this book in the handkerchief, Bob! Don't touch it, or I'll murder you! I'm gonna take plenty negatives of these little old finger-prints. I'll develop and print 'em right here, an' don't you believe I won't. Help me with this big camera and stand; bring over those two reflectors, too, while I get some plates! Oh, boy! This is the real goods!" Half an hour later, when the excitement had subsided and the two men were waiting for the negatives to dry, Bob remarked: "Well, Bill! We're off to a fine start, but don't forget it's only a start! It's going to be some job to prove this is a murder and to pick out this dirty hyena from a couple of million men in Illinois, but I'll gamble we do it."

"I'll gamble *you* will, Bob Rollins! If it wasn't for you, we'd both be sittin' on the bench right now, signin' a suicide verdict like the rest of them flat-feet. But what's gonna be the next act in our show?"

"I don't think that's hard. This man we're hunting for wanted the formulae on those cards, that's sure. That's what he came for. That's what he opened the safe for; and I know, now, that's why he poisoned Stevens. He got the cards. The proof of that is he altered the chemical symbols on some and carried off one card—or so I believe. I believe, too, that the last two things were done so that nobody else could reproduce this process after Stevens' death. He didn't take the other five cards away with him, for that might have aroused suspicion of robbery—*yet he must have copied them before he altered them.* You're a chemist, Bill; how long would it take you to copy the chemical symbols on those five cards and be sure each one of 'em was right?"

"I'd be a damn fool to do it, Bob! It would take almost a day. I'd photograph 'em, of course, same as I did those finger-prints."

"What camera would you use, Bill? The big one or that little one over there?"

"I dunno! The big one, I guess; that's the best."

"So, after you'd committed the robbery and murder, you'd saunter downstairs and stroll through the streets with three big double plate-holders under your arm and a guilty conscience? Eh, Bill?"

"Gee whiz, Bob! You make me feel like a dummy—I forgot the big camera takes plates. I'd use the little one with films, of course. Anybody would who had brains—which it seems like I haven't."

"Never mind the brain stuff, Bill; you've got plenty. I agree with you that this man probably used that small film-camera over there. We know there are no finger-prints on the outside of it, for you dusted it for prints yesterday, but it's just possible—although I doubt it—that this slick artist might have left some prints on the inside somewhere. Anyhow, we'll try it and see. Come on, Bill, you open it up!"

The inside of the opened camera was thoroughly dusted with finger-print powder, but none other than the prints of Stevens were observed. Bob was just about to close up the bellows and put it away when Hackett said: "See here, Bob! This shutter's stuck. The lens is wide open right now! It has been ever since that . . . left it."

The somewhat vacant look on Rollins' face implied a question.

"Don't you see what this means, Bob? It means that at least one of his films was over-exposed, and it's probably as black as your hat. I hope the whole damned batch is ruined. It could be. Just suppose that blessed old shutter got stuck on the first picture he shot! Why, old Mr. Lens would be keepin' open house from then on, and every damn film would be gettin' light-struck the minute the film came opposite the lens.

"Sufferin' Moses! This is the biggest joke I ever seen. Here's a guy commits murder and three or four hundred other crimes, an' all he gets out of it—mebbe—is a bunch of black films that wouldn't print a pound of butter. Oh Mister! But then, mebbe the luck ain't so good as that. Mebbe he took two shots at each card and mebbe the shutter only got stuck on the last shot. Then he'd have at least one good negative of each card! Oh gosh! Don't let's think of that! What's the program now, Bob?"

"I was just looking round, Bill," said Rollins. "I'm pretty sure this man didn't bring any films with him, for he couldn't be certain what size this camera needed. It's likely, then, that he used film from this stock. If he did, he probably took the boxes away with him, but perhaps he didn't. Yes, here's two empty boxes. That means he took two shots at each card."

"True for you," replied Mr. William Hackett.

"All right, then! Now let's sit down and do a little more thinking," said Bob. "Get that pad you had before, and put down these thoughts, even if they are erratic. We can fix them up in sequence later.

"In the first place, we haven't proved yet that anybody poisoned Stevens. His finger-prints on that whisky-glass, the 'good-bye' note which he left in his own handwriting, the sole key to his room lying on the desk before him, all continue to indicate suicide, despite what we've dug up so far. We know that somebody got into this room and did what we've learned, but that doesn't debar the possibility of Stevens having taken his own life. For instance, this slick robber might have somehow secured a duplicate key, might have entered the office when Stevens was absent, done his work, and departed. After the man had gone, Stevens might have returned, discovered that someone had stolen his process, become desperate at the thought of his life-work being wasted, locked the door, put the key on the table, written that 'good-bye' letter, put a few cyanide crystals in a glass where a spoonful of whisky had been left over from some previous dosing, drunk it down, and died.

"Here's another possible theory, Bill. Let's assume that Stevens suddenly found that his first few successful color-photos resulted from a chemical fluke; that he couldn't reproduce his successful pictures, that his supposedly perfect process is years away from perfection, that he must start all over anew, that he became desperate, drank the poison, and left that note and key.

"Suppose that after this had occurred, our burglar enters with his duplicate key, finds Stevens dead, coolly goes ahead with his photo-stunts, polishes all the things which might betray his presence, and calmly walks out with his photo-copies of Stevens' formulae, leaving the body of Stevens precisely as it was when he entered. Of course you and I, Bill, are certain in our own minds that Stevens was *mur-*

dered, but that is not yet proved. Here is the whole question: murder or suicide? That question hinges on two things: First, is this key the *only* existing key to room 713, and did Stevens, when buying it, prevent the possibility of its duplication? Second, *could* the man who robbed Stevens of his secret obtain possession of such a duplicate key?"

Hackett was eager to reply. "Listen, Bob! I suppose you know where that lock came from and who made that key, don't you?"

"Yes! Here is the address. Miss Stevens handed it to me this morning. Do you want to undertake the job of making *certain* as to whether or not a duplicate key was made, or could be made, for the lock on that door?"

Hackett strode across to the chair on which lay his coat and hat, put them on, handed Rollins the shorthand notes he had just transcribed, and said:

"I expect to be back inside of two hours, at least. When I do get back, you can bet every dollar you've got that I'll have every fact you want to know about that key. I'll stake my life on it. So long!" An hour later Bill knocked on the door of room 713, and Bob let him in.

"I've sure got the goods on that key stuff, Bob. I went over to Banister's, where Stevens bought it, and saw the superintendent, Mr. Morgan, personally. You know Banister's is the most reliable hardware store in town, and Mr. Morgan remembered selling that lock to Stevens six months ago. He knew Stevens well, and when Stevens came in and asked for him, Mr. Morgan gave him personal attention and made the sale himself.

"Stevens said that he was absent-minded and wanted to buy a lock which was fixed so that a man couldn't go out, no matter how forgetful he was, without locking the door every time. He wanted a heavy strong lock and didn't care how much it cost him. Morgan suggested a spring lock, but Stevens wouldn't listen. Morgan then told Stevens that they had one sample lock made by a concern in Birmingham, England, which he thought would fill the bill. The lock was solid, with heavy tumblers and bolts. You couldn't put the

key in or take the key out unless the bolt stuck out of the
lock—which meant that the door was locked. You noticed
yesterday, Bob, that this lock works just like that. You said it
was a nuisance, but mighty good for a forgetful man. Well,
Superintendent Morgan said that Stevens told him that the
lock was just what he wanted.

"Then Stevens asked Morgan about the key. There were
two keys, of course, and Stevens asked if he could have one
of them slightly altered. Morgan said he could, and that the
firm's own locksmith would do it. So Stevens and Morgan
went down in the basement of Banister's. They stood there
while the firm's locksmith altered one of the tumblers and
filed a deeper slot in the middle part of one key, so that it
would unlock the bolt from either side."

"Where did Stevens put the key after the alteration?" asked
Rollins.

"Stevens then put that key with his other keys in that little
leather key-case we saw yesterday. He kidded with Morgan
about it and remarked that if he ever lost that one key, the
door would have to be blasted with dynamite. Then Morgan
asked Stevens if he wasn't going to have the duplicate key
filed to fit the lock, the same as the original. Stevens said:
'No! There's only going to be *one* key to this lock, and that's
this one right here.'

"Morgan warned Stevens that if he ever lost that key, the
Banister firm would have to send over to Birmingham to get
a key-blank with tiny corrugations of that type. It seems they
don't make that sort of corrugated key-blank in America, and
it would take about four weeks to get another from Birmingham. Meanwhile Stevens would be locked out, unless he had
somebody jimmy open the door.

"Stevens said: 'I'm not going to lose that key, unless
somebody takes it off my dead body.' My God, Bob! Ain't it
funny about Stevens' saying that? I'll bet a million that key
was taken off Stevens' dead body.

"Seems to me, Bob, that settles this lock and key business,
but, the way I see it, we are in a deeper hole than ever. By
thunder! I can't believe Keller or Houdini or anybody else

could lock that door on the outside, throw this key through three inches of solid oak, and have the damn key land in the middle of this desk within a foot of Stevens' hand, while he was laying here dead. That's the one thing in this whole case that cooks me. The fellow who can do that stunt is sure some wizard."

Rollins rose wearily and started to put on his overcoat.

"You've certainly done one fine job, and we're on our way for fair. And listen, Bill! Don't worry any more about that key-throwing stunt. I'm no wizard, but within ten days I pledge my word to go outside, *stay outside,* lock you in this room *alone,* and drop that key right under your nose on this desk-top."

VI

As THE COMRADES walked toward the elevator, Rollins turned suddenly, with this remark: "Do this tonight, Bill; it is mighty important! The poisoner we're trying to land is probably a known criminal, with a police record standing against him. If so, the Police Bureau will have his finger-prints and we can compare our prints with theirs. We must be certain about this before we make another move. That comparison may settle the whole case if he has ever been convicted in this state. I want you to make photo-enlargements of each of those five finger-prints on Stevens' memo book. Then take the enlargements over to the Bureau, and see if you and Heywood can identify them. Phone me at the Sanford early tomorrow morning how you come out, will you?"

"Sure!" said Hackett. "Good luck to you, old scout!"

Rollins was thoroughly weary after he had dined. His in-tention had been to take a short stroll for exercise, board the L for home, and get a good night's sleep. The first two pur-poses were successfully carried out, and at half past nine o'clock Bob was in his room at the Sanford preparing for bed, when the telephone rang.

It was Detective Sergeant James O'Connor on the wire. "Is that you, Rollins? I hate to roust you out tonight, but I wish you'd run over to the City Hospital as quick as you can. There's a dame over there that's pretty near croaked and she had your personal card in her pocket. Her head's caved in, an' she's busted up so bad that she's likely to go west any minute . . ."

"Wait a minute, Jim!" shouted Bob, thinking instantly of Nora. "Who is she? Is she young or old? What does she look like? What has . . ."

"Hold your horses, Bob; I ain't seen her an' I dunno how she looks an' I can't tell you nothin'! All I know is that one of the boys picked her up, rang for the ambulance, and took her to the hospital. The doc there phoned us five minutes ago that she didn't have no money or purse an' nothin' on her person to go by except your card in her coat pocket. That's why I rang you up. Are you goin', or ain'tcha?"

"Sure, I'm going, Jim. As quick as a taxi will get me there. Phone the hospital right off, will you, please? I'm on my way this minute."

The agony of mind that Rollins suffered during that ride cannot be told. His thought was of nothing save Nora; he could think of no one else who could possibly have his personal card, with his residence address on it. The moments consumed in reaching the hospital accident-ward seemed hours to him. No one there could tell him whether the stricken woman was young or old, and only when he *stood at* the bedside and saw the silent, scarcely breathing form did Rollins recognize the face beneath that blood-soaked bandage and know who was the victim.

It was Sarah Vasch!

No person at the hospital could give any particulars of the tragedy, but the nurse stated that skull-fracture and concussion would probably end the patient's life before many hours elapsed.

"There is just about one chance in a hundred that she may live," the doctor told Rollins when Bob saw him. "We shall operate at once. Probably the police can tell you how it happened. I know nothing about that whatever."

At headquarters Sergeant O'Connor gave Bob a hearty welcome. "Glad to see you, Rollins! Wish I could have finished up that suicide business we started on yesterday, but I was assigned to tackle somep'n else an' couldn't."

"Yes, I was sorry you had to go to court . . ."

"Court, hell! I spent two hours at the county jail pumpin' a coupla hit-an'-run souses that killed a kid. That's where I was. Did you know that woman, Rollins?"

"Yes, Sergeant! I've known her for ten years—she's one of the finest old women that God ever made. How did it happen? Do you know?"

"Not a thing yet. The desk-sergeant has booked the case. Haven't had time to look myself. The guy who saw it is right here in the station. He's an A-1 business man, an' several of us fellers know him well. He insisted on stayin' until you came, and whatever he says, you can depend on. His name's Lester—Stacey Lester. Wait a minute an' I'll introduce you. Hey, Mr. Lester! Come on over here an' meet my friend Bob Rollins. He wants to talk to you about that woman that got slugged."

"Slugged!" thought Rollins. "Sarah Vasch slugged! An inoffensive, sixty-year-old woman beaten up so badly that her skull was fractured!" The thing was unbelievable.

Stacey Lester proved to be all that O'Connor had represented. Two minutes of conversation convinced Rollins that here was a personality far above the average. After Bob had explained who the victim was, and his knowledge of her character and her work, Mr. Lester remarked:

"I think I'd better tell you the whole story first, Mr. Rollins, and then I'll be glad to supply any missing details. The Sergeant's stenographer can take down what we say.

"At about nine fifteen tonight I was walking along the west side of Wabash Avenue, south of Van Buren Street, under the L. It was dark there, and, for a wonder, very few people were on the street. About fifty feet in front of me, walking in the same direction, toward Van Buren, was a short woman and a man of about your size. They seemed to be arguing or quarreling. I couldn't hear what they said, but that's the way they acted. Suddenly the woman gave the man a little push backward and waved her hand as if she were saying: 'Keep away from me.' Then she started to walk off very fast toward Van Buren Street.

"The man called after her. I couldn't hear his words, but she stopped and he caught up with her and said something. With his left hand he pointed northward toward Van Buren Street as he spoke. The woman turned again from him to look in the direction where he pointed and I noticed she was holding a little handbag at her side. They both were then fifty or sixty feet away from me, and I didn't get a good look at either of their faces, though I could see the man was younger than the woman.

"The instant the woman turned her back on him, that damnable butcher of a man smashed her with all his might on the head. He did it with a short club or slung shot—I couldn't see which it was—and down she went like a slaughtered ox.

"While he was striking the blow, he grabbed her hand-bag and then ran toward Van Buren Street like a streak. He was gone round the corner before I even got to the spot where that poor woman was lying. There was no possible use of chasing him with that much of a start, so I got hold of an officer and told him the facts; called an ambulance, and went to the hospital with her. After that I came down here and waited for you."

Rollins reached across the corner of O'Connor's desk and grasped Lester's hand. "You're a *man,* Mr. Lester, and I'm proud to know you! But tell me; how hard was that blow? Haven't you exaggerated it a little? I can't believe it!"

"Listen, Mr. Rollins! The blow that man struck was simply tremendous. It wasn't meant to stun that poor woman—it was meant to kill. It's beyond my understanding how anyone could receive a smash like that and still be alive. I told the exact truth when I said that blow would have slaughtered an ox."

"Could you give me any sort of description of the man? Any physical peculiarities, for instance?" inquired Rollins.

"Nothing facial, or as regards clothing, for his back was toward me all the time. I did notice, though, that he stooped forward a little at the waist and walked as if his hips pained him—but that didn't stop him from running; no, sir!"

"Did anyone else see the blow struck, Mr. Lester?"

"Not a soul! Of course there was a crowd right afterwards, but I'm sure no one saw the blow but me."

A few minutes later the two had shaken hands in mutual esteem and departed—Mr. Lester for his home, and Rollins to a telephone booth, whence he was soon talking to Eleanor Stevens.

"Sarah has had a bad accident," he explained. "She is in the City Hospital now with an injured head and can't be visited for a few days. I just left her half an hour ago. There's nothing we can do, sweetheart, so don't worry about it, and I'll explain tomorrow evening, after the funeral. Keep Alice with you, honey, and don't let her return home until Sarah is well."

It was long past midnight before Rollins reached the Sanford and went to bed.

The murderous attack on Sarah Vasch somehow linked itself up in his mind with his own adventure of the night preceding. In both cases there had been a sudden unexpected onslaught, and he well remembered that tremendous blow upon his shoulders which had been aimed at his head. If that terrific smash had landed on Rollins' skull, he would now be in a similar condition to poor Sarah Vasch—or worse. Why should that footpad have tried to knock him out? Bob had been entirely at the mercy of the robber; the pistol thrust against his ribs precluded any resistance; what sense or reason could there be in the man's endeavor to maim or kill? Rollins perceived at once that the attack on Sarah was subject to deductions like those made regarding himself. A third conclusion was likewise inescapable. Sarah Vasch knew the person who had tried to kill her. If she recovered, she would perceive and divulge the motive of the assault and name the man.

Meanwhile, for the moment, Rollins could take no action. He could only think—and the final thought which drifted through his mind as his eyes closed in slumber was: "Is the murderer of Alexander Stevens concerned in this?"

When Rollins rose the next morning, his head was clear, the mental turmoil of the preceding night had been thrust aside, and his sole purpose now was to make this—the day of Alexander Stevens' funeral—as easy as possible for Nora.

Just before breakfast Hackett phoned and gave the result of his search for the killer's finger-prints in the Police Bureau.

"No record of any prints like those of our man among the Cook County convictions for felony in the past twenty-five years, Bob. He may have been arrested and not convicted, but he isn't a known Chicago crook, that's certain. See you at one o'clock, old scout. Good-bye!"

"All right so far!" thought Rollins. "Now to see what I can do to help the best girl on earth on the hardest day of her life."

The minister who was to officiate at the obsequies was an old friend of Nora and was known to Rollins as well. Bob interviewed him briefly before the ceremony, telling the pastor confidentially that he was aware of facts which clearly proved that Alexander Stevens had died, as he had lived, a man of honor and a Christian gentleman. The burial service, therefore, was impressive and inspiring, and the minister's eulogy brought moisture to many eyes.

To Nora especially this was a welcome relief. Now she could give unrestrained vent to the sorrow heretofore locked in her bosom, and let tears carry away her mental burdens.

By noon the body of Alexander Stevens lay darkly in its final rest, and Mother Earth had closed around him.

On leaving the cemetery Rollins exchanged but one brief word with Nora. As she passed him, coming from the grave, with Alice at her side, he heard her murmur: "Only you, Bob dear! That's all I have!"

"God bless you, darling!" was his whispered answer.

To Rollins the journey downtown seemed scarcely to last a moment.

When he descended from the L to the street and strode toward the Meyers Building, where he was to meet his friend, Rollins' soul was bursting with resolve to find and destroy the man whose deeds had created this day of sorrow.

At the entrance to room 713 he encountered Hackett waiting.

"How was everything at the funeral, Bob?" said Bill as they entered the room.

"Pretty sad! Don't let's talk about it. I've got just one job to do, Bill, and every thought and act is going to be clamped

to that job. Now let me tell you what happened last night"—
and Bob related all that had taken place since they parted.

"This may or may not help us," he continued. "Meanwhile
we've got just one really sound fact to build on in hunting
for this killer. That fact is that Stevens hadn't even approached success in his discovery until about five weeks ago,
and it's only about ten days since he really perfected his
process. We are sure, then, that the man who killed Stevens
must have learned about Stevens' 'almost discovery' some
time within the last five weeks, and only in the last week or
so could he know that the invention was perfected. That nar-
rows down the time wonderfully.

"The next thing to consider is who could have got close
enough to Stevens to know that he was on the verge of discovery and to know ten days ago that the discovery was a
completed fact. Stevens wasn't blabbing about this thing. I
know of only two persons whom he told—his daughter and
Sarah Vasch. Two days ago, however, I learned of a man
whom Stevens might have told. That man is his former partner, Edward Folsom. Stevens' daughter told me that both
Folsom and Stevens were experimenting three years together
on these color-pictures. Yesterday Miss Stevens handed me
this letter which she found among her father's papers. Here it
is, Bill."

Rollins produced an envelope postmarked: "Los Angeles,
Calif.," and read its contents, as follows:

DEAR STEVENS:

Got your letter yesterday and glad to hear the news. You
and I surely worked hard enough on that accursed job. I
wish the three years *I* put in on it were paid for. I could
certainly use the money. Maybe you'll get it yet, but don't
be too sure. You know we thought we had it twice, but she
fizzled out on us both times.

Remember that nothing is finished till it's *done*. Regards
to Nora and yourself. Feeling a little better lately with my
new treatment, but still have pain. Let me know SURE if
you get the process right. Might be coming east myself be-

fore Christmas. If I do, I'll look you up. Keep trying and don't forget that *I* did some of that trying, too.

Yours as ever,

E.F.

Hackett almost overturned his chair in his excitement. "Hooray!" he shouted. "We're on a hot trail, Bob, as sure as I'm a foot high. Notice them underlined words. He underlines 'I' twice—thinkin' of himself, of course. Thinks he's entitled to be paid for the three years he put in. Wants Stevens to tell him 'sure' if he gets the 'process' right. An' he puts his 'sure' in capitals. Says he 'might' come east before Christmas. Say, Rollins, I'll bet a million dollars this guy Folsom is the bird we're after. I wouldn't wonder if he was in Chicago right this minute."

"Maybe he is, Bill, but how are we going to find out? We don't even know his Los Angeles address. We've got no other letters from him to go by. Miss Stevens writes on this envelope: 'This is all I can find, and I've looked everywhere.' What's your idea of this thing, Bill?"

"Sufferin' Moses!" said Hackett. "You and I ain't got enough dough to go to California hunting for him on a wildcat chase, that's sure. As far as I am concerned, Kansas City would be my limit, an' I'd probably starve while I was walkin' back. It's a darn shame we've got to waste such an elegant tip as this. What are we goin' to do about it, Bob? Can't you think up something?"

"Yes!" said Rollins. "I've thought of a lot of things and I'm hopeful that one of those ideas may possibly work. When I was talking to Miss Stevens Monday night, she mentioned that Folsom carried a good-sized life-insurance policy in the Marathon Life. Do you personally know anyone who has a fairly important position in their home office here, Bill?"

"Sure!" said Hackett. "My niece's husband is manager of one of their departments."

"Do you know him well, Bill? Would he do a favor for you if you asked him to and gave a valid, truthful reason for asking it?"

"I'll say he would. Yes, you bet he would! I'd make him."

"All right! Now get this straight, Bill," said Rollins. "I want you to call up this relative of yours and tell him it's very important that you get into immediate touch with Edward Folsom, formerly living in Los Angeles, who carries ten thousand dollars with his company. Ask him to find out Folsom's policy number from their index department. Then let him take that policy number to the Marathon's renewal department. Let him then look for Folsom's renewal card in the files of that department and make a memorandum of Folsom's last address. That's the address which Folsom instructed the company to send their premium notices to. When he finds the address, ask him to telephone Folsom's last address to you here, as quickly as he can. Emphasize its importance. It's strictly against the insurance company's rules, Bill, so you'll have to put it up to this lad pretty good and strong."

"Here! Gimme that phone," said Hackett.

Twenty minutes elapsed. Each minute seemed ten times its length. Tumultuous thoughts rioted through both the comrades' minds. Would that bell never ring? What would be the answer? Finally came a tinkle, and Bill had the receiver off the hook before the ringing had fairly started.

"Yes! Yes! This is me! Yes! This is Hackett . . . Oh, you got it all right? What's that? Are you sure? On what date did you get that change-of-address notice? November 1? All right! Give me the street number again . . . Say, spell the name of that apartment building. What's that first letter? P or B? Oh, B as in 'blockhead'! . . . No! I didn't say you were a blockhead, Henry. You're a prince! I'll buy you the best cigar you ever smoked next time I see you. Good-bye, old scout! Thanks a lot! Good-bye!"

Hackett hung up the phone and turned to Bob. He was gasping and his hands trembled. Finally he mastered his nerves, strode over to Rollins, and said: "Listen, Bob! We've got him. Here's the exact words that Henry just told me: 'On November 1 the insured, Mr. Edward Folsom, removed from the city of Los Angeles, California, to the Blenheim apartment building on east Sixty-third Street in the city of Chicago and State of Illinois!' Amen! Selah! Kismet! Whoopee! Say, Bob, got a cigarette? If I don't smoke now, I'll blow up. What! Not even a stogie? Well, I'm gone to get some! Back in two minutes!" And William Hackett jumped toward the entrance, unlocked the door, and dashed out.

It was nearly ten minutes, instead of two, before Bill returned, without the cigarettes and with little breath. Carefully relocking the door, which had, of course, remained partly open since his flying exit, he pulled his chair close to that of Rollins.

"Listen, young fella-me-lad! Things are doin'!" he said. "When I opened the door just now, some guy was streakin' it down the hall like a scalded cat. He'd been listenin' at this door as sure as hell. He went down them six flights of stairs as if the devil was after him. He was, for I was just one flight behind. I didn't get a clean sight of his face, but he's a spry little guy and he's got somep'n wrong with one ear.

"He was just goin' round the corner of La Salle when I got outside, so of course I lost him. If it hadn't been for the damn patent lock on this door, I'd have nailed him sure. This little game we're sittin' in is commencin' to get real interestin', ain't it? Honest, I believe I'm gonta like playin' tag with these birds. All right, Rollins! What's the next thing you got up your sleeve?" And Hackett stopped.

"Are you sure he was listening at this door?" said Rollins.

"Absolutely. I heard his steps start from just outside when I commenced to turn that damn key!"

"That settles it, then! While we're looking for the man who killed Stevens, he is spying on us," said Rollins. "And that spying means murder, if I'm right about poor Sarah Vasch. All right, Bill, go on!"

"Just a minute, Bob! Would you mind saying why you hoped to get Folsom's last address through the Marathon home office?"

"If you had kept up ten thousand dollars' worth of insurance for ten years or more, Bill, and then got some disease that made you uninsurable, wouldn't you keep the company *advised* of your address-changes, so that you wouldn't overlook your premiums and be lapsed?"

"I certainly would!" said Hackett. "Is that the case with this Folsom? Is that why you hoped to learn his address from the Marathon?"

"That's it, Bill. Now let's get down to business again. We know that Folsom wrote *one* letter to Stevens at his home and that he came to Chicago right after he wrote it. From that letter we must infer that Folsom hoped Stevens would share the profits of the color-process with him, if Stevens perfected it.

"I don't like the tone of that Folsom letter, Bill. It sounds to me like a man who had determined to make the other fellow pay up. Folsom's immediate departure for Chicago makes that inference still stronger. Now! Assuming that my inference is right, we can be sure that Folsom got in touch with Stevens by phone or letter or both, right after he reached this city. All this is plain simple logic. It just *has* to be so.

"If Folsom simply called on Stevens and discussed the color-process, we're out of luck, Bill. But Folsom had arthritis, and that's a painful disease. Sometimes it is unbearable. A four-day trip from California might be a severe undertaking for an arthritis patient. He might be in terrible shape when he got to Chicago, and maybe laid up in bed.

"Folsom certainly wouldn't use a telephone to discuss this thing with Stevens. It's too delicate a matter. I figure it that Folsom would do one of two things: he'd either phone Stevens, asking him to call at the Blenheim Apartments, or he'd write a letter to Stevens demanding that he call; and he'd do it soon. Remember, too, that Folsom is certain to be in pain, which means that he is probably irritable and impatient. He isn't going to wait many days for Stevens to call on him. He's going to *compel* Stevens to call, if he can.

"You can see from this why I am positive that Folsom wrote at least one letter to Stevens after he reached Chicago. We've got to find that letter, if such a letter exists. Miss Stevens says she can't find any other letters of Folsom's at the house. Possibly Stevens got one and destroyed it, but I think not. The only other place to look for such a letter, Bill, is in this office, and that's our next job. Let's tackle these two Broadway files and see what we can find. You take one and I'll take the other. Let's go!"

"How'll we do it, Bob? Sort out all the bills and circulars and business letters and personal letters in separate piles and then go over each pile afterwards if we have to? Do you think that's the best way?"

"That's probably as good as any, Bill. Come on, get busy!"

For one solid hour the two self-appointed sleuths examined every word of script in the two filing cases, but without avail.

Bob noticed that nearly every letter was endorsed with some comment in Stevens' handwriting. Not a line, however, which could, by any stretch of imagination, be attributed to Edward Folsom was located.

Shelves, boxes, packages, were examined without result. One typewritten letter, dated November 15, on the letterhead of Schwartz and Melden, Cleveland photo-supply house, seemed sufficiently ambiguous to offer a possible clue in another direction.

The document read as follows:

I confirm our telephonic appointment for an interview on Saturday morning, November 18, and trust we may reach a satisfactory decision on the important matter under discussion.

CHARLES H. DUNCAN

Bob pocketed this for further investigation. Aside from this the search had been entirely futile in results.

Hackett was disconsolate, and Rollins was beginning to assume a like mental attitude.

Finally the latter said: "Look here, Bill, do you remember my saying that we were not going to run around aimlessly, but were going to use brains and logic to master this job?"

"I sure do!" said Bill. "Haven't we been doing it all along? How in hell would we have got this far if we hadn't? I'll say *you* have been using some brains!"

"Have you seen any indications of brainwork in the last hour, Bill? Haven't we both been rummaging through these *papers* over and over again like a dog scratching his flea-bites? Do you see any signs of reasoning or logic in that? I don't!"

It would seem that Mr. William Hackett had wisely decided that, on this point, silence was golden—and accepted his own decision.

Mr. Robert Rollins, likewise, appeared to concur, for during the next three minutes no word was uttered by anyone in room 713.

Finally the voice of Rollins broke the spell: "Bill, what would you think of a chemist who wore an eighty-dollar suit regularly while working in his laboratory?"

"I'd think he was a damn fool," replied Hackett promptly. "His eighty-dollar outfit wouldn't sell for eighty cents in a week!"

"If a fellow gets a letter he wants to study over and think about, where is he likely to put it, Bill?"

"In his coat pocket," said Hackett. "Oho! I see what you're thinking, Bob. You're thinking that Stevens perhaps got a letter from Folsom and mebbe put that letter in the pocket of the *working-coat* and forgot he'd done it. But you're away off there, Bob. Stevens' working-coat is hanging on a nail in that dark-room. I seen you look through the pockets of it yourself—so that's N.G." Hackett's expression was that of an eminent college professor imparting wisdom to a backward child.

"You're quite correct, Dr. Hackett! I suppose you and your associates in the Chemists' Guild are accustomed to wear the same working-coat each working day throughout the year. However, a potential millionaire, like our late friend Mr.

Stevens, might feel warranted in purchasing and using *two* working-coats. Thus, while one was at the laundry, he could wear the other.

"Superintendent Donovan told us that this room was last cleaned on Friday of last week—the day before Stevens died. My inference is that the person who regularly cleans this room was accustomed to take away Stevens' working-coats on some special day each week and send them to the laundry. I hope she did it last Friday, and I humbly pray that there was a letter from Folsom to Stevens in the inside pocket of that coat. If such a letter exists and *if* Stevens put it there and forgot it, the laundry people will undoubtedly find it in the coat pocket, and, since Alexander Stevens' name was surely on the letter, the envelope, or both, they will return it to this building with that coat. Let me think a minute. Today is Wednesday; Saturday's laundry ought to be finished and back here today, and the coat is probably downstairs right now. The Lord knows how I pray that a letter may be in the same package.

"Suppose you go down now, Bill, and ask at the superintendent's office if there is a laundry package for Alexander Stevens. If there is, please bring it up here, just as it is. Don't open it, please, till you get back in this room."

Hackett got up, stood for a moment silently looking at his friend, held out his hand, grasped the hand of his comrade, shook it, grinned, turned, unlocked the door of room 713, and went out.

Ten minutes later he returned with a flat brown-paper package under his arm, which he handed to Rollins. "There you are," said Bill.

Bob opened the package. On the top of its contents lay a small gray envelope, with a slip attached, marked: "Found in coat pocket."

VII

"YOU CERTAINLY HIT THE NAIL on the head that time, Bob," said Hackett, as they left the building, "and I'm sure stuck on that system of yours—makin' your brains save your legs. Why, us two fellers could have spent a month and a thousand dollars runnin' out to California an' back, an' even then we wouldn't have learned what was Folsom's Chicago address. We probably would have found that he had moved back to Chicago, but that wouldn't have told us where he was now. This way we got the whole dope in about twenty minutes without stirrin' from our chairs.

"Look at this here letter from Folsom to Stevens, too! We didn't even know there was any letter except the one Miss Stevens gave you. You said that yourself. Then, after we'd curried this office with a fine-tooth comb, you go over there, plant yourself in that chair, an' spend about five minutes thinkin' about it. Pretty soon, after you get through with your reasonin' about it—out pops the answer. Honest, Bob! It makes me think of those Sherlock Holmes stories where he says: 'Why, Watson! That's elementary,' et cetera. You don't say that, but you *do* say: 'Go an' get that laundry, Bill, and you'll probably find that letter'—and we find it right there. Believe me, Bob, it's some stunt. Wisht to goodness I could do it."

"Listen, Bill," interjected Rollins, "you don't seem to understand what I mean by reasoning things out. There's nothing that requires particularly acute powers of observation about it. It's just plain simple logic and nothing else. I couldn't possibly tell from the fiber of a piece of cloth or a crease or rubbed spot on a coat-sleeve or a worn place on the heel or sole of a shoe what sort of work a man did or what his habits were. I don't believe anyone can. It's simply using your brains, that's all. Think over what we've just done, and you'll surely see it."

"Yeah! I see all right!" said Hackett. "But seein' and doin' are some different, believe me. Gee! Here we are at the La Salle already! Let's hustle in and feed our faces! I'm starved. Besides that, I want to see Folsom's letter. Come on!"

Rollins and Hackett were fortunate; they secured a two-chair table distant from the orchestra, and while waiting for their orders, Hackett studied the contents of Folsom's letter to Alexander Stevens. That once elusive document ran as follows:

DEAR STEVENS:

I have been thinking things over since you left, and your proposition to give me half the first-year profits of our process is absurd. Nobody knows how much this thing will earn during the first year. It might produce $5,000 or maybe $100,000. I put in three years' hard work with you on that thing.

I only quit because I was sick. Except for my illness we would now be co-inventors. You and I would share fifty-fifty on it.

Your idea of giving it to the public is crazy. What right has the public got to use OUR invention for nothing, after we have had only one year's profit from it? That process will net fifty million dollars in ten years and you know it. I'm not going to let you throw away *my* money. Here I am, a sick man, suffering like hell, and with mighty little cash left. With half a million dollars I could hire the best doctors on earth. I could bring them from Europe or England, or anywhere, and could probably be cured in six months. *I'm not going to stand for your offer and that's final.*

You have GOT to give me a legal agreement to patent our process in all countries; to manufacture all plates and films; to run this thing on a partnership basis, and to divide all profits between us half and half. That's what I am *entitled to* and that's what I *want*. If this arthritis of mine keeps

up, I won't last one year anyway, *and I swear to God you won't live ONE month if you don't sign up and act square.*
Yours,

E. F.

While Bill was studying this missive, the waiter served their orders, and both started eating.

Presently Hackett looked up from his reading, gave a long, low whistle, and handed the sheets back to Rollins.

"Well, Bob," said he, "you said there had to be a motive for everything. If this letter don't show a motive, what does? Here's this guy Folsom saying that Stevens *'won't live ONE month'* if he doesn't come through with the goods. Notice he puts the word 'one' in capitals too. He sure wanted Stevens to know he meant business. Gee Whittaker! That's a hot letter. If Folsom ain't the bird we're after, I'm nutty. Honest, I pity that guy Folsom! It looks to me Folsom's crazy. You can see he really thinks the three years he and Stevens worked on that color-process entitle him to a half-share. Let's see that letter again! Yes, that's just his very words— *'entitled to,'* and they're underlined at that.

"What's the pencil notation on the top of the letter, Bob? Did *you* write it? I can hardly read it, it's so scrawly. What does it say?"

"It's Stevens' handwriting, not mine," said Rollins. "You remember most of the correspondence at the office that we looked at today had been scrawled with his memos. As near as I can make out, it says: 'Undoubtedly demented. Desperate! Might do anything. Consult C.D.' I'm not sure about those two last initials, they're so scrawly. Looks like C.D. or G.D. anyhow, as far as I can judge.

"Let's see! 'C.D.' Wait a minute, Bill! Let's look at the letter from that Cleveland concern which I put in my pocket this afternoon. Yes! Charles Duncan wants Stevens to keep an appointment on November 18—that's the day Stevens died. We'll surely have to look this lad up tomorrow and see whether this Duncan chap is the 'C.D.' that Stevens refers to.

"Well, Bill, I'll pay the check, but you stay and finish your dessert. It's me for the North Side now! See you at the Meyers Building at ten sharp tomorrow morning! So long, old boy! Be good!"

For the next half-hour Rollins rode northward on the L, his mind intensely absorbed with Folsom's letter and the obvious deductions therefrom. The train was two-thirds empty at that hour, although he observed one man on the front platform.

When Rollins stepped off at Bryn Mawr Avenue, there were only two other persons who alighted. Bob, coming from the rear car, was the last passenger to reach the stairway, and, before descending, he delayed a few seconds on the platform to light a cigarette.

Still cogitating, he commenced a slow descent, his left hand sliding on the wooden hand-rail. At the fourth step from the top his right foot halted in mid air as if paralyzed, and refused to advance forward. Only his slow motions and quick grasping of the hand-rail saved him from pitching head-first forty feet downward, to the bottom of the stairs.

Instantly his hand went to his right shin-bone, just above the shoe-top, where he seemed to feel some strong pressure. As he grasped for its cause, the pressure loosened and his fingers encountered a strong cord stretched loosely across the stairs a little above ankle height. The right end of the cord he perceived was looped around the iron staircase framework, while the left end hung across the stairs and fell at unknown length toward the ground below.

Rollins quickly reeled in the loose cord and tried meanwhile to get a sight of the person who, ten seconds before, had pulled taut that cord across those steps and against his ankles. He observed a slender figure darting behind a signboard, and that was all.

The entire plot was instantly obvious. The two persons who had gone downstairs ahead of Rollins had encountered no obstacle, for the cord had probably been slackened and lay supine in the angle of the steps. When Rollins, after lighting the cigarette, had started to descend, the watching plotter

below had pulled tight the cord, which, had Bob been mov-
ing at customary speed, would have tripped and thrown him
headlong.

Bob shuddered. Plunging forty feet, to land, head-first, on
cement or iron meant sure disaster. It might spell death. The
memory of Hackett's dash down the hallway and stairs of the
Meyers Building that afternoon, chasing a slim man, flashed
to his mind. Only one inference could be drawn from these
two incidents. It was certain that the murderer of Stevens
knew that Rollins was hot-foot upon the trail, and only
through persistent vigilance would Bob remain alive. On his
way to Nora's home no essential caution was omitted.

That evening's talk with his beloved and with Alice was
largely about Sarah Vasch. Rollins gave the girls a concise
account of the assault on Sarah, as told to him by Stacey Lester. "As I see it," he said, "some man, well known to Sarah,
was reckless enough to attempt to murder her on a busy
street, within possible sight of dozens of people. It's a mira-
cle that he escaped. Nobody who had an ounce of brains
could fail to infer two things from such an act: First, this man
must have nerve, courage, audacity, and cruelty without
limit. Second, the motive for such a deed must have been
tremendously powerful for him to risk his own liberty by as-
saulting her *then* and *there.* Since the man and Sarah were
undoubtedly acquainted, why could he not kill her later with
far less risk? Why must the assault be committed *then?*

"We all know Sarah! The poor woman had no money,
wouldn't harm a fly, and didn't have an enemy on earth. She
wouldn't even dispute with anyone. Her only fault was gossip, and she admitted that herself. Remember what she said
night before last when I questioned her. The only possible
motive that I can conceive for the instantaneous decision of
this unknown man to kill poor Sarah was to *silence her
tongue.* She must have known some fact so potentially dangerous to this man that he dare not risk letting her remain
alive an instant longer."

"But, listen, dearest," interrupted Nora; "Sarah never went
anywhere except to the movies. She had a few women

friends among our neighbors, but, except for the last month, she hasn't gone downtown twenty times in ten years, I'm sure. How could poor Sarah get hold of a secret that would hurt anybody, Bob?"

"That's what I'm trying to find out, sweetheart. You say: 'Except for the last month, she hasn't gone downtown.' How about this last month, Nora dear?"

"She's been out three or four evenings every week, Bob. Of course I never asked her about it—in fact, I never thought about it until now. Sarah's sixty and homely and an old maid besides, so there was no danger of a scandal with her. I haven't the slightest idea where she went or whom she met, Bob dear."

"Didn't she ever mention the name of even one man whom she had met or visited, honey?"

"Not one, Bob darling. The only possible thing I can think of is one day about five weeks ago I came into the kitchen, and Sarah was actually singing—something I never heard her do in my life before. I said: 'You must be happy, Sarah!' and she said: 'I am, Miss Nora! You'd be happy too if you'd found somebody you loved and hadn't seen for over twenty years!'

"Then I asked her who it was, and she said: 'Oh, it's no sweetheart or anything like that. Just someone I'd lost track of and used to care a lot about. He's younger than me, so don't think you're going to have to get a new housekeeper,' and she laughed."

"That's the man we must search for, dearest! If Sarah lives, I know she'll tell us, but meanwhile perhaps we can find a letter or an address among her things which will give us a clue. Do your best in the next day or two, Nora; then let me know, no matter how trifling the thing may be."

Not a word had passed Rollins' lips regarding his adventure with the footpad or his lucky escape on the Elevated stairway that very evening. Eleanor Stevens was to have no anxieties about her lover to increase her burdens.

At ten o'clock Bob said good-bye to his sweetheart and Alice and, with Nora still holding his hand, watched from the porch the moonbeams filter through the clouds.

"I hate to say anything to bring up sad thoughts, Nora, but I want you to do one little thing for me. Will you, dear?" said Rollins.

"Bob, darling! I'll do anything in the world you ask. What is it?" she answered.

"Please don't do anything about your father's last policy for the next few days, Nora. Don't submit it as a claim or sign any papers or speak to *anyone* about it. Just let it rest until I tell you. It won't be long; and Nora, dear, please tell me something—the same thing you whispered to me yesterday. Say it to me again!"

And Nora told it to him again.

Rollins arrived at his quarters in the Sanford Apartments, a few blocks from the south end of Lincoln Park, at eleven o'clock. His room was on the fourth floor, fair-sized, steam-heated, with two windows facing toward the south. Although modern and with elevator service, the quarters were not expensive to maintain and afforded every convenience.

Having some furniture in storage (which had accrued to him on the death of his mother, several years before), Bob had furnished the room himself. Aside from the usual bedroom comforts, a three-foot alcove in the wall contained a marble wash-bowl, faucets for hot and cold water and running ice-water, a large closet with shower-bath and toilet, and a small closet for his trunk and wearing-apparel.

The location of the hotel was excellent for a young unmarried man who worked downtown, and Rollins had occupied his present room for two years—ever since the structure was built. In consequence of this he was treated by the management more like a friend than a tenant, and most of the help were known to Bob by their first names. He could get to any part of the Loop district in half an hour; a small but excellent *a la carte* restaurant in the basement furnished meals at any time he might desire; he was reasonably close to theaters and stores; in fact, Rollins was entirely content with his environment.

Not being especially tired or sleepy, Bob looked round for something to read. His eyes at once rested on the scrap-book of Alexander Stevens' verses, which Nora had loaned him two nights before. He picked it up and started to glance through its contents.

There were more than a hundred rhythmic effusions in the book—all neatly typed and each bearing a well-chosen heading. The verses were of every possible sort: humorous, sad, gay, sympathetic, or inspiring. Rollins envied the talents of the man who had written them. No names of persons appeared affixed or prefixed to any poem, and they seemed to have been filed in chronological order, if one were to judge from the contents.

Rollins did not attempt to absorb or digest any verses in entirety, but merely to get a general idea of their character with a view to more thoughtful study later. Glancing at his watch and observing that it was not eleven thirty, Bob was just about to lay the scrap-book aside and retire when the closing line of a three-stanza poem almost at the last page caught his eye. He read the line again.

Strange how familiar it seemed! Where had he heard or seen that same phrase before? The lilt and swing of the rhyme aroused some subconscious memory. He must surely have read the last part of that poem in some book or magazine. Was Alexander Stevens a plagiarist?

Bob looked at the heading of the poem.

TO A BELOVED FRIEND (Born October 31, 1870)

Whoever had received the original of those three stanzas on his or her birthday must now be well along toward sixty years of age.

Rollins read the whole poem again. The first two verses were unquestionably novel to him. So, too, was nearly all of the third. It must be that last line or two which persisted in nagging at his memory.

Determined to rid his mind of this vexatious problem, Rollins drew his chair close to his writing-desk, seized a pencil and paper, and copied the final quatrain of the poem, studying each line as he inscribed it:

> So may He, who Love created,
> Shower upon me from on high
> Many loyal friends like you, dear,
> Ere I bid the world good-bye.

Over and over again Rollins repeated aloud these four lines. "Stevens wrote this poem to a woman," he thought. "Men do not call other men 'dear,' even in poetry. This woman must be older than he, for Stevens was born in 1874—four years after the birthday of the one who inspired these verses. From the rest of the poem it is probable that she is a widow, for Stevens in the first stanza speaks of 'your lonely way,' and this would also indicate that she has no living children. The fact that she is four years older than Stevens is almost proof that this is no love-affair, and the entire poem gives evidence of a loyal high-minded affection of entirely different character from passion. Stevens *must* have known her intimately for a long time. He could not write as he did unless this were so. Surely, too, she is a good woman and probably a religious one. He asks that God may send him many friends like her 'ere I bid the world good-bye,' and, from what Nora says, he probably wrote this poem in longhand, signed his name to it, and sent it to her just before her birthday, October 31.

"My God!" Rollins almost shouted. "Stevens writes a longhand note saying:

> 'Ere I bid the world good-bye'

and Stevens' last letter, lying on his desk almost under his dead hand, reads: 'I bid the world good-bye—Alexander F. Stevens.' "Except for that first short word 'Ere,' this poem's ending line—which in the original surely bore his signature—is precisely like the note bearing his last farewell. If Stevens had killed himself, he might subconsciously have remembered the last line in this poem and have chosen it as a farewell message. But Alexander Stevens was murdered; hence he did not write that note just prior to his death. The fountain-pen on his desk contained different ink from that of the 'good-bye' note. The last line and signature of the original copy of this poem have somehow got into the hands of the man who killed Stevens. That man has cut the poem in two pieces just between its last two lines—he has somehow erased the word 'Ere' from the bottom piece. He is the one who placed that bogus 'dying message' beneath the hand of one already dead!"

Rollins rose quickly and took from his pocket the brown envelope which contained all the papers found on Stevens' body after death. Taking from the envelope the small blue slip which, in Stevens' handwriting and bearing his signature, gave his "good-bye" to the world, Rollins held it close against the frosted globe of the electric light.

"Yes, by God!" he shouted; "the erasure is plain! The letters 'ERE' have been scratched out. The paper is thinner and more transparent just before the word 'I.' This finishes the proof. God help the man who did it."

VIII

ON THURSDAY MORNING at seven o'clock Rollins called up Nora. After two or three minutes of waiting she came to the phone.

"What is it, Bob dear?" she asked.

"Nora," said Rollins, "I want you to put on the best thinking-cap you've got! This is tremendously important! Your father had a woman friend, probably a widow, about fifty-seven years old; and I don't think she has any living children. She is certainly a good woman, and, I believe, a person of refinement. I don't know whether or not she lives in Chicago, but if she does, she probably attended the funeral. Your father liked her and held her in very high esteem. One of his last poems, written recently, was his birthday greeting to her. Do you know who she is, dear?"

"Let me think a moment, Bob," said Nora.

Rollins waited—waited. Finally his sweetheart spoke again.

"Bob, I've done my best, but I just can't think of any woman nearly sixty years old who was Daddy's dear friend. You see, I've been away at college and only returned home this year. I've lost touch with Father's friends and almost forgotten some of them. I just don't know her, Bob."

"All right, Nora," said Rollins. "I'll try to find out in some other way, and if that doesn't work, we'll talk it over again. Good-bye, honey!"

Immediately after his futile talk with Nora, Rollins telephoned to Hackett's home and got him on the phone at once. "Bill," said he, "I want you to go to the County Clerk's office right away and find out where the births of children born in Cook County are registered. The person I'm looking for was a female born October 31, 1870. Get a list, if you can, of every female infant born in this county on October 31 of that year. After you've got that list, go to the Marriage Registrar's office and try to learn from their records if any one of the female infants on your list has since been married in this county. They've got indexed registers of marriages. If you find that any of them have been married here, learn the husband's full name, nationality, marriage date, and residence. Do your best, Bill, and try to have the dope for me at ten o'clock. Maybe the person we want to find was born or married outside this county. If so, we're up a stump, but let's try it anyhow. Good-bye!"

Ten fifteen found both Rollins and Hackett in room 713, of somber memory. Rollins first told Hackett of last night's adventure on the L platform. Bill then produced a list of eight female children born in Cook County on October 31, 1870, of whom three had since been married in or near Chicago.

Bob then explained to Hackett what he had discovered in the scrap-book the night before, showing the poem, and winding up by saying: "We've simply *got* to find this woman, Bill! Whoever murdered Stevens surely stole from her that birthday poem which Stevens had written to her, and planted that last line of it on Stevens' desk after Stevens had been killed. I realize our chances of finding her in this way are mighty slim, but we must do our best. Any suggestions, Bill?"

"Suggestions, hell!" said Hackett. "Listen, Bob! I ain't entirely useless. I can take orders, obey orders, an' draw my salary, but you know damn well I couldn't suggest to a pussy-cat. You do the suggestin', Bob, an' I'll do the sawin' wood. What do you want done? That's all I want to know."

"Well, Bill," said Rollins, "this man Folsom, judging from his letter, is either half-insane or a criminal. Here is a general description of his appearance, and here is an old photo of him I got from Miss Stevens. Take it, Bill. We also know that he's money-mad, or pretty near it. We know he lives in the Blenheim Apartments now. These things are all we've learned so far about him.

"What we need to learn is: Is he physically strong enough to walk, ride, and use his muscles, despite his disease? How strong is he? Does he stay indoors constantly? Or does he leave the building for one or more hours daily? Is it likely from his visitors, if any, that he employed your 'spotter' and my 'tripper'? In other words, what are his habits, his customary routine; and what men visit him? Finally, where was he after half past eight on the evening of November 18?

"If you can find out a fair share of these things, Bill, it will help us tremendously. You realize that a man who is crippled physically could not have climbed these six flights of stairs, committed a murder, and escaped. Will you tackle this job, Bill, and meet me here at four o'clock to compare notes?"

"I'll tackle it, an', believe me, I'll do it!" said Hackett; and in two minutes he had started southward.

Rollins, too, was out of the office shortly after Hackett departed, and made a bee-line for the Public Library and the alcove where directories of America's principal cities are filed, for reference.

Knowing the full name of the husband of each of the three women listed by Hackett, he traced, as best he could, each name from one year's Chicago directory to another, starting with the year of the wife's marriage. The work was long and tedious, as in each instance the marriage dated back over twenty years. The names of two of these prospects had vanished from all Chicago directory pages over ten years before. In the other and final instance the name of Edgar A. Halgard appeared in the 1918 directory as with "Residence, 6840 Michigan Boulevard."

The 1919 directory gave the name "Rose M. Halgard" at the same address—indicating that Edgar was away or dead, and that Mrs. Halgard was now the head of that household. This same name and address persisted throughout all succeeding Chicago directories up to the current year, and Rollins found it also listed in the current telephone directory on a shelf near by.

"Just about one chance in a thousand that this is the woman!" he muttered, as he took down the receiver and put in his call for Mrs. Halgard's number.

In a moment a feminine voice replied: "Hello!"

"Is this Mrs. Rose Halgard?" said Rollins.

"This is her residence," said the person replying. "Mrs. Halgard is away from town at present, but is expected home tomorrow or Saturday. Who is speaking, please?"

"My name is Rollins," said Bob. "I'm calling Mrs. Halgard on a personal matter. I'll phone her again tomorrow or Saturday. Thank *you* very much."

Two minutes later Rollins was talking on the phone to his beloved. "Nora, dear, do you know or did you ever hear your father speak of a Mrs. Rose Halgard, who lives on the South Side? Think hard, sweetheart, before you answer. I want to be sure."

"Why, Bob, you old darling! Of course I know Auntie Rose. Is she the one you asked about this morning? But you said she was fifty-seven years old, and I don't believe Aunt Rose is even fifty. She doesn't look over forty-five. You know she isn't my aunt, or any relation, but I've known her for years, and she's the darlingest woman in the world. Do you want to see her, Bob?"

Rollins could scarcely speak from excitement. He hesitated, stammered, and finally managed to blurt out: "Yes, honey! But I'll see her when she comes back. She's out of town now. Good-bye, Nora, dearest!"

It was a full hour before Bob Rollins had regained his composure. Now the quest was on the verge of reward. Now the hours of uncertainty and doubt were ended. Now the distant shadow of a noose was crawling, creeping, slithering nearer to some human fiend who thought himself secure, through astute planning and devilish conceits. And there, on a seat near the telephone booth in the Chicago Public Library, sat the youth whose brain and logic would infallibly weave from some far-scattered trifles the deadly rope which clings and spareth not.

It was now one thirty o'clock. Rollins had eaten no luncheon, but he could not afford to stop.

"I may as well call up Schwartz and Melden in Cleveland and see what I can learn about their man Duncan and his appointment with Stevens last Saturday," he thought. "Now ought to be a good time to catch him."

Leaving the library, Rollins went directly to a near-by hotel and, through the telephone operator, put in a person-to-person call for Mr. Charles Duncan of the Cleveland photographic supply house. In about ten minutes he had his man on the wire, and the following conversation ensued:

Rollins: "Is this Mr. Charles Duncan?"

Duncan: "Yes. Who is speaking, please?"

Rollins: "My name is Rollins. I am in Chicago and am calling on behalf of Mr. Alexander Stevens, with whom you had an appointment last Saturday."

Duncan: "Good! That's fine! I wondered why he hadn't written. Does he want to see me? Is he ready to fix things up?"

Rollins: "I can't say for sure, but if you can be at the Meyers Building here at eight o'clock sharp tomorrow morning, we can decide matters then. You can get the midnight train tonight, and of course we'll assume your expenses. Can you come?"

Duncan: "Sure I'll come. You want me to come direct to Stevens' office, I suppose?"

Rollins: "Yes, please."

Duncan: "All right! I'll be there. Say, Mr. Rollins, has this man Folsom got any real authority in this matter? He's writing me, but I haven't answered him yet!"

Rollins: "Don't answer him until we've talked things over. And, say! Bring Folsom's letter along with you when you come, will you?"

Duncan: "Sure, I'll bring it! Thanks for calling! See you in the morning. Regards to Stevens! Good-bye!"

Rollins hung up the phone, paid his toll charges, lit a cigarette, and pondered. "Not the least doubt about it," he thought. "This man Duncan is on the square. He has no idea that Stevens is dead. His frankness, the quickness of his answers, the fact that he's glad to hear from Stevens, wondered why Stevens hadn't written, and sends Stevens his 'regards' lets him out. Gee! Wasn't it lucky, too, he mentioned Folsom and his letter? Anyhow, whatever story he's got to tell will be the truth, whether it helps us or not.

"Sufferin' cats! This sleuthing game is sure darned costly business. I'm almost broke now, and I'll have to pay Duncan's expenses tomorrow. Got to get to the bank now and haul out half of that eight hundred dollars. Well, I can't help it, so there's no use kicking."

Arriving at the Meyers Building, Rollins had scarcely seated himself when he heard Hackett's knock at the door, and rose to admit him.

"Well, Bill, what's the news? How did you come out?" he said.

"Fine!" said Hackett. "Just you wait! I'll give you an earful! But say! What you been doin' all this time, boss, while us poor workin' guys have been buildin' up civilization? You went off like a clam an' never opened your face. Been loafin' all day, Bob?"

"No indeed, Bill!" said Rollins. "Had fine luck today and we're getting closer to that skunk every minute. Listen and I'll tell what I've got, and then you can make your speech. Better put this down, Bill. It'll keep your shorthand in practice and we can look it over any time later and be sure we don't miss anything.

"First I'll tell you what I learned from Miss Stevens last night about poor Sarah Vasch, and then I'll tell you all about today."

By four thirty Hackett had heard and transcribed a clear, concise, and complete account of his friend's doings since their parting.

When Bill heard the news about Mrs. Halgard, and Nora's confirmation of the fact that her "Auntie Rose" and Mrs. Halgard were identical, he upset two chairs, bruised his hand hammering a table-top, kicked over the waste-basket, and otherwise demonstrated his joy. His reaction when told of the coming visit of Charles Duncan at eight o'clock on the following morning was a little less hilarious. The doings of Sarah Vasch seemed to him scarcely worthy of hearing. Upon the still unknown killer of Stevens, however, he bestowed a multitude of his choicest longshore epithets.

"Now then, Bill, let's listen to your story," said Rollins.

"I don't want to string it out too long," said Hackett, "but I gotta put in everything that counts, too. Anyhow, I'll try and make it as short as I can, so here goes!

"You're right about this guy Folsom! If he ain't bug-house, I am. I got down to the Blenheim all right, and I seen from the mail-boxes that George L. Folsom had one of the apartments. Of course, he wasn't our man because the initials were wrong, but he probably was a relative that our Folsom was stayin' with.

"Well, I was standin' in the hall tryin' to fix up some scheme to get in an' learn somep'n about Folsom from somebody when a feller, nearly fifty years old, opens the hall door. He seen me lookin' at the names in the boxes an' says: 'Can I help you?' 'I dunno,' says I—an', believe me, I was doin' some darn quick thinkin'. 'My name is Jones. I'm from the Marathon Life Insurance Company, and one of our policy-holders, a Mr. Edward Folsom, notified us about a month ago that he'd moved here. Do you happen to know if he's staying with Mr. George Folsom?' (Lemme tell you, Bob, my mind was goin' like a streak.)

" 'He certainly is,' said this bird. 'I am George Folsom, and Edward Folsom is my uncle. He's been with me nearly three weeks. He's not in just now, and I don't know just when he'll be back. Can I do anything for you? I rather think he'll be home soon.'

" 'Well, if that's so, I guess I'll wait,' says I. 'It's a pretty long trip to come out here again. Brrrr! Awfully raw day, isn't it?' says I, kind of shivering.

" 'Yes, indeed it is!' says this George. 'Won't you come up to my apartment and wait for my uncle? It wouldn't be hospitable to let you freeze in the hall!'

"Say, Rollins! That George Folsom is sure a conundrum. We went up in the elevator an' sat there in his 'den,' as he called it, for about an hour gassin' about all kinds of things. I didn't hear half he said, for I was figurin' out what the hell I'd say to old man Folsom when he came home. Finally I got an idea. They don't come often, Bob, but I get 'em once in a while.

" 'Do you happen to know if your Uncle Edward has his policy here so I could see it?' says I.

" 'Oh, yes!' says George, 'I'll get it'; and he went into one of the bedrooms and in a minute was back with the policy an' handed it to me.

"I've seen lots of policies and I saw right away that this was a straight twenty-payment life, about eleven years old, with no frills, like disability benefits, but it did have double benefit in case of accident, just like Stevens took out.

"I pointed out this clause in the policy to George Folsom. 'That's what I want to see your uncle about,' says I. 'He pays an extra premium for that double indemnity, as we call it. It's an addition to the policy an' not a part of it, but the extra premium charge is based on folks who have their normal faculties and not on folks who have lost one or more of 'em. Of course, we couldn't give a blind man double indemnity for accident for the same price as a feller who had eyesight. I understand your uncle has been in bad shape several years, and possibly his powers of locomotion are affected so that he'd be more likely to get killed by accident than a normal man. That's what I wanted to see him about.'

"Of course, Bob, I was lying, for the double-benefit accidental-death clause is just as much a part of a feller's policy as the rest of it. However, it was printed on a separate slip of paper an' attached to the policy, so I figured probably George Folsom would believe it *could* be a separate thing—and he did.

"Well, of course, he told me all about old man Folsom's illness after that, an' backed it up with all sorts of illustrations. It seems Edward Folsom some days can walk around as good as anybody. Other days he can just about wiggle and doesn't go out at all then and suffers awful.

"Finally I says to George Folsom: 'Suppose you give me an illustration of how it works with him. Take last Saturday and Sunday, for instance. What did he do those two days?'

"So George told me: On Saturday old man Folsom was gone all morning until about two P.M. Then he came home an' stayed in till after supper; left about seven thirty P.M.; said he was going to the movies, and the nephew didn't know when his uncle got back, for George went to sleep in his chair till after eleven P.M. When he woke up, his uncle was home and in bed.

"Sunday was different. That day old Edward Folsom was pretty bad; stayed indoors all day, and laid down most of the time. One of the worst days he'd had.

" 'Your uncle used to be Alexander Stevens' partner, didn't he?' says I. 'Who's Stevens?' says he. I didn't answer, but, believe me, I thought a lot. I could see from his eyes he knew all about Stevens, but didn't want to admit it. I'll bet he's in cahoots with his uncle.

"I was just gettin' ready to leave when old Folsom blew in, walkin' as good as me. He looks just like his picture, only awful worried. Them little whiskers of his make his face haggard-like, an' he'll snarl one minute an' be like an icicle the next.

"First thing he said when he came in, an' before he noticed me, was: 'I took a little walk down Michigan Boulevard to Seventieth Street, George. Stepped in to see Rose, but she's out of town. Hello! Who's this?'

"The nephew introduced me, under the name of Jones, and right away, before either of 'em could say a word, I pipes up to the old man: 'Well, well, I'm certainly glad to get acquainted with you, Mr. Folsom. If I'd known you were in as fine shape as you are, I certainly would never have come down to see you.'

"Then I gave Edward Folsom a little of the spiel I'd given to his nephew an' wound up by sayin': 'Our company has been misinformed as to your condition. So long as you remain indoors when your attacks become serious, you are no more susceptible to accident than any man in Chicago, and of course your policy is O.K.'

"Well, sir, all this time old man Folsom stood there like an iceberg, boring me with his eyes. Honest, Bob, they looked like they were on fire, an' kept gettin' redder-like an' more glary. His face was like a stone, and not a muscle of his body moved, except his fingers twitching. I never saw a more devilish look on anybody in my life. The guy is rarin' crazy, Bob, an' oughta be in Dunning this minute.

"I could see he didn't credit a word I'd said, an', believe me, I was edgin' for the door all the while I was talking. When I got through with my spiel, he still stood there, sayin' nothin', but just lookin'—lookin'.

"Finally he spoke up. His voice was like an ice-box, an' them little whiskers of his was all a-quiver. 'What credentials have you to prove that you represent the Marathon Life? Show me your business card or any other papers with that name on them'—an' his fingers twitched worse than ever.

"Believe me, Bob, I saw it comin', an' it's a damn good thing I did. I was just tryin' to invent some sort of an alibi when he made his leap and I went through that door an' down them stairs like a singed cat, with old Folsom hell-bent after me. An', believe me, the nephew was helpin' in the chase. There's somethin' wrong with that bird too. I know it. Not a doubt of it! Mebbe he got George to help. An' say, Bob, remember how Folsom said he had just called on 'Rose' on Michigan Boulevard an' she wasn't home? How does that hitch up with this dame Mrs. Rose Halgard, who lives just about where old Folsom was strollin'—an' who's out of town too, by the way! Whoopee! She's the lady that got that poem Stevens wrote, an' I'll bet a million Edward Folsom's the bird that stole it. If Mrs. Halgard knows Edward Folsom, our case is cinched—but they won't hang Edward Folsom. Never! He's as crazy as a bed-bug, an' that's a fact. But he, or mebbe George, put out Stevens' light all right. You bet one or the other of 'em did!" and Hackett stopped.

"I'll admit, Bill, it begins to look that way. Did you learn of any visitors to Folsom who might possibly be the skinny chap you chased yesterday, or the one who almost dumped me down the L stairway last night?" said Rollins.

"No," said Hackett; "but old Folsom could easy have hired somebody by phone or letter. There's a thousand of those toughs in Chicago would butcher a man for half a grand. Nothing hard about that!"

Rollins looked at his watch. "Goodness, Bill, it's after six! I've got a splitting headache and a little fever, I guess. I'm going to get some tea and toast and then sail for home. Heavens, I'm thirsty! Give me that glass while I get a drink. That's a pretty sure sign of fever all right. Let's shut up shop for the night! Come on, Bill! See you at eight tomorrow!"

At the street door Rollins and Hackett parted, the latter going westward. Rollins stood for a moment watching the retreating form of his friend. "It's a darned shame," he thought; "here's poor old Bill losing a good steady job just through me. If I hadn't almost begged him to make that extra print of Stevens' desk, with the old man's body half-lying on it, and give the print to me, Bill would have his job yet. He did it entirely out of friendship for me. Nothing else! And what have I done for him?" Bob thought. "Not a blessed thing! I've chased him all over town doing this and that; I've ordered him round like a collie dog and he's done every darned thing I asked, without letting out a peep. Not one complaint! Not one single word of blame for me, although he knows I got him into all that mess! Darned if it don't make me ashamed of myself. Look at the two splendid jobs Bill pulled off today! I'll bet there isn't another man on the police force who could have got the dope on old Folsom like Bill. He's as loyal as they make 'em, and for quick thinking in an emergency, nobody can beat him. Yet here he is, almost broke, fired from a job he's had for six years, but still cheerful and willing to go the limit, just for friendship. I'll say Bill's a wonder, and the least I can do is to try to get back his job for him. It isn't too late, for he'll still be a member of the Police Department until Saturday. I'm going over to see In-

spector Devine right now and do my damnedest anyhow."
And Bob started to pay his moral debt.

Arriving at the Police Headquarters, Rollins found Desk-Sergeant Ryan just going on duty for the night shift.

"Good evening, Sergeant! Has Inspector Devine gone home yet?" asked Bob.

"Hello, Rollins!" said the Sergeant. "No, he'll be here for some time yet, I reckon. We're mighty busy now with these damned hold-ups and rackets, and, believe me, a police job is no cinch, with all that's doin' lately, and that's no fairy-tale."

"Do me a favor, Sergeant, will you? Ask the Inspector if he can see me for five minutes," said Rollins. "Smoke this while we're waiting."

"The Inspector has got somebody with him right now, but I'll ask him if he's got time to see you. Wait here a minute, Rollins"; and Ryan disappeared into the Inspector's private office.

An instant later he returned. "It's all right; the Inspector will give you five minutes," he said. "Go right in, Rollins. The boss ain't feelin' any too good from his rheumatism, but good luck!"

When Bob entered Inspector Devine's office, it was with a sense that he was attempting a useless task. Devine's reputation for efficiency was enviable, but, as to discipline, he was a martinet. He gave no excuses for his own failures and accepted none from others. With him orders were things to be obeyed, and the detective staff under his charge knew it. Although of medium build and height, there emanated from him a force of personality much greater than his physique.

As he looked up from his writing and said: "Take a chair, Rollins," his tone was icy, and Bob's hopes well-nigh vanished.

The Inspector had been talking to a visitor just as Bob came in. A plate of tongue sandwiches and a cup of coffee stood before him on the desk. "Just step outside for five minutes and wait for me," said Devine to his caller. "I'll see you as soon as I've finished with this gentleman"—pointing to Rollins—and the caller departed to wait on a bench in the ante-room.

"Now what is it, Rollins?" asked the Inspector sternly.

"I came to see you about Hackett," said Bob. "He's lost his job because I imposed on his friendship and got him to make an extra photo for me in that Stevens suicide case. It's all my fault, Inspector; I'm entirely to blame. I've known Hackett for over three years. I like him. I've done him some little favors and I know he has always looked on me as a good friend. I gave him my promise not to use that print without his permission, and I personally destroyed the photo in his presence the day after he told me of his discharge. He saw me do it, and will tell you so. I'm here to beg you to keep him on, Inspector. No harm has been done. Hackett's a mighty good man, and a credit to the force. I'm the man who led him astray. Won't you do it, Inspector?"

Devine tilted back his chair, grunted, munched another sandwich, rocked back and forth, grunted again, looked out of the window, toyed with his pen, frowned at Bob.

"So!" he said, and his words were frigid. "Rollins, tell me this! How could you run this department, keep up discipline, and maintain the essential secrecy of police work if your men violated long-established rules, gave out confidential information, and blabbed their stuff to any reporter who asked 'em? And would you overlook that sort of thing if you were me?"

"Inspector," said Bob, "you're perfectly right! I understand and appreciate the justice of your decision. I'm not questioning it. But I am the cause of all this. It's my doings that made Hackett disobey the rules. I'm the real culprit. Won't you give him one more chance?"

Another moment of studious indecision for Devine, another thirty seconds of frowning thought, while he consumed the rest of his sandwich. Finally the Inspector reached for a pen, seized a sheet of his official writing-paper, wrote a few lines on it, signed his name on the bottom, put the note in an envelope, wrote William Hackett's name on the outside, and handed the envelope to Rollins.

"There!" he said; "give that to Hackett and tell him he's the luckiest guy on earth to have you for a friend. He'll be suspended thirty days without pay, but we'll keep him on the P.D. rolls. Tell him to hand that note to the Sergeant a month from now, when he comes back. That's all, Rollins!"

"By thunder, Inspector, you're a prince!" said Bob, as he put the envelope in his wallet. "I'll never forget this. Good night, and thank you a lot!"

"Do you know why I did this, Rollins?" asked Devine.

"No," said Bob, wonderingly. "Why?"

"Well," said Devine, "it was because I've been thinking that old Stevens' desk-top and room was too damned clean, and that maybe we didn't dig deep enough into that mess of his. Only for that door-key I'd feel sure that we hadn't got to the bottom of his case. But that key settled it with me. It would with anybody. That key couldn't get there unless Stevens put it there, unless somebody had a duplicate. Of course, if you've got some real evidence to show us, we'll reopen the case. Suppose you come round in a day or two and we'll talk things over. I understand that one of Stevens' policies isn't likely to be paid because of its suicide clause. Too bad! I didn't know Stevens personally, but, from all I hear, he was a fine chap. Going home now, Rollins?"

"Yes," said Bob, "I don't feel any too good. Sort of shaky! Got a cold coming on, I guess. Thank you again, Inspector, and good night!"

Rollins stood talking to Sergeant Ryan for a moment after leaving Devine, while the Inspector recalled his former visitor.

"Good news, Sergeant!" he said. "The Inspector has suspended Hackett for a month instead of firing him. Bill will sure be a happy man when he gets the news, and, believe me, I'm a happy kid right now. Good night, Sergeant!"

Thirty minutes later Rollins was in his own room at the Sanford and, despite his influenza symptoms, felt decidedly better. He washed up, cleaned his teeth, took a good long drink of ice-water, filed his finger-nails, dusted off his shoes with the freshly discarded towel (strictly against house rules), threw the towel under the marble set-bowl, opened his room door, locked it, and went down in the elevator to the Sanford lobby.

Joe Atwood, the room-clerk, was up on a tall ladder putting new screws into the trolley roller of the folding doors leading into the dining-room.

The letter-boxes for tenants of the Sanford were at the left end of the hotel desk. Bob reached over and thrust his room key into his letter-box.

As he started to enter the dining-room, Bob was about to walk under Atwood's ladder, when Atwood shouted: "Hey, Rollins, don't do that! You may not be superstitious, but I am. No use taking any chances. Walk around this ladder, son! You never can tell!"

"Say, Joe, I thought you had a decent job here!" said Bob. "How long since you've been carpenter as well as clerk?"

"About five minutes," said Atwood, "and I'll be one for about an hour yet, it looks like. The screws on this darned trolley and track were too short, an' the doors got to sagging so that you couldn't hardly get into the dining-room. Don't ever believe I'm looking for this kind of a job, but there ain't anyone else here now to fix it. In this joint a guy has got to do everything."

Rollins ate a very light dinner—in fact, it was more like a breakfast. He chatted with a young man—one Percy Fosdick—at the adjoining table and came to Percy's rescue when a common friend, another diner, revived some time-honored jests on Fosdick's first name. It was nearly seven thirty when Rollins left the dining-room. Largely owing to the good news in store for Hackett, Bob felt almost like himself again.

Joe Atwood had just completed repairs on the folding doors and was stowing away his ladder as Bob went into the telephone booth on the right side of the Sanford lobby.

"Nora, dearest," said Rollins a moment later, "I'm so full of good news I can hardly speak, but I can't talk about it over the phone, and I'm so bunged up with a cold, I've got to go to bed. If you want to hear all about it tomorrow morning, I'll tell you how you can get to do it."

"How, Bob? For goodness' sake, tell me! Can't you come out tonight, dear? Please do!"

"No, honey, don't ask me. I've got to doctor this cold. But here's what I want you to do. You telephone to your Aunt Rose right now, and if she hasn't got back to town yet, telephone her again tomorrow morning. I want you to bring her with you down to your father's office between ten thirty and eleven o'clock sure. I'll be there. If she isn't in town tonight, find out from her maid, or whoever is taking care of her house, just where Mrs. Halgard is. Then wire her tonight to come back to Chicago by the next train and meet you downtown tomorrow morning before fen thirty. Will you do it, dearest?"

"Certainly I will, Bob. Maybe she'll be where I can reach her by telephone tonight. Is there anything else, dear?"

"Yes, honey," said Bob. "If you get Mrs. Halgard on the phone, be sure and ask her to look up that last poem—three stanzas—that your father sent her. It's the one she got from him about three weeks ago, on her birthday. We've just *got* to have that poem, Nora, so be sure she brings it with her, won't you?"

"Don't worry, Bob. I'll get in touch with Aunt Rose tonight, no matter where she is, and I'll have her come with me tomorrow—and bring the verses too—if it's humanly possible to do it. I suppose you want to take your medicine and go to bed now, so good night, Bob darling!"

"Good night, sweetheart!" said Rollins—and, as he hung up: "God bless her! She's too good for me or any man on earth.—Give me my key, please, Joe. I'm going to take a bath and some aspirin and hit the hay!"

The clock in the Sanford lobby marked seven forty-five as Atwood, now behind the desk, handed Rollins his room-key and wished him good-night, and Bob rode up to his room.

The bed-covers had not yet been turned back by the maid, and Rollins sank wearily into his arm-chair for a few minutes' thought before taking a hot bath and retiring. His brain was now clear. He sat with his back to the lights over the bureau, and facing the little alcove in which the marble washbowl stood.

The towel with which he had dusted his shoes less than two hours before still lay where he had tossed it, under the washbasin. Evidently Kate had not made her final rounds to clean up for the night.

"I didn't know my shoes were muddy tonight when I cleaned 'em," he thought. "It's a darn shame for a fellow to use a hotel towel to dust off his shoes, anyhow! I ought to quit it. Look at that streak of mud there!"—as he fixed his eyes on the otherwise white towel under the bowl.

"Gee, that isn't mud. Too yellow and straight for that!" Rollins rose, switched on the dome light in the ceiling, and looked again.

The object lying on that towel was a partly burned paper match.

IX

ROLLINS SANK BACK into his easy chair, looked again, and thought. For some reason his mind reverted to last night's peril on the L. A safety-match! He hadn't used a dozen in a year! Not since Nora had presented him with a patent cigarette-lighter last Christmas! Bob stared at the match again. He reviewed all that he had done two hours ago when he had washed up in the room before dinner.

He had dried his hands, dusted his shoes lightly, and tossed the towel under the bowl. But that match lay on the top of the towel! Yes, and he could see a tiny scorched spot on the linen where the still hot match had landed.

Rollins shook his head and laughed. "Pshaw! It was Kate, the maid. It must be!" And yet Kate was fifty years old, sober as a judge—and he was sure she didn't smoke! No, it couldn't be Kate! Yet it must be! Anyhow, he would find out. She must be somewhere on his floor.

Rollins jumped up, opened the door, and walked quickly down the hall. "Kate! Oh, Kate!" he called. "Where are you, Kate?" Almost before he could repeat his call, a pleasant Irish face beneath iron-gray hair projected itself from a nearby doorway.

"What is it? Oh, it's you, Mr. Rollins. Do ye want yer bed turned down; or is it clane towels you're afther? Sure, I've been so busy, with the housekeeper away an' me with double wurrk, that I've had no toime to fix up yer room yet."

"That's all right, Kate," said Bob. "Have a cigarette; it'll do you good. All the girls are smoking now, you know!"

Kate's smile left her face. She looked Bob squarely in the eye and said: "If I hadn't known ye for two years an' didn't think ye were jokin' now, I'd never sphake to ye agin in me loife. Me, smokin' cigarettes! Me! Huh!" and she turned away.

"Wait a minute, Kate," said Rollins. "I didn't mean to offend you; yet I wasn't joking. Do I understand that you haven't lit a match in my room any time today?"

"Av coorse not! I nivver lit a match there. Whoy should I? I've not been in your room since this marnin', Mr. Rollins, that's flat!"

"I believe you, Kate! Here's half a dollar to prove it," said Bob; "but have you seen anybody go into my room in the last three hours? Anybody?"

"I have *not!*" said Kate. "Did someone sthale somep'n? Is there anything missin', Misther Rollins?"

"Nothing so far!" said Bob. "Just wait here till I call up Atwood. Oh, say! Go round to my room and stay outside the door until he comes up! That's a good girl, Kate!"

Rollins called the hotel desk from the hall telephone, and the clerk answered. "Listen, Atwood! Come up to my room as quick as you can. It's important!" said Rollins.

Less than three minutes later Rollins, Atwood, and Kate were standing at the door of Rollins' room.

"I want you, too," said Rollins to the elevator boy, whose curiosity caused instant response to the summons.

"Now!" said Rollins, to the wondering three beside him; "somebody's unlocked my door and been in my room since I went down to dinner. This burnt paper match is the proof of it. Both Kate and I will swear we didn't put it there, and I haven't lit a match here this year. The question is, who did get into this room, light that match, and toss it on to that towel?"

After fifteen minutes' consultation and a thorough search of the room the four were no wiser than before. Nothing appeared to have been stolen. No one but well-known tenants had ridden on the elevator. Atwood agreed to question the other two bell-boys and pump them dry; Kate returned to her duties, and the elevator boy took Atwood down. Bob was left alone.

"I can't get it out of my head that the lad who got in here came on business," muttered Rollins. "He must have walked up, and folks don't walk upstairs for fun. He must have walked down, too! If he came up while Atwood was working on those doors, he could have swiped my key out of the box, provided the bell-boys were upstairs on calls. Anyhow, it's certain he had a purpose in coming.

"It's almost certain, too, that he knew I was eating dinner and out of my room just then. That means he must have been watching my movements—like that rope-artist on the L last night.

"I can't see that he took away a thing, although he had plenty of time to do it; so I'm pretty sure he didn't come to steal. The fact that nothing here is disturbed means that he tried to leave no trace of his visit. That means, then, that he intended I should never suspect anyone had been in the room.

"Another thing is certain: this lad did not come here to *help* me. His purpose must have been to *injure* me in some way. Now, what other way could he injure me except by robbing me? There can be only one other way; he meant to do me physical injury. How can a man injure another physically in a place like this? I've looked over every inch of this room and the toilet, and there's no one here.

"Poison, then, is the *only* way that he could injure me physically. Now how could my fine lad apply his poison—to the outside of me, or to my interior? An outside way would be absurd! I'm not going to jab myself with a poisoned needle. Well, how about poisoning me on the inside? I can't see how he could dope that ice-water, unless he did it downstairs in the cooler. If he did that, everybody in the hotel would be on the way to heaven! He hasn't bored a hole in the ice-water pipe, or the water would be leaking here somewhere. The faucet top is O.K. Let's see how she runs! When I took a drink just before dinner, it was all right!" Wrapping his hand in a towel, Bob turned the circular handle of the ice-water faucet. A steady but very slow stream of water resulted. As he watched it run, the character of the stream changed. It forked into two smaller streams, then became steady, then forked again.

"Something in the faucet-nozzle!" said Bob. "Away up, too, I guess. Let me get that corkscrew knife of mine. Ah, there she is! There's that . . . skunk's calling-card again!"

Rollins held in his hand a little piece of rubber sponge, similar to that used in most homes for bathing. The sponge was about the size of a very small acorn. Through its center was thrust a small hairpin, curved at about the same radius as the curved nozzle of the ice-water faucet. The bottom of the rubber sponge had been pushed up into the faucet about half an inch above the opening of its nozzle. The curved hairpin had held the sponge firmly in place inside the faucet opening.

On the top of that tiny piece of sponge were five or six small white crystals, only slightly dissolved by their brief immersion.

Robert Rollins' face set like a sphinx. He seized an envelope from his desk, dropped the sponge, hairpin, and crystals into it, locked his door, dashed for the elevator, and ran through the hotel lobby, hatless and disregarding Atwood's questioning shout.

Half an hour later Bob had returned from a visit to his friend Harding, whose drug-store was a block away. The crystals on the sponge had been analyzed. Twenty men would have died from swallowing the contents of that envelope: cyanide of potassium.

"What was the big rush, Rollins?" said Atwood as Bob re-entered the Sanford lobby.

"Nothing much," said Rollins. "Did you find out anything, Joe, about the lad who paid his little visit to my room?"

"Yes!" said Atwood. "Henry, the bell-boy here, says there was a short, slim, dark lad, with a sort of puckery face, waiting for someone here for about ten minutes while you were eating dinner. Henry got a sixth-floor call, and when he came back to the lobby, the lad was gone. Henry said he'd recognize him anywhere. His left ear-lobe was split as if an ear-ring had been torn out of it. Hey, Henry! Come here and tell Mr. Rollins about that bird with the split ear," said Atwood.

Henry was only too glad to give Bob all the information he could, and (still more gladly) pocketed a dollar bill with a yard-wide grin. "I'd know that guy among a million," he said. "Besides that ear of his'n, his face was jest full of little tiny wrinkles, all criss-crossed like. B'leeve me, if I ever lamp that bird, Mr. Rollins, I'll foller him to hell-an'-gone, the lousy pup!"

Rollins thanked both Atwood and Henry and returned to his room again. All desire for sleep had vanished. Where had he seen such a face as Henry described? That he had seen it—and recently—he was certain. Was it in Sergeant Ryan's office? Possibly—but he was not sure. Well, it would come back to him. Hold on! Hackett's spry lad yesterday had also something wrong with his ear. That was it.

And now for tomorrow's plans. He could not foresee, of course, what he might learn from his coming interview with Charles Duncan and with Mrs. Halgard in the morning. No use theorizing about either until he had talked with both and learned what they knew.

Now, as to the Folsom end of the case, Hackett was positive that Edward Folsom had poisoned Alexander Stevens, perhaps assisted by George. Nearly all the evidence thus far obtained tended to confirm Hackett's belief. If Folsom's letter to Duncan, which Rollins hoped to see in the morning, showed Edward Folsom's finger-prints upon it, and if these prints were identical with the five prints developed by Hackett from Stevens' memorandum book, the case would be complete. Edward Folsom's guilt would be proved.

Bob recalled that Edward Folsom had been absent from his nephew's flat on both the morning and the night of Stevens' murder. Thus, he *could* have committed the deed, unless he proved an alibi. His motive for such a crime was unmistakable. Folsom knew Stevens' habits well. The character of Stevens was such that he would have accorded Folsom an interview at any reasonable place or hour, despite the latter's threats and animosity.

Then, too, Folsom was an expert chemist. The formulae of the color-process as inscribed by Stevens on the cards, which were still in Stevens' safe, would be child's play for Folsom to comprehend.

But wait! With Folsom's knowledge of chemistry, would he be likely, while altering the card-formulae, to make those glaringly foolish changes in chemical symbols which Hackett had instantly noticed? Would not Folsom have changed the formulae in such a manner as to make them seem practical to the eyes of another chemical expert? He surely would, if his mind was functioning sanely.

But was Folsom really sane? Might not his mental state when altering the formulae (if he did it) have been such that powers of reason were not really applied to the task? To Rollins, the guilt or innocence of Edward Folsom hinged more on these questions than on any finger-print evidence that could be produced.

Finally Rollins thought long and deeply upon the bogus farewell message of Alexander Stevens. That Mrs. Rose Halgard had received the birthday poem containing the ending line: "Ere I bid the world good-bye" he did not doubt. Neither was there doubt in his mind that some person—still unknown—had secured from her somehow all of those verses, or at least the final stanza. Who was that person? . . .

The voice which greeted him on the phone at six thirty the next morning seemed a continuance of a happy dream. It was Nora.

"Bob, dear," she said, "I had to catch you before you got away. Auntie Rose was visiting her niece—her real niece, not me—in Joliet, Illinois. I found out last night from Julia, her housekeeper, where she was, and got her on the phone in Joliet, before she went to bed. She's been there a week, and she didn't know that Daddy was dead until I told her. She feels frightfully about it and she's coming to Chicago by an early train today and going straight home. She promised to look up those birthday verses that Daddy wrote and meet me at Marshall Field's at ten o'clock. Then we'll come right over to Daddy's office and meet you there. I'm so glad we found her, aren't you, darling?"

Rollins gladly devoted five full minutes to expressions of gratitude—and other sentiments. At seven thirty he had finished breakfast.

At five minutes before eight Bob unlocked the door of room 713, admitted Hackett, who had been waiting in the hall, went in himself, and left the door slightly ajar, awaiting Charles Duncan's arrival.

Charles Duncan, sales manager for Schwartz and Melden, the well-known photographers' supply house in Cleveland, was a man of his word, for promptly at eight o'clock his knock sounded at the door, and Hackett gave him admittance.

After preliminary self-introductions between these three strangers had been completed, Mr. Duncan asked: "When will Mr. Stevens be in?"

"Haven't you heard?" said Rollins.

"Heard what?" asked Duncan.

"About what happened to Mr. Stevens!" said Bob.

"No," said Duncan, "I haven't heard anything. How could I, when I just got off the train? What's the trouble? Auto accident, I suppose? Those cussed things are always busting somebody's legs or ribs. Is Mr. Stevens well enough to see me? I surely hope so. I'd hate to see this deal fall through now, after we've got this far."

Satisfied at last that Mr. Duncan had no knowledge of Alexander Stevens' death, and that he fully expected to meet Stevens personally that morning, Rollins briefly told the story of the reputed suicide. "Frankly, Mr. Duncan," said he, "Mr. Hackett and I are convinced that Mr. Stevens did not kill himself, but that he was poisoned by some person who was determined to steal that color-photo process for his own use, and leave no one else on earth in possession of the methods for producing it. I asked you to come on to Chicago because we both know you had probably talked with Mr. Stevens last Saturday, November 18, the day he died. I didn't tell you that Mr. Stevens was dead, or you might not have been willing to come. I will gladly reimburse you for your expenses and the time you are losing, and we both hope you will tell us everything you can which is likely to help us learn the truth about this sad affair. Mr. Hackett will take down what you say, if you don't object."

Duncan was unquestionably surprised and shocked by Rollins' revelations. Before Bob had really completed his story, he put out his hand to Rollins and said: "Don't say another word about money, Mr. Rollins! You may pay my fare if you want to, but that's all. Stevens was as fine a man as I ever met and I'm far more sorry over his death than over losing his business. Better let me tell you the whole thing in my own way, and then you can ask whatever questions you like. Here's my story, and I'd be glad to have you take it down, Mr. Hackett.

"Stevens wrote me, on or about November 15, asking me to meet him here in this office at nine o'clock Saturday morning, November 18. He said he was planning to order several thousand dollars' worth of plates, films, and printing paper, coated with a new special emulsion for color-photography and would like to discuss our prices. Of course I was glad to come, and wrote him to that effect. His letter is on file at our office now, and you can have it whenever you need it.

"I got here promptly at nine o'clock last Saturday morning and came direct to this floor. The colored elevator boy who took me up this morning was the same one that brought me up and directed me to this room last Saturday. The boy will remember it if you ask him, for he recognized me a few minutes ago, when we rode up together.

"When I got here, Mr. Stevens opened the door to my knock and invited me in. He was just saying good-bye to another visitor who was leaving—a man whose face I recalled, though not his name.

"Mr. Stevens seemed pleased to see me, and we got down to business at once. We talked for about three hours last Saturday—from nine to twelve.

"Stevens showed me some really wonderful—simply marvelous—photos, produced by his new color-process. He wanted us to supply all ingredients for the emulsions except two, and those two chemicals, or combinations of chemicals, he would supply himself. He was to send his own man to Cleveland to help make the emulsion, and that man was to stay at our plant and supervise its manufacture. Stevens was to make up his own two-chemical combination here in Chicago and ship it to his man at Cleveland in our shop. When our part of a batch of emulsion was ready, Stevens' confidential man would mix with it the requisite quantities of the chemicals that Stevens had shipped to him from Chicago. By this scheme nobody but Stevens could possibly know the entire formula, and nobody except Stevens' confidential man could obtain any of the two secret chemicals or compounds and analyze them.

"I saw at once that this was a really stupendous proposition. Through being sole producer of Stevens' secret emulsion our firm would be the largest photo-supply house in America within five years. It meant millions of dollars to us as well as Stevens, and I promised to submit to him the precise cost figures this week.

"Just before I left this office, somebody knocked at the door. Mr. Stevens let the man in and introduced him to me as a Mr. Folsom, who at one time used to be Stevens' partner. This man Folsom didn't appeal to me a bit. He seemed to know who I was, where I came from, and what I was there for. He acted as if he owned the place and butted in constantly—talked about 'our' process and all that. Stevens didn't argue or fight with him at all. He just let this man Folsom talk right on, but tried to pacify him as best he could. Everything that Folsom said about the process had a 'we in it. '*We* are going to do this,' or "*We* don't propose to do that.' My train was leaving shortly after noon, and I wanted to get home before Sunday, or I surely would have stayed over and found out what this Folsom person had to do with Stevens' affair. I didn't get a chance to ask Stevens about it, for Folsom stuck close to him every second until I left. It didn't seem to matter much at that time, for Stevens and I had practically finished our discussion before Folsom came in.

"This week—as I told you over the phone, Mr. Rollins— our firm got a letter from Folsom, and I've brought it along, as you asked. Pretty nearly everybody in our office has studied it several times, and I'm frank to say that I think this Folsom is a little bit 'off' in his upper story. I think you will agree with me after you have studied it. That's all there is, Mr. Rollins. Do you want to see Folsom's letter?" and Duncan stopped.

"Yes, please," said Rollins. "Frankly and confidentially, Mr. Duncan, most of our evidence indicates that Folsom has long been half-insane. He is convinced that he is entitled to a half-share in Mr. Stevens' discovery, became determined to get it, and may have poisoned his former partner in order to obtain it. Mr. Hackett and I have some finger-prints which we fully believe were made by Mr. Stevens' murderer. We asked you to bring Folsom's letter with you so that we might dust it for detection of finger-prints and see whether Folsom's prints are identical with those of the man who, as we believe, actually murdered Stevens. May we have Folsom's letter, Mr. Duncan, and see what we can find?"

"Sure thing, Mr. Rollins! Here it is. Let me see you do this thing; I'm interested!"

Hackett used more care in his experiments with Edward Folsom's letter than with any similar job in his life. Both front and back of the letter were dusted separately, and every smudge compared with the finger-print photos taken from Alexander Stevens' memorandum book. Bill worked upon it fully half an hour and finally laid the paper down in disgust.

"How many fellers have you got in your office, Mr. Duncan?" said he.

"Twenty-six," said Duncan. "Why?"

"I reckon there's no doubt the whole bunch handled this sheet all right," said Hackett. "I never saw so many different smudges on a piece of paper in my life. I'll bet every one of them guys in your shop pawed over this damned thing twenty times and held it upside down and slantwise while they did it. There's two prints on the left side and one print of a thumb on the lower right-hand corner that might be the ones we're after, but those have been smeared by somebody else, so I couldn't swear to it. Damn it all! I'm sorry, Bob, but we've just got to get some good clean prints offa Folsom's own hands—ones that we know are his. This thing here wouldn't go in court at all. Any good lawyer would have us gibbering like a coupla idiots if we tried to build our case on the smudges on this letter."

"Well," said Duncan, "I'm tremendously sorry the letter hasn't helped you, but I hope some of the rest of my story has. I surely wish you both all possible success. The man who could deliberately murder a man like Mr. Stevens is beyond the pale, whether he is sane or insane. Are you through with me now, Mr. Rollins? May I go?"

"Yes indeed, Mr. Duncan," said Rollins; "and you have helped us a lot. More than you realize! I think the contents of this envelope will prove that my word as regards your expenses is good, and Mr. Hackett and I thank you most sincerely. I'm going to the elevator with Mr. Duncan, if you don't mind, Bill," he went on. "I'll be right back."

On the way down the hall Rollins remarked: "You said you recalled the face of the man who was leaving Stevens' office when you entered it last Saturday morning. Do you remember his name now, Mr. Duncan?"

"No, I don't—I just can't think of it. If I'm not mistaken, he used to work for us in Cleveland over twenty years ago and left to take some city job. I can look it up when I get back and call you up or wire you if you think it's important."

"I wish you would, please. Every little thing is important in this matter. The least trifle may tell me what I want to know. Please phone or wire as soon as you can. By the way, was the elevator boy who took you up awhile ago the same as then and did he see this man?"

"Yes, the same boy. But I couldn't say whether he saw Stevens' caller or not," replied Duncan.

The elevator had just reached the seventh floor as the two stood before its steel door and shook hands in parting.

Harry Flood, the colored operator, grinned at Duncan. "Come again, boss! You're sho' welcome!" he said.

"You mean the little tip is welcome! But you won't have to guide me on my next trip, so maybe there won't be any tip," said Duncan, smiling.

" 'At's all right, boss! I likes tips, but they's some fellers I like, too. Don't do no harm to git liked, does it?"

The car shot down, with Duncan waving good-bye to Rollins. Bob turned to go back along the corridor to the room, then hesitated, turned back, and rang the elevator bell.

When the car arrived again at the seventh floor, Rollins boarded it for the down trip. "All out of cigarettes, Harry," he said. "Guess I'll go down and get some—if you don't charge me too much for the ride. How about it, Harry?"

"No charge for you, boss! 'Free rides for friends' is my motto!" To an observant person it would have seemed extraordinary that a well-dressed white man should make three round trips up and down the elevator shaft of a building, solely for the sake of joking with the colored attendant. Stranger still was it that he should forget to leave the car and purchase the cigarettes for which he had initiated his journey. And still more incomprehensible was it that Mr. Robert Rollins drew a full package of cigarettes from his pocket, lit one as he walked down the hallway of the seventh floor, and was smoking it when he entered room 713.

"I'm expecting Miss Stevens to bring Mrs. Halgard up here almost any minute, Bill," said Rollins.

"Sufferin' Moses!" shouted Hackett. "Did she get back to town all right? And is she comin' here? *Wow!* Now we'll get somewhere, Bob. How's it happen Miss Stevens is comin' along? Loosen up, you miser! Tell your buddy somep'n once n'a while! Ain't I in on anything you know, or do I give all an' get nothin'?"

"I didn't have a chance to tell you before, Bill. Duncan was here and I couldn't," said Rollins; and forthwith he gave a concise account of his telephone conversation with Nora that morning.

"Say, that Stevens girl must be one peacherino!" observed Hackett. "I'll bet there ain't another dame in this burg that woulda stuck on the job an' put it across like that! Likes her little Rollo—I mean Rollins—I guess! Eh, Bob?"

"Shut up, you darn fool!" said Bob. "I've got another nice little piece of news for you, Bill, that I didn't have a chance to spring yet. Sit down, Bill, and be ready for the flash! Here it is! Mr. William Hackett has been reinstated in his former position with the Chicago Police Department, commencing one month from this date. Mr. Robert Rollins will assume responsibility for William Hackett's loss of income due to one month's suspension. How's that, Bill?"

"What!" yelled Hackett. "My old job back! My darling, beootiful old job! *Oh wow!* D'ya mean it, Bob? For the luvva Mike, don't fool me on this, old scout! Honest, I couldn't stand kidding on that line. Is it true?"

"Absolutely! Cross my heart! I've got a letter in my wallet over Devine's signature, commuting your sentence to one month's suspension, and I'll take care of the pay part," said Rollins.

"You will, like hell!" said Bill. "I've had more damn fun this last week than I ever had, an' what the hell's the use of havin' fun without chippin' in your share in the kitty? I'm on vacation for a month, Bob, an' if you try to slip me any coin, I'll spend the next thirty days in the hoosegow for beatin' up my former pal, R. Rollins. Gimme that letter, I want to see it!"

"No, sir!" said Bob. "That letter goes in this safe right here and now, and you can take my word for it that it's all true. You can have the letter twenty-nine days from this date," and Rollins swung open the door of the unlocked safe, took Devine's letter from his wallet, put the envelope in the safe, closed the door, and locked it.

Coincident with the slamming of the safe-door came a rap on the panels of room 713, to which Bob, with almost lightning speed, responded.

As he expected, it was Nora, and with her stood a pleasant-faced exquisitely gowned woman, whose apparent age, to Bob, was well under fifty years.

Rollins knew, of course, that the likable woman who smiled at him and Hackett must be Mrs. Halgard, and the sole lonely fly in his porridge was that he lacked nerve to kiss Nora before her "Aunt Rose" and his friend Hackett.

Nora, however, refused to be bound by any frigid conventions. She calmly kissed her sweetheart on the precise frontal location nature intended. Then she introduced Rollins to her pseudoaunt. Bob, in turn, reciprocated by introducing Hackett to the ladies, and everyone was soon comfortably seated.

Rollins had dreaded having Nora Stevens visit the scene of her father's tragedy, yet almost the first word spoken in that fateful room on this eventful day came from Stevens' daughter.

"Bob," she said, "and you too, Mr. Hackett—Auntie Rose knows just how I feel about coming here after all that has happened in this room. At first it just seemed I couldn't bear to see even this building again. The very thought of it was terrible, but ever since poor Daddy was buried, and Bob and I knew we had only each other, I just resolved—determined—that I would not shirk anything. I know I've got to stand it. No matter how much I regret or pray, nothing can ever bring Daddy back. Crying and being miserable isn't gong to help—and the more I give way, the less chance there is of finding out who did this awful thing. Let's go right ahead, honey! Let's make believe that I was poor Daddy's dear friend, just like Auntie Rose here, and you, too, Bob darling! Don't mind me at all! I can be brave and I will!"

Nora stopped, and Bob leaned over and kissed her lips. "They don't make 'em any braver," he said.

"Bob," said Nora, "won't you please take charge of things? You and Mr. Hackett ask Auntie Rose and me anything you want, and we'll tell you everything we know. Go ahead, dearest!"

"All right, honey, I'll start, then! Mrs. Halgard, I suppose Nora has told you all she knows about this terrible thing, hasn't she?" said Bob.

"Oh yes, I think she's told me all she knows herself—but I'm sure you've found out a lot more, Bob. You see I'm going to call you 'Bob' right away, so as to get in practice. It won't be long before I'm your Aunt Rose, and then I'll have to—shan't I?" said Mrs. Halgard.

Bob looked steadily at the sweet, placid face of the kindly woman whose voice had uttered those happy words. No wonder Alexander Stevens had been proud to call her friend. No wonder that he had found, through her, real comfort and inspiration. No wonder that Nora had named her "Auntie Rose," "the darlingest woman in the world."

"All right, Aunt Rose!" he said; "I've got to get some practice too, you see. You don't mind, do you?"

"Of course not, Bob. Now make believe you're a lawyer and ask me questions. Mr. Hackett, Nora says Bob told her you could write shorthand. Won't you take down what Bob and I say, and then we won't forget it? You'll do it for me I know, won't you?"

"Honest, I'd do anything in the world to please you, Mrs. Halgard. Let's commence now! Start the questions, Bob," said Hackett, solemnly.

Bob: "That's fine, Bill! Here goes! Now, Aunt Rose, I'm going to tell you and Nora one of the things that I do happen to know which I haven't told Nora yet. When Nora's father died, the police found a blue slip of paper, about three inches in length and seven inches wide, lying right in front of him on his desk. It had evidently been torn from one of his letter-heads." Rollins then took from his wallet Alexander Stevens' bogus farewell message and showed it to Mrs. Halgard.

"You see, Aunt Rose, that he wrote on that slip: 'I bid the world good-bye,' and signed his name. I found in this scrapbook a typewritten copy of a birthday poem he sent to you. The ending line of the last stanza of that poem was: 'Ere I bid the world good-bye.' If you will hold this slip of paper to the light, you will see that something has been erased just in front of the words: 'I bid.' The erasure is only about a half-inch long, and I believe the word 'Ere' was formerly on that paper, but has been scratched out. Do you recognize this paper, Aunt Rose, and is it, or is it not, the lower part of the sheet containing Mr. Stevens' last birthday poem to you? Look at it! Both sides!"

Aunt Rose: "It certainly is, Bob! It's precisely what you said, and I'll prove it. If you'll turn that paper over, Bob, as I did just now, you'll see a place on the back of it where I spilled a tiny little blot of ink from my fountain-pen while I was writing Alex to thank him for the poem. See, there's the little blot!"

Bob: "Aunt Rose, I'm proud of you. We were morally certain before that this was so. Now you have given us positive proof of it. Now for the next question, Aunt Rose! Did you succeed in finding the remaining sheet or sheets of that poem, from which this blue slip has been torn off?"

Aunt Rose: "No, Bob, I haven't found any part of it, and I've looked everywhere. I had it in my writing-desk, but it's gone."

Bob: "When did you see the poem last—and where?"

Aunt Rose: "Let me see! Oh, yes, I remember now! I gave a dinner-party last week Thursday, just the night before I went down to visit my niece in Joliet. That was November 16, wasn't it? We had twenty-four altogether at the party, but only ten came to dinner. The others came later. After we were all through dinner and were getting ready for bridge, somebody started talking about poetry, and I remembered the beautiful birthday poem Alex wrote for me a few days before. I mentioned it and said how nice it was and how lovely it was of Alex to send it. Somebody said he'd like to see it, so I went upstairs and got it out of my desk and brought it down. Quite a number of the guests looked at it, and everybody said it was a darling. I thought Julia put it back in my desk, but she didn't know anything about it when I asked her this morning."

Bob: "Who was it said he'd like to see the poem, Aunt Rose? Do you remember?"

Aunt Rose: "No, I don't. Wait a minute! It was Edward Folsom. He used to be your father's old partner, Nora. You remember him? Yes, he was the one who wanted to see it first. I suppose it was because I said Alex had written it, and he knew Alex so well and was interested."

Bob: "How did you come to invite Mr. Folsom to the party, Aunt Rose? Did you know him well?"

Aunt Rose: "Yes indeed, the poor man! I knew him when he was with Alex, but, I must say, I didn't like him very much. Of course I was sorry when he became ill and had to go away; and when I met him two weeks ago on Michigan Avenue and saw how forlorn he looked, I was sorrier still. He told me he was living with his nephew, George Folsom, at the Blenheim Apartments, and how lonely he was, so I just couldn't help asking him to come over with his nephew, George, the next Thursday to my party. I thought perhaps it might cheer him up."

Bob: "Can you remember everyone who was at your party? Could you make a list of those who came to dinner and another list of those who came afterwards?"

Aunt Rose: "Oh, yes! Shall I do it right now? It won't take five minutes. I'll hurry."

While Mrs. Halgard was inscribing her two lists of guests, the other three sat talking, and watching her sweet puckery frowns as she tried to remember the names.

Mrs. Halgard was doing her clerical work at Alexander Stevens' desk—not in the chair where he formerly sat, but opposite. Suddenly she dashed her pen down and made violently vigorous motions in search of her handkerchief. That necessary article of apparel was grasped just in time to suppress an explosive sneeze.

"My goodness! I almost didn't," she gasped. "Now, where did that fountain-pen go? I had it right here," she said, looking on the floor. "No, it isn't there; and it isn't here," she continued, as she looked on the desk. "Isn't it funny how things disappear like that? Where can that pen be?"

Everybody at once started a search for the elusive fountain-pen. They looked in every possible place, upon, under, and near the desk. Not a sign of it anywhere! Not a trace!

Finally Bob said: "Let's reason this thing out. I've never seen any puzzle that logic won't solve. All we have to do is to eliminate the places where we know the pen is not, and we'll find at once where it is. We know it must be near the desk. We're sure, too, it must be in one of three places: *on* the desk, or *under* the desk, or *around* the desk. We've eliminated the *on* and the *under* already; hence the only place in space where the pen can be is *around* the desk. We can see three sides of the desk, and, since the pen is clearly not around either of those three sides, it must be behind the desk. Let's pull the desk away from the wall and take a look at the back of it."

Hackett and Rollins seized the desk by its sides, and together moved it outward three or four inches from the wall. Instantly the sound of a falling object was heard. On the floor, close to the wall at the back of the desk, lay the fountain-pen.

Hackett bent over and looked at the back of the desk, which was now visible. "Aha!" he said, "there's an inch strip of molding running the whole length of the desk; the molding was tight up against the wall, so that's why the lost pen didn't fall, Bob. The molding held it up. It's wonderful how simple a puzzle is when a fellow has found the answer. Let's move the desk back, Bob," he said. "Hello, what's this?" and Bill leaned down to pick up a second object from the floor.

"Stop! Don't touch it!" shouted Rollins, and he grabbed Bill's arm. "Let it lie just where it is until we think this thing over. Whatever that thing is—and it looks like a little tiny cornucopia of yellow paper—it's been there a good while. You and I, Hackett, haven't moved this desk since Mr. Stevens died, and I feel sure the janitress hasn't. That paper must have fallen there before Mr. Stevens died. There's just a chance that it may mean something and we mustn't overlook the chance. Here, Bill, take this handkerchief and pick it

up through that. Don't touch it with your fingers! Be careful!"

When retrieved and laid tenderly on a clean blue letterhead on the desk, the mysterious yellow paper proved to be, in fact, a very small cornucopia. It was nearly two inches long from pointed tip to its widened top. While not flat, it had evidently been somewhat crushed by pressure. From a crease extending straight across the cone at its widest end, it could be seen that a flap of the paper had once bent across and closed the opening of the cone.

Tenderly taking up the little cone through his handkerchief, Bob tapped its open end lightly upon the blue letter-head. At the fourth tap a tiny white crystal about twice the size of a pin's head lay on the blue paper. The crystal had been wedged in the small end of that little yellow cone, had become loosened by the gentle tapping, and now lay upon the letter-head before their gazing eyes.

Everyone present in that room breathed an almost noiseless "Ahhhh!" Rollins held up his hand for silence. "Get your powder and dust this cone, Bill. Dust inside as well as out. Whoever glued up this little devil must have used his bare fingers—so there *must* be prints on both sides of that paper. Go to it, Bill! Make it the best job you ever did!"

Five minutes later Hackett looked up from his work. "They're here, folks! Prints on both sides!" he said. "That damnable . . . held this cone between the thumb and two fingers of his left hand while he loaded it with cyanide. Damn him! Maybe I don't know those prints! I don't have to look. I'd swear to 'em among ten million! They're from the same fingers that opened your poor father's memorandum book, Miss Stevens, and left his dirty tracks there to lead him to a rope. God pity the devil who made 'em!"

Rollins held up his hand again. "I'm sure you're right, Bill," said he, "but let's test a tiny part of this crystal and get the positive proof. Go ahead, Bill, get your stuff ready, but be sure and save part of that crystal for evidence."

Not a word was spoken while Hackett worked. The last ultimate, indisputable proof of crime—a proof which the most obstinate man could not reject—was to be put in their hands.

Presently Hackett stood up and turned to his watchers. "Got him!" he said. "Potassium cyanide!"

A few minutes later two women, with somber faces, and eyes still moist with tears, had left the near-final scene of tragedy, and only Robert Rollins and William Hackett remained in room 713.

X

AFTER THE TWO WOMEN had left and the evidence as developed by the morning's discoveries had been locked in the safe, together with both of the lists which Mrs. Halgard had written, Rollins and Hackett started to go out to lunch.

"I want to see that watchman, John Harvey, again," said Bob. "I haven't a doubt that this murderous devil of ours came in and walked up to Stevens' office while Harvey was out for his tobacco. That's one of the things we're pretty sure of, but Harvey didn't say he had gone out twice. If Harvey didn't leave his post a second time and stayed awake, he must have seen that skunk go *out* of this building."

Young Mr. Harry Flood, the grinning elevator boy, whom both Bob and Bill had so often encountered in the past four days, took them down. Harry had evidently treasured the memory of Rollins' little conversation with him that morning. "I'm gonna be here till six, boss," he said. "You know me! Don't forget the number if you want anything."

"All right, Harry," said Rollins, "I'll remember"; and the two comrades left the elevator at the ground floor. There they stopped a moment to speak to the building superintendent, George Donovan.

"Can you get in touch with John Harvey this afternoon?" asked Rollins.

"I certainly can," replied Donovan. "He'll be here at one o'clock today if he isn't dead—and it's a pretty hard job to kill a Scotchman. We pay off at one o'clock Fridays here, and he might lose a day's interest on his money if he didn't show up. Don't worry, he'll be on hand all right!"

"That's good!" said Rollins. "Ask him to come up to room 713 for a minute when he comes in, will you?—and thanks a lot. We'll be back from lunch then."

If all the days of the week were pay-days, John Harvey would surely have qualified for "alertness championship" honors, for he was waiting in the hall, before the door of 713, when the two comrades returned. A big cigar and the most comfortable chair in the office (and his pay envelope in his pocket) put Harvey entirely at ease.

After bewailing, in his rich Scotch brogue, the fact that Rollins' previous questioning had compelled him to admit to Superintendent Donovan his brief desertion from duty in quest of tobacco, Harvey gave some information that seemed really worthwhile. To Rollins' inquiry if he had seen anybody at all in the lobby of the Meyers Building after ten o'clock last Saturday night, Harvey described a long-haired stranger with a brown Vandyke beard who had entered for a moment at half past ten, failed to find the tenant for whom he was seeking, and departed. This bearded unknown was positively the only person who could have got in or out, for Harvey had locked up all hall doors at eleven o'clock and had punched his time-clocks regularly thereafter.

John Harvey left room 713 with an extra cigar, an extra thank-you, and an extra dollar. He was content.

His retreating footsteps were still sounding in the hall when Rollins picked up the telephone and gave central the number of Police Headquarters.

"Hey, Bob, whatcha doin', you crazy nut? I'm supposed to be in my dyin' agonies. For God's sake, don't tell 'em I'm here," cried Hackett.

"Don't worry, Bill! Lots of confidence you've got in me— I don't think!" said Rollins. "Is this Police Headquarters? Can I speak to Desk-Sergeant Ryan? Oh, is this you, Ryan? How's the old boy today? This is Rollins talking—yes, Bob Rollins! I'm at room 713 Meyers Building, on Adams, near La Salle Street. Have you been to lunch yet? . . . No? That's good! . . . No, I didn't mean good for you; I meant good for me. Say, Sergeant, if you can spare ten minutes and come up here, I'll buy you any lunch you can eat . . . No, sir, I said any lunch you could *eat!* All right, but five dollars is my limit, remember! Hop on a car and come over right off . . . Atta boy! Who wouldn't be a cop? Car-fare free! Everything free—even if the Eighteenth Amendment . . . Yes, yes! Nobody could coax *you*—but I'd hate to try. So long, Ryan! See you in fifteen minutes! Be good!" and Bob hung up.

"Now, then, Bill," said Rollins, "let's have a little confab before Ryan comes. You noticed what Harvey said about that chap he saw with the short brown Vandyke beard. You noticed another thing, too—and that is that Harvey's description fits Folsom to a T. There's a third thing which makes it look as if this is the skunk we're after. That thing is the *time* that Harvey saw him.

"I figure that it would take just about one hour of solid, steady, systematic work to do what was done in this office last Saturday night. Remember, Alexander Stevens died at nine twenty-eight. That's certain! This fellow had to rob Stevens of his book and keys, open that safe, photograph those six cards, alter the cards, put the cards back, polish the safe-dial and knob, leave that good-bye note, wipe off the desk and chair-arms, finger-print that whisky-glass with Stevens' fingers, and clean up all litter. Besides that he had to use up three or four minutes telephoning to Stevens' home and four or five minutes on the most important job of all—transporting that door-key from outside this locked door to the top of Stevens' desk.

"Nobody living could do all that in much less than sixty minutes. That makes it ten thirty when he's through his dirty job and ready to go downstairs. It's a certainty he wouldn't stay in this building a second longer than he had to; and he must have known that Harvey locked the building up at eleven o'clock. He surely knew all about how this place was run. It is practically unbelievable that somebody else left here between ten thirty and eleven without being seen by John Harvey.

"If these deductions are correct, this brown-bearded fellow is our man! Just put that down on your collar, Mr. William Hackett. We can be practically sure of it. The next question is: 'Is this man identical with Folsom?' Let's reason about that for a few minutes and let's take *both* sides of the question. Here's the first side: that Folsom is not the poisoner.

"Folsom may be half-crazy, but he's far from being a fool. You and I know, Bill, that men with brown Vandyke beards are a mighty scarce article nowadays. I know only two, and I'll bet you don't know any more than that. Folsom knows that fact just as well as we do. Folsom knows his appearance is distinctive—that mighty few men in Chicago wear a beard like his. Another thing, Bill! If you ever saw evidence of an alert, keen mind, you've seen it on this job. Every detail shows studious, far-sighted planning—not crazy, impulsive action.

"Now, then! Are we to believe that the man who was keen and shrewd enough to plan such a murder as this could be so idiotic as to come to the scene of his crime and go away from it wearing such an advertisement as a Vandyke beard—if that was his *own* beard?

"Reasoning from that angle, you'll agree that Folsom—in spite of the mass of evidence pointing to him, and in spite of Mrs. Halgard's additional evidence today—is unlikely to be the man who murdered Alexander Stevens. We positively know that Folsom is mixed up in the deal somehow, but this line of logic tends to indicate that he didn't commit the actual crime. If this reasoning is sound, it means then that the skunk who poisoned Stevens was disguised—but why disguised to resemble Folsom? A supersmart crook like this man could have selected and worn twenty disguises far more effective and easier to put on than this one. The only possible inference could be that he wanted to impersonate Folsom, and that's why he chose Folsom's particular get-up. Only an actor, with expert knowledge of make-up, could impersonate another man, in both speech and appearance, in daylight; but almost anybody could do it at night when no talking was needed. There's no need to discuss now the *why* of such an impersonation—if there was one, for we don't know there was one. Pretty nearly all the evidence so far points squarely at Edward Folsom.

"Now let's study this thing from the other angle and assume that Folsom is the actual poisoner. Are there any logical reasons why he should enter and leave this building
without any attempt at disguise whatever? The answer is
yes—plenty of reasons!

"First: If Folsom had been observed by the watchman
when going up to Stevens' office that night, he had a valid
reason to give, and Stevens would back him up by assuring
the watchman that he expected Folsom's visit.

"Second: A bearded man must shave off or dye his beard
to attempt disguise. If Folsom had done either of these two
things, he would have aroused Stevens' suspicions, and Stevens would not only have wanted to know why, but might
not have permitted Folsom to come into this office. In other
words, disguise would have created distrust.

"Third: A man who constantly wears a beard *can* disguise
himself perfectly in three minutes, with a razor, and his best
friend wouldn't know him. Such a man is always prepared
for a vital emergency. He doesn't have to carry any imple-
ments except that razor; and after using that, he has a disguise that baffles description, whether in day-time or at
night.

"Fourth: Preparing an unshakable alibi nowadays is not at
all difficult for a clear-thinking man who has ample time to
do it in. Folsom had all the time in the world at his disposal.
He could fix things up so that no jury could convict him. He
could point to the fact that he was no fool, and that only a
fool would murder a former friend by poison without assuming some disguise, when the poisoner must know that he
would be at once suspected. The very openness of Folsom's
coming and going would tend to acquit him.

"Well, Bill, we've looked at both sides of this thing, and
I'm frank to say that the odds clearly favor Folsom's being
the murderer; but we can't *prove* it yet. If we had clear cop-
ies of Edward Folsom's finger-prints and if—mind you, Bill,
I'm saying *if*—his prints are the same as those on that little
paper cone we dusted this morning, *we've got him.*

"In other words, we *must* somehow get clear prints of Folsom's fingers without his knowledge; for if he even suspects we are trying to get those prints, he'll shave off that beard and vanish. That's the thing we've got to study out now, Bill, and let's both give our best thought to it.

"Meanwhile, we can't afford to overlook the other angle—that some other man, whose motive is unknown, planned this crime and tried to impersonate Folsom. If there's any real validity to that theory, this hypothetical man had to secure, somehow, a brown Vandyke beard. It had to be the same shape and color as Folsom's, and it must be a false beard that could be put on quickly. That eliminates the use of actors' curly hair glued on the face and trimmed to the proper shape. Our assumed impersonator couldn't carry hair, glue, shears, and mirrors with him and thus fix himself up on short notice to resemble Folsom. That means a regularly manufactured false Vandyke beard, made by a costumer who knew his business. This hypothetical villain, then, had to *buy* such a beard. The question is: *'Where?'*

"Now we are down to brass tacks, Bill, on this impersonator stuff. Chicago is pretty big, but I'll bet there aren't twenty costumers or masquerade people who could sell a specially tinted brown Vandyke beard today if you offered 'em a hundred dollars for it. Four out of five of even the best costumers would have to *make* it, and this man couldn't wait to have one made. As I figure things, it was late Thursday night, at Mrs. Halgard's party, before he decided that beard was necessary, so he must have bought it and the brown wig last Friday. While we are waiting to get Folsom's fingerprints, let's try to find out where that beard came from and learn who bought it. If we find such a purchase has been made by someone who *could* be the impersonator, that will let Folsom out. Otherwise he stays in!

"Hello! I'll bet that's Ryan coming down the hall right now. Get out, Bill!"

"I'm gone!" said Hackett. "See you here about six o'clock, Bob! Good-bye!" and he strode toward the hall.

"Welcome the coming, speed the parting guest!" quoted Rollins, as he unlocked the door to let Hackett out and Sergeant Ryan in. "How much is the bill for that lunch you haven't eaten yet, eh, Ryan?"

"Shure, I have eaten it, me bhoy! It's thirty-five cents, me lad; two sandwiches and coffee, and you can thank your lucky stars I had it furrst instead of afther. What's up, Docther Rollins?"

"Sit down, Sergeant," said Bob. "That alleged lunch of yours doesn't count. We'll start all over tomorrow and do the job right. Only remember, a five-spot's the limit. Are you on?"

"Shure, I'm on! Tomorrer at one! I'll meet ye at the station an', believe me, I'll show ye what real *eatin'* is! Now what's the game, Rollins? Make it snappy, me lad! Toime's short!"

"I'll make it short, all right!" said Bob. "Listen, Ryan! Twice in the last two days some bird tried to cripple me. No fooling, Sergeant! Cross my heart! I didn't see the lad myself, but I've got his description. He's about forty-five years old and rather skinny, with black hair. He's got a puckered sort of face—lots of criss-cross wrinkles on his cheeks and neck. Oh, yes, his left ear is slit too—as if he used to wear an ear-ring, and somebody tore it out. You know lots of crooks, Ryan; do you know this one? Think now! Think hard!"

Sergeant Ryan threw back his head and let out a perfect bellow of laughter. For two or three minutes he rocked to and fro in his chair, started to speak, and then laughed again. Rollins thought he would never stop.

"For the love of Mike, what's the matter, Ryan?" he said. "You may think it's funny to get sent to the hospital or bumped off, but I don't. What's the big joke? Tell me, so I can laugh too!"

"Haw! Haw! Haw!" howled Ryan. " 'Think an' think hard,' is it you're sayin'? Better do a little thinkin' yourself, me lad! I don't believe there's two guys on earth that answer the description ye jest gimme. Why, you was within two feet of this puckery guy yesterday. He had just come outa the front office an' was settin' on a bench alongside half a dozen other crooks in my room as you went out. We were goin' to pump him. That's Puckers! Every dick in town knows him. He's been in hock half a dozen times, and if he wasn't such a good stool, he'd be a lifer right now. By gorry! This is the best joke ever; you'd make a helluva a fine detective, Rollins! See a man sittin' almost in front of ya one day an' then call the cops to round up that same guy the day after"— and Sergeant Ryan exploded again.

Now Bob recalled that row of bums he had seen in Ryan's office the day before. "That was where the elusive subconscious memory of such a face originated," he thought.

"That surely is one on me!" said Bob. "It just shows that a fellow has got to be cut out for your business if he wants to make good. For Heaven's sake, don't breathe a word about this to anybody, or the boys would never quit giving me the raspberry. Promise me now, Ryan! Be a good sport and don't tell anybody. I'll make it a dinner besides that lunch if you do. Is it a go?"

"All right, Rollins, me lad! It's almost too good to keep, but ye're a nice bhoy an' I'll promise. Now what do ya want to do to this *guy* Puckers? Swear out a warrant an' jug him? We *can* do it! I can put my hands on him any minute of the day, an' if you say so, I'll send one of the bhoys afther him—but I hate to do it. He's too good to lose, that guy!"

Rollins thought a little before he answered. "All right, Sergeant," he said. "I won't rob the department of a good stool. I thought maybe he meant to kill me, but it's possible he was trying to get revenge for writing up some not too virtuous lady friend of his in the *Leader*. I suppose that must be it. It must be! What time do you go off duty tonight, Ryan?"

"Six thirty sharp!" said the Sergeant. "Why?"

"I'll tell you what we'll do then. You and I will have a swell dinner tonight at the La Salle. It's on me, of course! Not a five-dollar limit, but go as far as you like! Meanwhile, you get one of the boys to lasso this Puckers bird an' keep him in the jug under the station until seven o'clock. Don't tell him why or let him get wise to what's coming, and, for Heaven's sake, don't let him talk to anybody.

"Then, at sharp seven o'clock, you take him with you over to the La Salle. I'll hire a private dining-room there and be waiting in it. The bell-captain will show you both where I am. Bring Puckers in there with you at seven fifteen sharp. You and I will have our big feed and let Puckers drool while he's watching us.

"After we're through, I'll give Puckers the third degree, but I've got to have something on him before I do it. Listen, Sergeant! When you get back to the station, you send over to the Bureau and get all the dope they've got on Puckers. Get his complete criminal history—photos, finger-prints, arrests, sentences, everything. Send a boy over to me with the whole dope as soon as you get it. Be sure! That will give me a chance to look it over before tonight, and I'll have it all in my head when I start giving Puckers the works.

"After you and I have pumped him dry and scared him to death, we'll turn him loose, and I'll bet a million he won't bother me again. Oh, Sergeant! I'll bring Bill Hackett along! You don't mind, do you, so long as it's my party? Here's how we'll handle Puckers"—and Rollins told him. "I'll bet we'll have a whale of a time, and I know Bill will enjoy it. How about it, Sarge? Is it a go?"

"Is it a go? Will I do it? Haw! Haw! Haw! I'll say I will. Listen, me lad! I'll bet we have more fun than a barrel of monkeys. So long, Rollins! Don't forget there's no limit on the eats. I'll send a boy over with Puckers' dope. See ya at seven fifteen. Be good!" and Bob was alone again.

Now was Rollins' chance to study Mrs. Halgard's two lists, which had reposed in the office safe since Nora and her Auntie Rose had gone. It would probably be two hours before Hackett came back, and he could do much more efficient thinking while alone.

First, however, he must make that reservation for the Ryan "banquet" and assure himself and his guests a private dining-room for this very special occasion. No open dining-room would serve for the ordeal which Puckers was to face. That room in the La Salle must be very private indeed. If a soundproof vault had been available for the party, Rollins would gladly have paid double price for its rental.

Luck surely was with Bob Rollins that Friday afternoon. The La Salle arrangements went through as smoothly as a gigolo dancing with his most generous client. Not a hitch developed or even threatened. "Well-laid plans—good jobs," said Bob to himself, "and this has got to be the best job I've ever tackled.

"Now, then, we'll take those two lists of Aunt Rose and give them the once-over!" he murmured. "Onceover! Huh! I'll bet fifty times over will be a lot nearer what'll happen."

For one straight hour Rollins' mind was concentrated on those two columns of names and addresses which Mrs. Halgard had furnished. Of the guests who had partaken of her dinner, several were known to him by reputation, but none personally.

After twenty minutes' study of this list of dinner guests Rollins laid it temporarily aside and took up the other list, of the persons who had arrived later. On this list the first name which caught his eye was, naturally, that of Edward Folsom. "We'll put him out of mind just now. What I'm after is to find who *else* could have carried off that three-stanza poem. Let's see! There's George Folsom. Let's leave him out for a while, too.

"There are five women on this second list. Could any woman have put this across? Not a soul at that party knew that Rose Halgard ever in her life had received a birthday poem from anybody. Mrs. Halgard had no idea of showing that poem when the affair started. The person who stole those verses could not have had any such plan in mind when he or she came to that party. The purpose of stealing the poem entered the thief's mind *after* seeing the poem, not before. That purpose must have jibed in and harmonized with some half-formed plan previously conceived.

"A woman might create this scheme mentally, but she could not execute it alone. Any bright woman would realize that. She would need a man's assistance, and the profits of the color-photo process would have to be split with that man.

The man would have to do the killing, for a woman would have slim chance of entering and leaving this building unobserved. Later the bargaining or the manufacturing would necessarily have to be done by a man. No, the five women are eliminated. That leaves only the men to consider.

"Here's Adolph Muensch! He's got two millions if he's got a cent, and he's about seventy years old. Besides that, he's one of the biggest philanthropists in town. Gives away a quarter-million every year. Adolph, you're eliminated! Old boys like you don't commit murder."

Thus for an hour Rollins rubbed his forehead and studied those two lists—first one and then the other. Aside from Edward and George Folsom, no possible suspect appeared.

Unable to remain quiescent longer, Bob got up and paced the floor, then sat down and thought again. He shook his head. This would never do! Reasoning was to him fundamental to correct inference. *Elimination of the impossible in order to learn the possible* was his gospel—but sufficient facts upon which reason and logic might build an enduring structure were equally essential. He must have more facts! But whence? Facts right now! Where might he obtain them? Ah! What had the elevator boy said? "Any time!" Well! Now was the time.

Bob put on his hat, unlocked the door, relocked it from the outside, hurried to the elevator, and rang the bell.

Less than a minute elapsed before the gleaming white teeth and expansive grin of Harry Flood appeared in sight. "Listen, son," said Rollins; "ask Mr. Donovan if he'll put someone else on the car for half an hour. I know he'll say yes. Then you come to room 713 and see me. Do you see this? Would you think that two-dollar bill was unlucky if you got it? Or would you rather have a one-spot instead? How about it?"

"Say, boss!" said Mr. Flood, with a long, lingering look at the figure 2 in Bob's fingers, "Fridays I ain't one bit superstitious! No, sir! Friday is sho' my lucky day. Watch me come a-runnin'." For thirty minutes Robert Rollins and Harry Flood held earnest converse in room 713, and not once did the dark young man appear to remember that less than a week ago a dead man had sat in that chair before him.

The hands of Rollins' watch pointed to five o'clock when the amiable Mr. Flood ceased giving innumerable but candid answers to a host of mysterious questions, all of which (in his choice verbiage) "ain't got no mo' sense 'n a rabbit." Should Mr. Harry Flood embarrass his soul with worry for so trivial a cause? He should not.

It was almost five thirty when William Hackett knocked, for the last time that day, on the fateful door of the room where Rollins sat. Hackett's face was more than sober. It was somber, funereal. Without a word he came in, flopped wearily upon the nearest chair, stretched out his legs, put both hands in his trousers pockets, lifted his head, and looked across at Rollins.

"Well," said Bob, "no luck, I suppose, eh, Bill? Cheer up, old scout! You haven't been to *all* the costumers and masquerade-goods places in Chicago yet. You couldn't! I didn't expect you'd get the goods on this thing in one afternoon. You'd be a wizard if you did. Brace up, Bill! Tomorrow is another day! They can't keep a good man down."

Not a syllable from Hackett! Magnificent illustration of the sphinx-like qualities of a mortal when enthralled by novel, deep emotion.

"Oh, come, come! Nobody's blaming you, old scout! We haven't even started on this beard business yet. Besides, I've got a little news that may help the game along if we have any luck. What did you learn, Bill? Anything?"

"I reckon I'd better spin the whole yarn, Bob, an' then you can decide whether I learned anything or not," said Hackett. "Don't be scairt to butt in as I go along. I ain't sensitive. I mighta been once—but not now. Here's just what happened, so listen!

"Before I started out, I got to thinkin' this thing over—like you do, Bob! That reasonin' and logic stuff, you know—an' here's how I figured it out. This bird that wanted that false beard only had one day to get it in, an' that day was last week Friday. With his little job of murder on his hands for next day—an' probably a few other triflin' things, like safe-breakin' an' so forth to look after—he didn't have any time to waste.

"Another thing—as you said when we were talkin' about this mess—no small concern would be likely to have just the kind of whiskers he needed. He'd be a lot likelier to get what he was after an' get it quick by tryin' out some good-sized masquerade joint that had a store inside the Loop or close to it.

"Well, I couldn't be sure of listin' all the downtown costumers by lookin' in the telephone directory, because that's almost a year old and there must be lots of changes by now. So, thinks I, 'I'll phone to Information an' get the low-down on the whole thing'—an' I did. Information told me the new directory was almost ready to print an' said if I came over to the main telephone-office, they'd be glad to let me copy any lists I wanted off'n their records.

"Well, I went over there, an' they treated me fine. In ten minutes I had the addresses of every decent-sized masquerade-goods and costumers' shop within a mile of Madison and Clark. Listen, Bob, that system of yours is sure one peach! I'll say!

"Well, I routed 'em so's to save walkin', an' at the sixth place I hit, it looked like I'd struck oil. It's a concern on Wabash near Van Buren—Walker and Holmes, not a big shop, but pretty classy—and here's how I went at it.

"When I came in, I didn't see only one clerk, an' that was a pleasant-faced dame about thirty-two, an' I says: 'Good afternoon, miss, are you the young lady who sold my friend that brown Vandyke beard last Friday an' have you got another one in stock just like it? You see, he and I are going to impersonate the two Dromios from *The Comedy of Errors* at a Shaksperian *bal masque* next week, and we both think two beards like that would fix us up just fine!'

"Believe me, Bob, I stuck in the 'miss' and the 'young lady' as often as I could, an' I could see she wasn't peeved about it a bit. Say, Bob! I was scared stiff for fear she'd ask me who my friend was, or how he looked or somep'n, an' that's why I rattled on so fast that she couldn't get a word in edgeways. Finally I had to shut up. I wasn't out of breath, but my brains quit workin', an' I couldn't think of another damn thing to say, to save my life.

"The minute I stopped, she pipes up: 'Yes! We've got one and I'm awfully glad Mr. Donovan liked the Vandyke he bought. He was so particular about the shade of brown and we were afraid we hadn't trimmed it into the precise shape to suit him. He was so hard to please, I felt certain he never would come back or recommend us to anyone. But, you see, he did!'

"Well, sir, I was as cold as a pickled herring, Bob! 'Donovan!' thinks I. 'That Donovan guy must know this dame, or she wouldn't know him, an' if that's so, I'd better be on my way damn quick. How in hell was I goin' to find out whether this was a false lead or the real goods? Believe me, Bob, I was thinkin' like a racehorse, but finally I decided I'd take a chance.'

" 'Aha!' says I, 'I see Stumps is up to his old tricks!'

" 'What do you mean "old tricks"?' says the little lady.

"Why," says I, "it's just impossible for Stumps to meet a real pretty girl without tellin' his whole family history. I suppose the old sheik suggested a supper or a show or somep'n, didn't he? He *would!* If he didn't, it wasn't his fault.

" 'Why, no! He didn't,' says she, real sober. 'I wouldn't have gone if he had. I don't do that sort of thing. But, honestly, he wasn't fresh at all. Quite the contrary! Very sober! But what makes you call him Stumps?' ('What the hell else could I call him?' thinks I.)

" 'Oh, that's his old nickname when we were kids,' I says. 'But don't try to make me believe Stumps didn't tell you his name! He never left a nice girl in his life without doing that—an' you wouldn't have known his name if he hadn't told it,' says I. An' I tried to put on that wise look that says: 'I've got you there!'

" 'Really he didn't!' says she. 'I wouldn't have known his name at all, only one of his business cards fell on the floor, when he was paying for the wig and beard. Here it is! Look at it, if you don't believe me!'

"The poor girl was almost cryin' now, and honest, Bob, I pitied her. I'll bet she's a darn fine woman, Bob, an' somebody's lost a helluva good wife by not snappin' her up ten years ago. Yes, sir! Believe me, I know it!"

"Wait a minute, Bill," said Rollins. "How about that business card? Did you get it? Let me see it!"

"You wait yourself, young feller!" snapped Hackett. "Who the hell's tellin' this story? You or me? When I get round to it, you'll know all that's needed to know. I ain't never held out on a partner yet.

"Well, Bob, as I was sayin', I asked to see the beard she had in stock an' wanted to know could she trim it exactly like the shape of the one she had sold to my old friend Stumps. The girl says she'd rather not try to do that without havin' the other one to go by. 'They might spoil it,' she says, but if I'd bring back the beard that Mr. Donovan had, they'd fix 'em both up alike in ten minutes; so I left with the understanding that I'd bring down poor old Stumps' whiskers next Monday morning.

"Gosh all fish-hooks, Bob! If I'd had the money, I'd have bought that darn beard right there. The poor girl was so nice and sympathetic like. Believe me, Bob, that little girl may not be a spring chicken, but she's as fine a lady as I ever met, an' that's God's truth. Honest, Bob, if I wasn't damn near broke, I'd like to marry her tomorrow—an' be the luckiest guy on earth if I did."

"It wouldn't do you a bit of harm to do that very thing, old scout!" said Rollins. "You need somebody like that and I'm not fooling either. My suggestion is that you see the young lady Monday anyhow. You won't have to buy that beard or anything else, old top! Anybody that can think 'em up as quick and spiel 'em out as fast as you can, doesn't need any pocket-book. Folks *pay* to listen to *your* kind, Bill!

"I notice your lady friend sold this Donovan chap a wig as well as a beard. This begins to look as if we were getting somewhere, Bill. Let me present my compliments and congratulations! Honestly, I'm proud to be associated with a man whose brain can work as quickly as yours.

"It's quite plain to be seen where your interests lie at this moment, and I'm not blaming you for being human, but I am exceedingly anxious to see that *card.* The word is spelled CARD. I'll be glad to hear about the young lady a little later. Have you got the card, Bill?"

"You're all right most times, Bob, an' I can take a joke as well as the next guy; but, believe me, this ain't anything to joke about. Not by a damn sight! I'm tellin' you, young feller-me-lad, that us two birds are runnin' round in circles, like a pup tryin' to bite off his own tail.

"So you wanta see Stumps Donovan's business card, do ya? An' you think we're makin' progress when we find out who bought that damn wig an' beard, do ya? All right, then, Mr. Wise-Guy! I'll say we're right back where we started a week ago, only we've got *two* villains in our piece instead of one. There's your damned old card, an' I hope it bites ya!" and the slightly irritated William Hackett opened his wallet and dumped upon the table a business card, bearing the words:

Geo. L. Donovan,
Superintendent Meyers Building
Adams Street Chicago, Ill.

William Hackett slumped in his chair with the disgusted look of a spotted dog who has learned, too late, that the striped cat he's been chasing owns a scent and origin heretofore unknown.

Rollins studied the card intently, but without touching it. Although his face did not show it, he was inwardly much perturbed at this totally unexpected outcome of their quest.

"Did you get a good description of this particular Donovan who bought this beard and wig?" he asked.

"Did I?" Bill snapped. "So you think I'm nutty? Of course I did! Miss Allen described him perfectly. It's *our* Donovan—the guy who runs this palatial joint, the bird that don't furnish steam heat and hot water, the gazebo that'll probably raise Cain if we don't pay the rent for this room on December 1! That's who it is! Why, this poor little Doris Allen even described that big dark-brown mole on our Donovan's chin. She said Stumps told her it was a good thing the beard would cover it! Huh!"

Rollins for the next few moments went into one of his accustomed deep and studious reveries. Yes! he thought; Superintendent Donovan had a big brown mole on his chin. He had access at all times to all floors of the Meyers Building. On Sundays or holidays, in the absence of his employees or his tenants, he could enter the rooms on both sides of room 713; he could let himself down from the roof by a ladder or rope. Because of his position he could pump his help; could learn the habits, foibles, customs, and minor business secrets of his tenants. In fact, no calculator would dare fix a limit to the possibilities for evil of such a man if he selected the path of crime.

Who could say that George Donovan, with the sources of information at his command, had not long ago learned of the secret task on which Alexander Stevens was laboring? Was it impossible that Donovan had secured some expert locksmith who, with an entire day at his disposal, had picked the lock of room 713, made a duplicate key, and thereby given Donovan free access to that room whenever he chose?

With Alexander Stevens' trustful nature, was he likely to withhold from George Donovan any confidence other than the secret of his color-process? Given twenty-four or thirty-six hours to work, might not Donovan have secured admittance to Stevens' safe as well as picked the lock of that fateful room?

If Donovan had offered Stevens a drink of liquor in room 713 at nine twenty-seven on the evening of November 18, Stevens would never have dreamed of evil intent. How easily then might follow Stevens' poisoning and death, the picture-making, the locking of the door—with a duplicate key—and all the other acts in that sordid drama! Hackett had well said they were back where they started.

"Well, Bill," said Rollins, "don't let's worry about it! That won't help! There's nothing we can possibly do tonight to clear up even a part of this Donovan mess. The more thinking we do about it now, the worse off we'll be. Thinking means progress always when you've got *facts* to think about, but it isn't worth a tinker's cuss without a good bunch of *real facts.*

"What facts have we got, Bill?" said Rollins. "Just three! A description, a business card, and a mole—and Miss Doris Allen, nice girl that she is, may be a little off on two of those three facts. We've simply got to wait until tomorrow, Bill. Don't you worry, old scout! Trot along with me and I'll bet we'll nail that dirty rattlesnake's skin on a board and make a shopping-bag out of it yet! Listen, Bill! Miss Allen must have handled this card, and Donovan also; I'm sure *you* didn't. Did you get a sample of Miss Allen's finger-prints too, so that we can disregard them when we dust this card?"

"Sure!" said Hackett. "Here they are, on the firm's letter-head."

"All right! Hello! Who's that knocking? Oh, I know! Sergeant Ryan is sending over some dope I asked for. Let the lad in, Bill!—Yeaup! That's it! Here's the life-history of our sweet little Puckers! Thanks for bringing it over, sonny! Here, buy some Camels and think of me! Good night!"

"What you got there, Bob?" asked Hackett. "Good Lord! Something new again? By Godfrey! Ain't we got enough stuff to sleuth about without ringin' in a fresh lot?"

"Take it easy, Bill! This isn't work; it's fun! You and I are going to have the time of our lives tonight," said Rollins. "Sergeant Ryan dropped in for a few minutes while you were out, and I described this little devil who's been trying to break my neck and dose me with embalming fluid. Ryan seems pretty sure he knows this man. Says his pet name is Puckers. Ryan says in this note here that he's got this Puckers lad in the ice-box underneath the station right now, and here's a list of dear little Puckers' activities for the past twenty years or so. Got his whole criminal record, Bill! Ryan's going to bring Puckers over to the La Salle at seven fifteen sharp. I've got a small private dining-room engaged, and you and I'll be in it when Ryan comes along with this sweetfaced murderer of his.

"I didn't let on to Ryan that Puckers had tried to kill me. I just told the Sergeant that I had probably written some story for the *Leader* that had reflected on the moral character of Puckers' best girl, and that Puckers was probably sore and was trying to beat me up. It seems, from what Ryan says, that this Puckers is pretty valuable as a stool-pigeon, and they don't want to lose him; so I told the Sergeant we'd pump him good—maybe give him a little third-degree stuff—throw a stiff scare into him, and turn him loose.

"But that isn't what I'm after at all, Bill! Here's this little shrimp Puckers making two good strong tries on two consecutive days to put me in a coffin. The last one, when he put that cyanide in my ice-water faucet, came within an inch of doing the job. If I hadn't happened to see that burnt match on the towel, I'd have sure been a goner. That's the only thing that saved me—just that little trifle!

"Now, then! You and I know that there are a lot of tough men in Chicago that would commit murder pretty cheap, but I never heard of one that would kill a man for fun—without any motive. This lad Puckers must have had a motive. Now, *what* was that motive?

"I've got a scrap-book, Bill, of every story I've written since I started newspaper work. I've looked 'em all over, and there isn't one line in any of them that could have started Puckers on this rampage. I never saw him, that I remember, although Ryan says Puckers was sitting on a bench with a lot of other cheap crooks the other day when I was at the station. I remember looking at the bunch—there were five or six of 'em—I probably must have noticed Puckers, because when our bell-boy at the Sanford described the bird who'd been sitting in the Sanford lobby—and it looks as though he's the only one who could have got into my room and planted that poison in my ice-water faucet—I seemed to remember having seen a man of that description somewhere. I'm sure, too, he's the lad you chased downstairs the other day.

"Well, Bill, as I figure it, Puckers couldn't have had any personal motive for bumping me off. That means that somebody else wanted me put underground and hired Puckers to do it. There can't be any other reason, for nobody tried to rob me, and my death wouldn't profit anybody as far as cash is concerned. I've searched my mind for every possible way that any man could profit by getting rid of me, and there's only one: that is to prevent us from finding the murderer of Alexander Stevens and proving his guilt.

"Now, Puckers knows the man who did this, Bill! I'm *certain* he does, and here's why.

"First: Puckers has got a long criminal record, as these police cards show, and he's known to be a shrewd, nervy, resolute crook. You can see that borne out by the way he schemed out those two attempts on me.

"Second: men of that type, like Puckers, don't deal with go-betweens. They want to be sure of getting paid for their work. That's why Puckers surely knows his principal in this case.

"Third: with his easily identified phiz, Puckers wouldn't dare to tackle a job of murder unless he thought his principal would try to protect him if he were caught.

"That brings up another inference! The man who hired Puckers must be a man of influence. Puckers wouldn't have taken such big chances otherwise. Moreover, that man must have something mighty serious *on* Puckers. My idea is that he threatened either to send Puckers up for life for something which he could prove Puckers had done, or maybe to put Puckers under the sod if he didn't obey orders. In other words, I think Puckers was forced to tackle the job of murdering me and didn't dare to refuse.

"That brings up another inference, Bill! Unless Puckers and his principal had been good friends, or mighty close to each other away back—the Lord knows how long—this principal couldn't have known enough about Puckers' past to have him under control and make him try to murder me.

"Now, there you have the dope, Bill, the way I see it. Let's you and me study up these cards, get the low-down on every arrest this man has had, and have the whole business in our heads, so that Puckers will think we're wise to all he's done since he was a kid."

Never did an ambitious schoolboy anxious for high graduation honors study a text-book more thoroughly than Rollins and Hackett reviewed that criminal record. Finally Rollins looked at his watch and whistled.

"Whew! Six fifty o'clock!" he said. "Come on, Bill! Let's hustle over to the Hotel La Salle. I want to put you wise as to just how you and Ryan and I are going to handle Puckers at this party tonight."

XI

THE COMRADES ARRIVED at the Hotel La Salle a few minutes earlier than they expected and were at once escorted by the hotel steward to the small private dining-room which Rollins had reserved.

The room was about twelve by fifteen feet in dimensions. In its center was a round table with service for three, and a small vase of flowers as decoration. Four plain chairs and a writing-desk had been moved aside so that those dining might do so unimpeded. The usual dome ceiling light furnished illumination.

Sergeant Ryan, with his reluctant charge, would probably not arrive for twenty minutes or so; hence some little time remained in which to memorize the doings of Puckers and discuss them.

"Whaddya goin' to do, Bob, when Ryan brings in this guy Puckers? Are you goin' to call him that or give him his right name?" said Hackett.

"I'm going to call him by his right name—Stanislaw Brodski—and I want you to do it too, Bill. Let the Sergeant do as he likes."

"Have you got the campaign all mapped out? Do we eat first an' then give Puckers—I mean Brodski—the works; or what's the rules in this darn game? I never played it before."

"That's what I wanted to speak about, Bill! I told Ryan this afternoon precisely how we were going to handle this whole affair from soup to nuts. I even had him rehearse the exact words he's going to say when he brings Brodski in. The Sergeant knows, too, how we're going to conduct our dinner-table talk and repartee and so forth. A lot depends on that. If this lad thinks we're only guessing, we'll get nothing. If he thinks we *know,* he'll tell us plenty.

"Here's the idea, Bill: this Puckers—I mean Brodski—doesn't know how much we know about him and the man he's working for. You and I know we couldn't find a single finger-print of anybody on that ice-water faucet in my room after he'd shoved that piece of rubber sponge, loaded with cyanide, up into it. The faucet looked as if somebody had wiped it off with a towel, and that's probably just what Brodski did.

"However, he can't be sure he didn't forget himself and take hold of that nickel pipe with his bare fingers. You see, Bill, that ice-water pipe is so small that you couldn't even put your forefinger into the nozzle. You could just about get your little finger into it, and that's all. Now, Brodski had to push up that little piece of rubber sponge (with the curved hairpin stuck through it) into the nozzle far enough so it wouldn't show and couldn't come out. To do that, he had to use his little finger and he couldn't do it with gloves on. His finger wouldn't go in the nozzle if he'd worn even a rubber glove.

"Now I propose first to make Brodski believe that we've got perfect finger-prints of his hands from that ice-water faucet. He may think he's covered his tracks, but he can't be *sure*. I'm also going to impress on his mind that, with his known criminal record, a deliberate attempt at poisoning, such as this, means a life sentence for him—and no commutation.

"I'm going to assert that we have two witnesses at the Sanford who saw him in the lobby, and that one of them saw him go upstairs, come down a few minutes later, and put my room-key back in my letter-box. You see, Bill, he can't be sure that all this isn't so.

"Finally, I'll make him believe that we *know* who his principal is, and all we want from him is a confession to clinch our proof.

"Now for our talk at the table. Ryan knows all of Brodski's record, and so do you and I, for it's all on those police cards and clippings. We know how many times he's been arrested, indicted, and tried and what terms he's served. We know the names of over twenty crooks he's palled up with, and we can make him think we're wise to where most of these pals of his are right now.

"That's what we're going to do, Bill! While we three are eating dinner, we'll keep shooting questions at him constantly—first one of us and then the other. We'll skip round all over the lot, so Brodski can't imagine what we're trying to get at. For instance, Ryan will ask him: 'When did you see Hickey last?' Then you'll ask him: 'What's the last conversation you had with Wurtz?' Then I'll ask him: 'Didn't you suspect that Sullivan was a stool?' and so forth. We'll ring in every crime he's been arrested for and ask questions about every crook he's ever known, and by the time we get through, he'll think we know about a thousand times more about him than he could believe was possible.

"Then after dinner I'll handle him alone. Ryan won't say a word, and you keep your trap closed, too, Bill, except to play into my hands.

"The object of this whole thing, of course, is to convince this man Brodski that his *only* chance of ducking a life sentence is to come across and confess *who* hired him to poison me, and *why*.

"Now, have you got the whole theory of this, Bill, or shall I explain some more?" asked Bob as he finished.

"I've got it all, Bob," said Hackett. "But what are you goin' to do with this guy Brodski if he stands pat and won't loosen up?"

"I think he'll see the game is up and squeal on this skunk he's working for. If he won't do it now, he will within a day or two. If Brodski keeps his mouth closed and is afraid to betray his principal tonight, we'll take him over to my hotel, the Sanford, handcuff him, chain him to a staple in the wall, and keep him there until he delivers the goods. I've been living at the Sanford since it was built. I know everybody from the bell-boys up. I told the manager this morning just what I proposed to do if he was willing. He kicked pretty hard at first and was afraid of getting in bad with the law by practically kidnapping this Puckers—I mean Brodski.

"Here's what I told him. I said: 'Mr. Henderson, you're supposed to run a first-class apartment hotel. Nevertheless, you let a well-known crook steal the key of a tenant from behind your registry desk, go upstairs without protest from anyone, enter that tenant's room, put enough cyanide in the ice-water faucet to kill twenty men—with the unquestioned object of poisoning the tenant—and then let that crook come down to the lobby, put the key back in the letter-box, and walk out unmolested. That's just what happened!'

"Then I said: 'Now, Mr. Henderson, I've found that would-be murderer, and *I* propose to make him tell who hired him to kill me, and I want you to rent me a room so that I can keep this dirty crook there until he owns up. If you are not willing to do that much to help me find out who ordered this crook to attempt my murder, you'll find a full-column article about it tomorrow night in the *Leader,* and I'll take pains to see that the public knows just how the lives and property of your guests here at the Sanford are protected.'

"Believe me, Bill, when I got through, Henderson was eating out of my hand. He and I drove a big staple in the joist of a small unfurnished room right up under the roof and fixed things up fine for Mr. Brodski, if we have to take him there. We hitched a long, double steel chain to that staple, put a mattress on the floor, stood a chair and commode beside it in the corner, put heavy dark shades on the windows; and that little old apartment is waiting for Mr. Stanislaw Brodski right now if he doesn't tell us all we want to know. We may have to tickle his bare feet a few minutes with straws or feathers, or bluff him some other way, if he can't see where his best interests lie, but I don't think so, and I hope not. Anyhow, no man is going to try to murder me and get off with any: 'Please, mister, don't do it again' stuff. Shhh! Bill, here come Ryan and Brodski now. You let 'em in, Bill; I'll stand back here."

When Hackett opened the door of the private dining-room, the huge form of Sergeant Ryan at once appeared, pushing Puckers in front of him. Both officer and captive had evi-

dently disposed of their overcoats and hats in the hotel
check-room before entering.

Rollins was standing well at one side, on the left of the entrance, and at first neither Ryan nor his prisoner observed
him. For a half-minute the only person in the room visible to
the pair who had just entered was William Hackett. This
state of affairs, however, did not last over thirty seconds, for
Puckers' glance quickly swept all parts of these new surroundings, and the form and face of Rollins, his intended
victim, loomed before his vision.

The effect was terrific—almost pitiable. Puckers' knees
visibly sagged; his lips quivered; his fingers shook as with
palsy; and his pallor was a ghastly green. He tottered a step,
slumped into the nearest chair, grasped its arms, dug his fingers into the wooden side-pieces, and glared at Rollins as
though Bob were a ghost.

What were the thoughts of Stanislaw Brodski no man save
himself could know, but it is surely possible to infer what
was passing through his mind. Within the past three days he
had twice plotted and attempted the crippling and murder of
this man Rollins. Every precaution which his ingenuity could
devise had been used to keep his identity unknown.

On Tuesday evening he had "tailed" Rollins every step after the latter left the office. He had seen Bob mount the elevated stairway and had followed him. When Rollins stepped
into the last car on the train, Puckers had stood on its front
platform. As the train neared Bryn Mawr Avenue, he had
noted that Bob was preparing to leave the car; hence Puckers
had hastened forward through the train and was five or six
car-lengths ahead of Rollins when the train stopped. The instant Bob stepped off, Puckers had dashed for the stairway,
taking from his pocket a small ball of heavy fish-line, about
one hundred feet in length. The outer end of this cord was
already provided with a slip-knot loop. Reaching the fourth
step below the platform, Puckers had stooped to the left as if
to tie his shoes. On the left side of the elevated stairs—the
side toward the north-bound tracks—was some ornamental
cast-iron grille-work. Puckers had looped the noose of his

slip-knot over one of the projecting ornaments and had then quickly tossed his ball of cord through the aperture in the right-hand wall of the L stairway. The ball of cord had, of course, unrolled in falling and its end had noiselessly reached the ground below.

Through Puckers' action there was loosely stretched, ten inches above the fifth step, a strong cord ready to trip anyone who descended. Puckers had then stooped again and pulled in about three feet of slack cord and tucked it back in the angle of the steps, so that the cord might not trip anyone unless it was pulled tight, across the staircase, from below. The whole proceeding had consumed not more than three or four seconds. In fact, one passenger descended the staircase and passed Puckers while at his work, but observed nothing save that some man appeared to be tightening a shoe-lace.

This done, Puckers had raced down the stairs, run round to the outside of the station, grasped the dangling cord, and stood ready for his crippling or death-dealing mission. The entire operation had consumed approximately a half-minute.

Puckers had then stood waiting on the ground below, watching the figure of Rollins—perfectly visible on the well-lighted L platform above—approach the trap of danger or death. As Puckers thus stood, watching for his victim, he had seen Rollins take out his pocket lighter and had observed Bob's face as he fired his cigarette before descending the stairs. He had then waited three or four seconds until Rollins' figure reached the edge of the stairway. Then only had Puckers pulled taut the cord which was intended to trip Rollins and send him hurtling forty feet down the staircase.

Puckers had felt the pressure of Rollins' ankle against the cord, but that pressure had remained constant for one or two seconds; the cord had then been jerked upward, drawn swiftly from Puckers' hands; and he knew that his plot had failed. Swift flight behind a near-by signboard then was his only recourse—and thus he had acted.

At the Sanford last night Puckers had peered through the window and seen Rollins put his key in the box and go in to dinner. He had noted Atwood, the clerk, on a ladder, repair-

ing the diningroom doors, and observed the only bell-boy
half-asleep on a bench in the corner near the telephone. He
had then entered, sat down, and buried his face in a newspaper. A moment later he had seen the bell-boy step into the
dining-room. His opportunity at hand, Puckers had reached
across the desk, purloined Rollins' room-key from the letter-
box, and fled up the stairs as noiselessly as a wraith. No one
had seen him in the lobby, on the stairs, in the hall, anywhere.

The ten minutes devoted to preparing the death-trap in
Rollins' room had been free of all anxiety. He had gone di-
rectly to Rollins' wash-stand, scrutinized the faucets, and
made his preparations quickly, but without undue haste.
Rollins, he knew, was eating his dinner on the ground floor.
Puckers had locked Rollins' door immediately after entering.
There was no fear of interruption—there he was safe.

Puckers remembered every move he had made while standing before that wash-bowl and its nickel faucets. In his left-
hand coat pocket was a very small acorn-shaped piece of
rubber sponge. In that same pocket were a half-dozen small
hairpins. One of these he had thrust through the sponge.
Puckers recalled bending the hairpin into a curve approxi-
mating the curve of the ice-water faucet nozzle.

From his right-hand coat pocket he had then taken a tiny
quarter-ounce bottle containing a few crystals of potassium
cyanide. He had then shaken the crystals carefully on to the
top of the rubber sponge, pressing them firmly into its yielding pores. This done, Puckers had thrust the two pointed
ends of the curved hairpin into the ice-water nozzle and
pushed them—followed by the cyanide-laden sponge—away
up into the faucet-nozzle. A quick wipe of the faucet with a
towel and he was ready to leave.

Ah! That was a good job! Now for a cigarette and his get-
away! A light! A few puffs! A tossing away of the match!
An unlocking and relocking of Rollins' door! A swift flight
down the empty stairs; an instant's pause at the mezzanine
landing; a glance at the apparently vacant hotel lobby; out on
the street; and Puckers had gone.

Not a precaution omitted! The deadly draught in that room which he had left was waiting—waiting. Either that night or in the morning Rollins would certainly seek to quench his thirst from that seemingly innocuous faucet—and die! Yet here before him stood that same Robert Rollins, staring sternly, with steel-like gaze, into his own cowering eyes. And beside Rollins he heard the voice of Sergeant Ryan, saying:

"Well, Mr. Rollins! Here is the gintleman who called at yer room in the Sanford last noight. Shure, he must have been intoirely out of visitin'-cyards. Wasn't it koind of the dear soul to lave his noice little finger-prints on yer pretty ice-wather faucet. An' ain't it too bad the bell-bhoy who saw Misther Brodski goin' up an' comin' down thim sthairs was a toiny bit too shlow to bid the gintleman good-bye? I was shure Misther Brodski regretted his hasty departure from yer room, so I brought him with me tonoight to offer his apologies. I know ye'll be glad to mate Mr. Brodski, yer would-be murdherer, Mr. Rollins!"

"Yes indeed, Sergeant. Please make Mr. Brodski comfortable. He seems rather weak, don't you think? We can't permit him to injure himself by falling out of that chair. I think you'd better let Mr. Brodski place his arms behind his back, and then you might adjust some bracelets on his wrists. Rather tightly, please! We must not lose his valued society now that he is here. Ah, that's fine, Sergeant! Isn't it sad that a dear friend like Mr. Brodski must leave us so soon? I really shouldn't care to spend my entire life in Joliet. It must become monotonous after twenty years or so, but I presume a gentleman like Mr. Brodski, who has spent so much of his time there, has come to regard it as his home."

Rollins' brief speech sank into Puckers' very soul. With all his precautions, Nemesis had overtaken him. Puckers had wiped off that ice-water faucet, he felt sure, but had he not unconsciously *grasped it afterwards*? If *so,* his *finger-prints* would stand out like the headlines of a newspaper.

He felt certain no one had been in the Sanford lobby when he made his departure. But might there not have been some employee of the hotel who had observed his going, although unseen? Perhaps a bell-boy had been coming from the dining-room or basement just as he was going out and had his back to the lobby.

Puckers remembered that for about fifty feet he had walked under strong street-lights while passing the hotel front. He had not dared to glance sideways into the Sanford lobby as he trod those fifty feet. But there might well have been several persons in the lobby who had seen him. They might have entered as he was opening and closing the street door. Yes, it must be so! In what other way could the police have laid hands on him so quickly and brought him face to face with Rollins—the man he had twice endeavored to kill?

Less than twenty-four hours had elapsed since his last murderous attempt and here he was, in the clutches of the law, a habitual criminal facing life imprisonment. That nothing less would be his doom Puckers was certain. The influence which had hitherto protected him would not be without avail. Indeed, it was more than probable that the man who in the past had once saved him would now do his uttermost to jail him and keep him there.

Yes, that was what would happen. His principal would not dare to come to his rescue. Puckers had a well-earned reputation as a squealer. He knew it. Hence the man who openly or secretly aided him would be in constant jeopardy while Puckers was unjailed. But who would credit the accusations of a lifer?

While these thoughts were sweeping, lightning-like, through the mind of Stanislaw Brodski as he sat handcuffed, Rollins came and stood before him. Bob scrutinized his would-be slayer from every angle; he tilted Brodski's head up, down, this way and that, studied the helpless man from top to toe.

"It's all right, Sergeant," said Rollins. "He's the lad! I remember his being on the L Tuesday, and in the station-house the day before yesterday. This jibes up fine with what we know. Let's go ahead and eat. We can talk to Mr. Brodski while we're polishing off this dinner. Ring for the waiter,

Bill. And don't forget, Sergeant, the sky is the limit. This is my party, and, believe me, it's going to be a bird. Hackett, you'd better get out your note-book and take down any little things Mr. Brodski might like to tell us. They may come in handy."

It was a little after nine o'clock before the three friends completed their meal, and Stanislaw Brodski could do nothing but try to ease his handcuffed wrists and listen to the endless series of questions fired at him from three sources. Were these three men omniscient? It seemed there was nothing which they did not know already—and yet they sought for greater knowledge.

At first Puckers refused to answer, demanded release, threatened them with prosecution for illegal detention, insisted on his right to advice from counsel, threatened them with powerful political influences—all without the least effect. These three icy-hearted inquisitors of his seemed to find in his threats and protestations a tremendous source of amusement. The idea that Brodski, with three Joliet terms to his credit, with a well-known reputation as a stool-pigeon and squealer, should make threats or refuse to reply was absurd, ridiculous! Sergeant Ryan's guffaws over such idiotic folly could have been heard a block. Possibly a few hearty love-pats on the side of the face from Ryan's enormous palm may have influenced Mr. Brodski to change his tactics.

At all events, before Rollins' party was ready to adjourn, Puckers had been brought into a state of subjection which was pitiable. Almost every question propounded received a more or less truthful answer.

Hackett's shorthand memo book was half full of information regarding Puckers' associates, their doings, their joint adventures, and, as far as Brodski knew, their present whereabouts.

Not one word or question, however, had touched upon what was really the sole object of the evening's inquiry— proof regarding Brodski's principal, whose orders had instigated Puckers' attempts to slay Rollins.

Finally, at precisely nine fifteen, Rollins rose from the table, took a typewritten slip of paper from his pocket, walked to the corner where Brodski sat handcuffed on his chair, and stood above that unhappy scion of crime. Holding the piece of paper in his hand, and speaking in a calm, icy voice, Rollins said:

"Brodski, on this paper is our proposal to you. It is final and unalterable. It will be carried through to a finish. No pretests or threats from you can change one word of it.

"We have the description and finger-prints of the man who ordered you to murder me. We realize fully his position and influence. We know the motive which compelled him to employ you and force you to kill me. We know that you hope to escape penalty for your attempt at murder, because of him. We know you are in deadly fear that he will kill you if you betray him. I now hold up my hand and swear that every word of this is true." (It was.)

"Now, here is what we shall do. We shall take you handcuffed from this room to an automobile. Before entering the auto we shall blindfold you, and you will be driven to an unknown destination. You will be provided with bread, water, and a mattress, but no other comforts. Your handcuffs will be chained to the wall and will not be removed, even at meal-times. You will remain in that room until you have decided to give us a truthful, signed affidavit, duly witnessed, telling all facts regarding your principal and your dealings with him. Beside you, always, will stand a pitcher of water. In that pitcher will be placed the cyanide crystals contained in the rubber sponge which you put in my faucet and which you used twenty-four hours ago when you attempted my murder. If you care to drink that water, no one will prevent you. If you still withhold confession for more than three days, we shall use extremely unpleasant means to compel you to speak the truth. The application of feathers to a person's bare feet is trying.

"Now, Brodski, we know your principal" (this was untrue), "but our evidence against him has one weak link, and one only. That link you can supply. If you supply it, your principal will assuredly suffer death on the gallows and can never cause you fear again. Each day you will be asked for a definite decision. Here, then, is our proposal. I will read it to you, and when we have taken you to your place of confinement, we will leave it with you for study.

" 'If within five days from this date Stanislaw Brodski shall make truthful affidavit, supported by verifiable evidence, stating therein the full name, address, age, vocation, etc., of the person who persuaded, ordered, or, compelled said Brodski to attempt murder upon the person of Robert S. Rollins, and shall give all details of such conspiracy, said Brodski shall not be prosecuted for such murderous attempt, but shall be at once released from confinement and given his full freedom. Otherwise Brodski will be vigorously prosecuted for attempted murder.'

"That is all, Brodski. Sergeant, will you get Brodski's hat and coat and your own, please. When you come back, you can take off Brodski's cuffs, let him put on his overcoat, and then handcuff him again with his hands in front. He can conceal the cuffs by his coat-sleeves while we go out of the hotel.

"Hackett, go out and get our car and give the driver full instructions. The Sergeant and I will blindfold Brodski as soon as we get him outside the hotel. Meanwhile I will attend to the bill—" and Rollins finished.

Ten minutes later the blindfolded Brodski, now stubbornly silent, and accompanied by Hackett and Rollins, was in a hired limousine and being driven by a most circuitous route to the Sanford Hotel. Manager Henderson—previously prepared—was called outside by Hackett, and the manacled, blindfolded Brodski was conducted into a waiting elevator. Except for Joe Atwood, who had been fully informed of all arrangements, the Sanford lobby was deserted.

The elevator started without sound or jerk, and no man without eyesight could have detected its upward progress.

At the top floor the lift stopped noiselessly, and Brodski was led along the carpetless hall of that garret-like space to the candle-lighted room selected. The looped steel chain was linked around Brodski's handcuffed wrists; the chair was placed beside him, and the blindfold removed.

A small pitcher of water, a glass of water, and a loaf of bread stood on the commode, near the mattress.

At the door Rollins turned and addressed his sulky, silent captive: "Brodski, that glass of water is harmless; but don't drink a drop from that pitcher unless you want to wake up in hell. We'll be here on Monday for your decision. Twice a day you'll get a loaf of bread and another glass of real water. I suggest a frequent reading of that typewritten paper. Come on, Hackett!"

The door closed. The lock clicked! Rollins had told only a half-truth—the pitcher of fluid, save for a liberal dose of Epsom salts, was as harmless as the glass of water by its side. But Puckers knew it not.

As the self-appointed knights of justice descended in the Sanford elevator and stood in front of the hotel to "blow off Puckers' stink," as Hackett coarsely termed it, Rollins asked:

"Have you got that note-book with the shorthand stuff you took down at dinner tonight? Let me have it, will you? I want to put in a few things myself that Puckers whispered to me. I'll turn it over to you tomorrow, and you can transcribe it. It may come in handy yet!"

"Here she is, Bob. Don't lose it," said Hackett; and Rollins thrust the thick, heavy book into his inner left breast pocket. "Whaddya goin' to do now, Bob? It's a little early to turn in, ain't it?"

"I want to go over to the City Hospital and see how Sarah Vasch is. If they can only save her life, Bill, I'll give the doctor that does it a hundred dollars and be glad to do it. She's a lovable woman and I can't understand how anybody could possibly try to butcher her like that. Come along, Bill, I'll stand the taxi."

When the hospital was reached, they introduced themselves to the nurse, Miss Andrews, but were not allowed to visit the patient. "Miss Vasch was operated on, and is still alive, but delirious. She constantly talks to some man. We trepanned her skull yesterday, and there is a bare chance that she may live. It will be quite a while, though, before she can eat the candy you sent her, Mr. Rollins."

"Candy! For Heaven's sake, Miss Andrews! I didn't send her any candy," shouted Rollins. "Did some candy come for Sarah with my name on it?"

"It certainly did, this very evening, and your card was on the box. A two-pound box of chocolates it was, and came by messenger. Wait a minute, I'll show it to you." And the nurse flitted away, shortly returning with a box of expensive chocolates, beautifully wrapped, and with Robert Rollins' business card stuck under the silver wrapping cord.

On the card, in printed longhand, was written:

> To: Sarah Vasch
> c/o City Hospital
> With kindest wishes for speedy recovery

"Miss Andrews!" urged Rollins, with deep earnestness, "I did not send that candy, or that card. I'm convinced that the man who tried Tuesday night to murder that poor woman has today made a second attempt. Will you please get some doctor here who is well up on toxicology? I want him to examine the contents of this box. I am certain that one or more pieces of the candy in this package contain poison!"

Five minutes later two doctors and three nurses were gathered around a table on which lay a box of—apparently—delicious sweets.

"Doctor Sherman," said Rollins, "will you please examine these chocolates, one by one, with this pocket microscope? See if you find any piece that lacks in the slightest degree the smooth perfection of surface that should be produced in wholesale manufacture. If you find any such pieces, please put them aside for analysis."

Patiently, and with meticulous care, Doctor Sherman performed his task—and five chocolates from the top layer of the box rested upon the table.

A half-hour later Doctor Lloyd, accompanied by the others, reported that three of those candies contained sufficient poison altogether to wipe out the entire hospital staff. "Mr. Rollins, there are some people in this building who owe their lives to you. I hope—"

"Thank God—not me!" interrupted Rollins. "If you feel that way, let me ask that every person who knows of this matter swear a solemn oath of secrecy—to tell absolutely no one—until I give permission to do it. Will all of you make that pledge?"

Their assent was unanimous.

The clocks were striking midnight as Rollins and Hackett closed the City Hospital door behind them. At the near-by corner, beneath the strong illumination of the street-lamp above, both stood for a moment before departing for their respective homes.

"Bob," said William Hackett, "I'll never forget this night as long—"

Robert Rollins sank senseless at Hackett's feet! A sound like that of an auto back-fire had come from near by, slightly beyond Hackett's right shoulder. The left breast of Rollins' coat grew slowly dark; the crimson stain spread ever larger.

XII

BILL HACKETT WAS A MAN of instantaneous thought and action. When he saw, lying on the sidewalk before him, the senseless, bleeding form of his comrade, he realized that he could do nothing alone, and that delay might be fatal to the man whom, now, he almost reverenced.

Dashing to the Hospital entrance, only thirty yards away, he overrode all inquiries or protests, and in three minutes his friend Rollins was on a stretcher *en route* for the operating-room.

Meanwhile the heart of Hackett was a seething turmoil of rage. That Rollins had been shot by the same hand which had poisoned Alexander Stevens he had not the slightest doubt. The purpose of this second murder seemed to him equally clear. It could have no other motive than to put a final stop to the search for Stevens' slayer.

But how had this butcher of men chanced to be on the scene so opportunely? Hackett was certain that no other taxi had followed Rollins and himself to the City Hospital, for no other was in sight when the comrades had boarded their passing cab. It must, therefore, be that this dealer in bullets and poison had been close to the hospital when the comrades entered, had observed their coming and awaited their departure.

This meant that the murderer had a personal interest in some patient there. What patient? Who could it be but Sarah Vasch, to whom that same man had sent the poisoned chocolates, with Rollins' card?

It was clear to the mind of Hackett that the case of Sarah Vasch and the murder of Stevens were linked and inseparable. Despite his anxiety over the fate of his friend upstairs, Hackett's heart swelled with pride. At last he had proved that his brain was also capable of the same mental processes—reason, logic, inference—which he had so admired in Bob.

At this moment Doctor Sherman entered, holding between his fingers a small, dull, metal object, and with a smile on his face, "There she is, Mr. Hackett!" he said; "there's the little piece of lead that almost wiped your friend out of the world. If it hadn't been for that thick note-book in Mr. Rollins' left breast pocket, he would never shake your hand again. This bullet passed through his overcoat, his coat, and this note-book. The pages of the book must have somewhat deflected its course, so that it glanced from a rib and round under the flesh on his left side. We extracted it by a one-inch incision below the armpit. Mr. Rollins is certainly a fortunate man. Do you want to see him, Mr. Hackett? I'll let you in for three minutes, but that's all."

Hackett's heart was so full of joy that he could scarcely speak. "Doc, God bless your old soul! You're the best egg in the coop. Lemme in for a coupla minutes, will ya? I won't say a darned word, so help me!"

At the bedside of Rollins, a few minutes later, there were smiles on three faces, and Bob weakly held out his hand to his friend.

"I'm O.K., Bill," he whispered. "Out in two or three days, they say. Get on the phone this minute, Bill. Tell every morning paper in Chicago that I've been accidentally struck by a bullet fired at a speeding auto. Injury probably fatal; cannot see anybody! Make it strong, Bill, so it'll be in every sheet. Make 'em think I'll die sure! Get me?"

"You bet! I'll fix it, old scout. But how about Miss Stevens? Want me to put her next, on the quiet, that it ain't so? Mebbe I can roust her up by phone tonight, or early tomorrow morning before she sees the papers. How about it, Bob?"

"Yes, do that, Bill! Tell old Bostock, too! And tell Nora not to visit me at all. I'll phone her tomorrow. Good night, old boy! You're the best friend God ever made," and Rollins sank back exhausted.

Doctor Sherman now interrupted. "Don't talk any more now! I see what you want, and I think I understand why. Miss Andrews will be your nurse and will quietly spread the news that it's only a question of a day or two before you pass out. Now get a good sleep, and you'll be a new man tomorrow."

For the next twenty minutes the hospital telephone was kept busy. Every paper in Chicago was notified, and emphasis was placed on the fact that the fatality was accidental, with no blame imputed to anyone, although the person who fired the shot had not been located prior to the issue of that edition. Nora, too, when "rousted" from sleep and told the news, promised faithfully to abide by Bob's instructions as transmitted through Hackett.

When the latter gentleman visited his injured friend at nine o'clock on the following morning, he found Rollins propped up slightly on his pillows, and eating an invalidic breakfast.

"How're they comin', old scout? Did you see the papers yet? Say, they certainly give you a boost—that *Tribune* spiel about your bein' a reg'lar wizard at deductions was sure a pippin. They musta been lookin' in their morgue an' dug up that stuff from the *Leader* articles of a year ago. 'At's always the way! Sendin' bouquets to the fellers that's so darn near dead they can't smell 'em!"

"Maybe the *Tribune* will give me a job when I get out, Bill! This is my last day on the *Leader,* you know. Did you happen to phone Bostock? If you didn't, you'd better do it, and tell him I don't want any pay for this week's work, for I haven't written three columns since Monday. What is it, Miss Andrews?"

"There's a Mr. Bostock on the phone, Mr. Rollins. He's asking how you are. What shall I tell him?"

"Hey, listen! I'll do the tellin'. Where is that damn telephone? Lead me to it Miss Andrews, will ya?"

Mr. William Hackett must have had quite an extended interview with Managing Editor Ralph Bostock, of the Chicago *Leader,* and when he returned, ten minutes later, his grin was phenomenal, even for him.

"What did you tell him, Bill?" queried Rollins.

"Ne' mine what I told him. All you gotta do is put some whale-oil on your hair an' borrow Doc Sherman's safety-razor an' get slicked up. You're gonna have a visitor. He'll be here at ten thirty."

"Who's coming, Bill? Mr. Bostock?"

"Yeah! The Honorable Ralph Bostock, to see his used-to-be reporter Mr. Robert Rollins! Say, listen, Bob! Tell the guy somep'n of this mess we've been into. I'll bet he'll be eatin' outa your hand before he goes. An' lemme listen in while the big chief spouts, will ya?"

"I'll say I will. Sit right there and wait, Bill, while Miss Andrews plays barber, and then give her a tip out of my trousers pocket!" When Managing Editor Bostock arrived, his greeting to both was one of real friendliness.

"Mr. Hackett here made some exceedingly interesting remarks on the phone a little while ago. I'm delighted to see you in such excellent shape, Rollins! I noticed the *Tribune* article this morning was almost like an obituary—or a eulogy. Possibly both! Mr. Hackett said you had something to tell me. I'll be very glad to listen."

"I simply want to say, on my last day with the *Leader,* that you were perfectly justified in letting me go, and I'm not blaming you a bit for doing it. You had the goods on me, all right! I deserved to be fired, and it's a wonder you didn't lay me off long ago. I guess I'm a good deal like a cat watching a rat-hole. You could tramp on my tail all day and I'd never know it as long as I thought the rat was likely to come out.

"Honestly, Mr. Bostock, I haven't been worth the powder to blow me to hell in the last week. I'll consider it a favor if you'll tell the cashier that my services ended last Saturday. That'll set me square with my conscience, anyhow!"

"What's the trouble, Rollins? What is this thing that Hackett's been hinting at? I told you a moment ago that if you feel like telling it, I'll gladly listen," said Ralph Bostock, in a far more kindly tone than Bob had heard from him before.

Rollins thought a moment. "Well," he said, "there's a lot to it, and if you'd like to hear it, I'll give you the whole dope.

Remember, however, it's strictly on the Q.T. between you and me. I'll be broke in another two weeks, at the rate I'm going now, and I'm hoping I'll have some news to sell about then. Maybe you'll buy it. I know darn well I'll need the money."

In less than twenty minutes Rollins had given Ralph Bostock a concise synopsis of the Stevens tragedy and the assaults made on him personally, winding up by telling him the secret reason why he *knew* that Stevens' death was not suicide, but murder. At this news Hackett's eyes bulged like marbles. Bob did not disclose the other evidence he had secured, but simply asserted that he had a "barrel of it," and mentioned a half-dozen of the many points which he had dictated to Hackett as proofs.

Bostock sat and looked at Rollins silently, for at least two minutes.

"Bob," he said—and no living mortal had ever heard that managing editor call a reporter by his Christian name before—"Bob, your job as a reporter for the *Leader* is over today. However, if you care to consider a position as a special writer on our paper, I think it can be arranged, and the compensation will be satisfactory. You'll start next Monday. How about it, Rollins?"

"Mr. Bostock, you're a peach!" and Rollins reached out and grabbed his superior's hand. "But what's the big idea? How come?"

"The big idea, young man, is that *one big idea* is a good deal more valuable than a lot of little ones. I'm beginning to think that the *Leader* needs a few more 'single-track minds' that can concentrate on *one idea,* and I'm very much of the opinion that yours is that kind. Get well as quick as you can. Stick on this job until you finish it! That's all the orders I've got for you, Bob. Good-bye, and good luck!" And with another handshake with both Rollins and Hackett, Bostock left the room.

Of the state of mind of Robert Rollins, now "special writer elect" for the *Evening Leader,* suffice it to say that, despite his weakness, he was deliriously happy—and so was Nora, five minutes later, when through the hospital phone he had given the news to her.

"I shan't be able to get out for a day or two," he said. "But, Nora, dear heart, now we can see the rainbow which says: 'The storm is over.' "

As for Hackett, he was uproarious on his friend's account.

"No, sir, it can't be done! They can't do it! I always said they couldn't. You said it yourself yesterday, remember? Betcha life they can't," he shouted.

"Said what? Did what? Can't what? What on earth are you talking about, Bill?" asked Rollins, from his bed.

"Ya can't keep a good man down! Ya can't keep a good man down! Ain't no use tryin'. No matter if he's dyin'. Ya *can't* keep a good man down!" chanted Hackett in poetic frenzy as he pranced about the room. "Here we are, old scout! Both of us gets our jobs back! Me with a month's vacation thrown in, an' you with a boost in salary an' the right to put your name on top of your stuff. *Whoopee!*"

Great ecstasies are brief. When Bill's ardors had subsided, and the pulses of both had become normal, Hackett said:

"It ain't likely that Puckers will weaken and spill his story before Monday anyhow, an' mebbe not then. Perhaps he might swaller them Epsom salts, an' croak. Who knows? What are we goin' to do about this Donovan lead while you're sick, Bob? Here's good old Doris givin' us Donovan's description and his business card, an' you said yourself he was a likely prospect. Why not go after him? Why don't you do a little studyin' about him an' reason Donovan into this murder or out of it. Honest, Bob, I ain't foolin'. Just put Donovan through a course of logic and see whether he's a prospect or a suspect! You can do it, Bob. I'm bettin' all I've got you can."

"I was anticipating you'd say something like that, Bill," said Rollins. "But where are our facts? We can't reason without facts. I'll tell you what! You call up Superintendent Donovan's office; use the phone here and do it right now. Just find out if he's in—or when he'll be in. Then we'll know where we're at."

In a few minutes Bill had finished telephoning to Superintendent Donovan's office, and it was evident from his face that the news was not good.

"Hard luck, Bob! Donovan's away for a week trying to promote some scheme of his. He's somewhere in Illinois, but they don't know just where. Reckon we're up against it, old top. You see how it is! When the brains of a big concern like ours goes flooey, they gotta close up. Takes brains to keep the chimney smokin'!"

"Cut out the flattery, Bill! No man on earth can think quicker or clearer than you. What you told me, just before Bostock came in, about your deductions in connection with last night's affair proves it. Sarah Vasch's injury and near poisoning and Stevens' murder are no separate affairs. They are all of one piece, and that bullet I got belongs right with it. I'm hoping to be out of this place by Monday, and here are a few things you can do in the meantime. Put 'em down, Bill.

"First: get a good photo of George Donovan, if you can.

"Second: get one of his business cards, from his office.

"Third: dust the card Miss Allen gave you and see if there are any finger-prints on it besides hers.

"Fourth: photograph all prints on either side of that card and don't let your own prints get on it.

"Fifth: have that bullet which hit me examined by Professor Zweiss, today and get microphotographs of it. Maybe some day we'll find the gun that shot it."

By Monday morning Rollins' condition was such that Doctor Sherman said he might safely leave the hospital, provided he undertook no physical exertion whatever.

"Remember, Doctor, I'm supposed to be still here, and at the point of death. Tell everybody so! Keep this room closed, and let Miss Andrews act as if I were actually in it. Don't let a soul in the hospital, or out of it, know any different. Now get me a taxi please, and a big scarf to cover my face when I sneak out. Mr. Hackett will bring back the scarf. I'm depending on you, Doctor, and I know you'll see me through!"

"You bet I will!" said Doctor Sherman heartily.

At ten o'clock Monday morning, November 27, a feeble, bespectacled old gentleman, with his head enveloped to the eyes in a heavy gray muffler, hobbled with his cane from a taxi into the Meyers Building. Entering the elevator, he rode to the sixth floor—and walked up one flight after the car's descent.

A moment later Robert Rollins—minus spectacles and scarf—stood in room 713, ready to renew his interrupted campaign.

At ten forty-five—after six peculiar raps on the door— Hackett was admitted, and stood beside his partner.

"Bob, you old busted-up scallawag! You look so damn good to me I could almost kiss ya!"

"I'd a good deal rather get my kisses from somewhere else, Bill! Save yours for Doris Allen; perhaps she'll appreciate 'em."

"She *does,* Bob—an', believe me, I ain't stingy neither. The Lord never made a finer woman, and I mean it. But listen, old scout, Donovan won't be in town until next Monday!"

"Well, what if he isn't? Maybe we can get on without him."

"Swell chance!" cried Hackett. "How are we gonna find out if George Donovan is the guy who really bought that Vandyke beard offa Doris and impersonated Edward Folsom and murdered Alexander Stevens, when Donovan ain't in Chicago now, an' won't be for a week? Oh, all right, then, go ahead! Do some more of that reasoning of yours. We'd never get anywhere without it."

"I don't need to do so much of that now, Bill. You're developing."

"Thanks, Bob! I was talking to the janitor in Donovan's office this mornin', and he told me quite a lot about that bird, and it was worth hearing, too. Donovan's been here about six years, he said. He's a bachelor; lives in a furnished apartment on the South Side. He got a patent on a new floor-polisher, an' the janitor says it's sellin' fine. Donovan's had a lot of inventions patented. Here's an advertising circular of his with an engraving showin' Donovan's photo. See, Bob! Look at the mole on his chin! Here's one of his business cards, too; but how are we gonna get his fingerprints?"

"I can get a clear finger-print of every one of Donovan's fingers in ten minutes, Bill. Don't worry about that. You've done splendidly, and we've got facts enough now.

"Listen, Bill, I'll tell you what you'd better do. You take a little run over to your beloved Doris. Get her into conversation about that beard again. Tell her that George Donovan has gone out of town, and that you can't bring her that Vandyke beard he bought. Ask her if she can't trim that other beard which she's got in stock and make it the exact shape of the one her Donovan bought. Of course she'll say she can't do it.

"While you're talking, ask her if her Donovan mentioned his brother, the famous inventor. She'll say no, of course, because there isn't any such brother. Then casually show her this circular with our Donovan's picture. You're supposed to have got it in the mail today, and you're going to show it to Stumps. If she identifies this picture as the man who bought that beard, we have fairly well established the fact that Superintendent Donovan of this building was concerned in the murder of Alexander Stevens. If she does not recognize this picture as that of her beard-buyer, then some other man—probably Stevens' murderer—has impersonated our Superintendent Donovan, and that man purposely dropped our Donovan's card in order to throw suspicion on our Donovan.

"Of course, you didn't make a date to see your precious Doris Allen until later, but—'eventually, why not now?'—eh, Bill?"

"Bob, you're sure some quick thinker, and if you can materialize all Donovan's finger-prints at twenty minutes' notice, I'll say you're a wizard for fair!" said Hackett. "Only don't kid me about Miss Allen, Bob. Believe me, she ain't no kiddin' matter with me. She's *wonderful!* Well, so long, Bob! I'll be back when I'm herel" and William Hackett joyously departed.

For the next hour Robert Rollins devoted his time to four things:

First: scrutinizing two business cards under a big reading-glass.

Second: comparing a number of finger-prints.

Third: studying a twenty-by-twenty-four-inch enlargement of the police photo of Stevens' body, recumbent on his desk. (Rollins had himself made this the day after he received the original print from Hackett.)

Fourth: thinking.

By the time he had finished these tasks Hackett had returned, with a look on his face that was both happy and forlorn, if such a mixed facial expression can exist.

Bill started to speak, but was interrupted by Rollins. "Don't tell me a thing yet, Bill! Run down the hall and bring me that step-ladder in the wash-room. I'm going to show you Donovan's finger-prints!"

"Like hell you are!" said Hackett. "Where's the guy that can develop finger-prints on a dirty step-ladder? I'd sure like to see that bird. There ain't no such animal."

"I didn't say the prints were *on* the ladder. I asked you to bring the ladder and promised to show you Donovan's prints after you'd brought it. Come on, Bill, get the ladder! I'm anxious about this myself!"

"All right, boss! You win!" And in a few minutes the ladder was brought.

"We'll just stand this ladder up in front of the door," said Rollins, "and you'll find a lot of Donovan's finger-prints all over the glass in that transom—you know we had to smash that transom light to get into this office on Monday when we found Mr. Stevens here, dead. Well, Superintendent Donovan put a new glass in that transom the next day. I was here and saw Donovan do it with his own hands. He had to bed the bottom of the sash with putty, and no one has cleaned the glass since then, so there ought to be a dozen or more of Donovan's finger-prints on that glass. There's nothing better than putty to make clear prints on glass. Go to it, Bill! Dust both sides of that glass and see what you get."

Ten minutes later Hackett descended the ladder.

"Not the same!" he said. "This guy Donovan's prints on that glass ain't any more like the skunk who killed Stevens than a racehorse is like a centipede. Well, that jibes up with what Doris said. The minute she saw our Donovan's picture, she says: 'Isn't it funny, dear, how brothers can be alike, yet so unlike?' I says: 'How come, Doris?' Then she says: 'Why, the man on this picture has got a mole on his chin, just like his brother who bought that beard, but their faces are not a bit alike.' There! Whaddya think of that, Bob?"

"That settles it! Our Donovan, the superintendent of this building, isn't in on this at all—but I'm telling you, Bill Hackett, that our Donovan is going to tell us who murdered Alexander Stevens—and he's going to do it before tomorrow night. He doesn't know it. Our Donovan thinks that Stevens committed suicide. If I should tell George Donovan now that Stevens was murdered, and that he had probably shaken hands with the murderer, he'd call me a liar. But it's so, just the same. Our Donovan's going to clinch this thing as sure as fate. Don't think I'm over-optimistic, Bill. I *know* it's going to be so; and if you'll run downstairs right now and find out just where George Donovan is and how we can reach him by telephone today, our job will be done. Finished!

"I don't give a continental tinker's cuss, now, whether Brodski confesses or not, or if poor old Sarah gets her senses back right away. They will make our case a lot stronger, if either or both happens—but we can get on without them. All I want now is to get George Donovan on the telephone, and get him *quick!*"

Hackett was tremendously excited. "My God! You don't mean it! How in hell can Donovan point out a murderer when he don't even know there's been a murder? Honestly, Bob, I just can't believe it! Are you sure?"

"Bill, I'm so certain of this thing I'd stake my life on it."

"But, listen, Bob," said Hackett, "unless Donovan knows something about this thing—unless he's mixed up in it somehow—it just *can't* be!"

"I'm telling you, Bill Hackett, that Donovan's as innocent as a new-born baby. He hasn't the slightest conception that there's been a crime committed, and if I should tell him right now all the facts that we know, and should say that he could give us help in finding the man who killed Stevens, he would think I was crazy and probably tell me so.

"Do you want to know, Bill, what I'm going to say to Donovan when I get him on the phone? I'll tell you the exact words, and I won't vary them by a hair. I'm going to ask him one question—just one—that's all. When he gives me his answer, I'm going to make him jump the first train to Chicago, no matter where he is now. He's got to come! Now, do you want to know what that question's going to be, Bill?"

"Do I want to know it?" shouted Bill. "I'll bust if you don't tell. For God's sake, Bob, spill it! What's the question?"

"All right, Bill! I'm going to tell Donovan first that I have got to ask him what will seem to him ridiculous—a most foolish question—but it is *not* foolish or ridiculous. I'll tell Donovan that his answer to that question will involve fifty thousand dollars in cash to an orphan girl, will probably clear an innocent man from a charge which might send him to the gallows, and, finally, will absolutely convict a murderer and *prove* his guilt. Here's the question I'm going to ask George Donovan:

"On what date did you last start having a bad toothache?"

XIII

MR. WILLIAM HACKETT got up out of his chair, walked over to his friend, and took the latter's hand. Slyly his fingers felt Bob's pulse. Stealthily he scanned the blue-gray eyes of his comrade.

"Don't kid me, Bob!" he said. "We've been together on this job almost a week now, an' I'll say this for you—that I never seen a man in my life who could dig up so much dope with so little work as you can. Honestly, it's wonderful. The best part of it is that this reasoning of yours cops the money every time. It hasn't fluked once so far; not once! An' I'm givin' you all the credit, Bob! Believe me, you deserve it.

"But when you start in tellin' me that you're goin' to segregate the damn skunk who gave Stevens that poison an' murdered as fine a man as ever breathed by askin' Donovan when he last had a toothache—that's goin' pretty far. You may think you know what you're doin' but I'll be jiggered if I believe it. I kinder thought, Bob, that you had a little fever or was sick mebbe, but you ain't got no temperature an' you look all right, so I guess that's off and you mean it. The only conclusion I can come to is that you've got some darn good gag up your sleeve an' want to spring it on me. All right, Bob! I'll bite! Let her go!"

"You don't have to," said Rollins. "The best way to learn whether I am getting insane or not is to let me make such a fool of myself that you can give me the 'raspberry,' as you call it. Isn't that so? Do you know of a better way to find out? All right! I'm going to telephone now to Donovan's office downstairs, inquire just where he is today, if they know it, and where I can probably catch him by phone somewhere around dinner-time. Then I'll phone to him directly. It's almost noon, now. Give the phone to me, please, Bill!"

As the hands of Hackett's watch pointed to twelve o'clock, Rollins hung up the receiver and turned to his friend. "Donovan is at Streator on business. He's supposed to be stopping at the Kelsey Hotel there. I'm going to put in a person-to-person call for him right now, and the chances are I'll have him on the wire by one o'clock or so. Don't go to lunch, Bill, until he answers our call. After that you can bring me some lunch. You know I'm supposed to be dying in the hospital, and I daren't show my face.

"While we're waiting, Bill, I suggest we do a little something for the good of the order. You know we've got excellent fingerprints of the man who poisoned Stevens, but we still have no proof of his identity. You have said repeatedly that you were convinced that Edward Folsom did the job.

"One other thing is true. Nearly every particle of real evidence which we now have, points to Edward Folsom. Really, if it weren't for two or three facts which I can't possibly make jibe with the rest of the proofs, I'd say you were probably right.

"Here's one of those facts in the Folsom matter, Bill: We have three letters signed by Folsom. One is the short note he wrote to Stevens, intimating that he might come east pretty soon. You remember that. The second is that long, threatening letter to Stevens, where Folsom—now in Chicago—tells Stevens that a halfshare in the color-process belongs to him, and that Stevens 'won't live a month' if he doesn't do the square thing and give Folsom half the profits. That's the letter that Stevens left in his working-coat. The last of the three letters is the one that Folsom wrote to Charles Duncan, in Cleveland—the one that had so many finger-prints on it.

"Now, the thing which sticks in my craw is this; you did your best on those first two letters, Bill, but your dusting of them didn't show anything but Stevens' finger-prints, either on the letter or on their envelopes. Stop and think a minute what this means, Bill! Any normal, right-handed man holds down the upper part of the letter-head with his left fingers while he is writing. With a left-handed man conditions, of course, are reversed, but in both cases the letter-head is held down by the hand which is not doing the writing. Everybody knows that the bare fingers of any normal hand carry enough secretion and exude enough moisture to leave a vapory film on any surface they touch. The whole science of developing, classifying, indexing, and identifying finger-prints depends on that fact. Your experience has taught you how much better a smooth or polished surface records a finger-print than other surfaces. It's your job to know it.

"Folsom's letter-paper *ought* to carry a clear print and we ought to have excellent finger-prints of both his hands right now—but we haven't. Why? The only reason I can think of is that he has worn gloves of some sort while he was writing those letters. Again comes the question: Why?

"Was it to conceal the fact that he wrote them? No, for he signs his own initials boldly; and we know from Miss Stevens' statements that both writing and signature are those of Folsom. Was it solely to conceal his finger-prints? If so, that would constitute a strong presumption that Folsom was engaged in illegal pursuits. Law-abiding citizens do not wear gloves for such purposes. If engaged in illegal doings, may he not have been a party, if not a principal, in the murder of Stevens?

"If we could get the finger-prints of Edward Folsom—some that we *know* are his—we could compare them with the prints we found on Stevens' memo book and on that little paper cone which held the cyanide. Then we should be dealing with a certainty. If the two sets of prints were identical, it would practically decide the case against Folsom. If the prints were not identical, that would let him out of the actual murder—although I feel positive that he, or his nephew, George, is mixed up in this somehow.

"We haven't any other document which we know was handled by Folsom only—hence the only logical thing to do is to get one. You can't get one, Bill, for Folsom would probably want to commit a real murder—on you—if you tried to hornswoggle him again! My suggestion, then, is that we arrange to get Folsom's fingerprints this afternoon; get them directly, and make sure that they are his, beyond any

doubt"—and Rollins paused, awaiting his companion's reply.

"That's sure a nice little job," said Hackett. "Just as easy as
rollin' off a log. Gimme that phone a minute, Bob, I'm goin'
to call up George Folsom, an' tell him Mr. Robert S. Rollins
desires him to tell his uncle, Mr. Edward Folsom, to come to
713 Meyers Building this afternoon, sure! I'll say it's very
important. If George asks why, I'll tell the dear boy that you
want a nice clear set of Edward Folsom's finger-prints. Oh
yes, and I'll tell George you'll pay the old gent's car-fare an'
treat him to an ice-cream soda, too! He'll sure come with
those two inducements—I *don't* think!"—and Hackett
paused in disgust.

"Now, Bill," said Rollins, "you know I've been talking
sense—not crazy stuff. Tell me this, will you? Do you know
anybody in the Western Union or Postal Telegraph offices
here in town? Anybody? Even a messenger-boy will do."

"Sure I do! I know three or four kids at the Postal downtown office. Why?"

"Is any one of those boys especially bright and reliable—
and if so, can you get him a leave of absence for a couple of
hours?"

"Oh, yes! If he's in, I reckon I can," said Bill. "He could
get off to go to his grandmother's funeral, you know. The
gag's a million years old, but it's still good."

"All right, Bill! You go out and get that kid, but, before he
leaves the telegraph office, have him swipe one 'received'
telegraph blank—such as 'messages received' are typed
on—one telegraph envelope, and one of those lists which
persons receiving a message must sign when the boy delivers
it. Have him get blanks that have not been handled. While
you're doing that, I'll get a little dope ready so we won't
have to keep the boy waiting. Will you do that, Bill?"

"Of course I will—but darned if I see why! Maybe you
know what you're doin', Bob, but I'll be cussed if I do!"

Nevertheless, like a good soldier, William Hackett obeyed
and went.

In half an hour Bill was back, accompanied by a freckled-faced but intelligent-looking lad of fifteen, who produced from his pocket a large envelope, in which were the desired official papers.

"Sure these papers haven't been handled, Bill?" said Rollins.

"Absolutely!" said Hackett. "I gave Shorty my gloves to wear when he swiped 'em, an' he'll do what I tell him. Won't you, Shorty?"

"I'll say so!" said the boy emphatically.

"All right!" said Bob. "Just wait outside in the hall for a minute."

After the boy had stepped out, Rollins remarked: "I'm going to send Edward Folsom a bogus telegram from his sister, Agnes, in Los Angeles, telling him she's leaving for Chicago today. When he signs for it on this clean receipt blank, we ought to have a good set of his prints. It's an old gag, Bill, but it pretty nearly always works."

"But what if he ain't home, Bob?"

"I'll see that he stays home, Bill. I'll phone Mrs. Halgard to keep him there. Ask Shorty to come in now, will you?

"Here, let me put your gloves on for you, Shorty! There! Now listen, son! I want you to take this envelope and this receipt form in your gloved hands and carry both of them that way until you deliver the message. When you get to this man Folsom's apartment, ask for Edward Folsom. And don't you deliver that message into any other hands but his. I will know whether you did or not. Make Edward Folsom sign for it, personally. Hand him this fountain-pen to do it. I know that pen is a little greasy, but don't wipe off the grease. Keep your gloves on every minute till you get back here. As soon as you get outside Folsom's house, I want you to put that signed receipt form in this large envelope which I am giving you now.

"Here's two dollars, son! There's three more dollars waiting here if you do just exactly what I've told you—and not a cent if you don't. Now let me hear you repeat my instructions, Shorty, and be sure you've got 'em right."

The freckled-faced boy had a marvelous memory, for his repetition of Bob's orders was almost verbatim.

While Shorty stood waiting for final orders, Rollins got Mrs. Halgard on the phone. "Hello! Is that you, Aunt Rose? This is your new nephew, Bob Rollins. Aha, so you knew the voice? . . . So did I, Auntie! Say, listen! Do you want to do me a favor? . . . Good! Please call up Edward Folsom and tell him that you're coming over to see him at three o'clock and ask him to stay home. If he's not at home or can't stay in, phone me right away. I'm sending him a message and I want to be sure that he gets it . . . All right! I'll wait."

About five minutes later, while all three were waiting, came another ring, and Rollins again answered the phone.

"Hello, Aunt Rose! . . . Oh, he'll stay in, will he? That's fine! . . . Yes! . . . About an hour from now you can phone him that you've got company and can't come today. He'll have my message by then. Oh, say! When that pen rolled behind the desk, your last list wasn't quite finished, was it? . . . I thought so . . . Yes, that's the one you forgot to put down, but I fixed it. You're a wonderful woman, Auntie! . . . Say, when you have your next party, send a card to Mr. and Mrs. Robert Rollins, won't you? And don't forget that you've got a date on Christmas Day to give a bride away . . . Yes! Nora to me! . . . Sure it's wonderful. Can't believe it myself . . . God bless you, Aunt Rose! Good-bye!" Rollins turned to the waiting messenger. "All right, Shorty! Mr. Folsom will be at home when you get there. Hurry along and hustle back!" Then turning to Hackett, he asked: "Well, Bill, any criticism of my scheme?"

"Criticism hell!" retorted the latter. "You ought to pay a thousand dollars a month to the telephone company, Bob. You do more stuff with that phone in ten minutes than you could do in a month of walkin'. I'll bet ten dollars that you don't walk ten blocks while we're finishin' the rest of this case, if we ever finish it. You'll stay right in here an' telephone. Is it a bet?"

"Sorry, Bill, I've *got* to stay here if I want to stay alive, so there isn't any bet. Show me a better excuse than that if you can. Hello! There's the telephone ringing again. I'll answer it, Bill. Wait a minute."

By his conversation, Hackett at once knew that George Donovan at Streator was on the wire. Bob was repeating the exact words—as to the date of Donovan's last bad toothache—which Bob had assured Hackett he would use. It was quite some time before Donovan became impressed with the sincerity and seriousness of Rollins' inquiry, and still more time before Bob could induce Donovan to return at once to Chicago. The matter was at last arranged, however, and Rollins turned to Hackett, saying:

"Put this down, Bill, just as I spiel it off:

" 'Donovan had severe toothache in left upper molar all day Thursday, November 16. Suffered nearly all night despite constant applications to relieve pain. Visited dentist, Dr. A.L. Bryan, at ten A.M. Friday, November 17, and had molar extracted, with immediate relief. Molar showed large cavity, reaching nearly into roots. Donovan will arrive Meyers Building Tuesday—tomorrow—ten A.M.' Have you got it all down, Bill?"

"Yes, sure I have. I've got it all down—but how in hell did you know that Donovan had a bad toothache lately?"

"Bill, if I answer you this once, and tell the truth, will you quit asking me about this until I get ready to tell the whole story? Honestly, now, will you?"

"Yes! Word of honor!" said Hackett.

"All right, Bill! I'll tell you and it's the precise truth. The way I knew that Donovan had a bad toothache lately was the same way I know when I'm getting close to the Chicago stock-yards—by my nose," said Bob.

Hackett laughed loud and long. He had to.

"Bob," said he, "your answer reminds me of the story of the one-legged feller. The kids in town were always pesterin' him as to how he lost his leg. They kept at it and kept at it, but he wouldn't tell 'em. Finally he got sore, an' says he: 'If I promise you kids to answer one question, will you promise to quit botherin' me about my leg any more?' The kids all hollered yes, of course. 'All right!' says the one-legged guy;

'shoot your question!' 'Our question,' says the kids, 'is: How'd you lose your leg?' 'Well, I'll tell ya,' says Peg-leg; 'it was bit off!' ' "

"Pretty good, Bill! I can see the resemblance all right—and I want to tell you that your story reminds me that I haven't 'bit off' anything since breakfast, and it's nearly three o'clock now. How about my eats? Are you going to bring me some grub in a paper bag or not?"

" 'Hell hath no fury like intestines scorned,' " misquoted Hackett. "It's simply marvelous, Bob, how that great intellect of yours keeps both of us down to solid facts. I'll feed my face first, and then cop a coupla sandwiches for you. So long, you old cripple! God bless you!"

Four o'clock found them again in room 713, still discussing the various angles of their ever-present problem.

"Bob, do you remember making me a promise three days ago? Think a minute. Believe me, I haven't quit thinking of it ever since you made it."

"I don't seem to remember, Bill. What was it? I never made you a promise that I didn't keep, and I'll keep this one if you'll tell me what it was," said Rollins.

"It's about that damned key," said Hackett. "Every once in a while I get to thinkin' mebbe we're both wrong or gone batty or somep'n. When I see these solid walls, them thick glass windows, and that three-inch door, I just can't see how that key could be on that desk in front of Stevens unless he committed suicide. I just can't see it, that's all!"

"I remember now. So you don't believe what I said when I promised to plant that key right under your nose on the desk while you sat in Stevens' chair, after I had locked the door from the outside? Eh, Bill?"

"Oh! I don't doubt you *think* you can do it, Bob, but, if you want to know the truth, I'm damned if I think you *can* do it; and if you want to know why, I'll tell you."

"All right! Fire away, Bill!"

"Well," said Hackett, "yesterday I went over this room with a hammer, every foot of it. I sounded the walls and floors. I tapped the ceiling. I examined the windows, and I couldn't put a piece of writing-paper between the sashes. The door fits so tight I could only shove a visiting-card underneath it. The top and sides of the door are protected by a heavy molding. A bed-bug couldn't get in there. The molding around the transom edges and those eight big screws in the transom make it as solid as Gibraltar. The nearest building is fifteen feet below this one, and thirty feet away. The glass in these windows is thick and frosted, and so is the transom. Both windows were locked tight when Stevens passed out. There's no continuous keyhole through the lock, and nobody could monkey with the transom without a ladder. You may have some sort of scheme that you *think* will throw a key through solid oak or brick or glass and make it land on a precise spot twenty feet away from the place where you stand, but you've got to *show* me."

"That's what I promised to do, Bill, and I'll do the showing tonight. You be here at nine o'clock sharp, when everybody's gone, and borrow a stop-watch from someone to time this little experiment. You can re-examine the room, windows, door, transom, lock, and key before we start, Bill. Then you are to sit there in Stevens' chair—just where he sat when he died—and hold the stop-watch in your left hand. The door is to be locked from the inside, and the key left sticking—on the inside—in the keyhole. Then I'll blindfold you, and you'll promise not to touch or remove that blindfold until I say: 'Done.' After you're blindfolded, and holding your stop-watch in your left hand, I'll take your right hand and place it in the middle of the desk, palm upward. You are to keep your hand there until I say: 'Done!' When we're all fixed like that, you're to say: 'One! Two! Three! Go!' At the word 'Go!' you're to press the stop-watch and I'm to do my stuff, until I have said: 'Done!' The instant I say: 'Done!' you press that stop-watch again, and you can then take off your blindfold. I'll bet you anything from ten dollars to a hundred that I'll not be longer than three minutes on the job. I'll do more than that, Bill! You'll feel that door-key strike the palm of your right hand before you take off your blindfold—and I'll be in the hall outside of that locked door before I've said that last 'Done.' Is it a bet, Bill? Come on! How much?"

"Bob," said Hackett, "nobody ever accused me of being a poor sport; but I'm not betting against a sure thing with any-body. You've been reasoning this thing out, just like you've done every other thing on this job. I know it. That's what you've done. I'll need all the coin I've got before this little vacation of mine is over. No, sir! There ain't no bet! Don't forget, though, Bob, that I'll keep my fingers crossed for the next fifty years when I see you comin'. An' say, let me con-gratulate you on your coming wedding, old scout! Hello! Who's at the door? I'll bet it's Shorty. I'll open it, Bob. Come in, Shorty! How did you make out?"

"Fine!" said Shorty. "Slick as grease! I saw the old guy an' give him the wire with no trouble at all. When he started readin' the wire, he says: 'Well, well, I'm surprised!' and handed me a quarter. After that I ducked. I was afraid he might grab me with one of them big brown mitts of his. Here you are! Do I get them other three bucks now, mister?" and he handed the envelope to Rollins.

"Sure!" said Bob. "You've earned 'em, son! Take 'em and be happy! Come on, Bill, let's get busy!"

"Hey, hold on a minute, Shorty!" yelled Hackett as the youngster was disappearing through the partly open door. "You're too good a kid to be usin' that Bowery slang. That's Eastern talk. We don't use it here. Nobody in Chicago says 'mitts' when they mean hands.' "

"Neither do I," said Shorty. "Ain't it all right to say 'mitts' for mittens? My mother always says it. This old guy Folsom had on a pair of big brown gloves all the while I seen him." And Shorty disappeared down the hall.

Rollins looked at Hackett. *"Sunk!"* was all he said.

His partner glared at Rollins. "Don't it beat hell?" said William Hackett.

"Listen here, Bob Rollins! If I should say out loud what I think of this guy Folsom, Sodom an' Gomorrah wouldn't be a circumstance to what would happen to this joint. Of all the slick ducks I ever seen, this bird Edward Folsom is the slick-

est. One minute—while he writes a letter threat'nin' murder—you'd think he was a plain damn fool. The next minute,
when another feller wants to get a signature from him that
nobody on earth can imitate—that's his finger-prints—he's
as wise as forty Solomons! Don't tell me that this Folsom
bird is wearin' gloves for fun! He didn't have no gloves on
when he made a grab for me a coupla days ago. I'll say he
didn't. If you coulda seen them big twitchy fingers of his just
quiverin' to get at my throat an' choke the gizzard outa me,
you'd know he could get along without gloves if he wanted
to. He's wearin' 'em for a damn good reason, believe me;
an' if that guy didn't bump off your friend Stevens, I'll eat
hay for the rest of my life, so help me, John Rogers!

"There ain't a damn bit of use lookin' for prints on them
papers now, an' you know it. I s'pose we got to do it, an' I'll
give 'em the once-over, but I'll bet a million they're as clean
as a whistle. Shorty's an A-1 kid. When he says a thing is so,
it's so, and you can bet your bottom dollar on it. Wait a coupla minutes, Bob, while I dust this receipt form. It ain't goin'
ta do any good, but I s'pose it's gotta be done."

Five minutes later William Hackett pitched the telegraph
forms—which had cost his partner five hard-earned dollars—into the waste-paper basket, expectorated disgustedly
upon them, sat down in his chair, stretched out his legs,
jammed his hands into his pockets, and voiced a war-time
epithet which will not be permitted—even under present-day
usage—to soil this page.

Mr. William J. Hackett, with Cassandra-like prophetic accuracy, had foretold the outcome. The documents were as
clean as a whistle.

"Now what the hell are we gonna do?" he inquired.

"Don't be so discouraged, Bill," said Rollins. "Nobody
could have foreseen this fizzle. Nobody is to blame. We did
our best and she fluked on us, that's all! Of course, I'm sore
about losing that five dollars, but getting peeved isn't going
to bring it back. Seems to me the best thing we can do is for
you to go out and get some dinner—bring me a little steak or
chops—and then we'll make a call on our dear friend

Stanislaw Brodski and see whether he's determined to live
on bread and water for another three days or not. I'll muffle
up so no one will know me, and we'll grab a cruising taxi to
the Sanford."

"I hope the darn cuss has drunk that whole pitcher of Epsom salts," muttered Hackett. "That would do him good,
anyhow! Say, Bob, that little pitcher we give Puckers is too
damn small. It only holds about half a pint. Let's get him a
good big one an' fill her up with 'poison,' so he'll he *sure* to
be an angel after he drinks it!"

"Don't worry about that pitcher, Bill. I'll bet Puckers has a
chill every time he sees it. He wouldn't put one finger on it
for a million dollars. He thinks it's loaded with cyanide, and
whenever he takes a look at it, he'll be making mental pictures of how I would look if I had drunk that same poison out
of my faucet. Anyhow, I'm not so much concerned now
about whether Puckers betrays his principal or not. I hope he
weakens and gives us the dope and I'm positive he will before his five-day probation is up. But if he won't, it will be
all right, anyhow! I've learned something today that clears
up half the puzzle. I've only got about six hundred dollars
left in the bank, but I'll bet every nickel of it that by six
o'clock Wednesday night we'll know who murdered Stevens, and we'll be able to prove it. That's precisely ten days
from the time we started!"

"Oh, you mean through Donovan!" said Hackett. "In other
words, you're going to be a sure-enough bloodhound, an'
nose out the criminal, eh? Regular *Uncle Tom's Cabin* stuff,
ain't it?—only our Eliza is a damn skunk that deliberately
poisoned as fine a man as ever lived. Believe me, our Eliza
ain't got no baby in his arms, but I hope to goodness he's
jumpin' on ice-cakes right now—an' damn thin ice at that. If
he ain't now, he soon will be. Say, listen, Bob! Did you
really mean you got a clue which is likely to lead to this cya-
nide-peddler we're after? Mind you, Bob, I promised not to
ask any more questions about it, but that ain't stoppin' you
from talkin' about 'noses' and such stuff—if you want to."

"All right, Bill! So long as it's a general topic, I don't

mind. Here's my slant on learning facts. We've got five senses to do it with. Four of them—taste, sight, hearing, touch—we use constantly. The other sense—smell—we use rarely; but if we were dogs, or jungle animals, we'd use it more than any other. The reason we don't is that civilization has largely banished our need for its constant use.

"Nevertheless, the sense of smell—if we develop it through use—can bring to our mind facts which no other sense can. In some vocations, such as detecting by aroma the qualities of coffee, tea, perfumes, liquors, and the like, men become wonderfully proficient. Some have been born with a keen sense of odors. Some deliberately cultivate that sense. All possess it in some degree. Of course, it's the same way with all our other senses as well. Keenness of vision, hearing, taste, or touch varies tremendously in individuals, either from heredity or from cultivation.

"It just happens, Bill, that I was born with a very keen sense for odors, while my hearing is a little below normal—largely because of a tendency toward introspection. An odor stimulates my memory and often creates a new train of thought; so, of course, I have cultivated it. It gives me pleasure, and everybody likes to do agreeable things. It's no credit to me that I had an over-share of it through heredity"—and Robert Rollins ceased his oration.

"Gee, that's interesting, Bob! Do you mean to say that you can detect human odors—like a dog who picks his master in a crowd by smelling everybody's shoes?"

"Oh no, nothing like that, Bill! Just a rather keen sense of smell, that's all. The peculiar part of it is that a particular odor, which I haven't smelt for perhaps twenty years, will bring to mind, in a flash of memory, the scenes and incidents which occurred on the occasion when I last smelt that same odor. I'm willing to bet you've had that same experience, Bill. How about it? Isn't it so?"

"By gosh, you're right! That's so!"

"Good for you, Bill! And how would you like to smell a big porter-house steak, smothered with onions, maybe—and do your smelling about fifteen minutes from now? How about it? Doesn't that arouse some of your lost memories, old boy? I'll bet it does. Will you cultivate my smeller, too, Bill? I surely could put it away."

One hour later Hacket had demolished his steak and had sneaked another one just like it to his partner, and both were delightfully content. Thence with caution by a cruising taxi to the Sanford Hotel. The plethoric pair entered the garret where Mr. Stanislaw Brodski was cogitating on the irretrievable "might-have-beens" of a misspent past. The door—unlocked by Arthur Henderson, manager of the Sanford Apartment Hotel—was open. Mr. Henderson handed the key to Hackett and retired. Messrs. Rollins, Hackett, and Brodski were alone together in that bare, comfortless room, and the following conversation ensued:

Rollins: "We're here, Brodski! What's your decision?"

Puckers: "For God's sake, Mr. Rollins, I can't do it! I dassent!"

Hackett: "You 'dassent,' eh? Why, you lousy hound, you wasn't scared to sneak up to Rollins' room and plant a pound or two of rat-poison for him to swaller—but now you dassent squeal on the dirty mutt who sicked you on to the job! Say, Bob, let's give this damn skunk a dose of them feathers on his feet right now! What's the use of waitin' two more days?"

Puckers: "You couldn't do that, Mr. Rollins! You couldn't! You know it's against the law to torture a man! Besides, you're a gentleman! You ain't the kind of feller that bats a guy in the jaw when he's got the bracelets on an' can't help hisself!"

Hackett: "Shut up, you snivelin' polecat. I'm the guy that's handlin' this thing, and don't you forget it. Don't ever believe I won't knock you to hell-an'-gone if you don't come across with your stuff. There ain't no gentlemanly compunctions about *me,* young fella-me-lad, cuffs or no cuffs. You ain't dealin' with no sensitive lily when I'm around. I'd a damn sight rather kick the guts outa you than not; an' if it wasn't for this fool Rollins bein' a friend of mine an' promisin' you five days to make up your mind, you'd be hollerin' murder this minute, you . . .! Believe me, I'm just itchin' to get a swipe at your rotten hide, an' what I won't do to you on Wednesday—oh, mister!"

Rollins: "We shall leave this room in precisely two minutes, Brodski. Are you ready to give your decision?"

Puckers: "Oh, my God! Oh, my God! Please, please, Mr. Rollins! You don't know what'll happen to me if I squeal. I won't be safe anywhere. You don't know this guy. He'll do *anything!* He won't stop at nothin'. I just had to do what I did, Mr. Rollins. He made me! I couldn't help it! He'd have put me on the drop sure if I hadn't. With this map of mine an' my slit ear an' every dick an' bull in Chicago knowin' me at sight, do you s'pose I'd have gone gunnin' for you if I didn't *have* to. If I squeal, I'm as good as dead tomorrow. Mr. Rollins, please!"

Rollins: "Time's up, Brodski! Better move that pitcher of cyanide out of his reach, Hackett. You can put it back alongside of his grub Wednesday if he doesn't come across and squeal before then! After that you can handle him, Hackett; I'll be through!

"We'll be here Wednesday, Brodski! That's the last day. Just read that slip of paper there and make up your mind. Remember! That will be our *last call*—and on Wednesday Hackett will start giving you the works. Let's get out of here! Come on, Bill! The smell of that skunk there makes me sick"; and the two inquisitors left behind them a shattered moaning wreck.

Rollins' face was almost as pale as that of his prisoner as he and Bill closed and locked the door behind them. His hands were trembling with emotion.

"It's no use, Bill! I never could carry this thing through alone. No matter how evil a man has been, I keep remembering what he might be—his possibilities for good if he'd only think right. I can't feel really revengeful at Puckers, and I shouldn't feel that way even if he had succeeded in poisoning me and I knew I should die from it."

"You can't, eh?" growled Hackett. "Well, believe me, I can. You just leave Puckers to me."

XIV

ON THEIR WAY BACK to the laboratory little was said, but as soon as the door of room 713 had closed behind them, Rollins remarked: "See here, Bill, suppose you run down the hall and see if all the offices on this floor are closed up for the night. If they are, I'll get ready to keep my promise to you about that key business. No use waiting until nine o'clock if everybody has gone home."

"Hooray, Bob! Honest, I'll bet I've lost two nights' sleep studyin' about that damn thing. I'll be back in a minute."

While Hackett was gone, Rollins took from one of the desk-drawers a certain object which he had bought the Saturday before in preparation for this event. This he stowed away in his rear pocket, where it was hidden by his coat. Two minutes later his comrade had returned, and seated himself at the desk.

"All set, boss! Ready for the big show! An' say, Bob, if you fluke on this thing, I ain't goin' ta razz you so very much about it. Between you an' me, you got about as much chance of pullin' off your stunt as a fried egg has of bein' hatched. Go ahead, though! You're the guy who's doin' the performin'."

"All right, Bill, we'll tackle it now, if you say so. Did you find anybody who would trust you with a stop-watch—or did all of the watches happen to be in some repair shop?"

"Listen, young fella-me-lad! A gentleman who manufactures literary compendiums loaned me his pet watch today, after I left you. He's got confidence in Bill Hackett even if he is a bookmaker—I mean manufacturer! The audience is now ready, kind sir! Do you want some help in hoisting the asbestos sheet, Bob?"

"No, thanks, Bill! The only thing I ask is that you examine the transom, door, and windows of this room again. Do it right now, Bill, so that you'll be sure I haven't flim-flammed you. Get busy, old scout! I'll fire when you are ready."

"All right, Gridley!" said Hackett. "I'll be sure, don't worry!" And he spent ten minutes testing every possible aperture that would have given passage to a needle. "Righto, Bob, start the races!" said he.

"Now then, Bill, lock that door with the key on the inside! Now pull your chair up to that desk! Now hold your right hand, palm upward, in the middle of the desk—right here! All right so far, Bill!"

"Right as rain!" said Hackett. "Go ahead, Professor!"

"Now take that stop-watch in your left hand and get ready to be blindfolded. What do you want me to use? Your silk handkerchief, or mine?"

"Mine, please, Mr. Houdini! I'm used to smellin' it!" said Bill.

"Well," said Rollins, "are you blindfolded, or can you see a little?"

"Blind as a bat, Bob! Cross my heart! An' I hereby pledge my sacred honor not to take this damn thing off till you say: 'Done!' "

"Then I guess we're all fixed, Bill. I'm ready. Now you're to count: 'One! Two! Three! Go!' When I say: 'Done!'—from out in the hallway—you can stop the watch and take off the bandage. You'll have the key in your hand by that time and you can let me in again. All ready, Bill! Let her flicker!"

"One! Two! Three! Go!" yelled Hackett, and pressed the stopwatch lever.

Rapidly, but lightly, running up and down the room could be heard the feet of Robert Rollins. The sounds lasted about a minute.

A few seconds later Hackett heard the door-lock click—which meant the door was open.

Then came another lock-click—the door had been locked from outside.

Twenty seconds or so later there was a peculiar scrunching sound. Then came a slithering noise, lasting perhaps thirty seconds. *A hard flat object struck Hackett's palm! His hand closed! It was the key!*

Perhaps five or six more seconds passed, when "Done!" shouted Rollins from the outer hall.

Hackett pressed the stop-watch and tore off his bandage from his eyes. Save for himself, room 713 was absolutely empty. His stop-watch showed the elapsed time to have been a hundred and sixty-eight seconds. Slowly Hackett went to the locked door, unlocked it with the key in his hand, held the door wide ajar, placed his left hand over his heart, and raised his right hand in a military salute.

Smilingly Robert Rollins walked from the hall into room 713 and took his seat opposite the other at the desk. The elapsed time of their silence was just about two and three-quarter minutes, the time required to perform what Hackett, ever after, persisted in calling "the Great Key Stunt."

"Listen, Bob," said Hackett, "I never would have believed that trick, or whatever it is, could be done if I hadn't seen it myself. When I felt that key slap into my open hand, I darn near fainted. That's true, Bob! Honestly, I did! Right now it don't seem real! Say, lemme look at them windows again! No, it ain't them; there's a thick layer of dust where they come together. Not a finger-mark on it anywhere, an' both windows are locked tight! Wait a sec', Bob; I gotta give that door the once-over again. Let's see if I can slip this key under the bottom crack. Nope, she won't go! Honest, did you ever do this trick before, Bob?"

"Never," asserted Rollins.

"Well, for Heaven's sake, how on earth did you find out how to do it, then?" queried Hackett, unbelievingly.

"Easily, Bill! There's nothing that is in the least degree mysterious about this 'stunt,' as you call it. You can do it yourself if you sit down and do some good hard thinking for about fifteen minutes. All you have to do is to eliminate the impossible methods, and that leaves the possible ways of doing it. You wouldn't have to do it *my* way. There are at least two other ways to work the trick. Don't ask me how I put it across. Use your own brains and logic and you'll be coming round tomorrow and shouting: 'Eureka!' and wondering why you didn't think of it before."

"For the luvva Mike, what's Eureka?" asked Hackett.

"Why, that's Greek. You'll be telling me: 'I have found it.' "

"Like hell I will! The only time I'll be talkin' that stuff will be after you've told me how you did it. Say, listen, Bob, be a good feller and loosen up. Just tell me the way *you* did the stunt. Never mind about them other ways. Cough up, will ya?"

"All right, Bill, just as soon as we've cleaned up this case, I'll do it, and that's a promise. Are you satisfied now?"

"Sufferin' Moses! It looks like that'll be never," growled Hackett. That gentleman's periods of depression never lasted long. He was not built of gloomy stuff. As Rollins looked at his friend and thought of their conversation that very afternoon, he could not refrain from thinking that few crimes or misdoings could bring sorrow to a world whose inhabitants had the disposition and principles of William Hackett. Impulsive, hasty, generous to a fault, Hackett was always dependable—a stalwart friend, whether in sunshine or rain. Though uncouth at times in language and accent, though given to the frequent use of strong expletives—many of them unprintable, even in these realistic days—he was possessed of a good education and, as Rollins had often observed, was alert-minded to the highest degree.

Bill Hackett was in truth "all wool and a yard wide." He was a real man, and his next remark gave proof of it:

"Are you goin' to eat an' sleep here in this joint durin' the rest of your natural life, Bob? You notice I sneaked you up a coupla blankets. Copped 'em offa my landlady this morning—she keeps 'em in the hall closet. But I couldn't swipe no pillows."

"Do you want to bet that I won't have to sleep here after to-morrow—? Answer that phone, please, will you, Bill?"

"It's Joe Atwood callin' from the Sanford, Bob. There's some mail there for you—a small light package, he says. Shall I go get it?"

"No, thanks. Let it go, and bring it down in the morning. Ask Joe if there's any address on the package to tell where it came from."

"Joe says it's from somebody named Stoddard in Milwaukee. Is that all right?" asked Hackett.

"Sure, I know Stoddard. That's all right. Thank Joe and tell him you'll get it when you come past there in the morning. I'm going to turn in now, Bill. You'll be here before eight, won't you? I hate to wait for my toast and coffee. Don't forget, too, that Donovan will be on hand at ten o'clock. Good night, old boy!"

"Good night, Bob! I'll be Johnny-on-the-spot with the eats. Always did want to be a waiter, but it's damn few tips I'd get offa birds like you. So long, old sleuth!"

Bill Hackett always kept his word—which is saying much for any man. At seven fifty in the morning he appeared with a shoe-box under his arm, in which were orange-juice, toast, eggs, and coffee—all in eatable condition and nothing spilled.

"Here's that Christmas package of yours, too, Bob," said he. "Bet a dollar I can tell what's in it! Wanta bet?"

"Nope, no bets, Bill. It must be cigarettes. It's too light for anything else. Give me your knife, while I cut—Hello! That's funny!"

"What's funny, Bob?" queried Hackett.

"Why, this postmark where they've cancelled the stamp. I can't see what town it is, but I know it isn't postmarked Milwaukee, and Harry Stoddard lives in Milwaukee. All right, you open her up, Bill, while I finish these eggs."

"Cigarettes! That's what they are!" said Hackett. "Fifty fat, long, cork-tipped Russians! Gee, they're expensive, Bob! An' here's a card! Look at it; nice printing, ain't it?"

> *Smoke these and be happy!*
> *Henry*

"Let's see that card and that wrapper again, Bill!" And Rollins studied both for several minutes.

"Let me have that knife again, will you, Bill?" said Rollins, soberly. Then, one by one, he commenced to slit lengthwise all the cigarettes in the top layer of the box, dumping the contents of each on a newspaper.

"What the hell!" queried Hackett, but the other motioned him to be silent. As the eighth cigarette was slit, Rollins held out his hand to his partner and showed the contents of the cigarette—opened like a split herring.

About one inch from the white end of that cigarette, imbedded in the tobacco, lay a thin, brownish piece of material. In thickness it was about the size of a wooden match, and its length was approximately one inch. It appeared to be coated with collodion or shellac, and its contents looked like powdered mustard.

Hackett stood and gazed aghast.

"Open that window, quick, Bill! Now run to the lavatory and bring me half a dozen squares of toilet-paper."

No errand was ever more quickly performed.

Placing the slightly twisted toilet-paper outside on the stone window-ledge, Rollins laid the brown capsule upon it, lighted one end of the paper with his patent lighter, grabbed Hackett's arm, and pulled him toward the open door of room 713.

Standing together in the hallway, the comrades watched the flames slowly eating its way toward the tiny mysterious cylinder.

Puff! A trifling explosion and that was all! Rollins started toward the window, but Hackett pulled him back.

"Hold on! Don't go in now! Wait till the fumes clear up! Don't you smell it, Bob?" he whispered hoarsely.

"Sure! I smell something, but what is it?"

"Nothing much, only a little prussic acid, Bob! Just a nice little bit of mild hydrocyanic acid, mixed with some inflammable powder and coated with collodion, that's all! Any time you want to practice playin' on a harp, just inhale a puff of that stuff, and in about two seconds you'll be leadin' the heavenly orchestra! Sufferin' Moses! This is the worst ever! Ain't there no limit to what that . . . will do? This is the fourth time he's tried to put you underground."

"It's the fifth time, Bill," interrupted Rollins. "I'm convinced now that the supposed footpad who held me up and tried to smash my skull last Sunday night was the same man. I believe poor old Sarah Vasch heard me and the girls talking about getting Harry Stoddard to hunt up Stevens in Milwaukee, that she went to the movies with this man, that he pumped her about how the family were taking Stevens' absence, and that she innocently told him all she'd heard. That's how he got hold of Stoddard's name, and I suppose he got Harry's address from a Milwaukee directory and put that name and address in the corner of that cigarette package before he mailed it."

"But what good would it do him to croak you after you'd talked to Stoddard, Bob?"

"Plenty, Bill! I hadn't got hold of Stoddard when Sarah left the house. This devil we're after thought he might put me out of business before I could learn that Stevens wasn't in Milwaukee. Anyhow, that's the way I dope it out. If Sarah ever recovers, I'll get the truth out of her, and I'll bet all I've got that my theory is correct."

"I reckon you're right, Bob, but how in hell did you suspect there was somep'n wrong with that box of cigarettes? That's what gets me!"

"Well, in the first place the postmark was not Milwaukee, where Harry lives. Second, every letter on the wrapper and on the card was a longhand printed letter—even the signature, 'Henry.' Third, Harry Stoddard hasn't been called or signed his name 'Henry' in the last ten years. He's always 'Harry' to his friends. Fourth, no friend sending a gift-card prints his name with a pen. Fifth, the box was beautiful and costly, but the wrapping was common brown paper. Are these enough reasons, Bill? If you don't think so, I can give you three more if you want them."

"That's enough, Bob! An' say, if you ever hear me makin' fun of your 'reason and logic' system again, just slam me a clout over the head with a ball-bat, will ya? Listen! I'll bet that's Donovan knockin'—I'll let him in, Bob. Don't stir! Well, well, here's Brother Donovan! Large as life and twice as natural. How's the little old tooth, son? Actin' up still, or is she behavin' like a little lady? Come in, me lord!" continued Hackett. "Set down an' take the weight off your feet. Here's a chair. Welcome to our city! Any message to me from the Streator girls? If I'd known you was goin' there, it woulda saved me a trip. Now I gotta go down an' tell 'em that a real nice Chicago girl took a fall for me last week, an' we're contemplatin' matrimony. Excuse me! I mean, *I* am—I dunno yet about her. Anyhow, I ain't sure about the day yet!"

"Good morning, Hackett," said Donovan. "Glad to see you. How are you, Mr. Rollins? Guess I'm pretty near on time, eh? Had a pretty hard job getting away this morning, but I made it. Have to go back there this afternoon, though. Can we get through our business by noon, Mr. Rollins? I'd like mighty well to get that one-fifteen train."

"We can get through by noon, Mr. Donovan, and maybe by eleven thirty if you've got a good memory. Everything depends on that," said Rollins.

"I'm afraid I'm rather obtuse, Mr. Rollins!" said Donovan. "In fact, this whole thing puzzles me tremendously. As I recall it, the only question you asked me on the telephone yesterday was: 'On what date did you last have a bad toothache?' I told you it was November 16. I said, too, that I had had the tooth pulled the next morning. That's all I heard you say, except that you wanted me to come up here today without fail. Don't you think a little explanation would be in order, Mr. Rollins?"

"Most certainly I do, Mr. Donovan! You are entitled to one and I'll promise to explain fully right now. Unless you regard me as demented, you must realize that I wouldn't have the audacity to ask you to disarrange your business affairs in this way except for a matter of extraordinary importance— which, I assure you, this case is. Please understand, too, that 1 shall insist on reimbursing you for your expense and time."

"Don't worry about that! Now, how can I help you—and what do you mean by saying that everything depends on my memory?" said Donovan.

"You'd better let me tell you the whole story," said Bob. "I'm not going to string it out, but here are the essential details. I think they will surprise you. As you know, Alexander Stevens died in this room, at nine twenty-eight on Saturday evening, November 18, and a coroner's jury pronounced it suicide. Mr. Hackett and I did not believe that verdict was correct. We had strong evidence leading us to believe that Mr. Stevens was murdered."

"What! Murdered?" almost shouted Donovan.

"Yes!" said Rollins. "I mean just that and I can prove it. But let me continue, Mr. Donovan, please. Hackett, here, and I have been quietly investigating the case, but so far have not been able to attach our proofs to a definite suspect. We know beyond doubt, however, that the murderer purchased from a certain Chicago costumer a brown Vandyke beard, which all our evidence seems to indicate was purchased for the purpose of consummating the crime. While making this purchase, our suspect dropped—intentionally, in my belief—one of your business cards. His intent in so doing, we think, was to cast suspicion on you." Here Rollins looked keenly at his visitor.

"My God! On me? Me a murderer! Why, you couldn't believe that, Mr. Rollins," cried Donovan.

"We don't believe it, Mr. Donovan. The proof of that is that I asked you to come here and talk this thing over. We are certain that your business card—which our suspect purposely dropped—came into his hands between November 16 and the night of November 18. Here's another thing we are sure about: that card was authentic. It was not a printed imitation of your business card. It was *yours.* Another thing we know is this: that card didn't come out of a desk or drawer or a box or any other place where you keep your supply of cards. It came off your own person. By the way, Mr. Donovan, in what pocket do you usually carry your business cards?"

"In my upper right-hand vest pocket, always," replied Donovan. "I never did carry a card-case. Too bulgy!"

"There's a fourth thing we are absolutely sure of, Mr. Donovan," said Rollins, "and I may as well tell you why. You handed that card out personally, for your right thumb-print is on it! I verified that by comparing it with your thumb-prints taken from the glass of that transom light, which you personally put into that sash a few days ago.

"Now for the fifth thing we know. Here it is: you personally took that card out of your pocket on November 16, 17, or 18 and personally put it where our suspect could pick it up on one of those three days. Finally, there is a sixth thing of which we are morally certain, but in which we may be in error. That fact is this: you did not put that card in your suspect's hands. I believe you laid it on his desk and left it there. Our reason for this belief is that no finger-prints other than your own appear on that card, except those of the clerk from whom our suspect bought the beard. This indicated extreme caution, to say the least, on the card-handler's part in thus preventing an imprint of any of his fingers from appearing on it, and I think you can draw your own conclusion from that premise."

Donovan shook his head in wonder. "I'm surely glad I've tried to live an honest life," he said. "If six inferences like that can be deduced from a man's business card, I can't see that a crook has any chance on earth. But tell me, Mr. Rollins, how do you *know* that I put this card on somebody's desk at some time during those three days? Might it not be possible that I did it a week or so ago, and this suspect of yours picked it up by its edges, put it in his desk or wallet, and used it later? Are you *sure* it was on one of those three days that I handed out that card?"

"Absolutely!" said Rollins. "And I'm morally certain it was on November 16 or 17."

"Well, Mr. Rollins," said Donovan, "all this is new to me! Just what is it you want me to do? You may be sure I'll do it gladly."

"I want you to retrace in memory, Mr. Donovan, every action you took during those three days. Recall where you went, whom you saw, and all about it. You certainly did not hand your card to a friend or near acquaintance. There would have been no need. But you might have been near some stranger in a business office and put your card on the desk as one customarily does. The stranger might have then picked it up by its edges, taken it away with him, and used it to impersonate you when purchasing the beard."

"I see now just what you want, Mr. Rollins," said Donovan; "and here's what I'll do. I'll sit here at this desk and make out three lists, one for each of those three days. On each list I'll write the name of every man or woman—for perhaps a woman got this and handed it to a man—whom I talked with that day. Then I'll study those names and put a check mark against each person to whom it was possible I handed my card on those days. After I've finished, you can study all three lists, Mr. Rollins, and we can talk over everything that happened at each place."

"That's fine, Mr. Donovan! Precisely what I should have suggested. Sit down right here. I'll wait."

In five minutes Donovan had finished his three lists, and handed them to Rollins, saying:

"I didn't give out one card on Thursday, November 16, that's certain. I had a rip-roaring toothache coming on that night and was doing my damnedest to stop it. I stayed in the office until four o'clock and went home. Didn't see a soul I didn't know. That leaves only November 17 and 18 to account for. On Saturday, November 18, I wasn't out of this building. Never gave a card to anybody. Now for November 17. Here's a list of twelve people I talked with on the 17th, and only four of them strangers. You'll notice I've checked those four names, but I'm positive I only gave my card to three of those four. I've put the names and addresses of those three on the separate slip, and we can talk about those first. Here they are."

Donovan handed to Rollins a paper on which was inscribed the following:

Miss Mary Stresinger—Hotel La Salle (public stenographer)

Dr. A. L. Bryan—Masonic Temple (dentist)

George L. Folsom—Banister Hardware Company (manager).

For an instant Robert Rollins' face hardened like a rock, but in another second he was himself again. "That's fine, Mr. Donovan!" he said. "Now let's talk about these three. We'll start with the beginning of the day. Tell me everything you did. Don't omit anything. I'll let Hackett here take down what you say, and then we'll be sure to have it right. Go ahead, Mr. Donovan!"

Donovan's story ran as follows:

"On account of my toothache, I gave out no dictation on November 16, and at night I had a dozen letters to be answered. On Friday, November 17, my toothache was terrible, and I determined to have the tooth out; so I telephoned to Dr. Baker, my dentist, the first thing in the morning, about eight o'clock. He wasn't in, and the office girl said he wouldn't be in until about two P.M. I couldn't stand the pain that long, and said so. She recommended me to Dr. Bryan, in the same building, and said he specialized in extractions. I asked her to fix up an appointment with him for me just as quick as she could, and let me know. In about five minutes she phoned back that Dr. Bryan would see me at ten o'clock and pull my tooth. Just about then I got a phone call from Miss Horton, my office clerk, that she'd have to stay out all day. Her mother was very sick, and she'd have to get a nurse.

"I thought of my unanswered letters, and whom I could get to typewrite them that day. I decided to try the La Salle Hotel. I knew they had a public stenographer, and I could stop there on my way to the dentist, so I did. I asked the girl, Miss Stresinger, if she could do my work that day, and she said she would come over to the Meyers Building at one o'clock. I left my card on her desk just as I went away. I didn't notice whether she picked it up or not.

"It wasn't nine o'clock yet, and I remember I had two tenants' keys in my pocket. They had lost their duplicates and wanted me to get others made, so I stepped into Banister's on the way to the Masonic Temple and left the two keys there. I didn't know the manager, who personally waited on me, but he seemed to look familiar, so I asked him his name. He hesitated a little, then said he was George Folsom, the nephew of Stevens' old partner. I remember then he had met me once in this building while his Uncle Edward was here with Stevens. When I left, I threw my card on the counter, and said: 'Remember me to your uncle.' My tooth was aching so I don't know whether he picked it up.

"From there I went straight to the Masonic Temple, to Dr. Bryan's office, and laid my card on the table of the girl in the waiting-room and told her of my appointment. She looked up my engagement hour and said the doctor would see me in two or three minutes. In about a minute Dr. Bryan came out with his last patient, and the girl said: 'It's your turn, Mr. Donovan'; so I went right in. Dr. Bryan pulled my tooth, and it stopped aching right away. He's a fine dentist, and very busy. There were two patients waiting when I paid my bill to the girl and left. I didn't see what became of the card. After that I came straight back to this building.

"Is there anything more you'd like to know, Mr. Rollins?"

"Only one thing more, Mr. Donovan," said Rollins. "Do you remember if anyone else was standing near Miss Stresinger while you were with her?"

"Yes," said Donovan. "While I was talking to her, a man came in to give her some dictation."

"How about Folsom? Anyone near him?" said Bob.

"I can't say. They were all very busy there. That's why the manager waited on me. Is that all, Mr. Rollins?" asked Donovan.

"Yes, Mr. Donovan. I'm certain from what you've told me that we'll find the man we're after. By the way, did Mr. George Folsom say anything about his Uncle Edward— whether he was well or not?"

"Not that I recall. Folsom didn't look any too good himself! He was pretty grouchy. He only talked a minute."

"I've never seen George Folsom. What sort of looking

chap is he?" asked Rollins.

"Oh, nearly fifty, smooth-faced, about my size and build. Sort of stern-looking! Strong, big chin, you know."

"Something like yours, eh?" said Rollins, with a laugh.

"I guess that's right, Mr. Rollins," said Donovan. "But he didn't have this beauty-spot of mine"—indicating the mole on his chin—"that's one thing he's got to be thankful for! Well, good-bye, gentlemen! No, no, I won't take a cent, Mr. Rollins! I'd give a hundred dollars this minute to see Mr. Stevens sitting in his old seat, right there! No, sir, you can't pay me for helping on this thing. I hope to God you find the man who did it!" And with a final wave of his hand, George Donovan departed.

No sooner had the door closed behind their guest than Hackett grabbed his partner by the arm in wild excitement.

"Don't you see, Bob?" he almost yelled; "this George Folsom knows everything his uncle knows about Stevens. He's wise to Stevens' lock and that key! Morgan told him! He's strong! Got lots of pep and determination! He could make up just like old Folsom with the right sort of whiskers. I felt he was a crook the minute I started gassin' with him at the Blen—"

"Listen, Bill," interrupted Rollins. "We can't take anything for granted now, no matter how it looks. What I want you to do is to take your notes and write out the full name of every person Donovan mentioned. Then we'll look up their telephone numbers. After that I'll phone to all of them and ask 'em a few things. We'll start with Dr. Bryan first. What's the number of his office phone?"

Ten minutes later Rollins was talking with Dr. Bryan.

"Dr. Bryan? . . . This is the coroner's office . . . Yes, Coroner Howard speaking. Yes! . . . Did you hear of the accident on Friday, November 17 . . . Yes, November 17 . . . Yes, to Mr. Donovan. You extracted his tooth at ten o'clock that morning . . . Yes, that's the man! You had a patient just before him, and one right after him didn't you? . . . Good! I want those two names and addresses, please . . . Yes, full names, please . . . No, we won't bother them. I'll send a man to get their statements . . . What's that? Repeat those names again . . . Couldn't get it; spell it, please . . . Thanks very much, Doctor! Oh, say! Who is your reception-room clerk, Doctor? . . . Oh, Miss Martha Ellis. May I speak with her a moment, please? . . ."

Rollins asked Miss Ellis a few questions while Hackett studied the directory for other numbers.

"Now, Bill, give me the telephone number of Banister and Company. Yes, the store. What's that? Thanks, Bill!

"Hello, central! Give me Main 4630 . . . Hello! Is this Banister's? Can I speak to Superintendent Morgan? . . . Yes, please. Is that you, Mr. Morgan? Say, this is William Hackett speaking . . . Yes, Hackett, the man you talked with a few days ago about that lock Mr. Stevens bought from you . . . Yes, that's me! . . . Say, Mr. Morgan, your manager, Mr. George Folsom, was going to give me the address of that Birmingham firm that made that lock, and I want to order a couple of extra key-blanks . . . Yes! Is he in the store now? Not in, eh? Too bad! Seems to me Mr. Folsom was out of town last week, too. When did he get back? Monday, the 20th, eh? That's good! . . . Thanks, Mr. Morgan, I'll call at the store some time this week. Good-bye!

"Now, Bill, what's the number of the La Salle Hotel? Thanks! No, I won't go over; I'll call 'em. You'll see why in a minute." Rollins put in a call for the La Salle Hotel.

"Hello! La Salle Hotel? May I speak with the room-clerk, please? . . . Yes, it's very important! . . . All right, I'll wait . . . Hello! Is this the clerk of the La Salle? . . . It's important that I speak to your public stenographer, Miss Stresinger. Thank you."

(Two minutes later.) "Hello! Is this Miss Stresinger? . . . This is George Donovan, Miss Stresinger. You remember I left my business card with you on your desk in the La Salle last week Friday, when I came over to get you to write my letters. There was a little pencil memo on the back of that card, and it was tremendously important. Did you keep the card? . . . Too bad! I wish you had! Maybe somebody picked it up to scribble on? . . . Oh, you did! You noticed it! . . . Good for you! I'll send you a box of candy tomorrow! That's fine! What's his name? . . . Spell it please! . . . All right! I'll call him up. Maybe he's got it yet. Good-bye!"

Rollins hung up the overworked phone and looked at Hackett. His face was waxen; his hands shook; his legs seemed scarcely able to support his weight. His appearance was that of a pugilist recovering from a knock-out punch.

"Hand me that writing-pad and an envelope, will you, Bill? I don't feel any too good, and I want to write something. While I'm doing it, please open that safe. Here's a memo of the new combination. I changed it last Tuesday. Don't forget that our stinking polecat knew the old one and used it! He'll never do it again, the damnable murderer!"

While Hackett was turning the safe-dial, Rollins wrote rapidly, put his missive in an envelope, sealed it, and wrote his name across the flap. "Come here, Bill," he said. "Write your name across this flap right under mine, will you?"

Hackett wonderingly obeyed. Rollins took the sealed envelope from Hackett's hand and placed it carefully in a pigeon-hole, beside a small book and some other papers. He then closed the safe, spun the dial, and turned to his comrade.

"Bill," said he, "I want you to memorize that safe-combination right now, and we'll burn the memorandum of it. Do you know what is in that envelope I just put in that safe? *It contains the name of Alexander Stevens' murderer,* and I'm telling you that even if we never get another piece of evidence, our case is complete. Here is that same name on this other slip, which I am now going to tear up. Look at it, but forget you ever saw it, until tomorrow noon. Then the world will know it!"

At that instant a knock sounded on the door of room 713, and Hackett answered. "A boy with a telegram for you," he said. Rollins opened the envelope, glanced at the message, and handed it to Hackett.

"It's from Duncan, in Cleveland. He's telling me the name of the man who worked under him in Cleveland over twenty years ago. See it there! *It's the same man, Bill!* That settles it!"

XV

WILLIAM HACKETT SAT in his chair, silent, motionless, staring into Rollins' eyes. Where smiles had always been, there now were none.

"Bill," said the latter gently, "I wish you'd go over right now, get Doris Allen, and invite her out to lunch. Never mind my luncheon, I'll get some later. After lunch you take her to the address on this card and arrange it so that she may get a look at the man whose name we both saw just now; but don't let her be seen by him.

"Then, and not until then, ask her if she ever sold him any masquerade goods. If she says she has sold a beard to that man, go with her to a notary public and get her affidavit covering the date and all the facts about that sale. Don't let the notary read her statement, but be sure it is absolutely clear and definite.

"While you are doing this, I am going to get Puckers' confession. He'll give it to me now, for I'll prove to him that I know who his master-in-crime has been. After that I'm hoping that Sarah Vasch will be able to talk. I telephoned to Doctor Sherman this morning at the City Hospital, just before you came in. He said Sarah was very weak, but was conscious and rational. She came out of her state of coma late last night. Trot along, Bill! I'm going to do some fingerprint developing on my own account now. I promise to show you a new set of prints of the fingers of Stevens' murderer when you get back here at four o'clock. God bless you, old man! Good luck!"

No sooner had Hackett left the room than Rollins took from the safe certain papers, dusted them lightly and meticulously with lamp-black by means of a fine camel's-hair brush, and blew off the trifling residue. Again opening the safe, he took from it the enlarged finger-print photographs of the fingers of Stevens' slayer, as they had appeared on the paper cone and upon Stevens' memorandum book.

All were identical. The evidence was complete.

Nevertheless, Robert Rollins was fully conscious that the work which he was to undertake in the next four hours was vital to a thorough rounding out of the case.

Assuming the slouch hat, ulster, muffler, spectacles, and cane which he had used when leaving the City Hospital, he hobbled down the six flights of stairs in the Meyers Building, spied a cab from the doorway, hailed it, entered it, and was driven quickly to the Sanford Hotel.

Making himself quietly known to the room-clerk, Atwood, Rollins was soon in the attic room where Stanislaw Brodski sat, handcuffed and—it is to be hoped—meditating on the ill-paid wages of wrongdoing.

Rollins closed the door and locked it. "What's your decision. Brodski? Remember, this is your final chance."

"My God, Mr. Rollins! I can't do it! I dassent do it. I ain't slept a minute since you left. Not a second! It means a rope for me if I squeal, as sure as fate! That guy is a devil! To look at him you'd never think it, but he is. He'd put me on the drop, and nothin' under God's heaven would save me. He's got enough proof that I croaked a guy to swing me forty times—but I didn't croak him. I'll swear it. If I don't squeal, they can't hang me. The worst they can do is jug me for keeps. But if I squeal, I'm gone!"

Rollins pulled the wooden chair beside Puckers' mattress. Facing the fear-ridden visage of Brodski, he began to speak. For fully ten minutes his low earnest tones reached his listener's ears. As the murmured words came from Rollins' lips, their effect on Puckers was amazing. Despair gave place to doubt—and doubt to hope.

Finally from the pitiful wreck of what once had been a man, there arose a being whose withered face shone with a light which had not been there since childhood.

"Oh, my God! Oh, my God! You ain't lyin', are you, Mr. Rollins? Is it true? I can't believe it! Will you swear to God you ain't lyin'? Can I be sure that . . . won't get his claws on me again?" And Puckers looked into Rollins' eyes with the gaze of a child who begs his mother to say: "All is forgiven!"

"Brodski, I swear that every word I've said is true! We'll let you out of here tomorrow noon if you tell us what we ask. After that you'll have three days to put Chicago behind your back, and no one shall 'tail' you till those days are up. From then on you're on your own, and I hope you'll travel straight. Remember! I give you my word that, in the same hour you leave here, the man who has forced you to these acts will go behind steel bars for good. Are you ready? Shall I bring up the typewriter from my room and take down your statement?" And Rollins waited for Brodski's answer.

"Yes, yes! Oh, yes! Get it! I'll tell it all, Mr. Rollins! Every bit of it! I'll sign it! I'll swear to it—an' it'll all be true!" And Puckers sank again upon the mattress, exhausted.

An hour later Manager Henderson and Joe Atwood had witnessed a legal affidavit to a long typewritten statement signed by one Stanislaw Brodski. Atwood, being a notary, affixed his seal, and each page of the document bore signatures of the persons who endorsed it at the end. None but Rollins and Brodski, however, knew what that document contained—an added seal upon the death-warrant of one unfit to live.

As the three departed from that garret room, and before its door was locked, Rollins said to Atwood: "Joe, fix up a real good meal for this chap and bring it up, will you? I'll bet he'll eat it all!" The smile on Puckers' face was almost a thing of beauty. With the assistance of Atwood a cruising taxi was secured to convey the seemingly decrepit Rollins to the City Hospital. Bob had telephoned to Dr. Sherman from the Sanford stating the probable time of his arrival at the institution, and the good doctor was at hand to aid the old gentleman in his tottering journey from the cab to the hospital doors.

When safely in Dr. Sherman's office, with his simple but efficient disguise removed, Rollins inquired: "Have you anyone here, Doctor, who can take down shorthand, and whom you can trust?"

"Yes indeed, Mr. Rollins! Your nurse, Miss Andrews, is a good stenographer, and she is absolutely reliable. Why?"

"I'm hoping that your patient Sarah Vasch will tell all she knows today," said Rollins. "And I want to get every word of it in writing. If Sarah thinks we two are alone in the room, I'm pretty sure she'll open up her heart to me, but I'm afraid she won't if someone else is present. Can you fix it so that Miss Andrews can hear what we say without being seen?"

"That's easy, Mr. Rollins! I'll put up a screen now, near the door of Miss Vasch's room, with a chair behind it. Miss Andrews can slip in, near the back of the screen, with a pad to write on, and she'll be there when I bring you in. How's that?"

"That's splendid, Doctor! Do that, will you, please? And let me know when Miss Andrews is ready."

About fifteen minutes later Rollins was led by Dr. Sherman to the little room where poor old Sarah was convalescing.

"Here's a good friend to see you, Miss Vasch!" said the doctor.

"I'm going to give you ten minutes together. That's all! Don't overexert yourself, now! I hope you have a real nice talk." And Dr. Sherman closed the door.

Sarah Vasch looked up at Bob with a wan smile. "I'm awful glad you came, Mr. Bob!" she whispered. "I see now that it's all my fault, but I didn't know he'd ever do anything like that."

"You mean your half-brother, don't you, Sarah?"

"Yes, Mr. Bob. I used to love him so when he was a little boy! You see, I was ten years older than he was. He went away twenty-seven years ago, Mr. Bob, and after not seeing or hearing from him for all these years I just *had* to tell him everything when we came together again."

"Let's see, it was about five weeks ago when you ran across him, wasn't it, Sarah?"

"Yes! And he was *so* good—except that awful night. We often went to the movies, and he used to take me riding, evenings, and when he did ask about the photograph-pictures and about poor Mr. Stevens and the life insurance, I told him, just as I would tell you."

"When you went to the movies with him that last Sunday, of course you told him how we were trying to find Mr. Stevens in Milwaukee through Harry Stoddard, didn't you, Sarah?"

"Yes, Mr. Bob! And he got real angry and sent me home. I thought it was because I'd asked him what he worked at now. He always was cross when I did that. I thought his name was still Vasch then. I didn't know he'd changed it."

"You poor old girl! I don't blame you for fainting when you realized that it was his voice you had heard over the phone the night Mr. Stevens died."

"Yes! That was it! The shock was awful, Mr. Bob. And the next evening, when I told him I knew it was his voice on the phone because he rolled the *r* in 'Sarah,' and when he dropped an envelope out of his pocket and I saw what his new name was that was written on the envelope, I couldn't help telling him that I was going to tell you all about everything. That's why he did this to me, Mr. Bob! But I don't love him any more now. I couldn't after what he did. But, oh, I hope they don't hang him. Please don't let them!"

"Just a few more questions, Sarah. Do you remember anyone named Brodski that your brother knew in the old days before he first left Chicago?"

"Oh, yes! That's Stan Brodski. He used to go with my brother all the time for a while when they were both young and before my brother left Chicago and disappeared. Mr. Brodski was terrible, I thought. He would do anything, Mr. Bob! He got my brother to help him rob a store once and they got arrested." Rollins made a few more inquiries about Sarah's brother, and then said:

"That's all, Sarah dear! Do you mind if I have Miss Andrews put down what you've told me, and will you sign it when she's got it done? It will help give Nora her father's insurance money, and you know she needs it."

"Yes! Oh, yes! I'll do anything in the world for Miss Nora! God bless you, Mr. Bob! Will Nora come to see me after this, do you think—after all I've done? Oh, I hope she will—but I won't blame her if she don't!"

Rollins stooped and kissed poor Sarah on the forehead.

"Yes, Sarah, yes, Nora will come tomorrow to see you. We're going to be married on Christmas! Good-bye, Sarah! Get well quick, so that you can take care of Nora again—and of me, too!" It was three forty-five when Rollins arrived at the Meyers Building, with the typewritten affidavit of Sarah Vasch, signed, sealed, and witnessed, in his pocket, and one minute later that document was in the office safe.

Another two minutes, and he was on the phone talking to Mrs. Halgard.

"Hello, Aunt Rose! This is your nephew, Bob Rollins. How are you, Auntie? . . . Oh, you've got rheumatism, eh? That's too bad! Who's your doctor, Auntie? . . . Dr. Clayton, eh? That's the same doctor who's treating Edward Folsom, isn't it? . . . Oh, he's got Dr. Alston, has he? Alston's a fine man! I know him well! Why don't you try him? Say, Auntie, don't forget that Christmas date and run away again! Nora sends her love. Good-bye!"

Another telephone call by Rollins:

"Hello! Hello! Is this Dr. Frank Alston? . . . How's your liver today, Doc? This is Bob Rollins talking . . . Yes, Rollins! Say, Doctor, I just heard you were treating Edward Folsom for arthritis. He used to be Alex Stevens' partner, you know, and Nora Stevens is anxious to know how Folsom is getting along . . . Pretty fair, eh? . . . Oh, he's got that too, has he? That isn't so good, is it? . . . He does have to, huh? Gee, poor Folsom has a tough time, doesn't he? Well, it's a funny world! Thanks ever so much. Take care of yourself, old boy! Good-bye!"

Still another telephone connection:

"Is this District Attorney Walsh's office? This is Robert Rollins of the *Leader* calling. May I speak with Mr. Walsh a moment, please? . . . Hello! Is that you, Mr. Walsh? This is Bob Rollins. I've got the biggest thing in your life for you if you can spare an hour for me; I mean it! . . . Yes, bigger than either of those two cases last year. It'll boost your rep higher than a kite, Mr. Walsh. Nothing like it in this man's town for many a moon! . . . 'Where to?' Oh, I'm at 713 Meyers Building. Give six slow knocks on the door when you get here . . . Yes, I know, but I'm not doing it for fun! They've tried to murder me five times in the last nine days; that's the truth. Isn't that reason enough? . . . All right, Mr. Walsh, I'll expect you in fifteen minutes. So long, old man!"

Rollins was just replacing the receiver on the hook when Hackett's knock was heard.

"I've got the goods, Bob," he averred solemnly. "Doris said: 'That's the man who bought that beard' just the instant she saw the . . .! She darn near hollered it loud enough for him to hear, but I shut her off. There ain't no doubt about this thing now, Bob. Here's her sworn statement. By God, if ever a guy deserved hangin', he's the man, an' he'll get it, believe me! How'd you get along, Bob?"

"Read these two affidavits and you'll see, Bill! District Attorney Walsh will be here in fifteen minutes. I'm going to show him all our stuff and put the case entirely in his hands. Take a look at these finger-prints that I developed while you were out. Recognize 'em, Bill?"

"Hell, yes! They're his, damn him! Where'd you get 'em, Bob? Say, they're beauties! Best I ever seen! For the luvva Mike, have you done anything else since I left?"

"Yes, I have; but I'll tell you about that later. Now read these two affidavits from Puckers and Sarah Vasch and shut up!"

For fifteen minutes there was silence. Then came six slow knocks on the door, and the admission of the District Attorney.

Had it not been for a previous long and sincere friendship, established by mutual liking between Rollins and Attorney Edward Walsh, such a meeting as this could not have been arranged. Now, however, the District Attorney had come because his friend Bob Rollins had asked him. That *was* reason enough.

"What's up, Rollins?" asked Walsh. "Hello, Hackett! Here I am right on the dot! Can you tell your tale in an hour? That's all the time I've got."

"That's O.K. And you can be sure it's mighty important business that compelled me to drag you down here today," said Rollins. "I know that the Grand Jury is in session now, and that you are presenting cases and asking indictments. I've got a most important case here that Hackett and I have just completed. All the evidence is in this room. I have three affidavits here and a mass of other proof. You can verify every fact I give you by the evidence right here and now. The whole thing is almost incredible, but it's true. I want you to let me tell my story in my own way and show you my proofs and then I hope you will agree with the plan I have in mind for handling it. The whole thing will take less than an hour. Will you give me that much of your time, Mr. Walsh?" and Rollins stopped.

"Of course I will. I wouldn't have come if I didn't want to help you. That's why I'm here," said the District Attorney. "Go ahead! Spiel out your story, Rollins, and then we'll talk about it."

"All right, Mr. Walsh," replied Rollins. "I'll start now, and Bill, here, can take down what I say. As I mention the specific items of proof, you can scrutinize them. I've got 'em all numbered, and you can pick 'em out in a minute. If you're in doubt on any point, we'll make it clear, and after I'm through, you can study these three affidavits thoroughly and see how they jibe up with my statement. Here goes!"

Fully thirty minutes were consumed by Rollins in telling his story. At Walsh's request the dictated report was to be transcribed as if told in the third person singular.

When Bob's voice ceased, the District Attorney's face was very pale, but his lips were fixed in a firm line, and never was stern resolve more apparent than in the set of his jaws.

"Rollins," said he, "you've sewed this thing up like a master! There isn't a loop-hole for that devil to crawl out of. I couldn't have believed such a thing possible, but I've got to admit it is so. It's iron-clad! It's air-tight, bullet-proof! A lawyer who couldn't win a case with this evidence would be an imbecile. I don't mind saying, too, that it's going to boost my reputation a lot. Now what do you want me to do?"

"This is what I want," said Rollins. "I want you to shelve everything else and bring me before the Grand Jury at ten o'clock sharp tomorrow morning. You can read this report if you like, and show my evidence to the jurors, but keep every soul out of that room except the jury and ourselves. The instant you get a true bill, you swear out a warrant, but pick your judge. As soon as we have the warrant, call in Sergeant O'Connor and one other officer to execute it. O'Connor can make the arrest downtown. He'll find this man easily enough. Finally, I hope you'll be near by when the warrant is executed, and I'd like Hackett and myself to be not far away. How about it, Mr. Walsh?"

The District Attorney thought a moment. "All right, Rollins! We'll fix it just that way. You be at the jury-room at nine forty-five. I'll be there waiting. I know they'll vote a true bill on that evidence, but be sure you have it *all!* Hackett can get Heywood to dig up those old finger-prints in the Brodski-Vasch case at the Police Bureau. We've got all the rest. Of course you'll bring Miss Allen and Flood and Donovan along to testify.

"Another thing, Rollins! O'Connor and the other officer must be warned to have their guns handy when they make the arrest. I'm not much at foreseeing trouble, but this man is just as likely to shoot his way out as not. If he finds he can't do that, he'll bump himself off if there's the least chance. Let's make certain he has no chance! And be sure we get his gun, to test it later with the bullet that hit you. Hold on! You boys had better bring all this evidence to my office at nine o'clock tonight and we'll go over all the details.

"Well, Rollins, I don't fancy the job we have on hand for tomorrow, but that's our duty, and if ever a man deserved what he's going to get, this devil is that man. George Vasch's days are surely numbered"; and, with a very thoughtful face, the District Attorney shook hands and left.

As soon as Walsh had departed, Rollins turned to Hackett and remarked:

"You heard what Walsh said about those old police records. I wish you'd call up Heywood, your assistant in the Police Bureau, and get him to dig up the photos and finger-prints of that old burglary case which Brodski and Vasch were indicted for twenty-seven years ago. You remember Sarah Vasch spoke about it in her affidavit. Heywood will do it for you, and you're still on the Police Department rolls. Tell him to phone as soon as he locates them, and then you can go over and get them. We've got to make a microscopic comparison of those old finger-prints with those which we've got of Stevens' murderer. That will be the last nail in this devil's coffin, and *no* power on earth can save him. While Heywood is hunting them up, you can type that report so as to have it all done before we get to the District Attorney's office at nine o'clock."

"O.K." replied Hackett; "I'll call up Heywood now"—and he did.

Just as Bill had started typing, he inquired: "Say, Bob, what in hell is the reason that Edward Folsom wore gloves when Shorty gave him that telegram and—probably—when he wrote them letters? If I could find out that, I'd be happy; damned if I wouldn't."

"I can tell you, Bill."

"For the luvva Mike, how did you find it out, Bob?"

"By telephone," answered Rollins.

XVI

As Rollins replied to Hackett's last question, he glanced at his watch and noted that it was precisely five fifteen. For a moment silence intervened. Then came a rumbling growl and a vociferous "Huh!" from his partner which seemed to indicate that Bob's answer had not been entirely satisfactory to the normally genial gentleman who had received it.

"Well, well, what's the matter, Bill? What are you so grouchy about?" inquired Rollins, with a smile.

"Grouchy, hell! Who wouldn't have a grouch when he gets half an answer like that? Found it out by telephone, did ya? Of course you did. Pretty near every damn thing you've doped out about this whole case has been done by telephone. Whenever you wanta learn somep'n, it's you to the telephone, and in two minutes you've got the answer. I'll bet you ain't walked twenty blocks in the last ten days. I'm not blamin' you, Bob. I'd give a million dollars if I could do it. I'm envyin' you, that's all. Hell, there's that cussed phone ringin' again. Lemme have it, will ya?"

"Wait a minute! I'll answer it," interrupted Rollins. "Hello! . . . Whom are you calling? What number did you want? . . . Are you sure that is the right number? What department do you wish to speak to? . . . No, I'm sorry; this isn't Mandel Brothers. I'm afraid you have the wrong connection. Good-bye!"

Rollins sat for a moment thinking. Then reaching for the telephone directory, he leafed its pages rapidly, found a certain subscriber, and turned to his partner.

"Bill, look at this! Here's the phone number of Mandel Brothers. Everybody in Chicago knows they close up for the day at five o'clock. You know that the phone number of this office is Main 3764, and that number doesn't bear the slightest resemblance to Mandel Brothers' number. Nothing like it at all. Yet here's a man who *says* he wants to get the glove department of Mandel Brothers. When I ask him what phone number he's calling, he hesitates nearly half a minute and then says he wanted to get Main 3762. Anybody who was not totally deaf would know that he was trying to disguise his voice, and when he rolled his *r*'s on that last word of his—'Sorry'—I knew that voice as well as I know yours. I'm telling you, Bill Hackett, that no man or telephone operator could be so far out of the way on a phone number as that; and I'm also informing you that we've just received a phone call from George Vasch—the man who killed Alexander Stevens."

"My God, Bob, I can't believe it. But why did—?"

"Think a minute, Bill," interrupted Rollins. "This man Vasch wanted to find out if you and I were here in this office. *That's* why he called—and now he knows I'm here because, like a brainless ass, I made no attempt to disguise my voice. I'll bet you anything you like, Bill Hackett, that Vasch has been calling up the City Hospital and trying to learn something about Sarah or me from that end. Wait a minute and I'll call the hospital and see." Two minutes later Rollins had his former nurse, Miss Andrews, on the wire.

"Hello, Miss Andrews! Do you know who this is? . . . Sure, that's a good guess. You hit it right the first time. It's Rollins. Say, Miss Andrews, I'm pretty sure the gentleman who sent those poisoned chocolates to Sarah Vasch has been telephoning to the hospital and trying to learn something about her condition and about mine. Did you get any call in the last . . . You did? Tell me all about it, please. Wait a minute till I get some paper and put it down."

It was fully five minutes before Rollins hung up the receiver, and his notes of Miss Andrews' statement filled two sheets of paper.

"Here we are, Bill!" he said. "Miss Andrews tells me that somebody representing himself to be Eleanor Stevens' brother (who doesn't exist) called up about an hour and a half ago and tried to pump her about Sarah Vasch's condition and asked when he or Miss Stevens could see her. Miss Andrews suspected there was something wrong because she reasoned that if *my* condition was to be kept secret, the same thing should logically apply to Sarah Vasch's. She told this man that Sarah was still in a state of coma—that her death might occur at any moment and that no visitors were permitted.

"Mind you, Bill, I hadn't said a word to her or Doctor Sherman about concealing Sarah's true condition. I forgot it, like a damned crazy fool. Only for Miss Andrews' brains and foresight, George Vasch would be putting Chicago behind him this minute as fast as wings or wheels could carry him. He knows mighty well that if Sarah Vasch ever recovers and tells her story, he's a gone goose. You heard me tell Miss Andrews to guard Sarah from the access of any person on earth except Doctor Sherman and herself, for Vasch would kill Sarah in an instant if he gets a chance. I told Miss Andrews that, too.

"But that isn't all, Bill. About half an hour after that first inquiry Vasch telephones the hospital about *me*. He represented himself to Miss Andrews as Ralph Bostock. He wanted to know how I was getting on and would like to talk to me. This time, of course, there wasn't the least doubt in Miss Andrews' mind as to the call being a trick, and she told this bogus Bostock that I was in very serious condition and could not be seen. She wanted to call me up here and tell me about the two calls, but didn't dare to for fear she might make a wrong move and upset things. Listen, Bill, don't you ever intimate to anybody again that I've got brains. If I had one tenth the brains of Miss Andrews, George Vasch would be behind the bars this minute.

"Here we've been showing a light in this room for at least an hour or so almost every night, especially last night. Vasch knows that I'm the only man who has the key to the laboratory and the right to be here. All he's got to do is to walk down our back alley half a block, look up, see our light—and he knows I'm on the job. I think last night was the first time he has done it, or I shouldn't be alive now—and that telephone call absolutely *proves* to me that Vasch is determined I shall *not* be alive tomorrow morning."

"Sufferin' Moses! We *are* darn fools, ain't we?" vociferated Hackett. "We'd better get our stuff together and sneak out of here while the goin's good. I can write up this report somewhere else just as well as here, and our evidence is all ready to pack up right now. I say, let's go!"

"No, Bill! I don't think that's the way," replied Rollins musingly. "If we act abnormally now, Vasch will jump the town tonight sure. We'll never get him. If we stay here, turn on the lights as usual, and let him carry out his plan, he'll think we're unsuspicious and—"

"For Heaven's sake!" interrupted Hackett. "Stay here an' get murdered? Not me!"

"I don't propose to be murdered any more than you do, Bill. What I'm trying to do is to foresee how he can possibly bump us off tonight and still keep himself safe. Can you see any way, Bill? Remember, Vasch is no fool! Far from it!"

Hackett pondered a few moments and then remarked: "I only see two ways, Bob. He might sneak up here after all the offices are closed, play some trick to get us to open the door, and then fill us full of bullets. Then he could—"

"Wait a minute, Bill! Look at the chances he'd be taking! He'd have to walk up and would almost surely be seen by the watchman and perhaps by some of the tenants. The noise of exploding bullets would be heard all over the building. He'd have to run down six flights of stairs after doing his job and would very likely be seen or stopped. Finally, suppose he couldn't trick us into opening that door. Mighty slim chance for his bullets doing any harm through that three-inch oak. Better lay aside that plan for the time being, anyhow!"

"I guess you're right, Bob! But, say, listen! He could sure lay for us both when we come out and shoot us up then! Yes, sir! That's the dope—"

"Maybe you're right, Bill, but I don't believe it. He'd have to wait outside for us, perhaps several hours or maybe all night. He can't know when we are going to come out or how many people are going to be in the street when he starts shooting. Remember, too, he's got to kill us *both*—stone dead. If either of us lives half an hour, we could tell all our stuff, and Vasch would be done for, sure. Besides that, he must make his get-away after this double killing, and that's no easy job with Clark Street only a hundred and fifty yards away. Maybe, too, you and I might leave this building separately. He couldn't shoot one of us and then hang round and wait for the other. Remember, the only place where he can be sure of getting us *both* is in this building or right close to it. Have you got any other suggestions, Bill?"

"I can't think of another darn thing, Bob. Vasch couldn't shoot us through the windows there, for they're made of frosted glass and he couldn't see us. The building across the alley is only five stories high, and the roof is fifteen feet below our windows. I give up, Bob. Can you figure it out?"

"As far as I can see," said Rollins, "there's only one method on earth that Vasch could be sure of bumping us both off at the same time, and that is by means of some kind of bomb. If he could somehow project an explosive bomb or a poison-gas bomb into this shop, he'd be fairly certain of doing a thorough job. You can see that he couldn't do it from the hallway, but he might propel a bomb through one of those windows if it weren't for those steel bars. They are only six inches apart, and if he threw a bomb toward the window, it might hit a bar, bounce off, and explode outside.

"The question is, then, how could Vasch be *sure* his bomb came through the window and exploded in this room? I've racked my brains and can only think of one way, so here's my dope:

"When I was a boy in the country, we kids used to stick a green apple on the end of a flexible switch and throw that apple half a block by swinging it overhand toward a target. The roof of this building is only about three feet above the top of those windows. If I had a bomb tied on to the end of a four-foot willow switch, I could lie down on the roof, gauge the exact distance, release the safety-catch on my bomb, and then swing it slam-bang between those bars through the glass and into this room. Of course, the switch would go along with the bomb, but that wouldn't matter. By the time the bomb went off, I should be sixty feet away anyhow, and in three minutes I'd be where no one could catch me. There's the only *sure* method, Bill, and I'll bet every dollar I've got that George Vasch has doped this thing out precisely as I've done it."

"Bully for you, Bob! You've got it or I'm a dumb-bell," cried Hackett. "All we gotta do is wait for him on the roof and nail him. We can leave the lights turned on here, hide behind a chimney, and jump him when he gets ready to do his stuff. That's a pip, Bob! Come on, let's go."

"Hold on, Bill! Wait a minute! Our chimney is about seventy-five feet from the roof gutters. He'll have a flash-light with him sure. We don't know whether he'll get on to the roof through this scuttle. I think not. He'll probably go up through one of the adjoining buildings, which are all about the same height as ours. He'll spot us sure before we can get to him. No, sir, it won't do! He'd probably shoot one or both of us and we'd lose him. If we call in outside help, we'll *never* get him."

"All right, Bob, you win! For the luvva Mike, give us your plan. Seems like I can't get nothin' right. But, for God's sake, hurry. Mebbe that . . . is on the roof right now."

"No fear of that," said Rollins soothingly. "He won't start anything until after our light goes on and he somehow makes sure we're both here in this laboratory. Here's my scheme. Tell me what you think of it"; and Rollins explained.

It was now nearly seven o'clock, and as Hackett strode down the hall toward the elevator, not a light gleamed in any room on that floor. The elevator signal was answered by John Harvey, the watchman, to whom the comrades explained that burglars might attempt entrance into room 713, and that no one but tenants should be permitted to enter the building under any pretense.

"Leave this elevator up here on the seventh floor, Harvey, will you?" said Rollins. "Mr. Hackett and I might have to use it quickly. I'll be responsible, and here's a dollar to prove it. No, we shan't need any help. It may not happen, anyhow, and if it does we're all ready for the gentlemen. Good luck, Harvey. If you hear any noise up here, don't mind it. See you later."

Rapidly returning to the laboratory, Rollins switched on the lights, while Hackett carried the small package of affidavits, photos, and other evidence to the elevator. The key to room 713 was inserted in the outside keyhole, the door was left a few inches ajar, and the comrades stood together in the hallway, peering through the narrow opening.

Less than five minutes elapsed before the telephone rang. Rollins answered the call. "Yes, this is Main 3764 . . . Oh, you wanted Main 3964. Too bad! I'm afraid you have the wrong number. That's all right! I'm sorry, too! Good-bye."

Rollins hung up the phone and joined his comrade in the hallway. "It's Vasch!" he said hoarsely. "Same rolly *r*'s in his 'Sorry!' He's on the job and there'll be hell to pay here in about ten minutes. The instant you see one of those windows smash, lock this door, streak it for the elevator, and down we go. On your toes, Bill! She's coming as sure as the Lord made little apples."

Slowly the moments dragged. Four! Five! Six! Seven! *Crash!* The upper window-light was shattered. Squarely to the center of the floor rolled an oval metal object slightly larger than a baseball with, apparently, a four-foot piece of buggy whip attached.

The door of 713 was locked instantly and the comrades were about ten feet from the elevator door when *bang!* came an explosion which caused floors, doors, and transoms to quiver and a few panes of glass to shower in fragments on the floor.

"Down we go!" shouted Hackett as they entered the elevator; and down they went.

In the ground-floor lobby sat John Harvey placidly reading his evening paper. "Anything doing yet, Misther Rrrollins?" said he, clearly evidencing the fact that he had not heard the explosion.

"Listen, Harvey, they tackled us, but their shots went wide and they got away over the roof. One of their bullets hit a little jar of explosives in the laboratory and smashed a few things, but I'll pay all damages when I see Donovan tomorrow morning. Keep your face shut to *everybody* about this, and you get a five-spot coming tomorrow night. Is it a go, Harvey?"

"Surrely, Misther Rrroilins! Not a wurrrd out of me. Good night!"

Twenty minutes later Rollins and Hackett were alone with District Attorney Walsh in the latter's office.

"Well, well," said Walsh, "you're quite a bit ahead of time, aren't you? That's good! Did you get that report typed, Hackett? Say, what's the matter with you two fellows, anyhow? You both look as if you'd had a shot of dope. Did something happen?"

"I'll say it did!" responded Hackett. "Just another little would-be murder by Mr. George Vasch that didn't quite come off. Shall I tell Mr. Walsh about it, Bob?"

"Sure, go ahead, Bill! You know as much about it as I do." Briefly but comprehensively Hackett then reviewed the events of the past three hours. In conclusion he remarked:

"I dunno what was in that bomb, Mr. Walsh. I'm betting, though, there were slugs enough to wipe out an army. We didn't feel like lingerin' around long enough to find out. Anyhow, I'm sure of one thing. Bob and I would both be playin' harps right now if we'd been in the room when that damn pineapple went off. I've served one enlistment in the Marines, an' I know somep'n about bombs, but this sure was one peach. I'll bet little old room 713 is a total wreck right this minute."

"But," said the District Attorney, "what I can't understand is how you both anticipated the precise method of this attack. How did you know that it would happen tonight? What made you believe that the bomb would come through the laboratory window just when and where it did?"

"Say, listen, Mr. Walsh; this guy Rollins here has got old Mrs. Cassandra beat to a crisp. You give him three or four triflin' facts that nobody else would even think about, an' he'll prophesy to beat hell—and every damn thing will come out exactly the way he predicts it. Yes, sir! Every bit of evidence in this case Bob has reasoned out just like he did this attack tonight. When he explains, you can see just how he did it, but you can't do it yourself to save your life. Anyhow *I* can't, and, believe me, I've tried. Say, can I use that typewriter over there, Mr. Walsh? I can type this report in about twenty minutes, an' then you'll have all the evidence—every bit of it. The rest of it is in this package here."

"Surely! Go ahead and use it, Hackett," said Walsh. "And, say, Rollins, what does Hackett mean by this talk of his about predictions and reasoning and so forth? I don't just get it."

"Pay no attention to Bill, Mr. Walsh. He's just doing a little exaggerating to boost me, that's all. The indications all pointed to an immediate last desperate move on the part of Vasch to put Hackett and me out of business for keeps, and that bomb was the only way he could be sure of doing it. We knew that Vasch had a certain bunch of figures to add up. We added up that same bunch and got the same result a little quicker than he did. If Vasch hadn't used just the same figures we did, and if he had omitted something or made a mistake in his addition, nobody knows how things would have come out."

"Frankly, Rollins, I still don't see precisely what you mean."

"All right, let's see if I can make it plainer," said Rollins. "Suppose two good meteorologists observe a hundred sunsets and make predictions on tomorrow's weather. If they both use the same weather maps with the same barometer readings, the same wind direction and velocity, and so on, they'll both locate the same 'lows' and make the same weather prediction. Now do you see what I mean?"

"Yes, I believe I do. But suppose Vasch was a man of poor reasoning faculties and low intellect—"

"Then," interrupted Rollins, "he would probably have shot it out with us somewhere on the street, and maybe all three of us would be dead right now. All his past actions have indicated a determination to protect *himself.* Every move he has made shows that determination as a motive. That's why I figured he'd still formulate his plans with self-protection as one of his main purposes."

"All right, Rollins! We'll talk this over some other time. Now, while Hackett is finishing that report, I'd like to ask you some questions regarding a few things I'm not clear about. In asking them I shall speak of George Vasch by his correct name and not the alias he has used for twenty-seven years.

"All right! Ask all the questions you like, Mr. Walsh."

"Well," said the District Attorney, "I know that Sarah Vasch is the half-sister of George Vasch and that she was a sort of foster-mother to him for about ten years when he was a young man. Can't you explain that relationship a little more clearly?"

"That's easy!" replied Rollins. "Sarah was the daughter of Theodore Vasch's first wife. Her mother died when she was born. A few years later Theodore Vasch married again. His second wife was Loretta Folsom, Edward Folsom's elder sister. George Vasch is the son of Theodore and Loretta. He is eleven years younger than Sarah and he is a nephew of Edward Folsom."

"Good! Now I see! Has Edward Folsom any other relations living, Rollins?"

"Oh yes! He has another nephew, a sister, and a brother, but none of them are mixed up in this case."

"Another thing, Rollins. After Vasch and Brodski were arrested for that Chicago burglary twenty-seven years ago and we got their finger-prints, did Vasch go direct to Cleveland and take his present alias then?"

"Yes. He worked under Duncan three years. Then he took another job there along his present line for fourteen years. Ten years ago he came to Chicago, as you know. Brodski's statement says Vasch assumed his present alias for two reasons—first, because of the old burglary charge; second, because he hated the name Vasch. It sounded foreign."

"All right, Rollins! One more question and I'll quit. How many people besides ourselves know that the real name of this man is George Vasch and not the name he has used during all these years?"

"Only three persons, Mr. Walsh. Sarah Vasch knows and makes affidavit to it. Stanislaw Brodski does likewise, for Vasch practically forced him by threats to attempt to murder me. Edward Folsom knows, but his respect for the memory of his sister Loretta (Vasch's mother) keeps him silent. Stevens never knew anything about Vasch's past life except that Vasch was Folsom's nephew. Is that all, Mr. Walsh?"

"Yes, and thank you sincerely," said the District Attorney. "How are you coming along with that report, Hackett?"

"All done! Just finished the last sheet, and she's a pippin, if I do say it," commented that worthy as he placed the papers on the office desk. "But listen, Mr. Walsh! Do we have to wait for an indictment to arrest this hell-cat after all he's done? I haven't figured up how many crimes he's committed, but if they can jail a guy for spittin' on the sidewalk, why do we have to wait until tomorrow to put the clamps on this—?"

"We don't," retorted the District Attorney, "and we're not going to. Judge Withers is holding night court session right now, and Sergeant O'Connor is on night duty this week. I'll swear out a warrant right away and have O'Connor serve it as quick as he can reach Vasch's apartment. I'll put through the indictment tomorrow morning. We'll have George Vasch behind the bars before twelve o'clock tonight as sure as my name is Walsh. Step out in the ante-room for a few minutes, will you, gentlemen, while I get busy?"

In less than half an hour Sergeant O'Connor, holding in his hand a warrant for the arrest of George Vasch, alias — —, stood very soberly before Attorney Walsh, awaiting his final instructions.

"Are you sure you don't need any help, Sergeant?" asked Walsh. "You know what this man Vasch has done and what he's likely to do. Hadn't you better take another officer with you?"

"No, sir!" replied O'Connor. "Another man would only be in the way. I happen to know this man lives on the fifth floor of a South Side elevator apartment. I'll take a taxi to within fifty feet of the building, walk upstairs, ring the apartment bell, and snap the cuffs on him before I say a damn word. If he ain't at home, I'll go down and wait across the street till he comes in. I'll get him. Don't you worry. The—"

"May I ask a question, Mr. Walsh?" interrupted Rollins.

"Certainly. What is it?"

"Would you object if Hackett and I drove down in my sedan and parked my car half a block or so behind the Sergeant's taxi? We won't show up or interfere, I'll promise, and we may possibly be of some help after Vasch is arrested."

"How about it, O'Connor?" asked Walsh.

"O.K. Come along, you fellers! But don't you get any closer to me than half a block after you see me stop. Let's see, what time is it? Ten fifteen eh? Where's your car, Rollins?"

"Just outside this building, Sergeant. I got it out of the garage and drove downtown here while Mr. Walsh was arranging the details of this affair. Come on, Bill, let's go!"

XVII

AT TEN O'CLOCK on Tuesday evening, November 28, in a small high-class South Side apartment, George Vasch sat thinking. There were four rooms in the flat which he occupied, and upon the door facing the elevator was inscribed: "APARTMENT E-5." His domicile comprised a living-room, two bedrooms, kitchen, and bath. The front windows faced the street. A service stairway was located just beyond the rear hallway. The rear room contained a kitchenette, small refrigerator, dumb-waiter, and other light housekeeping appliances.

Vasch sat in an easy chair beside one of the living-room windows. No lights illuminated the apartment. A small table, upon which were smoking-utensils, stood beside him. The ash-tray was heaped with dead cigarette butts only half-consumed. No sooner had the smoker taken a few puffs from a fresh cigarette than he cast it aside and lighted another. The fingers of the man's right hand drummed ceaselessly on the table, and his nervous eyes were never still. For more than a week his brain had scarcely once relaxed.

Across his mind now floated a picture of the happenings of three hours ago. A telephone call, an exhausting race up seven long flights of stairs, a breathless run across two flat roofs, with scrambling climbs over their low dividing walls. He saw himself lying flat upon a roof-edge gazing downward at a window only a few feet below. Through frosted panes a light was gleaming there. Then came an upward swing of his right arm, succeeded by swift and instant downward motion—a shattering of glass—a leap to his feet, a swift retracing of his former route, and—*boom!*—an explosion which shocked his tense-strung nerves even though he was over fifty feet away.

Before his eyes passed a mental vision of his hasty yet careful progress to the street, to the elevated, and thence, southward, to the room in which he sat. Not for an instant did he bring to memory a chemist's laboratory wherein lay two dead men who would surely never trouble him again. That job was done. Let it be forgotten. "Sarah is the only danger now," he muttered. "I'll soon fix her."

And now, lightning-like, swept through his mind a flitting series of pictures of the past: Sarah in ecstasy at meeting him after so many years; her trusting revelations and answers to his queries; the tale of Stevens' inventive triumph; the blinding thought that millions waited for his taking; the plan—so deftly aided toward consummation through Stevens' own request that Vasch himself should intervene with his uncle, Edward Folsom, should pacify Folsom, and thus prevent him from annoying Stevens further.

"I'll talk to Uncle Ed and make him reasonable. Then I'll meet you here in your laboratory at nine fifteen tonight and tell you how he acts," he had said to Stevens on that fatal Saturday morning. How easy it was for a brainy man to lure a trusting fool to his death!

What a masterly plan he had created and how lucky he had been with most of it! No one in the Meyers Building lobby when he had entered, disguised as his uncle! A lavatory two doors from Stevens' office wherein to remove or replace his false beard. A dozing watchman to deceive when he departed. A made-to-order suicide message handed to him without effort by Rose Halgard! A genuine business card placidly waiting for him to use and impersonate Donovan while buying that Vandyke beard and wig! No one on earth except his uncle was aware that Vasch had ever met or talked to Stevens. Ah, he must not overlook the luckiest stroke of all—when Stevens, memo book in hand, had opened his safe and shown Vasch the formulas cards on that first visit! How could any sane man resist a gift of millions?

As to the killing of Stevens, why bother his head about it? With those gloves constantly on his hands two or three minutes after Stevens died; with his precaution to wipe off everything he could possibly have touched, and his forethought to carry away every scrap of litter, the job of getting rid of Stevens was almost perfection. Only three little mistakes: smoking that accursed cigarette and possibly spilling ashes; not putting on his chamois gloves the instant Stevens died; and being unable to clean the desk under the corpse without disturbing it. "Hell! A man can't think of everything. Nobody could possibly notice those trifles," he thought. "Anyhow, that note and the key trick clinched things."

As the mind of Alexander Stevens' murderer recalled these and other recent happenings, his glance wandered toward the hall closet, wherein a small wardrobe-trunk reposed.

"Damnation!" Vasch leaped to his feet and paced the floor like a maniac, while oaths poured in torrents from his lips.

"All for nothing! All for nothing!"—Thousands of times in the past ten days those words had hammered themselves upon his brain.

What an imbecile he had been to destroy that sixth card just to make sure that no one but himself could ever reproduce Stevens' color-process. He had left the other cards in the safe after altering the formulae, to prevent suspicion of robbery. Why had he not pocketed that last card instead of tearing it up and throwing it away? With that card—or its photograph—in his hands, he would be master of millions within two years. But now the two films of that card were black.

Surely he had used a camera enough to know that films were sometimes defective or were ruined by over-exposure. The other formula-films in the trunk were perfect; without a flaw and as readable as print. Every chemical symbol upon them was precisely as Stevens had recorded it—but what was their value now? The missing card, with its description of the rotating color-screen and the essential wave-lengths of light for printing, was indispensable—and was gone.

Could he not somehow pick up the scattered bits of that sixth card? Even if it required weeks of search, might it not be done?

Ah, but he had been so eager for its absolute destruction! Its fragments had been dribbled from his fingers, piece by piece! He had scattered them from a car vestibule along the structure of the L. There must be miles between the first and last fragments. A thousand men could not recover the torn pieces of that card—and without it the color-photo formulae were useless!

"All for nothing!" Again those maddening words! Would they never cease?

Yet was there no hope of rediscovering the light-intensities and details of that printing process?

Before his eyes drifted a picture of the intricate figures he had noted in his brief glimpse of card number six shortly after he had poisoned its owner. With such symbols he had never dealt. The abstruse directions on that annihilated card could never be reconstructed save by some expert technician, after months of experiment.

But what had caused this damning fiasco? Why should the last two films exposed in Stevens' office be absolutely black when developed? Had he by some accident turned the reflectors in such a way that their rays directly penetrated the lens and left card number six in shadow? Yes, it must be so!

"All for nothing!" Again that hideous refrain!

For two rolls of films, now utterly useless to any living man, he had wiped out one life and had been forced to plan other murders almost daily. For a few valueless scraps of celluloid he had deprived the world of untold beauty, throughout perhaps all future time. Again that maddening lilt! "All for nothing!"

And what of himself? What of his own safety? Why, the very first evening after he had bumped off Stevens, Sarah had gossiped to him the news that Rollins was trying to locate Stevens in Milwaukee, through Stoddard, and that he also was sure of the exact time of the phone call Vasch had made from Stevens' office. Damn the luck! He must put that reporter underground to shut his mouth. Punctured tires would force Rollins to walk to the L, and a smashed skull would do the rest.

What had Vasch got out of that encounter? A frightful knee-jab in the groin, which had half-crippled him for a week. The damn thing hurt him even now!

And that cursed idiot Puckers! Twice the shrimp had tried to kill Rollins, had failed both times, and now had disappeared. Not a trace of Puckers anywhere!

And then that awful night with Sarah! To think that his own sister, Sarah Vasch, would squeal! And if Sarah told Rollins, the game was up! What recourse had he save to kill her? Sarah Vasch must not go home alive, no matter what the risk to him! And yet, probably because of her piled-up mass of hair, his crashing blow had not been fatal, nor had the poisoned candy later. Vasch had been forced to watch the hospital constantly for news. Maybe, though, she might be dead *now!*

And that night near the hospital entrance, when he saw Rollins coming out, along with that witless Hackett! What had Rollins learned from Sarah? Vasch dared not wait to ascertain. Surely, with Rollins only thirty feet away, and himself, a good shot, behind a tree, he could put a bullet through that snooper's heart and settle his spying for good.

But it hadn't worked. Rollins was now back on the job again in that cursed laboratory. The lights proved that.

Damn that Rollins! Right from the start that hellish reporter had stuck his nose into this mess! Probably that suicide clause in the Marathon policy had spurred him on! With Rollins daffy over Stevens' daughter, that was doubtless the reason. If he had only known about that policy before— "Hell! A man can't possibly foresee every trifle!"

Well, anyhow, he was done with Rollins now, even if that fat prussic-acid cigarette had somehow fluked. "Who smoked that thing, I wonder," he mused.

"Let's see! Nearly eleven o'clock." Brrrr! "Now who in hell is ringing that damn bell at this time of night? It's the hall button, too. I'll just take a look out of the window and see what's on the street! Huh! Only a yellow taxi across the road and two doors north. And there's a brown sedan up in the next block."

Brrrr! "There's that bell again. I reckon it must be Sam with the cigarettes that I sent him out for an hour ago. Still, I'd better play safe and take something with me. Nobody's going to catch *me* sleeping at the switch. I'll just slip this slung shot up my right sleeve and keep my gun in my right hip pocket"—and George Vasch, placing his left palm against the door-jamb, grasped the door-knob with his right hand (in which the handle of the slung shot rested) and swung inward the fatal door.

Snap!—Instantly upon the opening of the portal the brawny right hand of Sergeant O'Connor shot through the aperture and clasped a steel handcuff around the left wrist of Vasch as the latter's palm rested against the door-casing.

"I arrest you—"

Smash!—The heavy-laden slung shot, impelled with terrific force by the sinewy right arm of George Vasch, crashed against O'Connor's upper forehead, and a second blow was delivered before the Sergeant's senseless body sank motionless to the floor.

Vasch stood for an instant gazing on that unconscious form, then stooped to search the body for the handcuff key. At that moment the sound of the uprising elevator became louder and Vasch hastily dragged O'Connor's body through the doorway into the apartment, closed the door, and commenced to search the body.

"Dead as a herring! Now for that key! Where in hell does he keep it? My God, I can't find it anywhere! And he's got some other officer down here with him as sure as hell! I dassent wait. They'll sure be here in a minute. Stay there, you ..." and Vasch ruthlessly kicked the unstirring form of O'Connor on the rug beside him.

"The back stairway! My only chance!" he muttered. "I'll have to get this hellish cuff off later. God, how that groin of mine hurts me! I must have strained it somehow. I can hardly walk."

Seizing his cap from the rack in the hall, Vasch painfully dragged himself down the four flights of service stairs, opened the side door of the building, and cautiously hugged its walls until he reached the front corner. Save for a manifestly empty yellow taxi across the way and a brown sedan at the northern corner of the block no vehicle was in sight and only two or three pedestrians.

"O'Connor must have come down alone in that taxi," he muttered. "I'll have to con that driver and get him to take me uptown. I couldn't walk a block with this cursed groin of mine. Damn that Rollins! He's the —— that gave me this."

Slowly crossing the road, Vasch approached the taxi standing beneath the street-light and stopped beside the driver's seat.

"The man who came down with you isn't going back for a couple of hours," he said. "You can drive me uptown to the Polk Street depot and then come back for him."

Robert Twitchett, taxi-driver and personal friend of Sergeant James O'Connor, straightened up in his seat, tossed his cigarette through the side window, and looked at George Vasch.

"All right!" said he. "You just go back and git O'Connor and let him tell me that! I'm taking orders from him"; and he pulled out a fresh package of cigarettes from his pocket, selected one, and lighted it.

"I tell you that O'Connor isn't going back uptown now," insisted the would-be passenger as he climbed into the cab. "Here's five dollars for your fare down here and back. The Sergeant will call another taxi when he's ready to go home."

"Say, listen, feller!" growled Twitchett. "What kind of a game is this? One minute you tell me that I gotta come back for Jim, an' the next minute you're lettin' on that he'll call another taxi when he's ready. Who in hell are you, anyhow? Jim told me he was comin' down here to make a pinch and I reckon *you're* the bird he was after. I'll see you in hell before—"

"Take a good look at this," commanded Vasch as he thrust a huge gun into the face of the astounded driver. "You turn this damn cab round and drive north like hell or I'll fill you so full of lead you'll drop through the floor. Step on it now— and rip off that top mirror. There, before you turn!—That's

it! Now give her the gas and remember what's jabbing you
between your shoulders. You won't have any more guts than
a fried chicken if you give me any more of your lip."

Robert Twitchett was a brave man, but he was also a wise
one. With eight inches of cold steel pointed at his back, there
was no recourse save obedience. He swung the cab round,
ripped off the narrow mirror, threw it into the street as he
passed the parked sedan, and drove swiftly northward.

While these incidents were in progress, Rollins and Hackett, who had arrived at their present location only a half-
minute later than O'Connor, sat in the front seat of the dark-
ened sedan and waited.

They dared not show any lights, nor dared they smoke. Not
for an instant did their eyes stray from the tall apartment
building in the middle of the block across the way.

"Jim's been gone a helluva while," remarked Hackett. "I
hope that damn cuss is at home. Say, Bob, see that bird
sneakin' along the side between those buildings? It ain't Jim,
is it?"

"No! He's got a cap on," said Rollins. "Look! He's crossing over toward Jim's cab and talking to the driver. Looks
like they're having an argument. See! He's getting in! I don't
like the looks of this thing a bit, Bill. What do you think?"

"Somep'n wrong, sure, Bob! Better start your engine! See,
the cab's turning this way. Hey! Bob! Look there! The
driver's thrown out his mirror. See it glitter! By God, *Vasch
has got away!* That's what has happened. Swing her round,
Bob, and go after 'em like hell. They're half a block ahead of
us now."

Despite Rollins' best efforts the yellow taxi was nearly two
blocks in advance of the sedan before he could make the turn
and was speeding northward.

With accelerator jammed down to the floor, Rollins was
getting every possible ounce of power from his engine, and
soon they were within a block of the car ahead. The street
was well-nigh free from traffic, with no lights to delay them.
Success now seemed only to depend on speed.

Slowly they drew nearer. Now less than a hundred feet separated the racing cars. *Crack! Zip!* A bullet pierced the sedan's windshield, and both comrades felt the breeze of its passing.

"Hit you, Bill?" questioned Rollins.

"Nope! All O.K., Bob! Step on it!"

Crack! Another bullet from the taxi, with no apparent result.

But now, for some unexplainable reason, the sedan was losing ground. Two minutes later it was nearly two blocks behind. Then, slowing up slightly, the orange cab turned to the left, straightened out in a westerly direction, and was no longer visible.

Meanwhile as Robert Twitchett, in obedience to orders, enforced at pistol point, threw out his mirror, George Vasch heard the growling whir of the starter in the sedan which they were just passing. A moment later Vasch perceived through the rear window that the sedan had turned and was speeding northward, pursuing him.

For such action there could be only one logical meaning. Some officer had accompanied O'Connor on his mission, had remained in that brown sedan, and was now chasing him toward the gallows.

As their speed increased and the sedan still gained, that inference became a certainty. When pursuer and pursued were but a hundred feet apart, Vasch had hoped that one or both of the shots he fired might be lucky enough to damage or kill; but the sedan, though slowed up, still hung upon the trail. And that accursed handcuff hanging by its chain from his left wrist! He had snapped it shut, but at every movement it dangled, flopped, and struck his knees or legs.

"Ah, that damn sedan is almost two blocks behind. Here's my chance!" he muttered.

"Hey, you! Slow down a little and turn west at the next corner! Then give her the gas up to sixty and keep her there, or I'll put four of these slugs into your guts," Vasch shouted to the driver.

With that gun-muzzle behind him, Robert Twitchett must, perforce, obey. He turned westward at thirty miles an hour and then stepped on the accelerator. The taxi shot ahead like a roaring wind!

Blind to all behind him, half deafened by the sound of his overloaded engine, Twitchett never knew when the right-hand door of his cab was opened by the man within. He did not see the form of his bandit passenger, standing on the running board and clinging with left hand to the handle of that unlocked door. He knew nothing of the crouching leap made by his unwelcome fare, just after the taxi swung round the curve, nor did he feel the jerk as that leap was suddenly checked in mid air. He did not hear the clank of that loose chain-bound handcuff as it swung forward and looped itself around the right door-handle of his cab. In the darkness he could not see the side of his taxi, nor could he view there the battered form of a murderer, suspended by a steel handcuff chain, bumping, scraping, dragging, bounding along the roadway at fifty miles an hour, below the swinging door of his speeding car.

XVIII

WESTWARD, roaring, plunging, bouncing, sped the taxi, and for three long blocks its senseless, trailing burden scoured the street. Some few belated pedestrians beside the road viewed the horrid spectacle of a man, seemingly roped by his left wrist to the open door of a cab, with legs and hips scraping the gravel. They yelled: *"Stop!"* to the driver, and motioned, but in vain. He could not see what trailed behind!

Only when Twitchett approached a well-lighted traffic-guarded boulevard and viewed in its center the welcome form of a stalwart officer did he apply his brakes and bring the cab to a standstill.

"What in hell are you doin'?" yelled the policeman. "Don't ya see the poor guy draggin' there? For the love of Mike! He's got one handcuff on his wrist, an' the other one's caught around the door-handle. Well, whaddya know about that?"

Robert Twitchett and Officer Daniel Gallagher soon released the unconscious man and bore his tattered form up to a grassy bank beneath the light and well above the sidewalk. Twitchett then explained what had happened.

"Look at him!" quoth Gallagher. "Pants and shoes nearly all torn off'n him. Damn near all the skin off his legs! Left arm broken above the wrist an' only hangin' by the tendons! My God, the man's a wreck! Is he alive yet, I wonder. Let's look him over an' see! Who is he, d'ya know? His head is so plastered with dust his own mother wouldn't recognize him! Hello! What are you two guys buttin' in on this for? Git the hell outa here! D'ya think this is a circus?"—This to the occupants of an approaching car.

"Hold on, Dan Gallagher! Don't get wrathy! You know me! I can tell you all about this case!" interposed Hackett, as he and Rollins stepped from the brown sedan which had just driven up. "This man is a criminal escaping arrest, Dan!" Bill continued. "Jim O'Connor got one cuff on to him, but I guess this bird must have slugged or shot O'Connor before he could snap on the other. We chased this man from 'way down below Sixtieth Street, an' he damn near got away on us at that! We couldn't see what happened after the taxi turned that last corner, but I reckon his joblots here was goin' to jump out, hide behind somep'n, an' let us trail along after the empty cab! Don't you figure that was it?" queried Hackett of the taxi-driver.

"Yeah, I guess that's right! All I know is that he told me a fairy-tale about O'Connor and was pokin' a gun into the back of my neck all the way up an' makin' me step on the gas to a fare-you-well. I ain't worryin' any if the —— never comes to"; and Twitchett spat disgustedly on the sidewalk.

"What shape is he in now?" asked Rollins. "Do you mind if I see?" and Bob walked up the grassy slope toward the spot where the inert form of George Vasch was lying under the gleaming lights above.

As Rollins climbed the trifling rise, his toe stubbed against a bare tree-root, and he dropped unexpectedly to his knees.

Crack! At that same instant, a bullet pierced the air just where Rollins' head had been a tenth of a second before.

Instantly Officer Gallagher, Bob Rollins, and Bill Hackett were struggling desperately to wrest from the right hand of their fighting prisoner a revolver, which he gripped with superhuman strength. Kicking, biting, squirming, heaving with the urge of desperation, the man, whom all had regarded as half-dead, fought on! It was three full minutes before that struggling form was mastered. No man with a broken arm, however, can continue to repel the onslaught of three vigorous opponents, and George Vasch was at last a prisoner indeed.

Officer Daniel Gallagher most willingly supplied an extra pair of handcuffs, and this time their adjustment was secure.

"Will ye look at the dirrty thug?" said Gallagher. "Who in hell woulda thought it? After bein' dragged for half a mile or so, with divil a bit of skin on him below his hips, he puts up a schrap like that! Well, me bucko, you're tame now, so that's that!"

"Would you mind letting Bill Hackett have that gun, officer?" said Rollins. "I'm certain this man put a bullet into me a few days ago. Professor Zweiss has the bullet and we want to match it up and see if this gun fired it!"

"Sure! Take the gun, Bill! But what are we gonna do with his nibs, here? Shall I call the wagon?"

"Don't do that, Dan!" pleaded Hackett. "He's a headquarters fugitive, an' we'd oughta take him there. I'll call up Desk-Sergeant Ryan and tell him about this. Then we'll cart this bird to the station and ask Ryan to have a doctor there to fix that arm. You can report the case to your station an' then come along with us to see that his nibs keeps sweet! We'll drive you uptown. How's that, Dan?"

"If you want to see O'Connor, you'll have to hunt for him in hell! He was dead when I left him," interrupted the prisoner. "And say! What are you going to do about this broken arm? I've got to have a doctor right *now*. You've got no license to let me suffer like this!"

"Is that so?" remarked Gallagher. "You don't tell me! It's all roight for a guy like you to blow the head off a feller that was tryin' to help you, but *we* mustn't let a lousy, stinkin' murtherer suffer! No, that would be just too bad, wouldn't it? Say, you shut your damn trap till you get in the cooler! We've heard about enough from you! You do your telephonin', Bill! while I load this skunk into your sedan! Get in there, you dirty . . .! Say, Hackett, send an ambulance down to that flat for Jim O'Connor. Hustle, boy! Maybe we can save him yet!"

Not a syllable escaped the lips of George Vasch during the journey uptown. The hands of Rollins' watch marked a little past midnight as the prisoner and his three guards entered Police Headquarters.

Desk-Sergeant Ryan got up from his chair, strolled over, grasped the chin of George Vasch between his thumb and fingers, tipped the man's head back, and looked him squarely in the eyes. "So you're the lad that battered Jim O'Connor's brains out for doin' his duty! Take this hell-cat in there, Doctor, and fix up his arm. Don't be too damn particular about it. He ain't gonna need it long, anyhow."

Forty minutes later came a telephone call from the South Side hospital to which the body of Jim O'Connor had been taken. The actions of Sergeant Ryan after receiving that long message were like those of a half-crazy child. He thumped Hackett squarely on the chest, whacked Gallagher thunderously on the back, hugged Rollins, and let out a whoop that brought in three waiting patrolmen on the run.

"Jim's alive!" he shouted. "He woke up swearin' a blue streak five minutes ago. That . . . didn't even crack his skull. The only thing Jim wanted to know was if you guys had copped that skunk downstairs. I told the doc to tell Jim yes, and the doc says he grunted and asked for a seegar an' he's smokin' it now. God bless St. Patrick! No Irishman ever got killed by hittin' him on the head; that's *one* thing that can't be done!"

The proceedings in the Grand Jury room at ten o'clock on the following morning were almost perfunctory. District Attorney Walsh was able not only to present all the evidence previously secured, but also to recount the flight and capture of George Vasch on the evening before. Aside from Rollins and Hackett, only three witnesses testified, and an indictment was at once drawn against George Vasch for willful murder.

On leaving the Grand Jury room Walsh motioned Rollins aside. "I want you and Hackett to come up to Inspector Devine's office promptly at one o'clock this afternoon. I'll be there with one or two others. Let me have that list of queries you dictated to Hackett right after Stevens died. I'm going to have Vasch brought in, and there will also be a friend of ours there who's going to use those questions in a way which will be *very* interesting, I'll promise you."

Save for the presence of Walsh, Rollins, and Hackett, the office of Inspector Devine was vacant at one o'clock when

George Vasch, manacled, and with his left arm in a sling, was ushered in.

"Sit down there, Vasch!" said Walsh, pointing to a chair. "Let's see! How many times have you tried to murder somebody in the last ten days? There's Alexander Stevens! You got him! There's Rollins! You tried to bump him off four times yourself, and you sicked Brodski on to him twice! There's your sister, Sarah Vasch. You smashed her skull and then tried to poison her. She's in the hospital yet. Then last night you tried to blow up Rollins and Hackett, and finally you wound up by blackjacking O'Connor and shooting at Rollins' car. We won't count that last. That was only target practice. That's a fine record, Vasch! Over a crime a day! You certainly ought to be proud of it! It shows what a wonderful brain you've got; eleven attempts at murder and one success!"

"Hold on, Mr. Walsh!" interposed Hackett. "This guy took a shot at Rollins again last night just before we brought him in—that makes *twelve* times in ten days, according to my figurin'."

"All right, Hackett, make it twelve times, then!" assented Walsh. "And look at the clever way you wiped out old Stevens! My, my, that certainly showed what a 'master-mind' can do when it gets down to business! Not a single clue! Not one—so *you* thought! Wore gloves! Cleaned off every single thing in that office! Flim-flammed that key on to poor Stevens' desk! Fixed up a dying message from Stevens in his own handwriting! Disguised yourself so as to throw the blame on your Uncle Edward if the suicide racket didn't work! Oh, you were *good!* Yes, sir! You were going to show the world how to pull off a *perfect crime*—a killing where the astute gentleman who butchers his victim leaves not a single trace—not one!

"Listen, Mr. George Vasch! In about one minute I'm going to introduce to you a man who was your best friend, a man whom you also tried to murder! He's got a list of two dozen little trifles which you didn't think of when you tackled that 'perfect crime' of yours. Besides that there's another two dozen items which my friend Rollins has discovered since! About forty-odd trifles, that's all! Come in, Jim! Just read to this marvelously brainy gentleman sitting there the full list of guilt-indicating items which I read to the Grand Jury this morning, all of which Bob Rollins, here, has doped out in ten days. Mr. George Vasch, possibly you know that this is James O'Connor!"

Sergeant O'Connor, his head swathed in bandages, entered, strode across the floor, pulled up a chair directly in front of George Vasch, glared into the prisoner's eyes, and commenced to talk. His voice boomed like a bass tuba as he looked squarely into the handcuffed man's face and shot his statements bullet-like toward the form of George Vasch.

First came some choice selections from the twenty-four queries which Rollins had dictated to Hackett shortly after the finding of Stevens' body. Then the Sergeant detailed a few striking items of evidence brought to light during the nine days succeeding. At frequent intervals O'Connor would stop, gaze at Vasch in ironical admiration, and murmur sarcastic comments, such as: "There's brains for ya! ... Ain't it marvelous how a guy can plan like that? ... Yes, sir! Absolutely perfect! Didn't leave one damn clue—except, maybe, a couple hundred dabs that didn't amount to nothin'. 1 suppose them Cleveland dicks you trailed with for fourteen years didn't bother with little things like them!"

Not a syllable came from the pallid, broken man who faced him.

Finally, when O'Connor had finished, he thrust the copy of Rollins' report into his pocket, stood up, reached out his ponderous hand to grasp the right shoulder of the prisoner, and thundered :

"Mr. Vasch, you'll mebbe recall that I was makin' a little speech to you in your hallway about eleven o'clock last night. Mebbe you think I oughta forget your gettin' peeved and givin' me that little tap on my bean, but I reckon now I'll just finish that speech that 1 was goin' to make. Whenever I start something, that job's *got* to be done and *I arrest you, George Vasch, alias Gregory Devine, Inspector of Police,* for the murder of Alexander Stevens! Take that damn snake out of here before I smash him!"

As Gregory Devine was led again to his cell, no word escaped his lips, but the devilish fire behind his eyes portrayed a hate unutterable.

Meanwhile, Rollins, by phone dictation, gave his paper a full account of Devine's partial arrest, his escape, the long chase, the final capture, and the eventual incarceration of the fugitive. This, together with a copy of Rollins' previous report to the Grand Jury, furnished the *Leader* with ample material for many future editions.

Editor Bostock was in his glory! It was the biggest "beat" in Chicago newspaper history, for the name and reputation of Detective Inspector Gregory Devine was known everywhere, and the whole city was anxious to learn the stirring news.

Devine's previous fourteen-year record on the Cleveland police force, and his six years of service, after promotion to the position of Inspector, in Chicago, were set forth in detail. Nothing was omitted, save such items as were tabooed by Walsh from publication, as being necessary to conserve the interests of the prosecution.

During the next five days Devine vouchsafed no word save to his attorneys, both of whom openly scoffed at this "unwarranted charge against a man of unblemished repute!"

Finally, on the sixth day of his incarceration, he asked that his half-sister, Sarah Vasch, be permitted to visit him, and the request was granted.

Escorted by Rollins, and with tears streaming down her cheeks, the age-stricken Sarah sat in a chair for nearly thirty minutes outside the steel mesh-work behind which her brother was confined.

What passed between those two the world will never know, but when that half-hour was over, and the trembling form of Sarah had gone forever from his sight, Gregory Devine's face bore a look of mental anguish such as no mortal had ever seen upon it before.

"Joe!" said he, to the guard. "Can you get me a pen and a piece of paper? I want to write a note to my lawyers—and bring me an envelope, too, if you will, please."

The writing-utensils were handed in, and Devine commenced his epistle, interrupting it shortly by a request for a drink of water, which he grasped by the edges as it was passed to him through the bars.

"Thank you, Joe! You're a good scout! And, say, tell Jim O'Connor I'm sorry I hit him, will you? Good-bye, Joe!" And Gregory Devine drank the cup of water, smiled, tottered for a few seconds on his feet, and sank to the cell floor, lifeless.

Hastily unlocking the cell door and shouting for help, Joseph Hardy, the guard, made every effort to revive his prisoner, but in vain. Gregory Devine had expiated his crimes forever.

A short, thick, lead-pencil from which the graphite was missing, lying on the cell floor, proclaimed the means of Devine's escape from prison and the world. In the hollowed pencil still remained a few tiny pulverized crystals of cyanide, and upon the floor lay a half-inch piece of graphite, which had plugged the pencil aperture. Only in death was the planning of that distorted mind of avail to him.

Of Stanislaw Brodski there had been no word or sign since the hour of Devine's actual arrest. Possibly a telephone message to Atwood, clerk at the Sanford, and the "accidental" loss of a handcuff key in Puckers' attic room might account for his vanishing. Who shall say?

The last written words of Gregory Devine, contained in the unsealed envelope, were never sent to his attorneys. They were published to the world. Here they are:

I did it. You can't beat the game. No man can foresee and fight a thousand damning trifles.

GREGORY DEVINE

The confession just recorded necessarily cleared from the name and memory of Alexander Stevens the stigma of suicide, and his daughter was now able to face the world with no shadow of the past to darken her future. As a result of this and the other evidence that her father had been murdered the Marathon Life-insurance Company promptly honored and paid to Nora the claim for fifty thousand dollars of insurance which they had carried upon the chemist's life. This amount, together with the ten-thousand-dollar policy which Stevens had long carried in another company, was sufficient to place Eleanor Stevens beyond the reach of destitution, had she no other source of livelihood or support.

In a wardrobe-trunk reposing in the apartment formerly occupied by Gregory Devine were later found ten clearly developed photo-films, upon which were plainly disclosed the full and correct formulae of Stevens' color-photograph process. In the envelope which contained these films were two others which were black from over-exposure. The ten perfect negatives, however, confirmed the findings of William Hackett.

On the morning after Devine's suicide Managing Editor Ralph Bostock called Rollins into his private office. Bob was glad to find his friend District Attorney Edward Walsh waiting there also.

"Sit down, Bob," said Bostock. "Walsh and I would like to have you do us both a little favor if you will. How about it? Are you willing?"

"Surely!" replied Rollins. "You're my boss, but you're my friend too, and you both know the answer without asking. Shoot the works, Mr. Bostock!"

"Well," continued the latter, "perhaps you don't know it, but your compatriot Mr. William Hackett has been telling some very queer stories about you and your doings during the past three weeks. Very strange indeed! Some of them so peculiar as to be almost unbelievable. Shall I tell you what he says?" and both of Rollins' friends awaited his response with quizzical smiles seeping through their would-be solemn demeanor.

Rollins studied the two faces for a moment and then laughed. "Now I know you are kidding me," he said. "All right! I'll bite. Tell me what Bill says about me. It can't be anything so very bad or you wouldn't be talking about my doing a favor for you, and such foolishness. Go ahead! Here I am."

"Very well, Rollins," replied Editor Bostock. "Hackett claims that you scarcely put your foot out of Stevens' laboratory to search for evidence during the entire time while you and he were trying to find out how and why Stevens was killed and who killed him. He told the District Attorney here that you performed absolutely *no* physical labor except lifting the telephone off of the hook and hanging it up again. He asserted to me that nearly all the evidence which you and he incorporated in your combined report was solely the result of inferences and deductions made by you from certain patent facts which should have been noted by *any* observant person. Walsh and I don't precisely look upon you as a defendant or prisoner at the bar, Bob, but anyhow there is Hackett's accusation. Now what have you to say about it?"

"Defendant declines to answer on the ground that it may incriminate or degrade him," replied Rollins with a hearty laugh, in which both of his inquisitors joined. "Seriously, Mr. Bostock, what do you and Mr. Walsh want to know? You've both done a lot for me and I'll gladly do anything I can to reciprocate. If you'll permit me to make one of those inferences which Hackett states are so prevalent when I'm round, I should say that you'd like to have me tell you *how* we got at the bottom of the Stevens case and pinned the guilt on Devine. If that inference is correct, I'll be glad to do it, provided Bill is present and also provided you'll bring in Griff Dawson also to hear it. You see, Griff and I had quite an argument about three weeks ago about crimes of impulse and those of premeditation, and I'm sure he will be especially interested in seeing his own theories disposed of. Will that be agreeable to you both? If so, suppose we get together in Mr. Stevens' old laboratory at five o'clock this afternoon. There are some pieces of evidence there which I couldn't transport elsewhere, and I should like to have you see them. They are essential to a proper understanding of what I have to tell. Is my inference correct, Mr. Bostock, and is that what you and Mr. Walsh are after?"

"That is exactly what Ralph and I want to know, Rollins. You've hit the nail on the head precisely and I'm sure nobody will object to having Hackett and Dawson in the family party," interrupted the District Attorney as Bostock was about to speak. "Ralph, you can round up Mr. Dawson and I'll get in touch with Bill Hackett and we'll all meet at the Meyers Building at five o'clock sharp. Meanwhile please accept a vote of thanks, Bob, from both Ralph and me for this favor (yes, it is a favor), and you can be certain we'll all be there."

XIX

EVEN THOUGH A WEEK had elapsed since the explosion of Gregory Devine's well-constructed bomb in Alexander Stevens' former laboratory, the repairs which had been made failed to wipe out all traces of its effect upon the room and its furnishings. The impact of scores of metal slugs had sadly marred walls, desk, tables, chairs, and chemical appliances. Nevertheless, to the four guests of Robert Rollins who now sat awaiting such disclosures as he might reveal, these scars of battle were unimportant. These men sought knowledge of no material character, but rather of the workings of mind.

"What should you like me to do?" inquired Rollins. "You know most of the facts already. Why not ask me such questions as you wish, and I'll try to answer them as well as I can. Suppose you start in, Mr. Bostock. Go ahead!"

"All right, Rollins! We all know the long series of queries which you dictated to Bill Hackett at the start of your investigation, all of which were inferential indications that this case was not one of suicide, but murder. What I should like to know is this: did you discover any *other* evidence which—inferentially or otherwise—pointed toward murder?"

"Yes, I did," replied Rollins promptly, taking from one of his pockets an enlarged photograph and unfolding it. "Here, you see, is a photo of the rear view of Mr. Stevens' body as it lay partially recumbent on his desk when we found him dead in this office on November 20. Hackett took the original of it. Take this reading-glass and look at that tiny grayish patch just below his collar-edge at the point between his shoulder and the center seam of his coat. *That patch was composed of cigarette ash.* In size it was a little bigger than a black ant. Had Mr. Stevens been standing erect when the ash-mound fell upon that spot, it would have fallen off instantly. The inevitable conclusion therefore is that the ash must have dropped on that precise spot *after* he had been poisoned. From that conclusion anyone could not fail to infer that some other person had been with Mr. Stevens in this laboratory after he died. My other inferences dictated to Hackett made this a certain fact. I feel sure that Devine noticed that ash-mound during the police investigation and purposely destroyed it by lifting Stevens' body upright in the awkward fashion he used. He seized the body by the collar and arm in lifting it. I tried to stop him, but he ignored me. At that time, of course, I believed this to be accidental, but afterwards I became almost certain that he had acted with intent to destroy that evidence before it was noted.

"Since I was now *sure* that Mr. Stevens had a visitor *after* his death, I was equally certain that the visitor must have been admitted into this room by Mr. Stevens *before* his death—-hence he was murdered and every particle of evidence which appeared to indicate suicide was manufactured by the murderer.

"Mr. Stevens' newly-invented photo-color-process was, from the very first, an indisputably clear motive. You will see, therefore, that I had, right at the start, only one problem to study—*who* had murdered him? Moreover, all of the supposed proofs of suicide became now valuable clues to locate the slayer."

"That's splendid, Rollins," remarked Ralph Bostock. "Of course I knew it before, for you told me about it at the hospital, but I wanted the others to have that same knowledge, especially Mr. Walsh. Suppose you tackle the questioning next, Ed. I don't want to monopolize it."

"All right, Ralph," said Walsh. "What I'd like to know, Rollins, is: when did you first begin to suspect that Devine was the murderer?"

"On the day when I went to Devine's office to intercede for Hackett and try to persuade Devine to retain Bill on the Police Department," replied Bob. "Just as I was going out, Devine made a remark to the effect that he understood one of

Stevens' insurance policies was not likely to be paid because of its suicide clause. Only four living human beings aside from Marathon Life employees knew about that policy, its date, and its terms. Those four persons were Eleanor, Mr. Stevens' daughter, Sarah Vasch, Alice Lane, and I. I knew that neither Miss Stevens, Miss Lane, nor I had told Devine; Sarah Vasch *might* have done so. All the evidence prior to that time pointed to a leak through Sarah as the means by which the murderer had obtained knowledge of Stevens' invention, and the attempt to kill Sarah by slung shot and by poisoned candy confirmed that conclusion as correct. It was therefore possible that Devine had been the recipient of Sarah's gossip and—because of her nature—must have been a close friend, or perhaps a relative, of hers. Instantly after I had reached this conclusion, I recalled a number of other suspicious acts which likewise pointed to Devine as being in some way implicated in the affair.

"When he first entered this room to conduct the police investigation regarding Mr. Stevens' supposed suicide, Devine told us that O'Connor had been called away as witness in an auto smash-up, and that he was handling the case of Stevens' suicide personally. A couple of days later I learned through O'Connor that this statement was a falsehood. O'Connor told me that he had been *"assigned"* to interview two men who had run over a child and had *not* been a witness at court. No one except Inspector Devine could possibly have "assigned" O'Connor to *any* duty whatever. Why had Devine lied deliberately and knowingly thus about an apparently insignificant thing? Men do not normally lie about trifling matters without a good motive.

"From the discovery of that falsehood I reasoned that perhaps Devine had told other lies during the police investigation in this office, and I remembered that he had required two of us to identify the body of Mr. Stevens. He also had made the remark that he "wanted to get familiar with this room." Both these comments of his were equivalent to saying that he had never met or known Mr. Stevens and had never visited this laboratory before the police inquiry. Then, too, Devine had failed to investigate that phone call or summon Sarah Vasch as an inquest witness. All of these facts combined caused me to suspect that Devine might, at least, know *something* about the case or perhaps be a party to it. Does that answer your question, Mr. Walsh?"

"It certainly does, Bob," replied the District Attorney. "But why stop just at this point? I'm getting mighty interested. What did you do then? Why not tell us some more? I suppose your next move was to find out whether or not Devine knew Stevens personally or had ever visited Stevens in this office, eh?"

"Correct you are, Mr. Walsh! That is precisely what I did," answered Rollins. "My first thought was to learn the facts through questioning Sarah Vasch, but she was in the hospital, unconscious, and might die at any moment. Then I asked myself who would be likely to know whether or not Devine had visited Stevens lately. The logical answer was simple. Devine surely would not walk up six flights of stairs to reach this office; hence one of the elevator boys might have seen him get off at this floor. Then I remembered that the colored elevator-operator, Harry Flood, had said to Hackett when we all went down in the elevator together after Mr. Stevens' body had been removed: 'Every time I see Devine, I envy him.' This indicated that he knew Devine by sight and had seen him several times, at least. On being questioned, Harry told me that he had taken Devine up to the seventh floor twice recently. Once was on November 16, and the second time on the morning of November 18. On both occasions Harry had seen Mr. Stevens greet Devine in the doorway of this room, shake hands with him, and admit him. On the last occasion Harry had directed a man—Duncan—to Stevens' office-door and had noted Devine coming out just as Duncan went in.

"I might say here, incidentally, that Duncan later confirmed this. Devine had worked for him in the photo-supply house in Cleveland twenty-six years ago, and Duncan recalled Devine's face, but not his name. A few days later, after Devine's guilt had been proved, Duncan wired me the name.

"Upon obtaining this positive proof that Devine was on familiar terms with Mr. Stevens and had visited him in his laboratory I remembered that Devine had explicitly stated to me, while visiting his office: 'I did *not* know Stevens *personally.*' Here, then, was a third lie coming from Devine— and this time it was clearly deliberate and *must* have had for its purpose concealment from me of the fact that Devine had been associated with Stevens. The scrawly 'Consult G.D.' on Folsom's threatening letter to Stevens, therefore, probably meant 'Consult Gregory Devine.'

"I was now morally certain that Devine was the instigator of Stevens' murder and had taken charge of the police inquiry to conduct it as he pleased, but I was *not* sure that he was the actual slayer. Mrs. Halgard's list of the guests who attended her party—at which someone had stolen her birthday verses and used the two ending lines as a supposed 'good-bye' message from Stevens—did *not* contain the name of Gregory Devine. I, of course, believed that list was complete. If this were so, Devine was *not* at that party, could *not* have stolen those verses, and could *not* be Stevens' slayer. I was therefore in a quandary and feeling pretty blue when Bill Hackett appeared with Donovan's bona-fide business card and told me how it had been dropped in the costumer's shop when a man, with a Donovan-like mole on his chin, had purchased a Vandyke beard and wig.

"I of course first assured myself that the card was not a bogus one. Comparison of it under a reading glass with one of George Donovan's own cards showed defects in printing on both which were alike; so this was settled. While studying the card through the glass, I smelt a very faint odor from it and soon placed the odor as being a mixture of oil of cloves and spirits of camphor. I was positive of this because I had several times used this mixture myself for toothache. The card bore not the slightest stain, hence it must have absorbed the odor of the two drugs without actually touching them.

"This is the way I reasoned about the matter: Druggists always keep these two drugs separately. They are mixed only when someone wants to use them to allay pain from a toothache. They are nearly always sold to customers in a tiny vial. The customer usually carries this vial with him and applies a drop or two to some cotton when he needs it to ease his toothache. This business card must have been in very close proximity to these drugs for a long time in an enclosed space in order to have absorbed the odor without being stained. In *what* place on a man's person is he likely to carry such a little vial together with some of his business cards? The only possible answer was: in his upper vest pocket, where both are handy and where the vial cannot upset. The patient's frequent withdrawals of the cork would, of course, account for the absorption.

"The next query I had to deal with was: Who had that toothache? Was it Donovan—or was it someone else? This was the most vital question of all."

At this moment, and for the first time, Griffith Dawson interrupted Rollins and interjected the following comments: "Of course I'm only familiar with the general outlines of this case and not with the details, like the rest of you, so I don't understand all this talk about Donovan's business card. Would you mind explaining what you were trying to find out about it and how the question of whether or not Donovan had the toothache enters into it?"

"Glad to do it, Griff! Here's the whole matter in a nutshell," replied Rollins. "If Donovan had the toothache very recently and if he had bought some clove and camphor mixture and kept the vial which contained it in his upper vest pocket along with some of his visiting-cards, it is clear that this particular card became impregnated with the scent of the mixture *while it was in Donovan's pocket.* If, then, he handed out that particular card to some person within the previous day or two and that person used that card to impersonate Donovan while purchasing the beard and wig (which the same impersonator later used as a disguise to impersonate Edward Folsom and murder Stevens), you can readily see that the unknown man who obtained possession of that card could be located by learning *where* Donovan had left that clove-scented card. Remember, Griff, that this card bore no finger-prints except those of Donovan and the costumer's clerk. Hence I reasoned that Donovan had laid the card on some desk or counter; that the criminal had picked it up *by the edges*—to keep his own fingerprints off it—and had used it in his murder plot.

"That is precisely what had happened. When I questioned Donovan, he told me the names of several persons in whose offices he had left business cards on November 17, the day before Stevens' murder. Donovan also corroborated my guess that he had suffered from toothache on November 16 and 17 and had used a vial of the mixture to ease the pain. Further, he admitted that he kept both vial and business cards together in his upper right-hand vest pocket. I knew positively that Donovan was not the criminal we were after, and his answers to my questions told me, beyond all doubt, who that criminal was.

"One of the places where Donovan had left his cards was the office of Dr. Bryan, a dentist in the Masonic Temple. Donovan had laid the card on the desk of Miss Martha Ellis, the dentist's clerk, as he came in to have his tooth extracted. As Donovan went into Dr. Bryan's operating-room, another man came out, whom Donovan did not observe because of his toothache. It is certain, however, that the outcoming patient noticed Donovan, observed the mole on Donovan's chin, planned then and there to impersonate Donovan while buying the false Vandyke beard, and secured Donovan's card, which was still reposing on Miss Ellis' desk—with that intent. The reason why I am so positive of this is that Miss Ellis told me, in answer to my questions over the phone, that she had seen this outcoming patient pick up Donovan's card *by its edges* and put it in his pocket while she was making change for him in paying his bill.

"Miss Ellis made no protest, of course, for the card was without value, but she observed it and remembered it. When asked the name of this outgoing patient who had performed this unusual action, Miss Ellis stated: *'It was Inspector Devine.'*

"I was now *certain* that Devine was the killer of Stevens, despite the fact that his name did not appear on the list of guests at Mrs. Halgard's party; so I called up Mrs. Halgard and asked her if she had not been so flustered by dropping the pen in Stevens' office that she had forgotten to include the name of one of her guests. She thought a moment and then said: 'Oh, yes! I guess I did forget him. Inspector Devine was there, too, with his uncle, Edward Folsom. I couldn't very well leave him out, after inviting Mr. Folsom's other nephew, George.'

"Except for one thing this disclosure practically settled the entire matter, and that one thing was the identification of the fingerprints of Stevens' murderer with those of Gregory Devine. While studying over this, I recalled my interview with Devine, when endeavoring to obtain Bill Hackett's reinstatement on the police force. I remembered that Devine had been eating some tongue sandwiches. I knew that his fingers must have become greasy from such a luncheon; I recalled that he had written a note reinstating Hackett; I reasoned that his greasy fingers must have left—despite the long time elapsed—a *lasting* finger-print record upon that note-paper; and, finally, I knew that this invaluable document was now in the laboratory safe in Stevens' office. All that now remained for me to do was to remove from the safe Devine's letter ordering Hackett's reinstatement, compare the fingerprints thereon with those made by Stevens' murderer when he handled the memo book and paper cone in Stevens' laboratory on the night of the crime, and see if all the three sets of finger-prints were identical. *All were identical. Devine was guilty.*

"You are all familiar with Stanislaw Brodski's confession and with the statement of Sarah Vasch, so I needn't speak of them. They added much to our knowledge of the details of the crime, but the case was complete without them. I think that is about all I can tell you except one striking thing which I think will interest you, Griff Dawson, more than any of the rest of you. This case was literally teeming—loaded—with tiny trifling clues, each of which helped to solve its problems. You remember Devine's last message said: 'No man can foresee and fight a thousand damning trifles.' He was absolutely right. It was the little things which he forgot or overlooked or overdid or did not know about that convicted him. I told you that same thing about premeditated crime three weeks ago, Griff, if you remember, when I asserted that premeditated murder is impossible of success if the investigators of the crime are capable and on the job. Seems to me that is about all, unless somebody wants to ask some more questions"—and Rollins stopped.

Scarcely a tenth of a second elapsed before Bill Hackett was on his feet. "Listen, fellers!" he shouted. "Have you forgotten about that key being on Stevens' desk right under his nose when we found him dead in his office?" Hackett then related briefly how Rollins had, a few days before, "tossed the damn key through three inches of solid oak right into my hand. I ain't workin' for either of you fellers," he said, referring to Walsh and Bostock, "but if you let this boy Rollins get out of here without givin' us the dope on that key stunt, you're no friends of mine, and that goes as it lays. Make the son-of-a-gun tell! *Make* him!"

Despite Rollins' protest Hackett's resolution was passed without a dissenting vote; hence Bob, whether or no, was forced to continue.

"The only reason," he said, "why I feel as if you are entitled to know about this is that it is excellent proof that a little study will solve any kind of puzzle or problem which any man can invent. After examining every inch of Stevens' laboratory I became certain that the key could be introduced into this room only from outside, by thrusting it in some way under the door. The crack under the door was not sufficiently large to admit the key; hence I reasoned that the crack *must* somehow have been widened to admit the key's entrance. There are only two known ways of widening such a crack—a lever and a wedge—and, in prying up such a heavy door, I felt sure either of these utensils would leave some mark on the threshold. I therefore looked for such a mark and found it. Here it is! See!"

All four of Rollins' companions trooped to the doorway and studied a plainly visible indentation about one inch wide and a thirty-second of an inch deep on the right-hand side of the threshold, perpendicularly below the lock.

"Having decided," Rollins continued, "that the key had been introduced in this manner, my next problem was by what route this key might be transported from the crack under the door to the center of that desk, twenty feet away, bearing in mind that I could not *aim* the key by my eyesight, nor could I *stop* it when it reached the center of the desk. Only three possible routes for transporting such an object from place to place are known to man: a straight route, a circuitous everhead route, and an angular route. The circuitous overhead route involved aiming and ballistics; hence I rejected it as impossible. The straight route was feasible, except that nothing could be devised to prevent the key from *sliding* several feet when it reached the desk-top. An angular route, therefore, was my only possible solution.

"No single force can propel an object on an angular route unless that object is compelled to glance off from a second object. *Two* forces are needed for such propulsion, and the only second force at my command was *gravity.* The key must *drop,* of its own weight, on the desk-center.

" 'From whence could and must the key drop to the desk-center?' I asked myself. The obvious and only answer was: 'The nearest object directly above it.' A glance at the desk told me what that object was. It was this brass T arm projecting from the wall about twenty inches, with its central T top directly over the desk-center and with electric light bulbs at each end of its arms.

"My next problem was: 'How may I furnish a straight pathway from the door-crack to the center of this T arm.' This involved the question of a straight path between two *unseen* points, and the only means known to man for such a pathway is a taut cord, wire, or rod stretched between those two points. If, then, I could somehow stretch a cord or pulley from the door-crack to the T arm, I could propel the key along this path, and, upon reaching the T arm, the key would drop to the desk-center.

"As soon as the word *'pulley'* flashed across my mind I knew that my problem was solved and here is the way which I used the other day while demonstrating to Bill that the thing not only *could* be done, but was so easy that it could be accomplished in less than three minutes.

"Before blindfolding Bill I had put into my pockets one hundred feet of strong silk trout-line and a short steel burglar's jemmy with a very thin curved end. The key to the door was in the inside keyhole, and the door closed. Hackett was then blindfolded and started his stop-watch, after which I proceeded as follows.

"I thrust one end of my line through the center loop of the key and then ran back with both ends of the line until the line was taut. The key—still in the keyhole—was then in the center of a fifty-foot loop of line, the two ends of which were in my hands. I then passed the two line-ends over the arms of the T bracket; one end over one arm, and the other end over the other arm. Seizing both line-ends, I then ran to the door, opened it, pulled out the key, passed *all four* lines under the bottom of the door. Then, still holding the two line-ends and the key in my two hands, I ran down the hallway until all four fines were taut.

"As now arranged, all four fines ran from the hallway through the crevice underneath the door (still partly open) and extended in a diagonally upward direction toward and around the T bracket. Being now in the hallway, my next move was to close the door, lock the door from the outside, pull out the key from the door, and lay the key on the floor of the hallway.

"After I had done this, I took the jemmy out of my hip pocket, stuck the thin curved end of the jemmy under the right-hand side of the door (in the bottom crevice next to the threshold), and jammed down with one foot on the end of the jemmy. This leverage pried up the door nearly an eighth of an inch and left ample room between door and threshold to thrust the key (still looped on the line) under the door and into this room.

"As soon as the key had been safely pushed through the enlarged crevice into the laboratory, I began to haul in both line-ends, hand over hand, as fast as I could. This hauling propelled the key along the floor, down the full length of the room, then up toward the T bracket, where it was pulled tight and stopped. The click of the key as it struck the bottom of the T bracket was quite distinctly audible in the hallway where I was standing.

"I am not quite sure that this explanation is perfectly clear to each of you, but if you will study this little sketch of the key being pulled upward toward the bracket, you will readily see how the lines were arranged.

"The click of the key against the brass T arm of the electric bracket told me that the key was suspended by the looped line directly above the center of the desk. I then immediately let go of one of the two line-ends and hauled in the other, winding the line in a ball as I hauled it in. As soon as the end of the line had passed through the hole in the key, the key, of course, dropped downward into Hackett's hand just below it. Meanwhile I had pulled out the jemmy from under the door and stuffed both jemmy and line into my pockets; after which I shouted to Hackett: 'Done!'

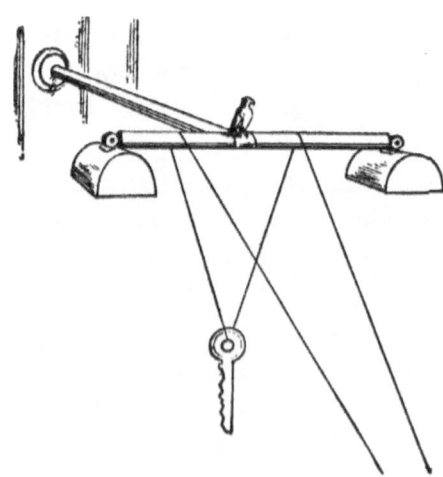

"If you will take a look at the upper side of the two brass side-arms of this T bracket, you will notice two bright streaks on the tarnished brass, caused by the friction of the two lines upon them while pulling the key from the door-crevice to the bracket. I observed these lines before I performed the experiment with Bill; hence I knew positively that Devine had used the same method when leaving this room after the murder of Mr. Stevens. This time I feel certain that there is nothing left to be explained."

"Wait!" shouted Hackett; "you're not through yet, Bob. No, sir! You've got to tell us why old man Folsom never left any fingerprints on the letters he wrote. You said you had found out why, but that's the last I ever heard of it and *I* want to know the answer even if these other guys don't. Come on, Bob! Spiel it out! I'll never quit pesterin' you until you do, and we may as well all hear about it."

"It was as simple as A B C," answered Rollins. "Mrs. Halgard told me over the phone that Doctor Frank Alston was Edward Folsom's physician. I called up Doctor Alston, whom I know quite well, and asked him what *other* ailment Folsom had besides arthritis. Dr. Alston told me that Folsom had a mild case of eczema of the hands and forearms. Alston prescribed an ointment which is rather greasy and Folsom rubs it on his arms and hands. Of course the grease sometimes comes off on the furniture. Besides that, Folsom can't write very well while the salve is on. His pen gets slippery and the paper becomes soiled. That is why he uses gloves a good deal of the time, except in company, and always uses them while writing. If I had possessed half the brains Bill gives me credit for, I should have found out that fact two weeks ago and saved any amount of thought and worry about it. By the way, gentlemen, it's now five minutes to six. I'm hungry and I'm pretty sure you feel the same way. Don't you think I have played fair and said more than enough? I say, let's adjourn!"

Mr. William Hackett, irrepressible commentator that he was, again leaped to his feet and held up his hand for silence. "Listen, fellers!" he commanded. "This session closes at six o'clock, and not before. You've listened to good old Bob for an hour and you've gotta stand hearing from me for five minutes. This Bob Rollins here doesn't toot his own horn half loud enough to suit me, so *I'm* goin' to do a little tooting for him. Do you realize what this guy Rollins has done in the ten days we worked together on this Stevens murder case? I'll tell you. Here's what he did: He saved Stevens' good name. He prevented the imprisonment and possible conviction of an innocent man. He pinned the guilt on the real culprit. He secured fifty thousand dollars' insurance for an orphan girl, which she would surely have lost if he hadn't used his reasoning powers the way he did. He's copped as fine a wife as any man could get, for he and Stevens' daughter will be married on Christmas.

"And look what he has done for me. He's taught me to use my bean instead of my legs. He got my old job back for me with a boost in pay and a month's vacation with pay besides. He's been instrumental in palling me up with the finest girl God ever made, and I'm telling you that, after New Year's Day, she's goin' to be called Mrs. William J. Hackett.

"But that isn't all. Bob suggested that I try to cancel out the alterations which Devine had made on Stevens' formula cards and get the correct formulae as they were before Stevens was killed. We have done it; we've found that rotating color-screen too, and I'm betting that we'll have the full specifications for the light-intensities as they were shown on the card which Devine stole or destroyed, before another three months have gone.

"Of course it may take a good deal longer than that. Nobody knows. We'll find it, though, no matter how long it takes. And listen! Do you know what this pal of mine, Rollins, and his wife are going to do after that photo-process is fully rediscovered and proved to be practical? I'll tell you. They are going to do precisely what poor old Stevens intended before he passed out: give the whole formula to the world for nothing.

"Well, I reckon my time's about up, but I'd just like to make one closin' observation. Three weeks ago, if anybody had asked me what I'd think of a guy, like Rollins, who wouldn't stir his stumps out of an office or turn his hand over physically to find out who murdered the father of the girl he was goin' to marry, I'd have said: *'That bird must be the laziest man that ever lived.'* Am I sayin' that now? *Not on your life!* Any lad who can get at the bottom of a murder, such as this, without usin' one damn thing except his own brains and a telephone can run for my money every day in the year. Yes, sir! I'm *for* him till hell freezes over.

"Well, fellers, your uncle's got a date over on Wabash Avenue to eat dinner with the finest girl on earth, an' you can bet there ain't anybody goin' to keep *her* waitin'. Let's all call it a day! So long!"

RAMBLE HOUSE's

HARRY STEPHEN KEELER WEBWORK MYSTERIES

(RH) indicates the title is available ONLY in the RAMBLE HOUSE edition

The Ace of Spades Murder
The Affair of the Bottled Deuce (RH)
The Amazing Web
The Barking Clock
Behind That Mask
The Book with the Orange Leaves
The Bottle with the Green Wax Seal
The Box from Japan
The Case of the Canny Killer
The Case of the Crazy Corpse (RH)
The Case of the Flying Hands (RH)
The Case of the Ivory Arrow
The Case of the Jeweled Ragpicker
The Case of the Lavender Gripsack
The Case of the Mysterious Moll
The Case of the 16 Beans
The Case of the Transparent Nude (RH)
The Case of the Transposed Legs
The Case of the Two-Headed Idiot (RH)
The Case of the Two Strange Ladies
The Circus Stealers (RH)
Cleopatra's Tears
A Copy of Beowulf (RH)
The Crimson Cube (RH)
The Face of the Man From Saturn
Find the Clock
The Five Silver Buddhas
The 4th King
The Gallows Waits, My Lord! (RH)
The Green Jade Hand
Finger! Finger!
Hangman's Nights (RH)
I, Chameleon (RH)
I Killed Lincoln at 10:13! (RH)
The Iron Ring
The Man Who Changed His Skin (RH)
The Man with the Crimson Box
The Man with the Magic Eardrums
The Man with the Wooden Spectacles
The Marceau Case
The Matilda Hunter Murder

The Monocled Monster
The Murder of London Lew
The Murdered Mathematician
The Mysterious Card (RH)
The Mysterious Ivory Ball of Wong Shing Li (RH)
The Mystery of the Fiddling Cracksman
The Peacock Fan
The Photo of Lady X (RH)
The Portrait of Jirjohn Cobb
Report on Vanessa Hewstone (RH)
Riddle of the Travelling Skull
Riddle of the Wooden Parrakeet (RH)
The Scarlet Mummy (RH)
The Search for X-Y-Z
The Sharkskin Book
Sing Sing Nights
The Six From Nowhere (RH)
The Skull of the Waltzing Clown
The Spectacles of Mr. Cagliostro
Stand By—London Calling!
The Steeltown Strangler
The Stolen Gravestone (RH)
Strange Journey (RH)
The Strange Will
The Straw Hat Murders (RH)
The Street of 1000 Eyes (RH)
Thieves' Nights
Three Novellos (RH)
The Tiger Snake
The Trap (RH)
Vagabond Nights (Defrauded Yeggman)
Vagabond Nights 2 (10 Hours)
The Vanishing Gold Truck
The Voice of the Seven Sparrows
The Washington Square Enigma
When Thief Meets Thief
The White Circle (RH)
The Wonderful Scheme of Mr. Christopher Thorne
X. Jones—of Scotland Yard
Y. Cheung, Business Detective

Keeler Related Works

A To Izzard: A Harry Stephen Keeler Companion by Fender Tucker — Articles and stories about Harry, by Harry, and in his style. Included is a compleat bibliography.

Wild About Harry: Reviews of Keeler Novels — Edited by Richard Polt & Fender Tucker — 22 reviews of works by Harry Stephen Keeler from *Keeler News*. A perfect introduction to the author.

The Keeler Keyhole Collection: Annotated newsletter rants from Harry Stephen Keeler, edited by Francis M. Nevins. Over 400 pages of incredibly personal Keeleriana.

Fakealoo — Pastiches of the style of Harry Stephen Keeler by selected demented members of the HSK Society. Updated every year with the new winner.

Strands of the Web: Short Stories of Harry Stephen Keeler — 29 stories, just about all that Keeler wrote, are edited and introduced by Fred Cleaver.

RAMBLE HOUSE's LOON SANCTUARY

A Clear Path to Cross — Sharon Knowles short mystery stories by Ed Lynskey.

A Corpse Walks in Brooklyn and Other Stories — Volume 5 in the Day Keene in the Detective Pulps series.

A Jimmy Starr Omnibus — Three 40s novels by Jimmy Starr.

A Niche in Time and Other Stories — Classic SF by William F. Temple

A Roland Daniel Double: The Signal and The Return of Wu Fang — Classic thrillers from the 30s.

A Shot Rang Out — Three decades of reviews and articles by today's Anthony Boucher, Jon Breen. An essential book for any mystery lover's library.

A Smell of Smoke — A 1951 English countryside thriller by Miles Burton.

A Snark Selection — Lewis Carroll's *The Hunting of the Snark* with two Snarkian chapters by Harry Stephen Keeler — Illustrated by Gavin L. O'Keefe.

A Young Man's Heart — A forgotten early classic by Cornell Woolrich.

Alexander Laing Novels — *The Motives of Nicholas Holtz* and *Dr. Scarlett*, stories of medical mayhem and intrigue from the 30s.

An Angel in the Street — Modern hardboiled noir by Peter Genovese.

Automaton — Brilliant treatise on robotics: 1928-style! By H. Stafford Hatfield.

Away From the Here and Now — Clare Winger Harris stories, collected by Richard A. Lupoff

Beast or Man? — A 1930 novel of racism and horror by Sean M'Guire. Introduced by John Pelan.

Black Beadle — A 1939 thriller by E.C.R. Lorac.

Black Hogan Strikes Again — Australia's Peter Renwick pens a tale of the 30s outback.

Black River Falls — Suspense from the master, Ed Gorman.

Blondy's Boy Friend — A snappy 1930 story by Philip Wylie, writing as Leatrice Homesley.

Blood in a Snap — The *Finnegan's Wake* of the 21st century, by Jim Weiler.

Blood Moon — The first of the Robert Payne series by Ed Gorman.

Bogart '48 — Hollywood action with Bogie by John Stanley and Kenn Davis

Calling Lou Largo! — Two Lou Largo novels by William Ard.

Cornucopia of Crime — Francis M. Nevins assembled this huge collection of his writings about crime literature and the people who write it. Essential for any serious mystery library.

Corpse Without Flesh — Strange novel of forensics by George Bruce

Crimson Clown Novels — By Johnston McCulley, author of the Zorro novels, *The Crimson Clown* and *The Crimson Clown Again*.

Dago Red — 22 tales of dark suspense by Bill Pronzini.

Dark Sanctuary — Weird Menace story by H. B. Gregory

David Hume Novels — *Corpses Never Argue, Cemetery First Stop, Make Way for the Mourners, Eternity Here I Come*. 1930s British hardboiled fiction with an attitude.

Dead Man Talks Too Much — Hollywood boozer by Weed Dickenson.

Death Leaves No Card — One of the most unusual murdered-in-the-tub mysteries you'll ever read. By Miles Burton.

Death March of the Dancing Dolls and Other Stories — Volume Three in the Day Keene in the Detective Pulps series. Introduced by Bill Crider.

Deep Space and other Stories — A collection of SF gems by Richard A. Lupoff.

Detective Duff Unravels It — Episodic mysteries by Harvey O'Higgins.

Diabolic Candelabra — Classic 30s mystery by E.R. Punshon

Dictator's Way — Another D.S. Bobby Owen mystery from E.R. Punshon

Dime Novels: Ramble House's 10-Cent Books — *Knife in the Dark* by Robert Leslie Bellem, *Hot Lead* and *Song of Death* by Ed Earl Repp, *A Hashish House in New York* by H.H. Kane, and five more.

Doctor Arnoldi — Tiffany Thayer's story of the death of death.

Don Diablo: Book of a Lost Film — Two-volume treatment of a western by Paul Landres, with diagrams. Intro by Francis M. Nevins.

Dope and Swastikas — Two strange novels from 1922 by Edmund Snell

Dope Tales #1 — Two dope-riddled classics; *Dope Runners* by Gerald Grantham and *Death Takes the Joystick* by Phillip Condé.

Dope Tales #2 — Two more narco-classics; *The Invisible Hand* by Rex Dark and *The Smokers of Hashish* by Norman Berrow.

Dope Tales #3 — Two enchanting novels of opium by the master, Sax Rohmer. *Dope* and *The Yellow Claw.*

Double Hot — Two 60s softcore sex novels by Morris Hershman.

Double Sex — Yet two more panting thrillers from Morris Hershman.

Dr. Odin — Douglas Newton's 1933 racial potboiler comes back to life.

Evangelical Cockroach — Jack Woodford writes about writing.

Evidence in Blue — 1938 mystery by E. Charles Vivian.

Fatal Accident — Murder by automobile, a 1936 mystery by Cecil M. Wills.

Fighting Mad — Todd Robbins' 1922 novel about boxing and life

Finger-prints Never Lie — A 1939 classic detective novel by John G. Brandon.

Freaks and Fantasies — Eerie tales by Tod Robbins, collaborator of Tod Browning on the film FREAKS.

Gadsby — A lipogram (a novel without the letter E). Ernest Vincent Wright's last work, published in 1939 right before his death.

Gelett Burgess Novels — *The Master of Mysteries, The White Cat, Two O'Clock Courage, Ladies in Boxes, Find the Woman, The Heart Line, The Picaroons* and *Lady Mechante.* Recently added is A Gelett Burgess Sampler, edited by Alfred Jan. All are introduced by Richard A. Lupoff.

Geronimo — S. M. Barrett's 1905 autobiography of a noble American.

Hake Talbot Novels — *Rim of the Pit, The Hangman's Handyman.* Classic locked room mysteries, with mapback covers by Gavin O'Keefe.

Hands Out of Hell and Other Stories — John H. Knox's eerie hallucinations

Hell is a City — William Ard's masterpiece.

Hollywood Dreams — A novel of Tinsel Town and the Depression by Richard O'Brien.

Hostesses in Hell and Other Stories — Russell Gray's most graphic stories

House of the Restless Dead — Strange and ominous tales by Hugh B. Cave

I Stole $16,000,000 — A true story by cracksman Herbert E. Wilson.

Inclination to Murder — 1966 thriller by New Zealand's Harriet Hunter.

Invaders from the Dark — Classic werewolf tale from Greye La Spina.

J. Poindexter, Colored — Classic satirical black novel by Irvin S. Cobb.

Jack Mann Novels — Strange murder in the English countryside. *Gees' First Case, Nightmare Farm, Grey Shapes, The Ninth Life, The Glass Too Many, Her Ways Are Death, The Kleinert Case* and *Maker of Shadows.*

Jake Hardy — A lusty western tale from Wesley Tallant.

Jim Harmon Double Novels — *Vixen Hollow/Celluloid Scandal, The Man Who Made Maniacs/Silent Siren, Ape Rape/Wanton Witch, Sex Burns Like Fire/Twist Session, Sudden Lust/Passion Strip, Sin Unlimited/Harlot Master, Twilight Girls/Sex Institution.* Written in the early 60s and never reprinted until now.

Joel Townsley Rogers Novels and Short Stories — By the author of *The Red Right Hand: Once In a Red Moon, Lady With the Dice, The Stopped Clock, Never Leave My Bed.* Also two short story collections: *Night of Horror* and *Killing Time.*

John Carstairs, Space Detective — Arboreal Sci-fi by Frank Belknap Long

Joseph Shallit Novels — *The Case of the Billion Dollar Body, Lady Don't Die on My Doorstep, Kiss the Killer, Yell Bloody Murder, Take Your Last Look.* One of America's best 50's authors and a favorite of author Bill Pronzini.

Keller Memento — 45 short stories of the amazing and weird by Dr. David Keller.

Killer's Caress — Cary Moran's 1936 hardboiled thriller.

Lady of the Yellow Death and Other Stories — More stories by Wyatt Blassingame.

League of the Grateful Dead and Other Stories — Volume One in the Day Keene in the Detective Pulps series.

Library of Death — Ghastly tale by Ronald S. L. Harding, introduced by John Pelan

Malcolm Jameson Novels and Short Stories — *Astonishing! Astounding!, Tarnished Bomb, The Alien Envoy and Other Stories* and *The Chariots of San Fernando and Other Stories.* All introduced and edited by John Pelan or Richard A. Lupoff.

Man Out of Hell and Other Stories — Volume II of the John H. Knox weird pulps collection.

Marblehead: A Novel of H.P. Lovecraft — A long-lost masterpiece from Richard A. Lupoff. This is the "director's cut", the long version that has never been published before.

Mark of the Laughing Death and Other Stories — Shockers from the pulps by Francis James, introduced by John Pelan.

Master of Souls — Mark Hansom's 1937 shocker is introduced by weirdologist John Pelan.

Max Afford Novels — *Owl of Darkness, Death's Mannikins, Blood on His Hands, The Dead Are Blind, The Sheep and the Wolves, Sinners in Paradise* and *Two Locked Room Mysteries and a Ripping Yarn* by one of Australia's finest mystery novelists.

Money Brawl — Two books about the writing business by Jack Woodford and H. Bedford-Jones. Introduced by Richard A. Lupoff.

More Secret Adventures of Sherlock Holmes — Gary Lovisi's second collection of tales about the unknown sides of the great detective.

Muddled Mind: Complete Works of Ed Wood, Jr. — David Hayes and Hayden Davis deconstruct the life and works of the mad, but canny, genius.

Murder among the Nudists — A mystery from 1934 by Peter Hunt, featuring a naked Detective-Inspector going undercover in a nudist colony.

Murder in Black and White — 1931 classic tennis whodunit by Evelyn Elder.

Murder in Shawnee — Two novels of the Alleghenies by John Douglas: *Shawnee Alley Fire* and *Haunts.*

Murder in Silk — A 1937 Yellow Peril novel of the silk trade by Ralph Trevor.

My Deadly Angel — 1955 Cold War drama by John Chelton.

My First Time: The One Experience You Never Forget — Michael Birchwood — 64 true first-person narratives of how they lost it.

Mysterious Martin, the Master of Murder — Two versions of a strange 1912 novel by Tod Robbins about a man who writes books that can kill.

Norman Berrow Novels — *The Bishop's Sword, Ghost House, Don't Go Out After Dark, Claws of the Cougar, The Smokers of Hashish, The Secret Dancer, Don't Jump Mr. Boland!, The Footprints of Satan, Fingers for Ransom, The Three Tiers of Fantasy, The Spaniard's Thumb, The Eleventh Plague, Words Have Wings, One Thrilling Night, The Lady's in Danger, It Howls at Night, The Terror in the Fog, Oil Under the Window, Murder in the Melody, The Singing Room.* This is the complete Norman Berrow library of locked-room mysteries, several of which are masterpieces.

Old Faithful and Other Stories — SF classic tales by Raymond Z. Gallun.

Old Times' Sake — Short stories by James Reasoner from Mike Shayne Magazine.

One Dreadful Night — A classic mystery by Ronald S. L. Harding

Pair O' Jacks — A mystery novel and a diatribe about publishing by Jack Woodford

Perfect .38 — Two early Timothy Dane novels by William Ard. More to come.

Prince Pax — Devilish intrigue by George Sylvester Viereck and Philip Eldridge

Prose Bowl — Futuristic satire of a world where hack writing has replaced football as our national obsession, by Bill Pronzini and Barry N. Malzberg.

Red Light — The history of legal prostitution in Shreveport Louisiana by Eric Brock. Includes wonderful photos of the houses and the ladies.

Researching American-Made Toy Soldiers — A 276-page collection of a lifetime of articles by toy soldier expert Richard O'Brien.

Reunion in Hell — Volume One of the John H. Knox series of weird stories from the pulps. Introduced by horror expert John Pelan.

Ripped from the Headlines! — The Jack the Ripper story as told in the newspaper articles in the *New York* and *London Times.*

Rough Cut & New, Improved Murder — Ed Gorman's first two novels.

R.R. Ryan Novels — Freak Museum and The Subjugated Beast, two horror classics.

Ruby of a Thousand Dreams — The villain Wu Fang returns in this Roland Daniel novel.

Ruled By Radio — 1925 futuristic novel by Robert L. Hadfield & Frank E. Farncombe.

Rupert Penny Novels — *Policeman's Holiday, Policeman's Evidence, Lucky Policeman, Policeman in Armour, Sealed Room Murder, Sweet Poison, The Talkative Policeman, She had to Have Gas* and *Cut and Run* (by Martin Tanner.) Rupert Penny is the pseudonym of Australian Charles Thornett, a master of the locked room, impossible crime plot.

Sacred Locomotive Flies — Richard A. Lupoff's psychedelic SF story.

Sam — Early gay novel by Lonnie Coleman.

Sand's Game — Spectacular hard-boiled noir from Ennis Willie, edited by Lynn Myers and Stephen Mertz, with contributions from Max Allan Collins, Bill Crider, Wayne Dundee, Bill Pronzini, Gary Lovisi and James Reasoner.

Sand's War — More violent fiction from the typewriter of Ennis Willie

Satan's Den Exposed — True crime in Truth or Consequences New Mexico — Award-winning journalism by the *Desert Journal.*

Satans of Saturn — Novellas from the pulps by Otis Adelbert Kline and E. H. Price

Satan's Sin House and Other Stories — Horrific gore by Wayne Rogers

Secrets of a Teenage Superhero — Graphic lit by Jonathan Sweet

Sex Slave — Potboiler of lust in the days of Cleopatra by Dion Leclerq, 1966.

Sideslip — 1968 SF masterpiece by Ted White and Dave Van Arnam.

Slammer Days — Two full-length prison memoirs: *Men into Beasts* (1952) by George Sylvester Viereck and *Home Away From Home* (1962) by Jack Woodford.

Slippery Staircase — 1930s whodunit from E.C.R. Lorac

Sorcerer's Chessmen — John Pelan introduces this 1939 classic by Mark Hansom.

Star Griffin — Michael Kurland's 1987 masterpiece of SF drollery is back.

Stakeout on Millennium Drive — Award-winning Indianapolis Noir by Ian Woollen.

Strands of the Web: Short Stories of Harry Stephen Keeler — Edited and Introduced by Fred Cleaver.

Summer Camp for Corpses and Other Stories — Weird Menace tales from Arthur Leo Zagat; introduced by John Pelan.

Suzy — A collection of comic strips by Richard O'Brien and Bob Vojtko from 1970.

Tales of the Macabre and Ordinary — Modern twisted horror by Chris Mikul, author of the *Bizarrism* series.

Tales of Terror and Torment #1 — John Pelan selects and introduces this sampler of weird menace tales from the pulps.

Tenebrae — Ernest G. Henham's 1898 horror tale brought back.

The Amorous Intrigues & Adventures of Aaron Burr — by Anonymous. Hot historical action about the man who almost became Emperor of Mexico.

The Anthony Boucher Chronicles — edited by Francis M. Nevins. Book reviews by Anthony Boucher written for the *San Francisco Chronicle*, 1942 – 1947. Essential and fascinating reading by the best book reviewer there ever was.

The Barclay Catalogs — Two essential books about toy soldier collecting by Richard O'Brien

The Basil Wells Omnibus — A collection of Wells' stories by Richard A. Lupoff

The Beautiful Dead and Other Stories — Dreadful tales from Donald Dale

The Best of 10-Story Book — edited by Chris Mikul, over 35 stories from the literary magazine Harry Stephen Keeler edited.

The Black Dark Murders — Vintage 50s college murder yarn by Milt Ozaki, writing as Robert O. Saber.

The Book of Time — The classic novel by H.G. Wells is joined by sequels by Wells himself and three stories by Richard A. Lupoff. Illustrated by Gavin L. O'Keefe.

The Case in the Clinic — One of E.C.R. Lorac's finest.

The Strange Case of the Antlered Man — A mystery of superstition by Edwy Searles Brooks.

The Case of the Bearded Bride — #4 in the Day Keene in the Detective Pulps series

The Case of the Little Green Men — Mack Reynolds wrote this love song to sci-fi fans back in 1951 and it's now back in print.

The Case of the Withered Hand — 1936 potboiler by John G. Brandon.

The Charlie Chaplin Murder Mystery — A 2004 tribute by noted film scholar, Wes D. Gehring.

The Chinese Jar Mystery — Murder in the manor by John Stephen Strange, 1934.

The Cloudbuilders and Other Stories — SF tales from Colin Kapp.

The Compleat Calhoon — All of Fender Tucker's works: Includes *Totah Six-Pack, Weed, Women and Song* and *Tales from the Tower*, plus a CD of all of his songs.

The Compleat Ova Hamlet — Parodies of SF authors by Richard A. Lupoff. This is a brand new edition with more stories and more illustrations by Trina Robbins.

The Contested Earth and Other SF Stories — A never-before published space opera and seven short stories by Jim Harmon.

The Crimson Query — A 1929 thriller from Arlton Eadie. A perfect way to get introduced.

The Curse of Cantire — Classic 1939 novel of a family curse by Walter S. Masterman.

The Devil and the C.I.D. — Odd diabolic mystery by E.C.R. Lorac

The Devil Drives — An odd prison and lost treasure novel from 1932 by Virgil Markham.

The Devil of Pei-Ling — Herbert Asbury's 1929 tale of the occult.

The Devil's Mistress — A 1915 Scottish gothic tale by J. W. Brodie-Innes, a member of Aleister Crowley's Golden Dawn.

The Devil's Nightclub and Other Stories — John Pelan introduces some gruesome tales by Nat Schachner.

The Disentanglers — Episodic intrigue at the turn of last century by Andrew Lang

The Dog Poker Code — A spoof of *The Da Vinci Code* by D.B. Smithee.

The Dumpling — Political murder from 1907 by Coulson Kernahan.

The End of It All and Other Stories — Ed Gorman selected his favorite short stories for this huge collection.

The Fangs of Suet Pudding — A 1944 novel of the German invasion by Adams Farr

The Finger of Destiny and Other Stories — Edmund Snell's superb collection of weird stories of Borneo.

The Ghost of Gaston Revere — From 1935, a novel of life and beyond by Mark Hansom, introduced by John Pelan.

The Girl in the Dark — A thriller from Roland Daniel

The Gold Star Line — Seaboard adventure from L.T. Reade and Robert Eustace.

The Golden Dagger — 1951 Scotland Yard yarn by E. R. Punshon.

The Great Orme Terror — Horror stories by Garnett Radcliffe from the pulps

The Hairbreadth Escapes of Major Mendax — Francis Blake Crofton's 1889 boys' book.

The House That Time Forgot and Other Stories — Insane pulpitude by Robert F. Young

The House of the Vampire — 1907 poetic thriller by George S. Viereck.

The Illustrious Corpse — Murder hijinx from Tiffany Thayer

The Incredible Adventures of Rowland Hern — Intriguing 1928 impossible crimes by Nicholas Olde.

The Julius Caesar Murder Case — A classic 1935 re-telling of the assassination by Wallace Irwin that's much more fun than the Shakespeare version.

The Koky Comics — A collection of all of the 1978-1981 Sunday and daily comic strips by Richard O'Brien and Mort Gerberg, in two volumes.

The Lady of the Terraces — 1925 missing race adventure by E. Charles Vivian.

The Lord of Terror — 1925 mystery with master-criminal, Fantômas.

The Melamare Mystery — A classic 1929 Arsene Lupin mystery by Maurice Leblanc

The Man Who Was Secrett — Epic SF stories from John Brunner

The Man Without a Planet — Science fiction tales by Richard Wilson

The N. R. De Mexico Novels — Robert Bragg, the real N.R. de Mexico, presents *Marijuana Girl, Madman on a Drum, Private Chauffeur* in one volume.

The Night Remembers — A 1991 Jack Walsh mystery from Ed Gorman.

The One After Snelling — Kickass modern noir from Richard O'Brien.

The Organ Reader — A huge compilation of just about everything published in the 1971-1972 radical bay-area newspaper, *THE ORGAN*. A coffee table book that points out the shallowness of the coffee table mindset.

The Poker Club — Three in one! Ed Gorman's ground-breaking novel, the short story it was based upon, and the screenplay of the film made from it.

The Private Journal & Diary of John H. Surratt — The memoirs of the man who conspired to assassinate President Lincoln.

The Ramble House Mapbacks — Recently revised book by Gavin L. O'Keefe with color pictures of all the Ramble House books with mapbacks.

The Secret Adventures of Sherlock Holmes — Three Sherlockian pastiches by the Brooklyn author/publisher, Gary Lovisi.

The Shadow on the House — Mark Hansom's 1934 masterpiece of horror is introduced by John Pelan.

The Sign of the Scorpion — A 1935 Edmund Snell tale of oriental evil.

The Singular Problem of the Stygian House-Boat — Two classic tales by John Kendrick Bangs about the denizens of Hades.

The Smiling Corpse — Philip Wylie and Bernard Bergman's odd 1935 novel.

The Spider: Satan's Murder Machines — A thesis about Iron Man

The Stench of Death: An Odoriferous Omnibus by Jack Moskovitz — Two complete novels and two novellas from 60's sleaze author, Jack Moskovitz.

The Story Writer and Other Stories — Classic SF from Richard Wilson

The Strange Case of the Antlered Man — 1935 dementia from Edwy Searles Brooks

The Strange Thirteen — Richard B. Gamon's odd stories about Raj India.

The Technique of the Mystery Story — Carolyn Wells' tips about writing.

The Threat of Nostalgia — A collection of his most obscure stories by Jon Breen

The Time Armada — Fox B. Holden's 1953 SF gem.

The Tongueless Horror and Other Stories — Volume One of the series of short stories from the weird pulps by Wyatt Blassingame.

The Town from Planet Five — From Richard Wilson, two SF classics, *And Then the Town Took Off* and *The Girls from Planet 5*

The Tracer of Lost Persons — From 1906, an episodic novel that became a hit radio series in the 30s. Introduced by Richard A. Lupoff.

The Trail of the Cloven Hoof — Diabolical horror from 1935 by Arlton Eadie. Introduced by John Pelan.

The Triune Man — Mindscrambling science fiction from Richard A. Lupoff.

The Unholy Goddess and Other Stories — Wyatt Blassingame's first DTP compilation

The Universal Holmes — Richard A. Lupoff's 2007 collection of five Holmesian pastiches and a recipe for giant rat stew.

The Werewolf vs the Vampire Woman — Hard to believe ultraviolence by either Arthur M. Scarm or Arthur M. Scram.

The Whistling Ancestors — A 1936 classic of weirdness by Richard E. Goddard and introduced by John Pelan.

The White Owl — A vintage thriller from Edmund Snell

The White Peril in the Far East — Sidney Lewis Gulick's 1905 indictment of the West and assurance that Japan would never attack the U.S.

The Wizard of Berner's Abbey — A 1935 horror gem written by Mark Hansom and introduced by John Pelan.

The Wonderful Wizard of Oz — by L. Frank Baum and illustrated by Gavin L. O'Keefe

Through the Looking Glass — Lewis Carroll wrote it; Gavin L. O'Keefe illustrated it.

Time Line — Ramble House artist Gavin O'Keefe selects his most evocative art inspired by the twisted literature he reads and designs.

Tiresias — Psychotic modern horror novel by Jonathan M. Sweet.

Tortures and Towers — Two novellas of terror by Dexter Dayle.

Totah Six-Pack — Fender Tucker's six tales about Farmington in one sleek volume.

Tree of Life, Book of Death — Grania Davis' book of her life.

Triple Quest — An arty mystery from the 30s by E.R. Punshon.

Trail of the Spirit Warrior — Roger Haley's saga of life in the Indian Territories.

Two Kinds of Bad — Two 50s novels by William Ard about Danny Fontaine

Two Suns of Morcali and Other Stories — Evelyn E. Smith's SF tour-de-force

Ultra-Boiled — 23 gut-wrenching tales by our Man in Brooklyn, Gary Lovisi.

Up Front From Behind — A 2011 satire of Wall Street by James B. Kobak.

Victims & Villains — Intriguing Sherlockiana from Derham Groves.

Wade Wright Novels — *Echo of Fear, Death At Nostalgia Street, It Leads to Murder* and *Shadows' Edge*, a double book featuring *Shadows Don't Bleed* and *The Sharp Edge*.

Walter S. Masterman Novels — *The Green Toad, The Flying Beast, The Yellow Mistletoe, The Wrong Verdict, The Perjured Alibi, The Border Line, The Bloodhounds Bay, The Curse of Cantire* and *The Baddington Horror.* Masterman wrote horror and mystery, some introduced by John Pelan.

We Are the Dead and Other Stories — Volume Two in the Day Keene in the Detective Pulps series, introduced by Ed Gorman. When done, there may be 11 in the series.

Welsh Rarebit Tales — Charming stories from 1902 by Harle Oren Cummins

West Texas War and Other Western Stories — by Gary Lovisi.

What If? Volume 1, 2 and 3 — Richard A. Lupoff introduces three decades worth of SF short stories that should have won a Hugo, but didn't.

When the Batman Thirsts and Other Stories — Weird tales from Frederick C. Davis.

Whip Dodge: Man Hunter — Wesley Tallant's saga of a bounty hunter of the old West.

Win, Place and Die! — The first new mystery by Milt Ozaki in decades. The ultimate novel of 70s Reno.

Writer 1 and 2 — A magnus opus from Richard A. Lupoff summing up his life as writer.

You'll Die Laughing — Bruce Elliott's 1945 novel of murder at a practical joker's English countryside manor.

RAMBLE HOUSE

Fender Tucker, Prop.   Gavin L. O'Keefe, Graphics
www.ramblehouse.com   fender@ramblehouse.com
228-826-1783   10329 Sheephead Drive, Vancleave MS 39565